Camarade

a novel

Theo Dorgan

MERCIER PRESS

Dedication

For Thomas McCarthy
true friend, true comrade

MERCIER PRESS

Cork

www.mercierpress.ie

ISBN: 978-1-917453-19-6
eBook: 978-1-917453-50-9
Audio: 978-1-917453-51-6

All characters and events in this book, except for those who are identifiably real and recognisable in the public domain, are entirely fictional. Any resemblance to any person living or dead which may occur inadvertently is completely unintentional.

Printed and bound in the EU.

PART 1

1

All things considered, I wonder if shooting that policeman made me the man that I am?

On the Rue Mouffetard this morning there was a man who reminded me, for a fleeting moment, of Sam. That gaunt, scribed face, now so world famous. I felt my hand rise unbidden in greeting, but the fellow turned away, a defeated slump in his shoulders that somehow irritated me. I miss my upright friend. Once, over whiskey, I asked him how it was that he flew free. Long silence, then: 'I suppose, I suppose I just refused.' That cold blank stare. Then, unexpectedly, he reached across and squeezed my arm. We veterans.

We come to our lives in different ways, those of us who are forced, shocked or tricked into waking. I mean, of course, our real lives – but very few people have real lives now, by which I mean lives over which they deliberate, lives they are prepared to answer for at the bar of extinction.

I have been awake in myself for what seems, when I think of it, a very long time. Whether this is good or bad, I cannot say. I have been, I think, exceptionally lucky: taking all in all, I have had exactly the life I was made fit for. From time to time, I have met others like me, people, for instance, who stare quietly for perhaps a fraction too long at what prompts an immediate emotional response in others – a car crash, a lovers' quarrel in public, the corpse of an acquaintance. I used to think of us as hungry souls, somehow defective in empathy. Not so, I eventually learned, not so at all.

What wakes us? Some very few, it seems, are born fully awake. I have seen infants in the Jardin du Luxembourg who could chill you with a look. I have felt that chill, then that sudden vertigo of mutual recognition. Always, I hurry by. Some others, and here I include myself, are woken by chance or so-called chance, generally it seems by some irrevocable act or gesture, a moment of absolute commitment to … anything. It can be anything. As long as one commits, as long as the act is irrevocable, cannot be unmade, cannot be explained away.

And therefore, I begin: all things considered, shooting that policeman was very likely what made me the man that I am.

2

Vincent called by last night. Two rings, a pause, two rings. He's done that from the first day he came here, I imagine he does it everywhere. An announcement: here I am, it's me. Twilight in the street below, a faint glow still over the rooftops. I tossed him down the keys, always amused at how he stands there, hands by his sides until the very last moment then, right-handed, snatching the keys from the air. His satisfied nod that my aim has improved. Vincent, who never wastes a gesture.

I left the door open, went to put coffee on. You shouldn't do that, he says, standing in the small hallway. Anyone might be hanging around on the stairs. I smile, he smiles, he knows I can see the landing from the kitchen. He knows I look down the stairs when I open the apartment door.

Vincent's a rangy Algerian, in his late twenties. A spring in him, in all that he does and says. As usual, he paces while the coffee brews. Vincent, he said, the second time we met, offering his hand and a mocking grin. Call me Vincent. A challenge, a small offering, a test. I said nothing, squeezed his hand, smiled. My silence made him my friend.

This is a grey suit night, a black silk tee-shirt underneath, the long sleeves a perfect half-centimetre past the cuffs. The gold-rimmed spectacles in his top pocket.

I was … around, he said, thought I'd pop in. Still pacing the room, checking to see what new books I've added to the crammed shelves. We sip our coffees at the tall window, watching the light fade.

So, he says, still looking away, I've thought about this and, well, I think you should write the book of your life.

Vincent, from time to time, to keep himself and for other reasons, steals cars – at least that's how I understand it. I don't really mind, one way or the other, but once when he claimed he was engaged in redistributing wealth I checked him: no, Vincent, you steal cars. It's a fact. Facts matter.

You should write the book of your life, he says. You should put down in words what it was to be here, what it was to be you.

This is one of the things I like about Vincent, he has a gift, sometimes, for knowing exactly what to say, exactly when it needs to be said. Somehow, he has snagged on to a stray thought that has been drifting like a small cloud out at the edges of my mind for some time now. Where did I read the phrase, 'at a certain point one becomes aware that one is dealing with time remaining'? No matter, it started me thinking, no, reflecting, on what a life I have had, what an *odd* life it has been. Not odd as in peculiar but singular, certainly singular. And, unshared. For the most part.

When did the idea start, that I should write it all out, leave some mark, some trace, some evidence that, once upon a time, there lived a man who had the life that I call mine?

No matter. I will, I said, I'll start tomorrow.

He put his cup down, satisfied. If I'd surprised him, he did not show it. Certainly I had surprised myself. Good, he said, that's good; OK, I have things to do. He gave me a long, appraising look. You sure? I gave him a slow wink. I'm sure. It's a good idea.

On the way out the door, putting on those spectacles, he looked back over his shoulder: you were thinking about this, yes? I was. I shut the door behind him, softly, listened in vain for his footsteps on the stairs going down, waited to hear the street door close.

I went to my desk between the windows that look on to the street; I sat down, I closed my eyes. I listened to my own breathing for a long time. I was wondering how to begin.

I rarely feel frail. I have what they call a sturdy build, a word I approve of. Sturdy. A good build in a soldier or sailor, you'd say, able for what comes.

When the last of the night had fallen into place, when the full dark was everywhere behind me in the large apartment, I stood and undressed where I was, in the front room lit by a yellow streetlight. Not questioning the impulse. Jacket over the back of the wooden chair, trousers neatly over the jacket, the rest folded and placed in a neat pile on the seat. I eased my bare feet out of their slippers, the better to feel the cool tiles of the bathroom underfoot when I'd go through. Standing before the full-length mirror, regarding my body, I felt, undeniably, frail. As if I could no longer have confidence in my bones. As if the sinews and tendons and muscles might fail in their job of keeping me mobile, alert and active. When that happens, and it happens to all of us from time to time, the thing is to look yourself straight in the eye, something most people, myself included, find it hard to do. To hold your own gaze without wavering, that's the thing. To call yourself back, to summon the will and bring it home firmly.

Next morning, this morning, I woke smoothly with a strong sense of animal power humming in my veins. I lay without opening my eyes, sending myself out to the different rooms, touching the walls, admiring the polished wooden floors, the few but tasteful rugs. Taking stock of myself, my own little world, so carefully and painstakingly assembled. When I saw that all was good, I rose smoothly, like a young man, showered, gathered my clothes from the front room, dressed and went out for bread.

As you step off my landing onto the wide spiralling stairs, the first wooden tread creaks. So does the first tread on the next flight down, and the first tread on the flight leading down to the hall. Henri did that, many years ago, loosened those treads so that I would always hear when someone was climbing the stairs. Too well-made, he said; a good carpenter all the same.

I make a point of starting my daily forays into the world by testing this little device of Henri's; a way, I suppose, of keeping him alive in my mind. No, better, since I must begin to think like a writer now, as an homage to his thoroughness and his care for me.

I have lived here for more nearly forty years, on the third floor of this shabby but decent building, one occupied apartment to each of the first three floors. For reasons I could never discover, the apartments on the floor above mine have been empty for decades. When I step down into the dark double-height hallway, when my foot falls on the polished, muted green tiles, I hear myself always give a small sigh of contentment. The place pleases me. Mine and not mine. Familiar, but always other. There is no hall like this in all of Cork where I was born. I register this every single time I go in or out, but now I rarely think about it. There is a kind of vanity about this, the hallway reminds me that I have made my life my own.

The French love their bread, I noticed this from the start, but more than their bread they love the idea of going to the *Boulanger*. I think it speaks to them of civility. They are a private people who fetishise, solemnise, every action conducted in public. Thus, it is not enough that I go to the bakery, buy bread, return home and make my breakfast. There are first the expected people on the street to be acknowledged, people one knows to nod to, people with whom one has spoken in the past and may again, people whom one is obliged to greet by name, by some minor inquiring courtesy. In the bakery itself one waits in the short queue for *Monsieur* or *Madame* to acknowledge one, to ask if one desires the usual. Ideally, to be fully in tune with the rituals, one then fumbles in a worn coin purse for the handful of coins required. Those who come to the counter with the exact change already in hand are frowned upon – but so discreetly that only the regulars notice the faint arching eyebrow of *Monsieur* or *Madame*.

I like all this. No, better, it pleases me. This morning, business concluded, baton under my arm, I decide on a coffee before retracing my steps. I do this seldom. I associate the impulse with some unacknowledged process arriving at its conclusion, the conclusion signalling itself by desiring a small espresso. I cross the street. It is early autumn, certainly warm enough to sit outside. The waiter arrives, takes my modest order, departs without a word. It is the young Spanish fellow with the ear-ring, the ponytail; there is nothing beyond appearance obviously interesting about him, I have taught him not to speak to me. He thinks I'm an old grouch. Good, it suits me.

So, what is it then old man? Ah. I have decided it seems in my sleep that, yes, I will write the book as Vincent suggests, and I will write it in English. I inhale the bitter aroma of the coffee, I take a first taste. So.

But, how to go about this? Well, obviously, a long tour from start to finish – well, nearly finish, eh? But, how tedious that might become. I did this, I did that, then I did this, that happened – no, boring, tedious, and somehow dishonest. And, the danger that I would be tempted to explain myself ...

As so often happens once you embark on something and an obstacle arises, the solution came by itself. I will write the book twice. Twice, Joseph? Yes, one strand faithful to the line from cradle to grave (now stop that), and a second strand like a diary in present time, recording whatever reflections are prompted by the unfolding story, how these bend and inflect my days as they take the stage.

Oh for fuck's sake, I scold myself, whatever happens, for the love of Jesus do not become an *author*! I hear the accents of my faraway Cork in that inner voice, and am suddenly buoyed up by the thought that I have never lost that bracing native instinct to pull down the high-flown.

My coffee's gone cold. I beckon to the boy, he brings me a fresh cup and now I am all practicality.

Will I need paper, then? The *papeterie* on Soufflot? No, this also, it seems, is decided. I will write direct on the screen; it would be prudent to save as I go on a flash-stick, yes? But of course. Flash-stick, not paper. Off to the shop then. No time like the present, Joseph, up and at 'em. I leave a small but excessive tip. A tentative smile from the boy as he clears the table; I smile back.

Breakfasted, cuff buttons unfastened, I switch on the laptop, open a Word file, label it 'Book'. All very efficient. Then, inevitably, I skive off, seduced by the day's news, the sorcerer's ease with which I can roam the world. *Libé*, BBC, *Irish Times*, today (superstitiously) *The Irish Examiner*. Equally predictably, in a sudden flush of distaste with myself, I log off. The perpetually cool Vincent, it makes me smile now to remember it, was astonished to find I own a laptop, even more astonished that it's a Mac. He was so embarrassed at letting his mask slip I hadn't the heart to tell him I have a high-speed broadband connection. He finds me disconcerting enough as it is. Sometimes, it's true, I enjoy feeling smug. Henri used say, a good weapon feels right by the intuition of the hand. That's why I bought a Mac. Machines should be fit for purpose.

I catch a stray thought, reel it back in to examine it: what I feel about this machine is like what I feel about the hallway below.

I open a second file and label it 'Time Present', record the morning so far. Now it would seem I am writing two books. Or, better, two books in one – noting time present as I record time past. Ah god damn it, concentrate you old fool.

Very well.

3

I was born in Cork in 1940. I was an only child, my parents died when the car in which they were travelling went into the river near Blackrock. They died in the car, as did the driver, a neighbour and friend. His wife, the front seat passenger, survived. Nobody ever told me how. (She moved away from the neighbourhood a year later. I know it was because she could not bear to see me on the street but I told this to no one, then or since. It was a look that would pass between us. I thought she was lucky to have survived, that's all, but she saw reproach in my eyes where there was none, and could not deal with it.)

I was ten when they died, this was 1950, I had begun to see things directly, to know things without having to reason them out. Perhaps this is why teachers feared me, without understanding that their dislike of me was, in fact, a kind of fear. I was ten, as I say, and grief-struck – but I decided, then and there, that I would choose where and when to show this grief, that I would decide in whom to confide this grief. Was I a kind of monster? Not at all. I knew this from the start. I disappointed the neighbours, of course, and the aunts and the uncles, the teachers, even the priest, by what seemed to them a serene, unfeeling composure. Disappointed, certainly, but now that I sit here and call it to mind, I see that I horrified them. 'Unnatural child', Mrs Buckley hissed to Mrs Kearney, as I passed by the day after the funeral. I heard the hatred in that, let me tell you, and I was angry, certainly, but in some other way unmoved.

I was a voracious reader, I could not for a long time work out where the boundary lay between things reported from the world beyond me and things made up in books.

Mrs Buckley hissed. I filed that away.

At the graveside, the day of the funeral, people kept telling me to be brave. This made me impatient. I knew already that I was brave, and brave had nothing at all to do with the deep silent darkness looming up all around me. I told myself to be patient. I looked around me, carefully, examining the crowd one by one, separating with a kind of unblaming dispassion the living from the already dead. I saw surprisingly few living souls, and they saw me. And they saw my grief and knew it was real.

In the years that were left to me in Cork, not one of those people, encountered in the street, ever failed to acknowledge me with a nod, a kind word or, sometimes, met in a shop, a coin for a comic or some sweets. I thought of them, without dwelling on it, as the good people.

I lived with my grandfather, Michael John. I first laid eyes on him, the phrase is exact, in the winter of 1945. We were living in his house, a big house in Blackpool, bigger by far than the houses of any of my schoolmates, and I knew from a very early age it was my grandfather's house. Granda, the first five years of my life, was 'away'. What 'away' meant I could not puzzle out, devious and cunning though I was, but when a neighbour or relative drew his name into the conversation my father or mother would be uncomfortable, evasive. There was a lot being said in silence, in a repertoire of held looks or fleeting glances that, meant to exclude or spare me, served only to pique my curiosity.

Then, in the winter of 1945, he reappeared. Stood on the stone doorstep, late afternoon, a leather suitcase at his feet. I knew him from the photograph over the fire, his wedding photograph, but how I knew him was a puzzle to me then, a puzzle to me yet. I mean that I knew him, not that I recognised him. Lean, hard, tanned and tall, with deep bruises under his eyes, his fair hair bleached near-white, he looked at one and the same time younger and far, far older than the man in the photograph. I remember knowing immediately who he was, this man who had never laid eyes on me, but I don't remember saying what for years after he'd swear I said. Looks me in the eye, he'd say, drawing out the moment, looks me up and down, leans up against the wall with his arms folded and says, well, is it yourself? Him about two foot tall, short trousers and grazed knees, always up to mischief. Is it yourself, says he. What would you make of that now?

I loved him from the start.

My father worked in Ford's, assembling cars. A good job, a job for life the neighbourhood sages would always say, leaning on the parapet of Blackpool Bridge. We had lodgers in the house but one room was always kept empty, a big double room with two tall windows, looking out on Great William O'Brien Street. This room was my grandfather's and within a day of moving in, or back, it was as if he had always been there.

My father was his son, and they got on very well together. Michael John had a particular kind of affinity with my mother, would sing to her in an idle moment with great fondness, his easy affection for his son doubled by his affection for my mother. He had a deft way of being part of the household yet never intruding, would disappear for a few days with the briefest of words, would always contrive to return in the early part of the day so that Mam could include him in the dinner arrangements without fuss. Ah sure aren't you always so thoughtful, Mam would say, and I am, sure, I suppose I am, he'd say and the two of them would laugh.

I studied him very carefully indeed, not from doubt, or from any kind of fear or anxiety, for in truth he had a way of projecting calm and steadiness wherever he went, wherever he was, but I knew from the start there was something he knew that I needed to learn. And he saw it, too.

I watched him, for instance, when someone would ask directly where he had been all that time. He had a way of answering that conveyed carelessness but that I saw at once was very careful indeed. Bit by bit, in the house, in the larger family and throughout the neighbourhood, the understanding spread over the next few years that he had served in the American Navy during the war. I knew he hadn't, I was already sufficiently hardened by trouble in school to recognise a cover story when I heard one, and he knew that I had him tabbed. By a careful strategy of modesty and misdirection, he encouraged a composite belief into existence, so that soon all Blackpool was under the impression that he'd had a good but hard war, had experienced things that, understandably, no man would want to talk about, let alone boast about.

Of course, as I'd go on to learn, Michael John had already a considerable reputation as a guerrilla fighter in the War of Independence, so that it was easy for people to add new tales to the corpus of smoky legend that clung to him. His reticence spoke of modesty to these simple people, and because simple people have always room in their lives for what's unspoken and mysterious, never once did anyone ask him directly what it was he'd been doing in the years he'd been absent before the outbreak of war.

A year after my parents' funeral, I asked him outright. What age are you now, he said, let's see, eleven is it? Eleven. You can ask me in four years time. Don't ask me before then. I shot one glance at him and shut up. I knew that look by then, I had no intention of pursuing the matter.

I did, on that occasion, have something else on my mind, though, and I sensed my opportunity. I'm having a bit of trouble in school, I told him. I'd have thought you were well able to look after yourself, he said.

It's a teacher, I said, and reached for a phrase I'd often heard but had never used, it's getting a bit beyond the beyonds.

To his credit he didn't laugh, but his eyes were dancing.

Would it help, do you think, he was quite serious now, if I went and had a chat with him?

I pretended to think about this for a minute, then nodded. He lives in Wolfe Tone Street, I added. Does he now? Number 34, I added. And you have an after-hours visit in mind, is that it?

I thought that might be best, I said. Considering.

Considering, he echoed, thoughtful now, and giving me a hard look. Are you maybe hoping I might give him a dig?

I was of course, but I thought it better to say no. Maybe you could, I don't know, let him see it's a possibility? This time he did laugh, in fact he roared. He had tears in his eyes from laughing.

We'd just finished dinner. I think, he said, I'll take a bit of a walk after we've cleaned up. I was heading to bed when he came in, the fresh night air clinging to his cold ears as he bent to give me a hug. Do you know what I'm going to tell you, he called up after me, the world is full of possibility.

Where did you walk to, I asked, trying to sound casual.

Where do you think, he answered, mockingly, and I went laughing to bed.

4

It was dark already when the phone rang. Vincent, I said. Silence, then: how did you know it was me? Because, Vincent, you are one of the very few who rings me here, and you're checking to see if I have started on the book. Silence again. I have, I said. Good, be careful back there Joseph, you know, in the past. I will, I will. We hung up.

Afterwards, splashing cold water on the back of my neck, I thought to myself that was an oddly perceptive thing to say. Even for Vincent. I shrugged into my coat, went thoughtfully down the stairs and out.

For some people the past is a forgotten country, a country you work to forget by force of will and circumstance. People like that, they push on from one day to the next, like skiers trying to stay ahead of an avalanche. I saw that once, in Zermatt; they came clear, those skiers, they were lucky, but the image pressed in on me. The Greeks of the classical age thought of the past as a landscape constantly before them, a living panorama; the future was always blank, therefore it made no sense to face forward. They thought of themselves as backing into the future. I'm like that, I find that a congenial thought. I hold the past in mind, constantly seeing it from new perspectives, sieving and parsing the various happenings that have held my attention, letting some things fall away as they outlive their usefulness, letting others float towards the foreground as I find some new understanding.

This habit, this constant practice of mindfulness, is emphatically not neurotic. I detest those people who nurture their past as a series of open wounds, and I detest even more all those, a surprising number, who are constantly editing their past into a mounting succession of petty triumphs, of promises vindicated, points scored, enemies done down. I detest, in short, all self-proclaimed heroes and victims.

But, I think this as I am ordering my dinner, taking a first sip of the one glass of red I have decided to permit myself, Vincent has a point. I should be careful how I write this life.

Facts are what matter, I tell myself, leaving the restaurant, nodding to neighbours, a stiff bow to the patron, ignoring the gaze of strangers. Fact matters, the rest takes care of itself.

I lay in bed, fingers interlaced behind my head, watching the play of light on the high ceiling. All down the years, whenever I have embarked on something new, always I lie down like this, letting the day settle, sending feelers out into the unknown, trying to sense the shape of what's to come. It's comforting, this thought, and I drift off to sleep luxuriating, the very word, in the feeling of being comforted.

Fool of an old man that I am, I pay for this indulgence when I wake with a stiff neck in the morning. Get up you fucking idiot, I tell myself, and I go through to soak a towel in hot water, wrap it around my neck, soak it again, wrap it again and so on until the stiffness eases.

I enjoy swearing at myself, I always have. Don't know why. I always swear in English.

Yesterday's bread will do if I toast it. Café au lait instead of my usual black, if only because watching the milk heat steadies me, stops me from fretting about aimlessly. I keep telling myself to get a grip, impatient to get going, knowing I need to find a pace from the outset.

It rained in the night, I can tell from the air. Good.

Thérèse loved toast, I remember that. And Marie-Louise considered coffee with three cigarettes, one after the other, sufficient breakfast. Good morning, good morning I address them, these figures from my life so long ago; they nod one after the other and head off again about their business. Each oblivious to the other, oblivious, also, to me.

This, I can see, shaking my head to dispel those ghosts, is a day that will need discipline.

So, no internet browsing today, we must be firm, we must be focused. I see I have already found an appropriate shorthand for the diary entries, yesterday's cryptic file notes swelling to narrative as I look at them. That's good then, saves time. I make it up to the moment and close the file.

5

Michael John kept on the lodgers after my parents died, the two he had inherited, old friends of his, and he added two more. As far as I could see, he made no effort to find work, so the steady income must have been sufficient for our needs. The lodgers were all of them quiet men, and as I grew slowly I began to notice that, solitary as each seemed to be, they had nevertheless a great deal in common. A kind of ease in themselves, a certain quality of attentiveness. And an inwardness that was like a muted sorrow, a shadow that would fall, some night by the fire when they would be taking a break from playing cards; one or the other would go away in himself, I put it like that, and presently I began to notice that when this happened the others would gather in around him. Nothing, of course, would be said.

Once, watching this, sensing that Mr McNamara was a bit more down in himself than was usual, I caught Michael John watching me. A slow, thoughtful look. Then he shook his head and I got up and went and made tea. To show I had understood, I made a point of handing the first cup to Mr McNamara. I have said that these men had a certain quality of attentiveness; he took the cup, looked up at me from his low chair and ... came back into himself. I saw it, and was startled. Only for a moment, but everyone saw, looked one to the other, complicit in understanding.

I saw them for what they were, comrades, and felt a fool for a moment that it had taken me so long to understand.

My grandfather stood, beckoned me to his side. The men straightened up in their seats, Mr McNamara by the fire, Mr Owens, Mr Murphy at the table, Mr Driscoll by the window. Joseph, he said, his hand flat on my shoulder, not quite pressing down, this is Tommy Mac, Tony Driscoll, Seanie Murphy, Tommy Owens. Each nodded back as his name was called, and now they were all looking at me expectantly.

That was the first time I felt electricity in the air, felt how it chooses words for you that you might not otherwise have thought to speak.

I stood away from Michael John, so's to include him in this band of comrades. Gentlemen, I said gravely, with a short nod.

At first I was furious when they burst out laughing, slapping each other on the back when the coughing took them, nearly falling out of their chairs – but then I saw it from their side, the absurdity of this little eleven year old with his solemn bookish airs, and I started laughing, too, crushed into my grandfather's side, feeling his ribs shake, his hand tousling my hair.

I mean, I really saw myself, from the outside, from across the room. It went by in a flash, but something inside me marked it, flagged it for further study.

I was a Fianna messenger when I was not much older than him, Seanie Murphy said softly to my grandfather. So you were, so you were, Michael John said, then: sit down here with us, Joseph, 'til I tell you something about these blackguards.

These disappointed men, he might equally well have said. All winter I heard their stories, of desperate ambushes, of fear on the street at nights, the exhilaration of combat and the sickening ice in the pit of your stomach in the dark of a barn somewhere out in the country, the night wind howling and the face of some man you'd shot beseeching you to explain, to explain ...

Not that anyone put it like that, not Tommy or Tommy Mac, not Tony or Seanie, nor yet Michael John. They had a shorthand for these things, they never explained anything to me, and I knew better than to ask questions. A phrase here, a memory haltingly aired, sometimes only a name, someplace I'd never heard of, someone they all remembered, I'd pick the information out of the fog of cigarette smoke (and Lord how they smoked) as the talk rolled on. Later, in bed, I'd let it all drift past me again, stitching the pattern together.

Bar Seanie Murphy, who had been on the Headquarters staff ('Oh always the cushy number' they'd rib him, until the night he told how it felt, signing the execution orders), bar Seanie they'd all been in the same flying column. In school they were teaching us songs of gallant wars and telling us stories of romance; at home I learned by indirection what fear was, what hunger and cold on the eve of battle was, what exhilaration was, and grief, and numb despair, and remorse.

When the Civil War came, to a man they had walked away. That was one of the few times I interrupted the talk. Why, I asked, why did you not fight on? That charge in the air again, the men looking at my grandfather. He put his cards down on the table with a sigh, and I heard a faint disappointment in that sigh: ah Joey, Joey he said, how could we shoot the men we'd been fighting for? No matter that we thought them in the wrong?

And I was ashamed, not because of that faint disappointment but because I should have understood. I felt I had let myself down. I should have understood.

In school, I had long since learned that nothing was more unwelcome, suspect even, than a wish to understand. I kept my own counsel, as a rule, I kept some perfunctory friendships but had no kindred spirits. Everyone else, it seemed to me, considered the acquisition of knowledge, such knowledge as we were being offered, an imposition and a burden. I found it hard to respect my teachers, I say this here freely and with no false pride; they had no sense that, young and unformed as we were, each of us was a person, and each of us had a right to understand. That they, conversely, had a duty to make their best efforts to explain.

How I got to be like this I do not know. I was always like this, I have always been like this. Somebody, Marie Louise perhaps, or maybe even Henri, would later say to me that had they enjoyed the misfortune of being my teacher, they would undoubtedly have strangled me. I said then, and I say it now, I would have understood.

I did my best to be inoffensive, I went out of my way, but this never stopped the charge passed from teacher to teacher, from class to class as I slowly made my way, that I was cheeky, forward, a know-all, full of myself.

I had a policy of polite invisibility where teachers were concerned, of speaking only when spoken to, of keeping opinions to myself. One day, though, it all got too much for me. We had a history teacher I watched carefully. Something not quite right about him. For one thing, he rarely hit us. For another, he was careful not to single me out too much in class, knowing the herd cruelty boys are capable of when one of their number is 'too smart for his own good'. On Fridays he had a habit of drawing some dry lesson out of the books and into the open air. This particular day we had somehow landed on Ireland's policy in the recent war. What do you think, boys, was De Valera right to keep us neutral? The usual sullen silence, then red-haired O'Mahony, the chemist's fat son, blurted out: we should have joined in with Germany, Sir. You know, England's difficulty is Ireland's opportunity? Big smug face on him, the fool. The teacher caught my scowl, flinched, looked away. Anyone else? No?

I stood up. Nobody ever stood in class unless told to, usually to answer some petty charge or other. I said: German fascism was a complete evil. We see what they did to the Jews, we see what they were. If Germany had won the war Ireland would be a slave state. Worse than under the British. But, they had a powerful and effective air force. So, if we had joined with the Allies, our towns and cities would have been levelled overnight. Destroyed. It's clear, De Valera did the right thing, the only thing he could have done. Your first duty is to protect your own people, after that you do what you can to protect others. For instance, you let American planes fly in over Ireland, you let thousands of Irish men join the British navy, the air force, the army. Please don't be stupid.

All this addressed to O'Mahony, intended of course for the teacher. Perhaps for myself – sometimes, as you're growing, the best way to find out what you think is to listen to yourself saying it. To take something you've read or heard and test it against your own understanding. Perhaps I was parroting something I'd heard from the men, perhaps I was putting together fragments of overheard conversation into an argument that made sense to myself?

You said all that? In class? Michael John was, for the first time ever, taken aback by me. And the teacher, what did the teacher say, what'd he do? He said that's a very interesting point of view and thank you both for your contributions and as it's a Friday I think I'll let you all go home early.

I think he's smarter than you'd think, I added.

Why so?

Because he saw that if he let us home early they'd all somehow think it was because of what I'd said, and they could see anyway that he was pleased by me, so maybe some of them would actually think about what I said. Smart.

And what about what's his name, the O'Mahony boy?

I looked at my grandfather with respect, impressed by his ability to cut through things. He tried to start a fight outside the gates on Fair Hill. Did he now, and what did you do? Oh, I gave him a dig. And what did he do then? I don't know, I said, he didn't get up so I walked away home.

Michael John turned away then with a grunt, ducking his face. Later, knocking a ball against a gable wall I realised he'd turned away so that I wouldn't see him laughing.

6

The habits of a solitary man are hard to break. I have not always been solitary, of course; I have shared my life from time to time, but I have passed long swathes of time on my own, and this has had its conditioning effect.

Not long ago, I was seventy.

Sometimes I treat my birthdays as full-blown social occasions, I invite people round, whatever people are filling my life at the time, I make big meals or, if I'm particularly in funds, I take a private room in a restaurant and lavish my friends of the moment with their hearts' desires – subject, of course, to the whims of the chef and sommelier, the indulgence of *Monsieur le Proprietaire.*

There have been bacchanals, there have been long intense evenings full of good talk, long comfortable silences. Once or twice there have been near-riots – when, say, there has been a decisive shift in some party line and my guests fall on one side or the other with the usual passions, noise and heat.

Equally, I have often chosen to pass those birthdays in quiet and seclusion. As this year.

Just now, sitting back to ease the stiffness in my shoulders, letting the child I was drift away until tomorrow, I went to take a book, an Irish history, from its accustomed place, and found it was not there. I couldn't be bothered looking for it, knew it would surface in its own time. Books can be like that.

It comes to me that I have passed many birthdays re-arranging my books, as one re-arranges the elements of a life, in search perhaps of some pattern of meaning.

I switch on the lamps and draw the heavy drapes, I pull the low, padded nursing chair to the centre of the room and sit down.

'Books,' Michael John would say, 'are the furniture of the

mind' – and then he'd add, 'always ask yourself why you're reading the book you have in your hand. Is it the book you'd take with you if you had to walk out the door right now, leaving everything behind?'

I knew what he meant, but I thought he was being much too severe. I made no discrimination in my reading as a child, and still don't. Anything and everything that comes to hand. Yet I sit here now, like an appraiser after a death in the family, and consider that I have built a particular library. Here, in this room, at least. There's every kind of book piled higgledy-piggledy on shelves in all the other rooms – and this, mind, is a three-room apartment – but here in the front room, there is order and choice in disciplined abundance. There by the door, floor to ceiling, my books on Ireland – histories, sciences and politics, then poetry, novels and biographies. The next bank, biographies, mainly political; the next again, by the window, religion and philosophy. Past the window, coming round to the door again, classics, French literature of all kinds – and finally, a double bay, world history and politics.

The day of my birthday, stripped to a singlet and track suit trousers, I gave from dawn to dark dusting and polishing shelves, arranging and re-arranging the books in here. (I like tracksuit trousers; I find the softness agreeable and somehow private – I wouldn't dream of wearing them outdoors, despise the old fellas I see in suit coats and track trousers shuffling to the shops).

I'm tired, I'm puzzled. What brought all this on? Ah, that book, now ... and I remember where it is – on the small console table in the hall. I meant to take it with me when I went out for coffee this morning. Did I mean to stay for coffee, then, after the baker's? What put that in my head?

Now why did I draw the drapes, why did I light the lamps – I hate overhead light, I avoid it except in the kitchen – dear god

I'm tired suddenly. Dark outside, that's why the drapes. The day gone.

Right then, brisk now. Sleep for an hour, dinner, a walk around, an early night.

I've always talked to myself, sometimes out loud – as a kind of treat to myself. Just lately I started wondering, do I talk to myself on the street? Now that I would hate.

I'm talking to myself now as I undress: don't forget to set the clock for an hour, any more than that and you'll not sleep later; decide now where you'll eat when you get up; don't forget to take an umbrella, it looks like rain again.

I start talking to myself again the moment I open my eyes next morning. I must have killed the alarm at some point. Get up, you lazy man. Get washed, get dressed, get out for bread. Get some fruit while you're at it, some milk, butter, salami and olives. Tonight, buy wine, when you've finished for the day. Right, coat, look outside, dry and bright, no umbrella then. Quick march.

Back in again, I stand on the threshold before entering the apartment, savouring the book-rich air, the smell of beeswax, the rich tones and halftones of the rooms I can see from here.

My life, I think, my place, all those years of living.

7

My fifteenth birthday. Michael John was at the breakfast table, tea made, hot toast on a plate between the settings, boiled eggs in their cups. All perfectly timed.

No school today, he said, as I settled in. OK, I said, suits me. We ate in silence. Do you miss your parents, boy, he asked, as he washed, I dried.

Yes, you mean on my birthdays, particularly like? Today, not so much. Last year, the year before, terribly.

He looked at me thoughtfully: I don't want you hardening your heart, boy, you hear me? But he knew it wasn't that, by now he knew me well.

He waited, so I thought about what to say, about what his question really was.

Granda, I hate it when people summon up their feelings, you know what I mean? When they go, right, I'm supposed to be sad so I better be sad, that kind of thing? He nodded. I'm used to them being gone, I don't like it, I often wish they were still here, but to tell you the truth that's more like wondering than wishing, if you know what I mean? I mean, wondering how they'd find me, how I'd be with them, you know?

We sat there for a while, each of us remembering the terrible nights I'd passed, the long noiseless nights of crying, the bouts of bed-wetting, the recurrent, draining nightmares.

Remembering, too, how he'd come and sit by my bed, calming me, how he'd gather the stinking sheets in the morning, how we'd never speak of the night before. How I'd walk out the door to school, composed in myself as if nothing had passed in the long night reaches.

Get your coat, so, he said eventually, we're out for a long walk an' you'd never know what the weather might do.

We were good walkers, Michael John and myself. We'd strike out Dublin Hill for the Black Man and on to Hyde's Brake, or bear off through Glenville and back through Glanmire. Long walks. Or we'd head out the Lee Road, follow the river out to the Angler's Rest, then on to Healy's Bridge and back in by Blarney Street. Some days were like route marches, purposeful and silent, other days more like long, chatty rambles.

Where'll we go, so, he asked, as I pulled the front door shut behind us. Sometimes he'd say this as if musing to himself. Today it was a flat question. My choice. A crisp fine day, a hint of cloud over Spangle Hill. My birthday, my choice. Things to be said, things to be heard. Instinct told me we'd be hungry before the day was out, and told me, too, that Michael John was in no humour for meeting friend or acquaintance along the way.

Straight out Blackpool, I said, Kilbarry, the back roads, circle away on down to the Blackstone Bridge. No, wait – I was trying to remember if anywhere along that quietest of our options there might be a chance for lunch. He grinned, patting the pockets of his Macintosh: enough sandwiches here for a column he said; right then young Joseph, right turn, quick march.

The usual jury of idlers on Blackpool Bridge: no school today then boy? I'm teaching him how to go on the lang, Granda said, sweeping us past in a gale of wind. And the right teacher you'd be, too, boy, someone shouted after him.

I knew spiteful bravado for what it was, and looked up at Michael John to let him see I knew. Ah don't be so hard, lad, don't be so hard, he said, everyone's just trying to get through the world.

What was I responding to there, I wonder, some corner-boy's wish to wound, some need to protect a man I had recently come to see was vulnerable? Michael John was a proud man, you see, and proud men are always vulnerable.

You're growing up fast, he said presently. That's a good thing in you, I've seen it before. I was confused: seen what? You saw that fella meant to wound me, he said, you wanted to shield me, that's good, but don't go judging him, that's not what it's about. You get me?

I did, then and after.

We stopped at the Grotto, at the last shop heading out; he sent me in for two bottles of milk and apples, and when I came out he had a satchel held open, the sandwiches in the middle. Here, see, the bottles to either side, that way they won't make a sound as you move along. He put the strap over one shoulder so that the bag fell diagonally across his chest. See, putting his hand on the bag, if you have to run it won't be swinging about the place.

Watching to see did I understand he was telling me more than he was telling me. Satisfied, that characteristic nod that I valued so much, he moved off at a steady pace.

By god, that man could eat up the ground. The same age as the century, as far as I could figure, he had the energy of a man twenty years his junior. We were out past Murphy's Rock before he took pity on me and called a halt.

I was nervous. We hadn't spoken of it for years, but I was remembering and knew he remembered the promise made four years ago.

Sit in here beside me now, he said, out of the wind, and don't interrupt me.

The Treaty broke our hearts, he said, mine and a good few more. I don't blame Mick, he was sent out to get a deal and that's what he came back with. I don't blame Dev for sticking to what his heart was set on – tho' it was very wrong to give them the powers and then refuse to acknowledge what they brought back. See if you can understand me now, he said. What broke our hearts was two things: that we wouldn't have the Republic we fought for, and the brute reality of the situation, that there was nothing we could do about it. I couldn't go with Brugha and Dev, couldn't, couldn't. To shoot our own? I couldn't. And then, how could I go with the Free State, and end up shooting the men I fought with? The men I fought for? D'you see this? Join with an army made up for the most part of men that were nowhere to be seen when we were fighting for them and theirs? D'ye follow me now?

Every word of what he said working its way into my brain, every inflection, the lapses into relaxed speech, him that was always so accurate and precise. I was memorising as he spoke, actually and deliberately committing his words to memory. Terrified that the words wouldn't lodge.

My father had a saying, he went on, 'never join anything except your hands'. I would have listened if I could, but I heard the words and despised him for them. It's a sad thing, you see, but I was always a joiner.

I went to America, like hundreds more. We looked out for each other over there. I got work in Pennsylvania, in a quarry, dynamiting and such. Tough work, good money. I brought that money home, bought the house, took in two lads as lodgers, lost men like myself, old comrades, d'ye see?

He broke off, leaning away to see what was puzzling me? Ah, your father. You don't know, of course, of course you don't know, who'd have told you? Stupid of me. Maybe that's where I should have started.

I met his mother in 1918. We were out on our keeping in North Cork, up around Millstreet. I married her in a month, your father was born the year later. When I went to go, she wouldn't come with me. The brothers saw which way the wind was blowing, they went for the uniform, and she went with them, sided with them.

The thing they hated in me, the brothers, she came to fear it.

Your father, the next time I saw him, he was the age you were when I came back in 1945. He didn't know me, he didn't recognise me. I went to visit her, she had the priest in to keep the peace you might say, and not a picture of me was there in the house. The child didn't know me. He stood there looking at me. He didn't know me.

A sudden aside, then: you knew me, though, didn't you boy?

I kept quiet, kept my head down.

He shook his head sadly, went on. And then, all of a sudden, the consumption took her. This would have been about, what, 1928? Seanie and Tommy Mac drove me back to the house, I marched in and took the child, not a man there with the guts to object.

And do you know what, that child took to me then. He gave me his whole heart and I gave him mine – or thought I did.

He was about the age you are now when a man came to visit me from America, an old friend from the Union days, from the quarries. You with your books, have you heard of the Wobblies now? I have, I told him, you'd be amazed what I know about. Don't be giving yourself airs now, behave yourself. Sorry, Granda. And that's just what I was, sorry I mean; he could see it in me.

Anyway, Snyder was a good man, a man I admired to tell the truth; the upshot of it was, he signed me up to the Lincoln Battalion and I was on my way to Spain. You've read about the Spanish Civil War, eh? Of course you had. Oh a far dirtier business than ours it was ... but that's for another time

We won't go into it now. Your Aunt Peg took your father in. That was a dirty oul' war, and when we were beaten I made my way, me and a comrade called Henri, over into France. I was making for home, you see, at least that was the plan, but Henri was a bright man, a big man in every way, he saw what was coming. You want to fight Fascists, Miguel? Then you stay here with me.

One day soon, we will be fighting them here. And that's what I did. I stayed, up there in the maquis among Henri's hundreds of cousins and second cousins and pals and neighbours, and that was a dirty fight, too, when it came. My third war, you might say, but this time we won.

And then you came home?

And then I came home.

To find your son married and me installed by the fireside? He looked at me sideways, head tilted, one eyebrow cocked. D'you know what, you have a very quaint way of expressing yourself sometimes. I have, I said, it must be all them books. Those books, he corrected me automatically, then saw what I'd done and was grateful for the cheek of me. As I'd meant him to be. Because bald as it is when I write it out here, that man was suffering as he spoke his story, suffering as I'd never imagined he could suffer.

After a long silence, he said: Snyder died at Jarama, the same battle as poor old Charlie Donnelly. Who's Charlie Donnelly, I asked. He shook his head, stood, stretched, looking away down the narrow valley.

I'd no right to be telling you these things, he said then, but you asked. Be careful what you ask for.

Oh I'm always careful, I said. He gave me a look, a very cold look. You are, he said, you are that. And you're always in danger of going that small bit too far.

8

Henri said that, too, more than once. Careful himself even when being reckless, he was a man who acknowledged the role chance plays in a life but would go to great lengths to manage his affairs so that random events were, as far as possible, provided for in his calculations.

He liked to sit here by the window, as I am doing now, looking down on the street from an angle, seeing what passed by without himself being seen. Careful, always.

Like Vincent, he liked to come by at night. Like Vincent, and this has only just now occurred to me, he had the knack of climbing the stairs without making a sound. Unlike Vincent, he had a key to the front door; Henri had the keys to quite a few front doors.

And now I am thinking of Vincent, my day's labour done, wondering if he'll drop by to see how I'm doing. As far as I can remember, I never mentioned to him that I was thinking of writing this account of my life. All summer I've been thinking of it – perhaps for far longer, unknown to myself? There is a certain sympathy between us, though I would not call it a friendship. Perhaps it is, and I'm just slow to acknowledge it? I am not surprised he should have suggested I embark on the work, not surprised that he may well have picked up some growing valedictory mood of mine, some instinct towards a summing up. Or a clearing? He has a witch gene of some sort, something we share, though neither he nor I, if we spoke of this at all, would employ such a term.

He is curious about me, of course, but there is a certain disinterest in his curiosity; I mean it lacks prurience, what my neighbours in old Blackpool would have called nosiness. To Vincent, I am an old man who teaches English, a chance acquaintance with whom he keeps in touch.

Which perhaps does no justice at all to our relationship, nor does it explain the faint sense I am exploring here, flexing my stiff fingers as I have seen my barber do, that I am writing this – account, is it? – for him.

Is that what I'm doing? No. Decisively not. So often this happens, as soon as we drag something out of the nebulous, frame it as a direct question, the answer comes clear and unbidden. Not for Vincent, though I have prepared a place in my anticipations for him to ask how things are progressing; I allow he may feel a certain proprietorial interest in the outcome.

Not for Vincent, I think, no. Perhaps then for ... nobody? Ach, foolish question old man. Too early to tell. What does your instinct tell you? That this will become clear at the end, if not at some point *in medias res*. Well then, why trouble yourself with questions now? A good point, you make the case well.

You could go in for law, Michael John said that, my school leaving year. You have that cold mind. He meant it well, as untroubled as I was by the fact that law, in Cork in the late 1950s, was a profession reserved for the sons, more rarely the daughters, of lawyers. A lawyer from Blackpool? No, I said, no, not law.

Mme Frenaud is going by, she looks up as she always does, as she has been doing since first I moved into this apartment. True to her bourgeois type, she has never once taken the simple expedient of stopping me in the street and engaging me in conversation. She would, I know, die before asking straight out: but what is it *Monsieur* does? She would dearly love to know, it has in its insidious way been a satisfying source of disquiet to her all these years. Mme's husband, long dead, was a middle-rank functionary under Vichy, a collator of forms, of files. The Party suspected his hand in the dossiers prepared in advance of the Vél' d'Hiv, but nothing was ever proved and besides, as Henri said, standing here once beside me, looking down as I am looking down now, how many hundreds of thousands would we have to pursue?

Mme somehow knows I am not the elderly proper man I appear to be. I dress with a certain casual formality, I have often under my arm a leather document folder, on my face a certain mask of propriety and reserve. My hair, *en brosse*, is always disciplined, and when I wear an old-fashioned beret, as I sometimes do in the rain, as I often do in winter, it is always set four square on the top of my head, just so. I am, in short, remarkably unremarkable for this quartier, but Mme knows, somehow, there is something about me that is not quite right.

When I die, when she hears I have died, she will say to someone or other, perhaps M. Hourcand, our jovial baker: there was something not quite, I don't know, about that man. And they will look at her with polite incomprehension.

I have a remarkable fund of information about my neighbours. Truly, I believe it would astonish them, how much I know about them. I derive no satisfaction from this, you understand; like all information it is merely ... useful. I have taken care to ensure they know little or nothing about me. Henri approved of, indeed admired, my ability to withhold information about myself. He did not understand, I think, that this had nothing to do with caution, nothing to do with him or with our relationship, or our work as I suppose I must call it. Once, ah I was young and perhaps over-bold, thinking to test his understanding as well as to clear some space for myself, I told him: there are no electrons in my outer shell. No, he said, and his pitying look was sufficient rebuke for my arrogance, no my poor dear Joseph, you are not a joiner. Then, seeing my dismay, at his words and at the fact that he had so readily understood me, he added cheerfully; and some day, you poor young man, you will learn that nobody ever really, truly joins.

I miss Henri. I miss Michael John. And I will miss dinner if I do not go now.

9

Granda, I had stopped at the foot of the stairs, on my way to bed, Granda, what you told me today, did my Dad know? Come here, he said, and folded me in his arms, his overcoat as yet unbuttoned so that I felt on my cheek the warmth of his chest. Of course he knew, did you think I wouldn't tell him? I loved him, do you not remember that?

I went back for the pictures, the flurry of memories, and saw what I saw. Understood what I knew. I looked back up at him, leaning into the circle of those sinewy arms. And he loved you, I said, and Mam did. A kind of wonder in me.

Good boy, he said, letting me go, reaching for his cap where it hung on the hallstand. Good boy. Your Aunt Peg ... Doesn't get it, I said at once. I was brutal, sometimes, in those days. No, he said, softly, she had a story running in her head, hadn't she? The disappearing heartless father, the neglected half-orphaned child ... ach I don't blame her. Nor do I, I said stoutly. He looked at me mockingly: well now and isn't that very good of you?

He stood in the doorway, surveying the street as he buttoned up his coat against the breeze. Come here Joseph, he said, and listen to me a minute. What I told you today? Yes, I said. Stays between us. Nothing to the lads, OK? And, well, you asked me something a few years ago, I've given you sufficient answer, all right? You were owed that, but nothing else. Don't ask me again. I'm not being hard now, nor treating you with disrespect. I have your measure, boy; you'll be up there in bed with your fingers laced behind your head, running it all over in your mind, listing the questions you'll want me to answer. Am I right? I blushed, yes you're right. Well, don't. Not now, not until you're ready for the answers. And how will I know that, I asked, bitter inside suddenly, I suppose you'll be the judge of that, will you? Ah now, he said, cop yourself on. Of course I'll be the judge of that, and so will you. D'you understand me? There are things in this life you have to be fit for to understand.

We stood there, side by side, looking out on the quiet street, mist beginning to gather around the street lamp in front of us, and it came to me, came creeping up into my mind, that one day Michael John would die, and that I would die, and that all this would go on or it would dissolve into nothing like a dream in which you have no further interest.

Would you look at the pair of ye? Tommy Mac came bustling towards us, rubbing his hands, that habitual gesture. Like a pair o' feckin' gargoyles from above on the front of St Finbarre's. Is it coming or going ye are? Michael John smiled at him fondly; ah Jaysus Tommy, he said, isn't that always the question? Are we coming or going? Go to bed now, you. And I went.

Would you like a sup o' tea? Tommy called up after me.

No thanks, Tommy, I said, but if there's a drop o' whiskey goin'?

Dear god, he laughed, but aren't you gettin' very cheeky all the same, g'way up to bed with you. And the street door and the kitchen door clicked shut with the same soft sound.

A year later the Border Campaign stuttered into life, and everything changed. None of the men had stayed in touch with what remained of the Republican movement. As far as I knew. Naturally, Cork being the size it was, they might from time to time socially or otherwise bump into men they knew from the old days, but of the new young pups, Seanie's phrase, they knew nothing – nor did they care to know. They had in common, the lodgers, a stoical acceptance of what had come to be. They shared my grandfather's understanding that the revolution they had fought for had been defeated, that Ireland had made the best peace it could with an incomparably more powerful enemy. Having made their war with no thought of personal profit, they were inclined, if I understood them then, to accept that they had gambled and lost. In this sense, and it is an important sense, they were utter realists. That they were unhappy with how Ireland had turned out was a given, but when Tommy Mac said one night at the cards that this was not the Ireland he had fought for (I think there had been some trouble at work, a friend unfairly dismissed, something like that), Seanie had cut him off: Tommy, boy, leave off, would you? Nobody asked you to fight, did they? You gave it your shot, we gave them what they have, and this is what they want to do with it, all right?

They had looked to Michael John, then, years of unspoken hurts, disappointments, crowding the room. There was real compassion in his voice, real adult compassion, I was hearing the colour of it for the first time, noting it down to think about it later, when he said: ah lads, lads, play the cards you're dealt, eh? Play the cards you're dealt.

On the Border business, Michael John was cold and concise in his dismissiveness. Play-acting, he called it, no hope of military gain, utterly uninstructed by politics, no material base in objective circumstances. Precise, magisterial, cold, this was a Michael John I'd never seen. The men considered what he'd said, and one after another they nodded agreement. They always took their line from Granda, but I liked it that they would argue if unconvinced, insisting that he defend and explain his line of argument.

I know that approaches were made, to each of them in turn, certainly to Michael John, but they were as one in their scornful dismissal of all overtures. As far as I could tell.

Granda's revelation that he had fought in Spain had affected me deeply. I read everything the city library could provide me with; I learned how to use the Reference section, would trawl through the newspapers of the period, piecing that desperate war together for myself. Not easy, since I could find little in those papers that wasn't, one way or another, inclined to Franco's side. Nobody reading this, if anyone ever does, will need to be told what the world was like then, nor will they need to be told how the world's press was remarkably unsympathetic to what I rapidly deduced was the key fact in the whole conflict: that Franco's rebellion against a legitimately elected Republic was just that, a rebellion against the expressed will of the people. I was black and white at sixteen, as young men and women should be, and no doubt my sympathies were engaged with Michael John.

The Right, as I liked to phrase it, privately to myself, was wrong.

I made my politics, such as they were, from this reading, from what I could deduce of Michael John's own views, and from the set of perceptions I formed for myself listening to the men and walking about the city.

And, of course, my politics took a certain fieriness from my hormones. I detested team sports, although I loved watching hurling or knocking a ball about by myself or with some casual acquaintance, but I was superbly fit from my habit of walking about the city or deep into the countryside for hours and hours on end. That and the endless reading to which I had long since become addicted made for a heady brew of energy which, when animal spirits kicked in, made me dangerously, unpredictably unstable.

We had just crossed over into the new year when the special branch came calling. A loud, insistent knocking, about 9 o'clock at night; who the fuck, I was thinking, already irritable, as I went to open the door. A big broad older man, a weaselly looking younger man with a gut on him that didn't fit with the lanky stretch of him – it annoyed me, just the look of him – and when the older man spoke, in a slow heavy voice, I had to turn my head, ask him to repeat himelf. I asked, he said, spacing his words out, is your grandfather in?

Ah for fuck's sake ... the younger man just shoved me aside. I turned, fast, was about to hit him a dig, anger coming over me, when the old lad, surprisingly quick, caught my fist in mid-air and snapped at the other fella: get back here, you. I think that perhaps I was the more surprised of us, taken aback by that sudden surge of rage.

Granda was standing at the foot of the stairs, his reading glasses on the tip of his nose, a book held down by his side, watching us all dispassionately. He looked through the young pup, nodded to the older man: Gerry, he said, civil. Ah Mick, how're things, could we come in for a minute?

The house was warm, Granda always kept the place warm in winter, but there was a chill in the air now, a kind of undischarged lightning I thought later, still seething, still in a slightly literary fever. The older men looked at us then, at the young cop and at me, from one to the other of us, back and forth, and I saw the same look of resignation in both their faces.

Ah, the one called Gerry said, with a certain weariness, closing the door gently behind him, ah Mick, young bucks, eh? Young bucks.

I stood aside to let this Gerry go by, and I saw a certain shrewdness in his eyes as he looked at me briefly, a faint flicker of amusement that was not unkind.

The younger one nearly stood on my heels, pushing into the kitchen behind me. The lodgers sat at the table, unmoving. Granda pulled out a chair for Gerry, who sat, waved a hand over his shoulder, said: Cassady. A grunt from the pup. Granda took the remaining chair, between Seanie and Tommy Mac; he didn't offer tea, an unusual thing for him, and Gerry sighed, understanding. Cassady, unable to keep still, started drifting around the kitchen, picking things up, putting them down again. Making his presence felt. Everyone ignored him, except me; I knew this insolence was aimed at me.

Silence settled on the men around the table, measured, expectant. I was waiting for Gerry to say something, but Granda spoke first. He leaned back in his chair, palms flat on the table and said: Gerry, we all know each other here, you had to call in, o'course, we understand that. I'll tell you now, and you know me, nobody here is having anything to do with this ... foolishness. That day is past. That day is done and gone, all right? Gone.

Gerry, his big, broad shoulders bowed, had his head down, listening to this, his hands folded one over the other, a man at prayer. He nodded once, twice, then lifted his head, looked each man at the table clean and mild in the eye. One after the other they inclined their heads, a formal gesture, their agreement.

Cassady was watching Granda, his feral instinct telling him Granda was the power here. He must have felt me seeing this, his head snapped round and he gave me a stare of such venom I know I physically recoiled.

Michael John saw this, and something unwound in him as he straightened, something animal, hyper-alert and very dangerous. This I had never seen before, but when I saw it, I knew I had somehow always intuited its latent presence.

Gerry saw it, too. He rose abruptly to his feet, said that'll do now, that'll do, go wait in the car. Making a point of not looking at Cassady. Who hesitated an insubordinate second or two before walking, stiff-backed with rage, out of the room.

Gerry stayed standing, his eye flicking for a moment to Seanie Murphy. Seanie who all those long years ago had signed the execution orders, Seanie whose level stare now acknowledged his former commanding officer.

Mick, Gerry said, your word was always good. I understood this as a question. Something I couldn't see passed between them, and when Gerry said, it was Mick, god knows, your word was always good, I saw my Granda soften, his eyes widen; only then did I register that he had been standing, too, since that look passed between Cassady and me.

Ah Gerry, he said, and I waited for more, but that's all he said.

On his way past me, this Gerry stopped, looked me up and down thoughtfully. I saw some kind of sadness, regret maybe, in his eyes. Over his shoulder, very softly, still holding my look, he asked: a good lad, Mick? Phrased as a question, but I knew, and everyone knew, it wasn't. The best, Granda said, and I felt a rush of pride, of other emotions I could not name then, and could not name now. Gerry, that thoughtful man, punched me lightly on the shoulder, to forestall the sudden emotion he sensed. Good enough for me, he said; and then, a warning expressly directed to me mind how you go, lad. You'll be grand.

That Cassady fella ... Seanie said. I had never seen him so cold. A cunt, pure and simple, Granda said. A dangerous cunt all the same, said Tommy Mac, giving me a thoughtful look. Adding, look how shocked the boy is at your language, Mick, would you ever mind your tongue. And they all burst out laughing, and after a second or two, for the relief of my own rage as much as to join in, I started laughing too.

10

Late afternoon, I've had enough. I close the memory file, close the diary file, save both to the stick. What did that young poet say, we buy memory now, we don't have memory any more. A bright young woman, later I might take down one of her books.

I open the windows wide, that Cassady leaves a bad smell, I feel him pushing against the edge of my mind and I don't want this right now, I'm not able for it. For him.

I go through and switch the water heater on. A long bath tonight, I think, already savouring the bone deep luxury, but a walk first, a slow steadying walk.

I'm out for a stroll, Michael John would say, want to come? Sometimes I would, sometimes I wouldn't. One way or the other, he didn't mind. We could walk for hours without saying a word to each other, hesitating at some turn, deferring to each other. Where to now? And on, then. For hours as I say.

That I miss, and miss it more as I get older. The long walks, the deep companionable silence.

Almost always in this city I walk alone.

I pull on socks, ease my feet into shoes without opening the laces.

Today, for the fun of it, I go down the stairs without testing the creaking treads, testing instead the lightness of my step.

There are walking canes, rubber-tipped, in a kind of open basket in the corner of the hall. They were here when I first came. Sometimes there's a fine spider's web from one of them to the fuse box overhead; I think I may be the only one here who will sometimes employ one.

Selecting a fine Malacca now, I note that I have decided to

walk as far as, and through, the gardens of the Islamic Cultural Centre. The cane is for poking leaves, turning things over, parting branches to look deeper into the undergrowth.

They have good teas there, mint tea will freshen my head, banish perhaps these insidious miasmas.

There's a gang of students outside the Collège des Irlandais as I reach the corner, the year's new intake of, if you please, Erasmus scholars. I'm not in the humour for those excited accents, I think, and continue on up towards Mouffetard.

A latecomer bustling up the street jostles me, accidentally. Jaysus sorry, he says, then, collecting himself, pardon, *M'sieu*. That eagerness to be part of the gang, that moment's dispassionate pity for a slow old man.

Past it, isn't that what they say, isn't that what the look says?

I observe in myself a malicious cold surge of rage. Then, softening, a kind of weary pity. For the lad gone by or for myself, I couldn't say. Maybe both. Oh once I, too, was immortal ...

On the terrace, under the plane trees, their still-dense heads of leaf absorbing the noise of the traffic from the Seine below, I bow my head over the steaming graceful teapot, inhaling the smell of crushed mint; that reminds me, disconcertingly, of crushed nettles. Those long walks into the country.

I am considering buying a pack of cigarettes on the way home when, of the two figures passing below me on the garden path, I recognise Vincent. He feels my eyes on him, it seems, for he turns without breaking stride, meets my look and passes on, still listening politely to the robed figure with whose short stride he is struggling to accommodate himself.

I know he saw me, I know he saw that I recognised him. He is wearing jeans, a black leather jacket, neat. He has sunglasses pushed to the top of his head. I will him to glance back, I approve that he does not.

I should not like to have misjudged Vincent.

That first time we met, and only briefly, Vincent misjudged me.

Sometimes, in the cool of evening after a long, hot summer's day, when I venture out for some few groceries to the Rue Mouffetard, I make the circle back home by way of the south side of the Panthéon. That long curve of tall buildings to the right side, the wide pavement, the empty road then the blank high wall to the left, between them they make a vault of space where the mind can rest, can settle into the hoped for cool of night. I was walking slowly, deliberately, and perhaps this lulled the boy somewhat, perhaps it exaggerated the sense he had of some feeble old man coming towards him. He had been jemmying a kerbside car, now he was leaning back casually, his face to the buildings, a long slim bar of some kind half-concealed by his body, the suit coat he wore over neat denim jeans worn loose. Algerian, I thought. North African. The occasional jerk of his elbow, of course, gave the game away, that and the fact that, looking around him as he worked the lock, he was being just that little bit too cool for his surroundings. Nevertheless, I could see he knew what he was doing. Coming abreast of him, having studiously avoided his gaze until then, I halted, leaned back against some doorway and stared at him frankly. He stopped what he was doing, adopted an aggressive stance, his shoulders rounding towards me, left hand behind his back. What do you want, old man? What're you looking at? A passable *banlieue* accent, I thought, though the roughness might just be contrived. A young man who could give a smooth account of himself. I like, I said, to watch a professional at work. It amuses me. He stared at me a moment, looked down at the briefcase standing beside him on the pavement. For a few seconds he considered the situation, then lifted his head and gave me a sunny, open smile. Come here, he said, giving a quick look around, come here and I'll show you. Out of town car, I said, having seen the plates. Exactly, he said, as I drew near, hired, see this little sticker here on the rear window? Ah so, I said, reduces the incentive a little for the cops? Exactly, he said. I had his approval now. See here, this little flat bar? I slide it down here, like so, I jiggle it and, hoop la! The door clicked.

OK old man, he said, reaching for the briefcase. I stood back as he sat in, jammed a screwdriver in the ignition, started the engine. He took some papers from the briefcase then, spread them on the front passenger seat. I saw the heading, *Faculté de Droit*. He took a pair of spectacles from his breast pocket, unfolding and fitting them in one smooth movement and, *voila*, a young, bespectacled law student, conservatively if causally dressed, heading home in the cool of evening after a hard day at the books. Upward mobility, assimilation in action. Bravo, I murmured, and he smiled acknowledgement.

Then it struck him, how odd it was that this elderly bourgeois should be so approving, so ... aware? That was a very different look he gave me then, very sober, very serious. What is it you do, old man? I teach English, I said. In a school? Then, answering himself, no, I think not. You live around here, he asked me then. I held out the shopping bags. Well, good, he said, we'll see each other again? Why not, I said, why not – should you find yourself in the neighbourhood. He liked that, and I who had already decided to like him for his insouciant ways, thought I could like him all the more for admiring my own *sang-froid*.

Here in the tea garden I run through the details again, that first encounter with my friend, if friend he is. Trying to decide whether or not he is a cop. Or something worse.

My young friend, Henri liked to favour me with his home-grown maxims when I knew him first: my young friend, when out of the blue somebody decides to be your friend, that man you must at once suspect him. You have a saying in your book, you Anglos, 'oh sharper than a serpent's tooth ...' He was teasing me, of course. I'm not an Anglo, I said, and betrayal isn't confined to Anglos. And besides, determined to punish him just a little, to stake a place for myself perhaps, besides the quote is inapposite. I blushed at my choice of word, but Henri smiled kindly at me. A forgiving man.

Inapposite, inapposite ... Oh Miguel, Miguel, he said, invoking my grandfather, shaking his head sorrowfully, half mocking, half serious, what have you sent me, eh?

Later, home from my walk, taste of mint still in my mouth, I lay back in the bath, the heat going deep into my bones, and asked myself, what put that thought into your head old man? Those days are gone. Finished.

But of course, common sense returning as I towelled myself briskly, roughly, the lad could be a cop and have no interest, no professional interest, in you. A very subtle cop.

Part of me, turning that thought over as I fell asleep, was perhaps a little piqued.

11

All through my final year in school, and for a year after that, the cop Cassady became the bane of my life. At night, moving the curtain aside having first turned off the light, I would see the glow of his cigarette in the car parked across the street. At lunchtime, when I'd dash home for a hurried bite, he might be parked outside the school gates or walking slowly back and forth in the street outside our house. Always those feral eyes on me, as if he was trying to make me feel the intensity of his hatred. At first, hot as I was in those days, I was merely furious, I'd have to will myself not to confront him, not to challenge him. My teachers had already learned to steer clear of my unspoken rage, anyone who knew me had learned, some with good reason, to fear my tongue. I had in me, in those burgeoning days, a capacity for viciousness when aroused that now I understand all too well, having burned through those passions, but at seventeen one is aware only of the power of one's feelings. I knew I reciprocated Cassady's hatred for me, I knew it was hatred is what I am trying to say, but I couldn't quite understand why he should hate me as he did. Or perhaps I did, maybe at some cellular level – after all I was aware that I was constantly keeping my own occasional violent instincts heavily repressed. I did not know then – how could I – that if I ever gave way to those instincts, I would be lost to myself forever. I did not know then that in time, after long study in managing myself, those instincts would fade to nothing.

I used to imagine, in hallucinatory detail, the raw surge of pleasure I would feel if I were to walk up to him, all innocent, and then smash him in the face without warning. I am not exaggerating when I say that learning to master and control that impulse was my first lesson in tempering the violent side of my nature.

He has it in for you, that young buck, Michael John said to me once. Autumn, late, we were walking out the Commons Road in the early dusk, a turn before dinner as we liked to say. I was scuffing dry leaves where they'd drifted against the Sunbeam factory fence. I was watching Cassady out of the corner of my eye, keeping pace with us on the opposite footpath, a few yards behind. I didn't think Michael John had noticed.

I wouldn't like to get between you, Michael John said, eyeing me mildly. Holding the moment now in memory, I see the dart of humour in his look; I didn't see it then.

I had a fella like him once. Fixated on me. This was before it came to shooting, mind. I suppose, now that I think of it, I wasn't much older than you are now. This fella, RIC man, he'd follow me night and day. As if he couldn't help himself. It would have come to one or other of us only he went and signed up to the Munster Fusiliers. Killed at High Wood, poor bastard; that was one dirty attack, that was. Do you know, I felt awful sorry for him after.

Something in his voice took hold of me. We'd stopped abruptly, and so, I noticed, had Cassady, who was staring at us avidly, openly. Granda, I said tentatively, concerned at his unfocused look, his sudden air of vacancy. I saw him come to himself, I saw what the phrase meant, I felt some undefinable sorrow pass through me. He looked at me so intently I started to fear for him again, and then he shook his head, still holding my look. Soldiers are fools, boy, never forget that. No matter what you're fighting for, what you get in the end is never what you killed for, and the poor bastards you kill, they wouldn't have got it either. Kennedy that fella's name was, he added, softening again, looking across at Cassady absentmindedly. Kennedy, from out by the Lough. One of his brothers went Sinn Féin after, I knew him slightly but we never spoke.

Come on, time for grub. Now – brisk, commanding: *aire! Clé iompaigh*, by the left, quick march. And we headed for home, as we had done so many times since my boyhood, backs erect, arms swinging crisply, *clé, clé, clé, deas, clé*, eyes dead ahead, our leather-soled boots ringing in unison.

Leaving the cop, to my vengeful satisfaction, bewildered behind us.

Maybe Michael John had a quiet word with his old comrade Gerry, maybe Cassady found someone else to torment, but he disappeared from my life around then. For a while.

That spring I made a friend, not meaning to. I was, as I hope I've made plain, a solitary boy, and content enough with that. I had Granda, to be sure, and the lodgers, and I wasn't entirely solipsistic, there were guys in school with whom I was friendly enough, or friendly enough as they saw it. There were a bunch of guys with whom I might hurl on one of the nearby streets after school, so little traffic in those days we would stop for a moment when someone shouted 'car!', resume when it went by. I would swop books occasionally with the guy who sat next to me in class, and was more or less an accepted member of the gang that would sit on the wall at break discussing girls, politics of a primitive kind, the characters of our teachers, what we might do when we left school. Known derisively as the swots, we were also known to be quick with our fists if need be, some of us anyway, so we would be left alone for the most part, if you discount the occasional mistaken attempt to bully one or another of us. There was a kind of comfort in that particular belonging, but I was, though I wouldn't have recognised it, quite lonely in myself.

I was haunting the history section in the City Library, as usual, reading to all sides of the narrow course prescribed for us in school, and one late afternoon I saw a boy of about my own age reach down a copy of Ernie O'Malley's *The Singing Flame*. He saw that I recognised the title, asked politely if I thought it was any good, and when I told him I'd read and enjoyed it, and that my grandfather vouched for it, he tucked it under his arm. About to go, he turned and put his hand out: Philip Kelly, he said; Joseph Roche, I said, and then added, they call me Joe. They call me Philip, he said, and laughed when I caught the ruefulness, said Phil will do.

Phil lived in Sunday's Well, a good suburb on the edge of the city, out near the Lee Fields. He went to Christian Brothers College, 'the cream of the city rich and thick' as we liked to say in my school. Cork was a city of social hair-triggers in those days, stratified by class divides that were Byzantine in their nuances, immutable as the rankings of Czarist Russia. Nothing, it was universally felt, would ever disturb that savage complacency, and cross-class friendships were quite rare. That never bothered us, neither did it bother Phil's family when I began to appear in their house, and if I expected it to bother the men when Phil started to drop around to see me, I did them an injustice. That first time, Granda looked at Phil thoughtfully, searching his face. Is your Dad John Kelly, he asked, John Finbarr Kelly? He is, said Phil looking back at him with an equal thoughtfulness, and he told me to wait until you asked that before giving you his best, Mick, he added. That cracked the men up; Tommy Mac shoved Seanie aside and said sit down here lad, and tell us what ails you, that you'd make a friend of this fella here.

We walked all Cork that spring, Phil and I, and when summer came we'd bicycle to Crosshaven to swim, to Kinsale and further afield when the day seemed to offer the prospect of light and sun from morning to late at night. And we talked, my god how we talked. About everything and anything, as young men do at that age if they are fortunate enough to find, in essence, an echo to what sounds in their souls. Phil was as bookish as I was, more given to sports but, like me, uncomfortable with the enforced loyalties of team games. He ran, walked, swam and rowed to test himself, to test this life as it bubbled and flowed inside him, and this was so much my own way, his animal spirits and inquiring mind so perfectly coincided with my own, that there was, we agreed, something Greek about our friendship – but we were Cork enough that we laughed immediately at the phrase and at ourselves. Jesus save us from becoming provincial intellectuals, I said; and, Jesus be thanked for Frank O'Connor who came to save us from ourselves, Phil responded, in the perfectly-caught singsong voice of the altar boy each of us had, for a short while, improbably in my case, been.

We were sprawled in Bell's Field, night coming on, the purple night of just past midsummer. The whole panorama of the Northside lay before us, the flat of the city, its shops and broad streets intercut with alleyways to the left and below, while before us rose Gurranebraher with its red-roofed terraces of new-built Corporation housing; Churchfield and Spangle Hill to the right of it, capping the ridge line, and down to the right, spreading out and away from the brewery chimney to the green cap of the new church, dubbed Dwyer's Fire Escape in honour of its patron, lay the valley of my native Blackpool.

The tower of the North Cathedral and the bell-hung steeple of Shandon stood proud before us, sandstone and limestone giving back the heat of the day, while on the far edge of Sunday's Well the last of the light came in sheets off the green steep-pitched roof of St Vincent's – like a castle, we said, on the Rhine, neither of us having yet set foot outside Ireland.

They want me to do law, Phil said, lying back in the dusty grass. Next year, after school, you know? What about you, Joe, any ideas? Not a thing, I said, not a notion. Phil sat up, concern in his face. But Joe, Jesus you have to do something, you know. I mean, with your brains ... and he got embarrassed then. I waved it aside, I know, I said, I know, scholarships, all that, don't worry pal, there's money there, Michael John has already said so. I didn't mean, he said. You did of course, but you didn't mean anything by it so forget it, right? C'mon Phil, we're beyond that surely? No, I just haven't a clue what to do with myself. Really, not a clue.

We lay back again in the dry grass, and presently Phil said: do you think you might be queer? Do you mean, I said, would I ride you? No, but I'd flah your sister!

I know what it is to want the ground to swallow you up. That was, suddenly, exactly what I desperately wanted. Theresa. There was a moment's pause and then Phil said, softly, ah poor Joe, I know you would, but she won't. Not now, not ever. We lay on, letting the moment ebb away, ripples quietening to the edge of a dark pool.

Are you, I asked him presently, when we stood to go, by some unspoken agreement, dusting ourselves down, taking a long look around. What, queer? Nah. Pity, I said, damn pity, what? Still laughing, we straggled across to where our bikes stood companionably interlinked, aslant on the hill, their handlebars glinting. Come on, he said, better chance of getting something to eat in our house, this time of evening; your Granda runs that place with military precision, there won't be a scrap left.

At the top of Richmond Hill, unbelievably, scowling as he leaned over the roof of his car, stood Cassady. Ah for fuck's sake, Phil said, then roared across at him, would you ever just fuck off, would you? Then he bumped over the kerb, swerved into the deep gutter that ran down the side of Fever Hospital Steps and sped away downhill, lurching over occasional drains, headlong and headstrong down where the car couldn't follow, me reckless behind him, and when we shot out onto Leitrim Street under the huge brewery chimney he had to swerve in front of a dark blue Ford Anglia while I, only just, managed to scrape behind it. The driver, white in the face, screaming unheard obscenities at us.

12

I am becoming mildly disturbed by this process, this business of retrieval. Not least by the serial nature of the thing. That I have gone all the way back, am marching so grimly forward, one thing after another. As if life were like that.

Off and on over this past summer, bits and scraps of memory have been appearing to me, fragmentary, uncertain, out of time and sequence: a face, an incident, a place, all in a slow foggy tumble. Something would come steady, clear, the projectionist tightening his focus, and then would dissolve, having caught my full attention for a moment. I did not expect then, if I expected anything at all, when I sat down to write this ... account is it? that this linear, disciplined progress, this route march through my life, would provoke such self-searching, such ... judgement.

I have not been to the doctor, to any doctor, for years. I have no sense of being unwell, nothing in the way of presentiment disturbs either my waking or my sleeping, and yet I feel I am drifting towards some kind of point, some resolution, that moment people report when they feel that up ahead some doorman is lumbering to his feet, turning his face towards one, ears attentively pricked for a particular footstep.

I have learned over the years, two principal tactics for dealing with doubt, at least the kind of doubt I am feeling now: either one lies down in a dark room, for days on end if need be, allowing the mists to thicken and swirl until something comes clear, or you can hand the process over to the body, to some decisive physical action. *Basta*! I strip clumsily but gather my clothes neatly, dropping them in the basket as I turn on the shower. Cold and hard, so that I panic, thinking it will be too much but then the light comes on inside again, that elemental rush, and I am brisk as a newborn as I step out and towel myself vigorously, humming away to myself as I dress in cords and tweed jacket over a favourite grey soft shirt, a green pullover. Brown brogues with this, I think, hah, and there I am, ready to go out.

Brisk as a newborn indeed, I think, time to stop making phrases old man, now take the stairs carefully won't you? That's right. And perhaps we might stop humming *Avanti Popolo* now? We have a certain neutral identity out here on the street, do we not?

I am always at my most cheerful when I catch this dialogue between me and myself – or perhaps it is that catching this chatter going on makes me happy? Ah who can tell, eh?

The Spanish boy brings me coffee, Americano they call it now, so surprised by my recent gesture, that calculated tip, that he greets me, half unsure, with a mumbled *Bonsoir, Maitre.*

Maitre, indeed. Someone's been talking, or he's been asking. I assume from this that the proprietor is present, and when I turn, having favoured the lad with a gracious nod, Honoré is indeed in his usual place behind the bar; we beam at each other, honours even in the hypocrisy stakes, and I note with satisfaction that, as usual, he is hovering close to the till. He must be, what, in his early fifties? I'd say so, but I have no doubt in my mind that had he lived through the war our dear Honoré would have been a willing, an enthusiastic, collaborator. Strange how types play true to type, how a handful of roles suffice for the human comedy to go grinding on. And on.

Honoré, now, has been dying to ask me for years and years what it is, exactly, that I do. Of my respectability, he is not in doubt: he observes through those slitty eyes of his how the old ladies greet me, how I defer to them in those small encounters on the street, in the bakery opposite; he observes how the old gentlemen bow to me, and how I bow to them; he observes how decorously, at suitably long intervals, we may linger a moment and chat inconsequentially.

I was here before he took over this café, he knows this, but he does not know for how long I have lived here; for all he knows I have lived here all my life, and such people bring out the unease in him, they touch on the raw nerve of a provincial come to the capital – from Rennes, if I am not mistaken? From Brittany, yes certainly.

Ah Honoré, you old fool, why would it never occur to you simply to ask me what it is you wish to know? But then, to be fair, I would have lied to him, wouldn't I? Yes, I would.

The boy comes for the money and, newly-emboldened, ventures an opinion on the weather. I answer in Spanish that I do not think it will rain and tipping the back of my head towards the interior give him a quick wink. What pleases him most, hearing his native tongue from me or the sly invitation to a little conspiracy I do not know, but when he accepts that I may be right he says it in loud, robust if non-native French. I for my part have always prided myself on my ear, and seeing him startle at my passable Basque accent I feel the momentary gratification of being one who knows. A small but dangerous vanity; I rebuke myself and get up abruptly, leave without looking back.

I am heading I notice, downhill, towards the Rue St Jacques. Ah, I think happily, wine, that's what I want. I like this small wine shop, tucked back from the narrow street on a wider section of paving, next to the shop that sells mostly art books. The young proprietor, open-faced and friendly as ever, greets me over the shoulder of some burly man with glasses perched on the tip of his nose, briefcase at his feet. The young woman, his companion, perhaps co-owner, I have never been able to decide, whom I suspect has read every word ever published by Cixous and Kristeva, gives me her secret smile, the one that says one must humour such people, with a nod, all but imperceptible, towards M. Burly. Her formal greeting extends this pleasant little by-play: ah *M'sieu*, she says, you have exquisite timing, we have just taken delivery of a new Cahors. Allow me ... and she pours me a little to savour, discreetly pushing a spittoon forward with, I observe, a shapely foot. Oh but she's quick, sees where my eye falls, is not displeased. Theresa, I think, with a spasm, oh Theresa, the buried memory that sent me lurching from my desk.

Is *M'sieu* all right? Her concern is genuine, I must look stricken. Ah, old people, we are struck by memories, out of the blue, you understand? Ah, and now she is definitely flirting, no doubt *M'sieu* has so many memories ... I meet her look, I see she is serious under the banter, that somehow she understands, even though of course it is not possible to say what it is she understands. Nevertheless ... one of us, I think, one of ours; and this shows in my eyes, this sudden impersonal judgement, this recognition, call it what you will, and she sees it register, acknowledges the moment briefly, and we agree to return to the world's business.

Mam'selle is right, I say, having tasted and spat, please wrap me four bottles, just the right blend of iron and fruit. Just so, she says, adding quietly: *Madame*. Not a rebuke, a reaffirmation of that moment just now: we are the kind of people, she is saying, agreeing, who like to know what's what. She smiles at the young man, and he smiles at me. M. Burly, poor chap, is at a loss and not liking it sensing, as he must often do, an atmosphere he could not possibly understand.

And damn it, I think, walking out firmly, turning left, crossing Soufflot towards dinner (and when did I decide on this?), that's the second time today, the second time in an hour, in a half-hour, you've felt that sudden prick of vanity!

Later, after a disappointing meal, not enough chilli in the curry, the lassi too sweet, I am dawdling home, becoming aware of a vague, sexual disquiet. Ah now, I think, I'm not dealing with that, and pick up the pace. I am practically marching when I round the corner and see a car, a small green Citroen, parked across from my door, exhaust drifting from it in a light grey, barely perceptible haze.

Transfer my bag to my left hand, the right sliding smoothly into my pocket to grip the can of mace I habitually carry. Don't break stride, I think, always keep stride, don't let them see you've noticed them, always keep the advantage. Vincent unfolds from the passenger side as I reach my door, still in that leather jacket. He smiles, holding his hands up in mock surrender. What's that you've got in your pocket, old man, he asks, no, let me guess. A knife would mean questions when your mugger goes to get seen to, right, which leads back, perhaps, to you, so ... I'd say a can of mace? Am I right? Big wide grin on him now, and on my face too. I flash the can at him – out, show, back in a flash – and he claps: bravo, bravo, never at a loss old man, I salute you! And he says gently, I brought Genevieve, this is OK? Good evening Genevieve, I say, with genuine pleasure, brandishing my bag of bottles, I must have had a presentiment you would call. She is out of the car, leggy, dark-haired and blue-eyed, truly a beauty, happy to see me. Joseph, she breathes, dramatic and low, making my ears tingle as she embraces me, ah Joseph, you impossibly beautiful man, how do you do it!

She is, of course, as we would have said at home, a complete chancer, but she never fails to delight me. This time I pardon myself the vanity; it's true, I am a beautiful man!

Come in, come in, I say, but you, prodding a finger in the direction of Vincent, have something to explain; he says, I know, I know.

I sniff appreciatively, following them up the stairs. White Musk, says Genevieve without turning around.

A large Ricard with ice for Gen who's driving, a diet Coke for Vincent, who's not. A large, restorative Jameson for myself.

Vincent sprawls on the nursing chair, his jacket hung carefully over the back, staring out the window. Gen, at the bookshelves, has her half-moon glasses on; unlike Vincent's, which are of plain glass, a prop, she needs them, keeps them permanently hung on a light cord around her neck. What are you re-reading these days, she asks. So, Vincent has told her I am embarked on my writing project.

Nothing in particular, I say, I've been picking things up, reading a few pages, putting them down. You know the way. She nods, says: so, not a history, then. Vincent looks pained. Not a history, no, not as such.

And not a memoir, she says thoughtfully. I suppose then you don't really know what it's to be yet, do you? A memoir wouldn't be exactly you, dear Joseph, would it? Am I in it?

Such delicate, calculated artlessness, no wonder it makes me happy when she comes to visit. It is of course Vincent who wants to know, and she's obliging him by going through the motions of asking me these things, but Gen, left to herself, is one of those rare people who are content to find things out when the time is right. She'd rather, for instance, that I finished this writing and put it into her hands, than that I give her a progress report or, worse, an outline of what I plan to make of it.

Perhaps, I say, I'll abandon it, perhaps I'll get bored, one never knows. She nods, grave, pulling her brows together as she has seen it done on TV. We're teasing Vincent now, of course, but my young fox is too quick for us both.

OK, OK, he says, that gesture of mock surrender again: me, too, I'll wait to buy it in one of those bookshops, you know. The ones full of people who've taken all day to decide what they should be seen wearing before they're seen buying just the exact right book of the moment.

Gen sits beside him on the floor, which I recognise as a prelude; I knock a large plain cushion on to the floor by the chaise longue, fold my knees neatly as I sit down. Gen, listening for the click and hearing none, makes an appreciative *moue*; I'm going to tell her, 'Glucosamine' but I refrain – the old have their health secrets, too.

My father married again after my mother died – Vincent has plunged in. I was six, seven. That man today is my half-brother, Hamid. You see yourself, religious, yes? OK, more than. A believer, you understand? No, Joseph, no, I mean a true believer, you get me? My mother was French, Hamid's mother Algerian. My father, he is what you might say live and let live; not so my ... his second wife. I do not wish to be unkind but, well, she is of the old school, eh? I like Hamid, to tell you the truth; there is something ... likeable about him. No, to be accurate, there was. Nowadays a political journalist would call him a Jihadist. One of those terrifying people who believe in the possibility of absolute things. No, the necessity of absolute judgement, you understand? Myself I think he's been playing with this stuff, but now it's started playing with him. He does not know truly what to think of me. We live such different lives, he and I, but, hey, family is family, eh?

I'm not sure how much of this I believe. It isn't exactly that I disbelieve him, it's more an intuition I haven't dealt with for some time, that Vincent is more than, or less than, an erudite car thief.

Our friendship, if we are to call it such, is based on some mercurial ability we share, to divine each other's minds. Now he reads doubt in mine.

Oh very well then, he says, exasperated, turning to Gen for support, didn't I tell you this fellow would ... ah never mind. Turning back to me again, he said: look Joseph, that first time, the car, those papers on the front seat?

Ah, I say, you really are a law student. I am, he says, and I do steal cars from time to time. But I am, sorry to say, a more or less respectable young man on his way, perhaps, to becoming wholly respectable. A 'huh!' from Genevieve at this, which earns her an elbow, lightly, in the ribs.

Vincent is looking at me expectantly. There's something ... and now Gen is looking at me, too. I sigh, I should have seen this coming. Which of you is in trouble, I ask, you or your brother? Genevieve flashes me a look of such intense adoration that I flinch, and then have to hurry to reassure Vincent who's jumped to his feet. No, no, it's OK, sit down, sit down, it's all right. Soothing him out of his sudden bitter fright, his instant conviction that I mean to disappoint him.

He's really wound up tonight, I've never seen him like this. He barges on: because, you see, that first time we met I saw there was something peculiar about you, old man. I've always been like this, I see something odd in someone, I get to know them, to see what it is. He makes a kind of helpless gesture with his hands and I see how his mother must have adored him, her oddly brilliant son. And then, when you agreed to teach me English, I mean teach me properly, at first, but you know this, it was a pretext, but then, you know, by bits we became friends. Yes? Tell me if this is true?

Of course it is I soothe, of course it is. Vincent, tell me what's wrong.

My brother, I don't know, I mean my half-brother, shit, he's been mixing with some fucking crazy nutjobs, OK, and the cops got onto him, I don't know, for something he won't talk about, right, and they strong-armed him into becoming a, a snitch, is that a good English word? Now either the cops are going to fuck him or the crazies are going to find out and kill him and he has no one to turn to except me and I don't know what to do.

I need to be careful here. I stretch, look away, waking up a level inside myself. Careful. Gen has her arms around him now, leaning in over him precariously. The boy has his head down, looks suddenly very much a child in need of his mother. I feel a sudden almost unbearable stab of loss; not his, mine.

Forgive me, Vincent says, for not acknowledging you today when I was walking. I mean, look Joseph you have, a, something about you. My brother, if he saw me, saw you, you would have frightened him, do you understand? And he is already so frightened.

Vincent, I say, I'll need a little time, OK? He steals a sudden glance at the laptop on the desk above him, nods. I didn't even ask how it's going, he says, rebuking himself, judging himself for this lapse in care. Yes, yes, I say, I need a few days, some things that will take a day or two, nothing serious. But Vincent, look at me my friend, we will take care of this, all right? It can be taken care of, look at me.

He looks right into me, perhaps sensing some larger amplitude in that 'we', and something he sees in there reassures him. He's on his feet in a second, Gen scrambling to stand beside him. I open my arms to them, not having meant to, and for a moment I feel their body heat warm me, I feel their deep faith in the world, that it will take care of them, and I feel ... renewed and desolate.

Go home, I tell them, turning away, go home, let me think about this.

When I turn around they are gone, stealing away down the

stairs without a sound, and I bless them for their tact, for their feline and unexpected trust.

I stand at the window after their car has crept away; scarcely breathing, unmoving, staring into space. For a long time. And on the verge of sleep, on the very edge, some little time later or a great deal later, I don't know, I hear that 'we', that 'we will take care of this', and I am wondering what Vincent thought I meant, or thought he understood, by 'we'.

I wake, dress and go out moving slowly, my thoughts at bay. The Spanish youth is leaving the bakery as I arrive, a big transparent bag of rolls in both hands. He holds the door open with his heel, murmurs *Bonjour Maitre* as I hesitate a moment, goes smiling off. I approve that he has not greeted me in Spanish, this lays a disquiet to rest. I am whistling as I go home to begin the day's work.

13

Theresa, ah Theresa. I am struggling to be severe in these memories, to avoid sentimentalities, clichés above all, but ...

Of course I was in the usual fever of youth, of course I was tormented by desires recognised and unrecognised, I needed sex, lots of it, I wanted to be swept away in a torrent of sensations, and I was uneasy all the time, wondering what to do with myself, where, after school, I should turn. All that. I was also, though, somewhere inside myself, already the cold calculator, the silent witness, the reserved and removed observer that living with Michael John and the men had made me. I make that sound ... trite. Yes, trite, but then sometimes life is trite, is it not?

Before ever I met Phil, Iit had become my habit, leaving the city library, to take Grand Parade as far as Daunt's Square, and then, more slowly, to follow the long sinuous curve of Patrick's Street, looking at girls in a day-dream, admiring that hair, those eyes, that particular slouching or elegant way of walking. I had built a gallery in my head, I would look for particular favourites in the passing groups: blue eyes, fringe, black curls, green coat, the one who never laughs, the dancer. These girls were, of course, no more real to me than I felt myself to be; I had no wish to speak to them, to learn anything about them, I had no wish to break the spell, you see? Life without consequence, a shadow-play where everyone was a projection, a living and vivid phantom.

It was, if you like, a kind of voluntary delirium. Also, in all the exact senses of the word, an entertainment. A kind of harmless make-believe.

One day, outside the Savoy, there was Theresa. She was standing with a group of girls from Scoil Mhuire, her heel propped on the step behind her, head tilted forward, looking up from under her fringe at some boy who was talking to her far too loudly. Her blue school uniform. Her long brown hair. That fucking idiot she was pretending to take seriously – I could see, even from the edge of the pavement, the discreet mockery in her eyes. She glanced sideways a moment and caught my look. I was shocked, accustomed to thinking myself invisible; I felt appalled, vulnerable, but she did not see me as such, merely registered my presence then looked away again.

The most succinct way to put this: I had ice in my belly, fire in my head. I was entranced, the word is exact now that I think of it.

For days, weeks, I did not dare to go in to town again, and every moment I held back was a torture.

In school I was soon in one kind or another of trouble, distracted, sullen, sarcastic, liable to say or do anything that came into my head. At home, at night, I would head for my bed after dinner was over, unable or unwilling to make conversation.

Sometimes I'd head out of the house abruptly on long, savage walks, pounding the streets, my feet hammering in the night. If that fucker Cassady was about, I did not notice him.

Of course I succumbed, as I'd known I would. The next time I saw her was outside the library, as it happens. She was going by in a gaggle of friends, how many I could not say, in her uniform again, as were they all, but on her it looked somehow different. I know now what a subtle art tailoring is, how a tuck here, an adjusted hemline there can make such a difference, but to my avid eye it seemed then that her blazer was perfect on her shoulders, her waist snug, her skirt exact in its accent of her behind as if such neat perfection was somehow foreordained.

I never quite lost that sense of awe at how appositely, how exactly, her whole being fit itself to the material world.

I followed that afternoon, at a careful distance, observing the route they took, learning for the first time their inviolable daily pattern: how they'd cross at the Fountain, bear left then right through the cavernous hopelessness of the English Market, never pausing but taking it all in; how they'd emerge on Prince's Street, how the girl with the short hair and glasses would peel off then towards South Mall, sometimes hurriedly, anxious, I thought, not to miss a bus or a lift; how they'd bear left, to stand a while outside the Pavilion cinema, chattering, always chattering, then move slowly on to the Savoy, the steps there a kind of meeting place where, likely as not, would be gathered a gaggle of spotty, loud boys from the 'better' schools.

She had a way of tilting her head when listening, just so. An insolence, somehow, in her dragging walk, in the cock of her hip as she'd stop to fiddle with a stray strand of hair, a snap of the wrist as she'd wave to some causal acquaintance that was both greeting and instant dismissal.

She was, imperious.

She was utterly self-absorbed.

She was a nightmare, and I was, again the word is exact, enthralled. For months and months on end.

I'm impressed, Michael John said eventually, at how seriously you're taking your studies. I looked at him blankly. I mean, he said, the amount of time you're spending in the library. A power of books you're getting through, isn't that right men? *Homage to Catalonia*, said Tony Driscoll, cigarette in the corner of his mouth, picking it up and looking at it thoughtfully. Again, he said; you're fond of this. Read it, have you? I said, and there must have been a sneer in my voice because he looked up at me sharply, put the book down, said I was there kid. Watch that mouth of yours, got up, still holding my eyes, and walked out of the room. That sense of pressure in the air. I looked at my Granda and what I saw there made me afraid of him for the first and only time. Ah Jaysus lads, what's wrong with you, it's a girl. said Seanie Mac, and I was so grateful to him I nearly started to cry; it's a girl of course, and she's too good for him, she has him mesmerised, amn't I right boy?

Get out, Michael John slapped me between the shoulder blades; with affection, I felt that, but hard enough that it was a warning, too. Get out and go for one o' them long walks you've been taking.

I went, gratefully, but first I climbed to the back room and knocked to apologise to Tony. Come here, he said, and he gave me a gruff hug. Mind that mouth of yours, you hear? I heard, and I went out into the night hunched over with gratitude, in a sadness I could neither name nor understand.

You're the boy who is everywhere, she said, the first time I went with Phil to his house. I couldn't speak. Fool that I am, it had never occurred to me she'd be home when Phil, famished after our long morning cycle, said let's go to my house, see if there's anything doing in the way of grub. She was in the kitchen, in a heavy sleeveless dress; I had never seen her arms, so slender and, like the rest of her, somehow exact. She dried a hand with a tea towel, I'm Theresa she said, cool, with a hint of mischief, and you are ... Joseph, I said. Joe, she said. You're welcome, Joe, and by some coincidence, looking at her brother in a slightly superior way, just in time for lunch.

He follows me everywhere, you know, she said over her shoulder. I know, said Phil, I've seen him at it but what can you do? You're a goddess, amn't I sick telling ya? She threw something at him, I don't know what, but he ducked with the ease of long practice, and there was such deep affection between them I almost forgot to be mortified by her casual phrase.

I wanted the ground to, yes, swallow me, but I was beyond saving; suddenly, in the light of that airy kitchen, the garden outside pressing up against the windows, brother and sister bantering and bickering, I felt the whole press of what I had been missing, and such large intimation of what life might yet hold that I decided, yes I decided, not to be dull and dumb, not to hold back ever again, to trust my life and my instincts and not care, not care ever again, about making a fool of myself.

Theresa, I said, I am a fool and a poor boy and some kind of idiot but I am utterly stone mad about you and have been since I laid eyes on you and what do you think of that now?

Bravado, yes, but a rush of clarity in my head that I hadn't felt for years, a sureness all of a sudden.

She looked at me gravely, her hands crossed under her breasts, the tea towel twisted in her grip. I think, she said, you are a fool and a poor boy and nobody's idiot but get in line, kid, get in line. Sure the whole town is mad about me.

And, to her gaping brother, close your mouth, you gom, and go lay the table. Then, casually, give me a hand here with the onions, Joe.

I was of course, as she meant me to be, immediately her slave.

That was a long summer, and I followed those bare arms, those long brown legs wherever we went in a kind of waking trance, as Pasternak says the young men followed the red flag, the death woman's kerchief.

I had no illusions of course, that my happy yearning for her body was in any way reciprocated, nor did I mind my slave status. I was content, surprising even myself, merely to be in her nimbus. Phil minded none of this, one way or another.

And when autumn came, her last year in school, I no longer had to follow her progress furtively through the streets. I was, as in ancient Rome, a family slave; almost family in fact, but still undefinably other. As such I was permitted to join in her royal progress, even welcomed, if guardedly, by her girlfriends.

When there was some boy she had decided to test her powers on, I might be snuggled into as she spoke to him, I would be permitted to take her arm as she swept past some stuttering loon or other, dispensing a wave or a frown as the moment deserved.

I grew to be cordially hated by total strangers, and to enjoy the experience, the immunity that her marked favour bestowed on me from the bother of having to fight some idiot or other.

That winter was when Cassady descended upon us after a long absence, and as I cherished that long enchantment with Theresa, I grew to loathe the man, his stalking and staking of me, his sweaty hatred.

There was the night he accosted me at last, as I'd somehow known he would do, at the back of Blackpool church. I had gone to buy biscuits in the little shop on the Commons Road where there was a bank of glass-fronted biscuit boxes, tilted to meet you as you came in the door. You took some from one box, more from another as you pleased, and brought the brown paper bag to be weighed by the smiling woman. Since my mother and father died, she had always added an extra biscuit, for the poor orphan boy as I understood, and where once I had found this embarrassing, now, hulking brute that I had become, I found it touching.

I always went there when some memory was unsettling me, when in the grip of some minor melancholia, a memory of early childhood, perhaps, something like that, and I was vulnerable and inattentive on the short walk home when a hand shot out of a darkened doorway, grabbing me by the knotted scarf, and Cassady's narrow, hot face shoved itself into mine. You think you're some smart fucker, don't ya? Whiskey on his breath, a wild dark light in his eyes, and a dark rank smell off him, sweat, and something else too, something sharp and acrid, a smell I would recognise years later as what some men secrete when in the grip of adrenalin-fuelled hatred. Riot cops, for instance. You think you're some smart fucker, don't ya, he repeated, shaking me. I was too stunned for a moment to react, and perhaps he mistook my rigidity, my shocked silence, for fear. He relaxed his grip for a second, and I dropped the biscuits, deliberately, at his feet. His eyes flicked downward and I hit him a good solid dig in the gut, a short-armed jab, power in my arm that surprised even me. Down he went, and I picked up my bag of biscuits. I was almost paralysed by adrenalin myself, the first time I experienced that curious feeling, but I recovered fast, fast enough to know that I had done something incredibly stupid. I ran for home, and as I pulled the hall door shut behind me, slowing my breath as best I could in case anyone was about in the house, I looked back and across at the alleyway through which I'd come. Nothing, not even a cat crossing under the streetlight.

Night after night I'd check from behind the curtains, scanning what I could see of the street. Nothing. I gave up those solitary walks, and when I did venture out at night, the odd time Michael John would suggest a walk, I'd have a wary eye out. Michael John saw this, of course, but said nothing.

Not that Cassady disappeared of course. He took to cruising Patrick Street in his car, always another branchman at the wheel, young fucker like himself, so he had time enough and plenty to put the evil eye on me. Day after day. Once, turning to watch him in the reflection from Lester's window I saw his eye fall on Theresa, and stay there for a long time. I remember the cold that came on me then, the deep-down ice-coldness in the bones, a kind of settling in my will that I noticed, remarked and filed away.

Theresa finished school, took a job in the bank, and if I saw her this summer it was most likely to be in her house, at the weekend. We had a new, a different kind of ease, now that she was drawing away from her own childhood, I was coming to terms with the end of mine. We had grown fond of each other in an unforced kind of way, and if she sometimes teased at the edges of my undiminished desire for her, it was not without kindness.

And autumn, as it will, came slowly, reluctantly, to an end. That night back then, my first night in Phil's hospitable house, still shaken by the mad rush down Fever Hospital Steps, our split-second avoiding of that Anglia, we'd sat in his kitchen as the light faded, thinking about the day, thinking about the year ahead.

I told my Da about that Cassady fucker, a few weeks ago, Phil said presently. Did you, I said, did you now. What'd he say? He said nothing to tell you the truth, then he asked me if you were involved in anything I said no – you're not, sure you're not? I just looked at him. No, Dad, I told him, definitely not. Me neither, before you ask. Good, he said, they're all fucking idiots, that crowd. You know, I think that's the first time I ever heard him swear. Then he got me to tell him all about that bastard Cassady and he said nothing again. Sat staring away out into the garden, we were in the kitchen. I was going up to bed when I heard him on the phone to someone, Gerry was it? Yeah, his name, Gerry.

I thought of saying something but, really, what was there to say?

Last year at school, it was getting serious. The teachers different somehow, more wary of us, walking around us. None of that mindless beating now; probably, I thought sardonically, from a strong sense of self-preservation – but perhaps also, to give those men their due, they wished us well, they were trying to do right by us. Like everyone else I put the head down, got stuck into the books, not the least idea what I meant to do after, but knowing there was a watershed up ahead. I meant to do well, for my Granda and his faith in me, but for myself also. I meant to do well because here was the next major test in my life and I wasn't letting anyone down, least of all myself.

The first was the funeral of my parents. How long ago that seemed to me then.

I did well in the exams, I did very well. The men were as proud of me as if each in his turn, rising to shake my hand, was my loving father, I the beloved son, but none was as proud as Michael John was, and when he took the results sheet in his hands, and beckoned me towards him, and folded me in a hug that had some kind of desperation in it, there were tears on his cheeks against my face, and a full flood of tears pouring out of me.

All the long summer I did nothing. If I knew then what I know now, that each life has its crises, its turning points, that the big moments are always preceded by a particular kind of lull, I might have had an easier time of it. I had resumed my solitary ways, but this time in a kind of disquiet. On my forays into town, almost always to the library, I might see Cassady, in fact I would often see Cassady, but all that seemed to have faded away. I had begun, in the phrase of the time, to take a drink, but I knew from the start I would be a moderate drinker, and a pint of Murphy's with a good book in the Long Valley became a feature of my days.

I saw little of Phil; his father had arranged for him to spend the summer in a solicitor's office on the Mall, get him a jump start, as he put it, for his law studies. Theresa I saw even less of; she had become the pet of some older women, was always off sailing at the weekends, or otherwise engaged. Beginning, it seemed to me, her ascent into an adult world as narrow and closed as it was mysterious and banal.

September was drawing in, that certain crispness in the air, that violet quality to the night sky outside the haloes of streetlamps. I was whistling as I came down the street, a parcel of books tucked under my arm, some mysterious buoyancy having sprung up in me from nowhere. I saw Dr Kelly's car outside the house, and stopped short. Phil's father. I let myself into the hall quietly, stepped carefully to the kitchen door. Michael John, Dr Kelly, the doctor speaking. Mick, something has to be done, it's getting beyond the beyonds. If I'd been at home last night, god alone knows what I'd have done.

Through the crack in the door I saw Granda reach out, put his hand flat on Dr Kelly's where it was drumming on the table. Bad enough the boy, he went on, if you saw the black eye on him, and I can't be sure but he has a cracked rib. Won't let me examine him. He's ashamed, I think, I think that's the worst of it for him. Ach, young fellas. But Mick, Jesus Christ in heaven Mick, to drag the girl into it ...

Once before I had seen something in Granda's face that struck fear into me. I saw it now, the skin drawn back over his cheekbones, the set of his jaw. John, John, he said, take it easy now. We have to think this out very carefully now. But he wasn't soothing his old comrade, he was considering a question of what was to be done, cold, analytical, implacable: you say Gerry's no good to us? No, he's been posted to the Border, that fucker has a new Super, Merrigan, a fucking Blueshirt. Merrigan, Granda, said softly, one of O'Duffy's heroes? More likely to give him his head than rein him in; no, that won't do.

I could bear no more, I pushed the door in, was startled to see how quickly they moved for men of their age, on their feet and facing me, hands bunched in fists.

I sat down, and neither man questioned my right to sit down. They saw, at least Michael John saw, I had been listening at the door. I was cold: Dr Kelly, I said, please tell me what happened, all of it please. Kelly looked over at Michael John, who gave me a long, hard look. Tell him John, he said, he's of an age, and this concerns him. Never taking his eyes off me.

Joe, he said, uncertain, you know I'm fond of you, but ... Tell him, Michael John said, and he wasn't asking this time.

Phil came home last night, the doctor said, staring at the table. He'd been down the Mardyke playing tennis, he was just coming up to the gate when ... Cassady, I breathed. He nodded, expressionless ... when this Cassady stepped out of a car, walked across casually to young Phil. I don't know if Phil said anything to him, he might have, you know what he's like, but your man drew back and gave him a punch in the face, I mean full force, I can tell from the marks, and Theresa saw it all from her room, you know, up above the front door? Poor Phil went down like a sack of spuds and your man for good measure gave him a hefty few kicks in the ribs.

Turning aside from me he said, Mick, in the name of god what ails that man? Why ...

Collecting himself, sensing my nearly hysterical impatience perhaps, he went on: well, Theresa flew down the stairs and out the gate, started in on your man. You know, battering at him.

He stopped, stricken, looked at Michael John. Mick, he said ...

Granda, not taking his eyes off the doctor, said: he grabbed her between the legs, Joe, she was only wearing something light, right John? John nodded yes, nightdress. He grabbed her between the legs and shoved her up against the hedge and he, he exposed himself to her, he said something like, maybe this is what ye need, haw? Bit of a baton charge, haw? You like that Missy?

He stopped, unable or unwilling to go on. I was implacable: and then?

Dr Kelly had gathered some force in himself, said matter of factly: then he, he just got back in the car and drove away. Tell me, I said, was he alone? Was there someone else in the car? The men looked at each other, questioning. No, Michael John said, I already asked. The doctor nodded agreement, no. So, no witness then, I said. They agreed, no witness.

I stood up, I put my hand out to the doctor, who rose, surprised, to his feet. Doctor, I said, my grandfather is right. Mick is right. Granda looked at me sharply. Mick is right, I repeated deliberately. This needs to be thought over very carefully. Please don't tell Phil or Theresa you came to see us, can I ask you that? I didn't dare look at my Granda now. Will you promise me that, I insisted. I will he said, I will. I saw that he would. Then I think we should leave it at that. You know how I feel about Phil, you know how I feel about Theresa. You know I brought this on you. Ah no, no, he tried to say but I wouldn't let him.

Dr Kelly, I said, my grandfather has very good time for you, and I trust you. You have been very kind to me. Please leave this with us. And I looked at my Granda then, and my look said would you please show Dr Kelly out; and if he was offended he didn't show it, he was always and ever the most gracious man I knew. He took John Finbarr Kelly by the arm, solicitous of the age that had suddenly come on the poor man, and he led him to the door, and down to his car, and waited there until his old comrade had collected himself, until he started the engine and drove away.

Come in, I said, taking my Granda by the elbow then, come in and sit here beside me. We were still sitting there when the men came home, in boisterous good humour after a card drive somewhere. They sobered quickly when I told them what Kelly had come to say, and that was a cold, dangerous sobriety came over them. Go on to bed, Mick, I said, we've time enough, and they parted to let him go by. I came in from the bottom of the stairs and Tony Driscoll gave me a hard stare: Mick now, is it? I looked at him. He said: fair enough, so.

We need to know everything there is about this fella, I said, looking at each of them in turn. Go to bed, Seanie Mac said gruffly, go to bed yourself. Leave it to us. They sat down in their usual half-circle, turning their backs to me, staring into the fire.

Always a fire in that house, no matter the season.

14

I need more information, I think, shutting down for the day, neither willing nor able to cast an eye back over what I have written. I splashed water on my face, texted Vincent: Collège des Irlandais, the yard, are you free, one hour? Faster than seemed reasonable he texted back: yes.

Shopping first, I have time. Mouffetard for vegetables, fruit, bits and pieces, two good lamb chops. I'll cook later, I say to myself, putting the things away, checking for keys, phone, wallet before leaving again. Sometimes I come in from shopping and empty my pockets.

Bells from the college chapel as I step through the door, a knot of people coming away from some class or meeting, a sideways flow as students emerged from the door to the residences on my right. Vincent is across the broad gravelled courtyard, by the artist's studio, a book in his hand. The red metal chairs always seem frail to me. I drag one around so that I am facing back towards the doorway to the street, I have checked already, there is nobody watching us.

So, Vincent says, putting away his book. So, I agree. Now Vincent, I need your half-brother's full name, his address, the names of the cops who are dealing with him, if possible their station. I need to know what they're asking of him, how deep in he is, what he's given them already. He has his glasses on now, is regarding me attentively. What's with the glasses, I ask, mildly irritated. He uses the back of his hand to indicate the yard, the banks of windows on three sides. The attentive student is listening carefully to what his professor has to tell him, he says, not mocking me exactly, explaining himself for once, a sign, perhaps, of a certain, unusual, agitation. You need to know these things, when? I don't like his casual tone. Vincent, I say, don't fuck around with me. This is a serious business. I can let it drop if you like, yes? Do you want me to let it drop?

He looks at me very thoughtfully, using his shoulders to show he isn't challenging me in any way. I am sorry, he says, formally. It is easy to forget, sometimes, that you are a very serious man; at once, of course. We sit there for a moment, both looking at the ground, until he is soothed and I am mollified.

Let me know, I say, rising to my feet. How much do you propose to tell ... Hamid, isn't it?

I will tell him, he says, that I am dealing with this, that there is a chance I can make it go away. I will tell him, I think, that my price is an end to these fucking Jihad fantasies, that we need a real politics for our people in this so wonderful country of France, yes? Would that, do you think, be a fair price?

And now he is challenging me, standing a little too close to me, face to face.

Vincent, I say, this is the first time you have spoken to me of politics.

Old man, he says, not unkindly, it has taken me a long time to figure you out.

Vincent, as I say, rarely fails to surprise me. I wave him goodbye over my shoulder as I turn abruptly to walk away. I don't want him to see the rush of affection I feel for him, but he calls softly after me: you be careful, old man. Adds, and Genevieve, she sends her love.

I smiled to myself, face tilted towards the weak sunlight overhead. Ah Vincent, Vincent. I sat on in a reverie after he'd left. I am thinking back to when we first met

A week or so after I had observed his elegant manner of stealing a car, a week or so after that first encounter, I was standing at the traffic lights at Rue de la Sorbonne when a soft voice at my elbow greeted me: *bonjour Maître*, it goes well I hope? In English. He surprised me, I admit it, I who do not care to be surprised. He surprised me by speaking in English, I mean. That he would appear again, sometime, somewhere, I had not doubted. This is how these things work.

If it pleased him to have caught me off balance, he had the grace not to show it, and in truth, someone less sensitive would likely not have noticed.

He wanted something, I saw this at once, and when he saw that I had seen, he smiled, agreed with a small benediction, a raised eyebrow, indicating a bar on the far side of the street. Coffee, I think, he said, settling on the terrace, and for you, Sir? Coffee also? Good.

We regarded each other calmly while we waited, in no hurry; you would have said, had you glanced at us, that we knew each other well.

I need to learn English, he said, stirring two sugars into his coffee, and I thought I would ask you to teach me. You speak English very well, I said ... but he stopped me with a raised palm. Sir, he said, I am aware that I speak English, I myself do not think I speak well. I think you are a man of ... nuance, is that the word? He gave a wicked little smile, more a grimace perhaps. I can explain myself to a policeman, he went on, but not, perhaps, to a judge?

I take your point, I said. Pardon? I mean, I said, that I understand the distinction you wish to make. The distinction I wish to make, he said thoughtfully, then seeing the opportunity for what it was, he leaned back, smiling broadly now, and with palms outspread, a chess player's final gesture, he said: but exactly, Sir, you make my point for me.

I have a pupil it seems, I conceded; I was amused, and allowed him to see that I was, at the adroitness of that lightning ambush.

There will be certain conditions, I went on. I charge doctor's rates, I see no point in working for less. Agreed, he said. I assume you will find the money in the usual way, I said. Most likely, he said, inclining his head gravely. I would much prefer, I said, that you do not pursue your vocation in this quartier. He was mock-disappointed in me: but of course, evidently, he said; *M'sieu* has naturally a certain reputation, he is of good character – amusing himself now. And, by the way, he added, that was by way of an experiment. Not an exercise in what you see fit to call my vocation.

Look, I said, switching to French, leaning across and putting my face square in front of him: I don't want the fucking cops turning up at my door, right? You do not bring any kind of trouble to my door, right?

Head down, he considered this thoughtfully, taking the glasses from his top pocket, adjusting them on his ears with a delicate gesture. One wishes, naturally, to observe a certain discretion, of course, of course, he said. A very earnest young man, you'd have thought, passing by, a young man with respect for his elders, and if you were of a certain age you would have nodded in approval. Then, having given me time to approve his performance, and still without raising his head, he reached in his pocket for a pen, a notebook, and carefully tore out the page on which he had written a phone number.

He sat up, handed me the page. *M'sieu* will no doubt have to reflect on the arrangements. When you have decided, please give me a call and we can perhaps begin? I folded the paper, tucked it away. Mobile number, unsurprisingly. Mobiles for the mobile, I thought distractedly, how mobile we all are now.

One keeps on the move, he said, and there was the bond again that I'd sensed the first time we met, the leap. How few they have been with whom I have shared this particular kind of understanding.

Let us call me Vincent, he said then, extending his hand, offering his side of a complex bargain. I permitted myself the ghost of a smile. Vincent ... I see. And let us call me, Joseph? I waved him off when he went to pay, said: I will call you soon. Soon? Yes, I said, soon.

Good god, full dark outside! I type this, and as I type I feel the question push at me from the back of my mind: what are you doing old man? Bah! I save and quit, just so. Pouf!

15

The day after his father, the doctor, had visited us, I called Phil. He had a tendency to boom at you on the phone, but now he sounded subdued, a hesitancy come over him that I sensed he would be a long time shaking off. Confined to barracks, he said, forcing some energy into his voice, bizarre thing happened last night. Yes, I said. Should have stopped playing, I suppose, the light going, you know, fella I was playing lashed a fucking great serve at me, smacked me right in the eye. Never saw it coming. You should see the fucking shiner! It wasn't like Phil to swear so much. Yeah, rushing on, I can barely see out of the eye. The oul' fella wanted to send me to the Eye and Ear last night, call in some quack he knows, but we said we'd let it be and it isn't too bad this morning but, ah feck it, I don't fancy goin' in to work with it you know?

Sounds bad enough, I said, masking as best I could my awareness of his true distress. He was frightened, I could feel it coming from his voice. I was going to push it, suggest I call up to see him, see what response that provoked, but either good sense or some instinct for mercy kicked in. Listen, I said, I'm doing a bit in the house for Michael John, painting and plastering, you know yourself. Maybe I'll give you a call after the weekend? Yeah, yeah, after the weekend. I so very much wanted to ask after Theresa, couldn't trust myself that far. So, steak on the eye, I suppose and a lie-down in a dark room? Yeah, yeah, something like that. See ya then, I said. Yeah, see ya. And Joe, thanks for calling, yeah?

In bits and scraps, in a few short days, the men assembled a remarkable amount of information. Reporting each evening to Granda. Through me.

If it is possible for tension to be matter-of-fact, that is how I would describe the atmosphere in the house.

My mother would cook for us all, and she was a good cook. After she died, after some initial confusion, we settled into some kind of unspoken communal arrangement. Each of the men, Granda included, would take it in turns to make the evening meal, all except Seanie who was, as Granda remarked drily one night, a born incendiarist. Seanie took on the shopping, one or another of the men, whoever it suited I suppose, giving him a hand when needed. I did the local stuff – bread, milk, tea, that kind of thing. This routine carried on, of course, but now each evening, before the cards came out, before one or the other headed out to the pub or to go visiting friends or to the pictures, when the table was cleared we would share out what we had learned. Or rather, what they had learned.

He drinks in Canty's, Tommy Mac reported. And in Foley's, The Swan and Gannet, Maher's sometimes, The Chateau lately, with Merrigan. That fucker, Tony muttered, and Michael John shushed him. He seems to favour Lenihan's Lounge, Tommy went on, shower o' cunts in there, and when he went to explain I forestalled him Staters, I know, Seanie gave me a list of places to avoid. Michael John snorted, breaking the tension for a moment. That's all for now, Tommy was somehow apologetic, but Granda said: good man, Tommy, that was fast; and I saw again, as so many times before, how a man would straighten to praise from my grandfather.

Night after night, dribs and drabs. He supported the Rockies (no surprise there, darkly, from Tony, a passionate Piarsaigh man); he lived on his own in a small house in Ballinlough; he was fond of a feed in the Metropole; he had a good singing voice. This last from the quiet man, quiet, neat Tommy Owens who could sing you at the drop of a hat any tenor aria you could think of. Has he now, Tony Driscoll said, savage and thoughtful, has he now?

Work, lads, work, Michael John said at some stage. We need to know his work routines. And this, too, they somehow supplied. He's been moved to the Watercourse Road. They couldn't stand him in Union Quay. Some of his mates are trying to get him shifted up the country. Gerry Carroll tried to have him sent back into uniform after young Healy, you know? A poor gom called Pat Healy had ended up in the North Infirmary having got a bad hiding coming back from a Sinn Féin rally one night. Is that so, Michael John breathed, that was Cassady was it? Seems like, said Tony, what I heard anyway. Is he free range or what, Michael John asked after a few days. How do you mean, I asked. Well, he seems to turn up day and night is what I mean, I was just wondering, do they not have shifts to keep to?

Look, I said, surprising myself as much as them, he probably has, shifts I mean, but he's a law unto himself that fella, it isn't work with him, he's obsessed, right?

The men looked, not at me, at Michael John. Who looked at me appraisingly. You're right, he said, I think you're right. And among other things, he's obsessed with you.

That was a cold moment, we all felt it.

Something was being passed to me, some responsibility that I had somehow volunteered for.

Somebody sighed, I couldn't say who to this day, somebody sighed and we sat back then. Tommy reached into the drawer under the table. Who's for cards, he asked.

It's a fresh night, Granda said, get your coat, lad. I never went night-walking by myself now, by a common consent that included my own. Granda, I saw, had taken to carrying a heavy blackthorn, with a casualness that spoke for itself. We climbed Water Lane, stopping as we had since I was a child to hear the water running behind the upright slab in O'Brien's wall where once there had been a well. New houses had been built at the top of the hill, on the stretch of Redemption Road between the hill and Farranferris Seminary up to the right. They did a grand job on those, said my Granda, did you know that ... I do, I said, I know; they all did the labouring on each others' houses, the builder was called the Happy Man because he was such an old grouch, they're all Piarsaigh players, the Happy Man cast the blocks himself on site ... I could make him laugh from the first time he came home, I could make him laugh still.

The third house up, a man and a young boy were standing at their front door, looking down on us from on high, the small hand in the big hand. Little curly-headed fella. How're the men, he called down, with a wave, and we burst out laughing – he couldn't have been more than three, four? Where do they come from, eh, Bert? God only knows, Michael John, god only knows, the man said.

We passed through the gates of Farranferris Seminary, its red brick and turrets, steep roof, going black in the dark of evening. We struck off immediately left around the small farmyard, its few cows settled for the night, the clank of buckets as Mr Buckley finished work for the day, and climbed past the grave of Danny Boy Cohalan, late bishop of Cork, until we stood at the foot of the Calvary, looking down and out across the night city. That fella, Michael John indicating with his foot the bishop's grave beneath us, little he thought when he excommunicated us all that his day was nearly done. I looked at him in surprise. Oh yes, he said, you mark my words. They're in the saddle now boy, but a time is coming when the Catholic church will go the way of all flesh. Everything men build, boy, you listen to me now, everything men build will fall again. It's the nature of things. Nothing is forever, boy, nothing is forever.

He was staring away down over the city, not looking at me but alert all the same, waiting to see if I'd heard him. My silence, I think, was answer enough. Good lad, he said, one o' the things I like best about you, you get things.

We walked away down the avenue of elms towards the seminary, and I looked at the rows of lights where boys sat studying into the night, and I imagined them quenched, one by one, until there was only, maybe, a caretaker's lamp near the side door. And one day, who knows, maybe that gone too.

A good heavy slab they put on him anyway, Danny Boy, I said. Oh no fear that buck will rise again, Granda agreed, and I waited from him to say something along the lines of 'ah sure he probably thought he was doing the right thing', for it was his habit to try to see both sides of a story, but no, he said nothing after that.

Seanie was waiting for us in the kitchen, a low lamp burning on the sideboard near the window. He's in the Watercourse Road, all right, he said. They've taken him off the street anyway. You know who, Granda nodded at this, you know who is after telling me they want to crucify him with paperwork until he asks for a transfer. They have him on twelve to eight. No overtime.

I was blazingly angry. Kelly, I said, rounding on Michael John, you told Kelly to say nothing ... Easy, lad easy. He sat me down, pressing down hard on my shoulders.

Kelly's word is good, he said, soothing me with his voice, but he couldn't do nothing at all. You have to understand Kelly, you see, doctors and such, they have a way of doing things. Look, what he'd have done, he'd have worked it so that he bumped into someone he knows, you follow me? Maybe a whiskey in the Imperial, right, a chat about old times. And it would've come around to this caper up North, right. And maybe while he's ordering another drink, right, he would've said something like, it must be hard keeping a rein on the young bucks, is it? And he'd've waited, and if your man came back at him, if he copped on that there was something behind all this, Kelly would have said, oh very casually like, I hear there's a fella called, what is it now, Clancy, Cassady, something like that? And if he got back Yes.. or I think I know who you mean then he'd have his invitation, you see now how it works? And he'd've gone on, letting on that he'd heard this as a doctor, you see, and said something like 'a bit quick with the boot, is he?' And your man would have got the message. The respectable classes, boy, the respectable classes. And he shook his head, sadly.

Now go on up to bed, up with you. Good man, Seanie, I heard him say softly as I went towards the stairs, and I turned, heard Seanie, head down, echo him quietly 'the respectable classes', saw him give Mick him a weary, defeated salute.

I heard the off-sound on the fourth step as I climbed, but I carried on up. Those men had hearing you would not believe, they'd have heard me hesitate, but in truth, as I recognised, closing the door of my room with a snap, I was beyond hesitation. I knew that as soon as I sat down heavily on the bed.

I'd found the gun when I was twelve, a long summer afternoon with the house to myself. I was running up to my room for something, a football, a catapult, something like that, when I stopped, came slowly back down, went around and in under the stairs. Somewhere inside myself I'd long before registered the anomaly, running up and down constantly as was my habit, the step that didn't sound quite like the others, but until now I'd never given it thought. Behind the riser, a false riser, making a neat shallow compartment; the false board with its line of coat hooks fitted with spring clips on the back so as to yield to a sharp firm tug. The heavy revolver in an oilskin pouch, dry on the outside but I could make out the film of oil inside. Two flat boxes of ammunition in another pouch, some kind of felt packing surrounding the three packages, tacked to the genuine riser.

I remember squatting there on my heels, intrigued. I remember how desperately I wanted to take out the gun, handle it, feel the weight of it, load it, swagger around the house with it. But I knew, thought coming through again, that the instant I opened the pouch the smell of oil would escape, and that one or another of those old boys, most likely my all-seeing, all-knowing Grandfather, would smell it.

Let the hare sit, Michael John liked to say, reining me in. I let the hare sit.

I sat on the bed now without moving, long after Seanie and Granda had gone to bed. I was thinking about Theresa. I was thinking about Phil, wondering why he hadn't rung, hadn't called round; I assumed his father had counselled him not to speak of the incident, wondering why he chose not to disobey him. Wondering, sadly, if our friendship would survive. Wondering about Theresa.

16

I am too tired to write any more today, too tired, even, to think of eating. I will sleep, I think, sleep for a while then rise and go out.

It came on to rain while I slept, and the soft noise on the roof, coming in through the bedroom window where it stood half open, must have soothed me, as the rain would in my childhood, in that long room under the slates.

I dressed and went out in search of dinner, wondering a little that I could not remember undressing. I felt the need for a certain ... invisibility, that's the word. I walked as far as the Sorbonne, dodging and feinting with my little umbrella, and I found a place that had only recently opened, a place I had not been before, and was satisfied.

After the pea soup, the cassoulet, two good glasses of something dark from near Toulouse, I felt myself utterly at peace. I have always enjoyed a certain kind of null retreat into myself, borne up into a place or perhaps a time where there is no sense of place, no sense of time past, present or, indeed, to come. I think of it as the professorial quiet, imagining a certain professor for whom the mind is a great expectant vault into which, if he is schooled in patience, presently a clarifying thought will introduce itself. This is, of course, a game I play with myself: with a few exceptions, the professors I have known have been vain, busy-minded, prattling and, when you come right down to it, dull. There have been, as I say, exceptions, but not even they had the magisterial calm I grant to that imagined professor of mine, and common sense told me to keep my fantasy to myself.

I enjoy, as I say, this sense of null quiet, and it gives me, when it comes over me, a kind of beatific aura, as if I were some kind of Buddhist sage.

The proprietor, as I paid, beamed at me as if by my presence I had brought him, or would bring him, some good fortune. In a doorway, as I made my way home, a young woman was weeping on the pavement, one would have said inconsolably, rain and tears streaming down her upturned face, and when I stopped to look at her she bristled at first, a perfectly sensible reaction of course, and then, her sobs subsiding, tentatively, she smiled at me. I smiled back, and with a last dismissive look up at the lit window of her faithless lover, she shrugged, opened her umbrella with a snap then tilted it so that it tipped off mine. Salute! We who understand this world! And also – the set of her shoulder, a certain tilt to the hip as she walked away: fuck him anyway. Who does he think he is?

And so much, I thought, chuckling to myself, looking up at that lit window, so much for you, pal. You'll never know what you missed.

There was a plain white envelope in the cage tacked to the inside of my front door, the flap sealed neatly with Scotch. I shook my umbrella out the door, collapsed it, shrugged off my Macintosh, folded that over my arm, extracted the envelope, humming contentedly away to myself, tucked the letter in my jacket pocket and, as I climbed the stairs, texted Vincent, bravo. I like to give myself little exercises in dexterity. He texted back as I opened the door: thank you.

I smoothed the single sheet flat as I booted up the laptop. What a strange word, I thought, 'booted'. I must look it up. I opened a new file, typed up the handwritten information, sent the file to print and when the machine began to clatter out the single page, I deleted the file. Vincent's envelope and original note I shredded, then burned in the fireplace. I put the new sheet in an envelope – gloves, old man, gloves – and I was done.

I slept well, decided as I showered that I would breakfast in that noisy place on Soufflot, near the antique apothecary. It is a favourite with students, always lively with the excited bird chatter of the young, and one never knows what extraordinary things an invisible old man will overhear. Sheer entertainment.

There is a phone box, one of the few remaining in the age of the mobile, near the Jardin du Luxembourg Metro, up against the railings. I keep my phone numbers, certain numbers at any rate, in a tatty old accounts book, the numbers disguised as sums of money. I had, in any case, memorised the number I needed to call.

Ah, he said, it is you. It has been some time. You are well? I assured him of this. I enquired after his health: it was good, he was glad to say. A certain awkwardness in the silence? No, I decided, merely the lifelong habit of caution.

We agreed on a place to meet, a time. I will not describe him, certainly there is no need to give his name; we have a long history of mutual trust, he and I, since he was my pupil and an all but unknowing protégé of Henri's.

Seated, presently, on a park bench, I handed him the envelope and when he'd taken the sheet out, glanced at it and slipped it into an inside pocket I took back the envelope. This one, I said, is a good fellow, it seems, but he has fallen into some trouble. Firstly, he has been somewhat swayed by certain ... followers of the Prophet – peace to his name, my companion finished my sentence. Always quick to the point, you see. Exactly. These two, now, they have conceived the idea of recruiting him as an informant. I see, said my friend, I see, and had he a beard he would have stroked it. So, let me guess: your good fellow, he will desist from foolishness? Most assuredly, I said. And the leverage these two idiots have on him? Will disappear, I said, when ... when I let it be known, discreetly, discreetly, that he is an asset of ours, he finished my sentence again. And, effectively, finished our conversation.

To my surprise, and pleasure, he embraced me as we parted. I had not expected such warmth, and I hope he was pleased that I'd patted him on the cheek as we stood there a moment longer, I hope he felt my enduring affection, my gratitude for his trust in me.

I would call Vincent later. I hailed a taxi, had it drop me off at the Panthéon. I went back to work.

17

I let a week go by before calling to see Phil. His mother met me at the door, and there was a certain hesitation in her greeting, perhaps I imagined it, that made me uncomfortable for the first time in that welcoming house. I was already ill at ease, but I was also, I knew this, somewhere else in another part of me, in an implacable frame of mind.

Phil's bruises had faded, and I knew by the way he walked as we headed out towards Shanakiel that his father's fears for his ribs had been unfounded. I had one thing only on my mind, and I grew increasingly desperate as we made small talk, walking along. He was full of his coming enrolment in the college, plans, fears, aspirations, talk of this fellow he knew, that fellow who'd been giving him advice. I felt cold towards him, a coldness that I had time to examine as he prattled on, and when I'd had enough of this self-examination, when I'd had enough of his efforts to keep me somehow at bay, I stopped and asked him, straight to his face: how's Theresa these days?

Only a moment's hesitation, but that told me all I needed, feared, to know. Theresa, well you know Theresa's away up in Dublin for a while. We've an aunt, my father's sister, Margaret, I'm sure you've heard her name brought up, she's not been the best, you see, the heart you know? And Theresa's gone to stay with her for a while, give her a hand out, you know?

The cold part of my mind gave him credit: of course they'd have had to concoct a story, and he'd have had time to make himself comfortable with it, but for an honest man, and Phil was extremely honest, he told his story with a fluent, offhand ease. He'll make a lawyer all right, I told myself sardonically, and then felt ashamed of myself. He was, after all, sparing me as much as protecting his family, and he was the kind who would feel it keenly that he had not been able to protect his sister, had indeed brought this gross and sordid disturbance to the family door.

And, my cold mind wasn't done with me yet, how could he not, deep in some part of himself, blame me for drawing Cassady down on them in the first place?

We parted with vague talk of seeing each other soon, good wishes from me for his coming enrolment in the college, his promise that he'd pass on my greetings to Theresa, to his father, and it was clear to me that each of us, for our very different reasons, was relieved.

I stalked that fucker Cassady, I stalked him with a cold, precise detachment. I put every bad detective story I'd read to good use in the coming days and nights, surprised and a little disturbed that what I had scorned as melodrama should prove so surprisingly effective in practice.

I kept from myself the obvious, indeed the only question: what, exactly, do you propose to do?

We had stopped speaking of him at home. For one thing, there was no more information to be had, nothing, as Michael John put it, of any practical use. A waiting game, Tony Driscoll said once, to nobody in particular, putting on his coat to go out: Jesus, I always hated the waiting.

I stood in doorways across from his pubs, I cycled past Watercourse Road station at four o'clock in the afternoon, at eight o'clock at night, my cap pulled well down over my eyes; I stood by a pillar in the Metropole one night, pretending to read the *Echo*, watching him shovel food uncaringly into his mouth.

He kept to his hours, I'd give him that. Never a minute late to start, never a minute early to finish. I was waiting for rain, I was waiting for a rainy night.

Directly across from the garda station, there is a garage whose side gate gives out on to the narrow beginning of Pope's Road. A good, deep, dark gateway, set in a high blank wall, a high blank gable at the other side of the road. There were very few cars in those days, and it was unlikely that anyone walking or cycling by would see me; I would hear them coming, press myself deeper into the darkness.

I feel the dry flakes of paint against my cheek, the rough splinters where something had gouged the door coming in or out. I smell the cat piss, I smell the rain, I smell old engine oil, I smell myself. I hear the rain hammering on the asbestos roof, on the concrete road, on the lone car at the station door, the particular sound rain makes hammering on a car roof. Heavy rain, black heavy rain. The dim light over the station door.

He stepped out, it was too far away to see his face but I saw his evil temper in every jut and angle of him. He looked up impatiently, looked around, fumbled a set of keys from one hand to the other. I stood out from the doorway but he didn't see me. I raised the heavy revolver, barely able to hold the weight of it in two hands. I pulled the trigger and felt the unmerciful kick of it, the roar almost unbearably loud, the shock running through me. It was a heavy gun, that Nagant, with a ferocious muzzle flash that blinded me for a second, but I was hallucination-sharp, I'd aimed for his legs through the gap between the projecting station wall and the car windscreen, but some feral instinct made him move in that last fraction of a second, and the gun kicked up, so that as I ran, as I ran like fuck for the lane beyond the station where I'd left my bike, I was certain sure I had killed him. A head shot, a head shot, the crazy refrain roaring in my head, and fuckfuckfuck oh dear Jesus what have I done what have you done what have you done. The roar of the gun still ringing in my head, the extraordinary unimagined stink of cordite, gunpowder whatever the fuck it was. Nauseous, nauseous, but I ran, so fast across the road I almost do not remember running and home home home home pedalling like a man in mortal fear of the devil and hell behind him.

I dragged the bike up the steps and fumbled through the front door. They were all there, the men and Michael John, the noise I'd been making had stopped them in whatever they were doing and they'd come to their feet. I threw the bike against the wall and Granda grabbed hold of me. What is it, what's happened – and then, oh Joe, Joe, what have you done. I could see the horror in my own eyes mirrored in his, and then he was hard, sharp and fast. Get out of those clothes, now, at once. Give me that coat, and he went for the pocket where the heavy gun was weighing me down on one side and he took it out, showed it to the men. Seanie took gun and coat immediately, rummaging the pockets to see what else was there. Get rid of that, Mick ordered and Seanie was already past me, into the hall, reaching for his own coat, gone. Tommy, run up and get him some clothes, Tony get these in a bag of some sort, we'll have to burn them. You, taking me roughly by the arm, come here by the fire, stand there. He went for a basin, a washcloth, a towel from the scullery and he scrubbed me as I stood there, naked, shivering, wild inside myself still with the shock of it all. Tommy Owens stood by the table, a large glass of whiskey he'd poured me in his hand, and I don't know exactly what the look in his face was but it made me start to cry. Shush, now, shush, time enough for that, time enough, Mick said, drying me roughly, helping me into the dry clothes Tommy Mac had brought down. Tony beside us was stoking the range, and when he saw Mick had finished with the towel he went and brought the bike through the house, out into the back yard and I understood what he was doing of course, a wet bike in the hall ... and then he dried all traces of rain from the lino, working backwards from the hall door and when he'd done that he came back in and started feeding my clothes to the roaring fire. He looked at the sodden raincoat for a moment, sniffed at the sleeve and Mick said go out and fuck that in the river.

Listen to me now, lad, sit down, drink that, good boy, listen to me now. You'll have to go away now, do you understand that? You'll have to go away, look at me, look at me little Joe, ah good man, good man. You're certain sure nobody saw you, now? You are? Good. Right. Answer me now, look at me, is he dead or wounded, this is important now. Is he dead or wounded, the rest you can tell me later, shush, shush. Well? A kind of dispassion came over me, a kind of monotone. I aimed for his legs, I said, but he moved, the gun kicked, I think it was his head ... Granda folded my head into his chest, then: ah Joe, Joe ... but whatever softness he felt, he overcame it. They'll be raging in there, he said, and they won't be thinking straight. They'll go straight for the Seán South boys and maybe they won't think of you at all, maybe not ever, or not for a long time. But if he's conscious at all, if he's conscious and able to talk, no matter what he might really think he'll tell them it was you, do you understand? Do you see what we're dealing with here?

My throat felt swollen, as if it wouldn't let words out.

Tony came back in, and Granda said we'll have to get him away, we'll sort that later, but now I want you and Seanie when he gets back to take this lad up to Lehane the teacher, in Spring Lane ... someone was fumbling at the door, we tensed, I think I stopped breathing and Tommy Owens reached behind him for a hurley. Seanie came in, and when he saw the towel on the hall floor he stood on that. Rain's easing off he said, and in answer to Mick's unspoken question said: gone, stripped, the parts down different drains, the bullets too. Good, Mick said, I'm sending the lad here up to Lehane in Spring Lane. Seanie was doubtful: but Mick ... and he stopped and I saw, I understood that his look meant 'but he's not one of us'. That was the part of me that had been ticking along since I'd burst in, sat back and watching me, the men, Mick, watching all that was happening, hearing all that was being said, filing it all away to examine when I'd got through whatever fog of feelings and confusions I was going through. I saw what Seanie meant, that's what I'm trying to say. I *saw*. That's all. Tony took Seanie by the arm, to steady him, you would say, but also, I thought, as a kind of warning to mind his manners with Mick: Lehane was with us in Spain, he said, is that good enough for you? Ah Jesus I'm an old fool, Seanie said – he had a way of turning things to the good that I'd always loved in him. Ah Jesus what am I thinking, sure this young buck might be learning Spanish yet! And he did what he thought might be a toreador's twirl.

Not under fucking Franco, Mick growled, he won't be dancing under Franco, may he rot in hell. Seanie responded with the universal hangman's sign, suspending himself from his own fist, tongue to one side. Now we were only busy, efficient and brisk. Tommy Owens slipped out, slipped back in with a case, Mick's old leather case that had stood on the steps beside him all those long years ago; you'll need clothes, he said. Seanie, Mick said, you and Tony. Here, Tommy Mac said, and he splashed whiskey on Seanie's front, and on Tony's. Good, Mick nodded, walk him up there quick but easy lads, you know the drill. Tell Lehane I'll be by tomorrow. Joe, listen, I'll have to sort some things out, OK? You stay quiet in Lehane's, I'll be by tomorrow, or it might even be the next day, it all depends. You'll be grand, sure isn't it a house full of books? He was trying to comfort me, in some awkward way, but he knew and I knew and everyone there knew that nothing would ever make this right, nothing would ever bring us back to where things had been. Away with ye, now.

Going out the door I felt suddenly stricken, as if my whole life had suddenly collapsed around me, because my whole life had collapsed around me, and I twisted, desperately, but the two men had a grip of my elbows and they forced me down the steps, half carrying me, and Tony said:: aisy, now, aisy now, we all went through this door, lad, we all went through this door – and it was the sadness mixed with the gruffness, even the cold in his voice, that steadied me all out through Blackpool. I looked back once as we climbed the steps by the church, but the angle was wrong and if Michael John, Granda, was standing in the door to see me off I didn't see him.

18

How far away that night seems, now. A night not unlike this, the rain beating at the window, emptying the streets, the few cars that go by hermetic and private, small beating worlds hurrying through a bigger world.

What does it say of me, I wonder, that one of the great pleasures of my life now is to stand at this tall window looking down on an empty street in the rain?

What I do when it rains at night, if I am not occupied, I stand here at this window and gaze at the world, and am very much at home.

I shape the phrase 'in a foreign city', testing it: 'at home in a foreign city'. This peculiar life of mine: my country in books ranged on the wall behind me; my country in front of me in these angles and tumbles of roof and chimney, the rain-grey plastered walls, the stately windows streaked with wet dust, the splashing street and the gutters down below. The thought sour in my mouth – do I *have* a country?

Old men, they say, are given to living in memory. Rubbish. We all live in memory, there is only memory: every breath we take, every word we speak is already committed to memory, memory is where we live, memory is every moment of the day until the sudden dark and no more memory, no more anything.

The trick is to sort, to order, to prioritise. Standing here I am pushing away the memory of that stricken, bewildered boy, I am pushing though his memories, the memories he was so desperately already storing up as they hurried through the sleeping city. The city that, in his panic, he was finally recognising as home even as he felt it, inexorably, beginning to slip away.

I am looking for a particular memory, and half-afraid to find it, that moment when he felt genuine fear, when I felt genuine fear, for the first time in his, my, life.

What, the thought struck me like a blow, rounding off Thomas Davis Street into the haven of Spring Lane, what if all this has already happened, what if this feeling of falling, falling is because all this has already happened?

When I said out loud, wonderingly, what if all this has already happened, and Seanie looked at me dumbfounded, Tony looked shrewdly at me, pulling me out under a street light and said, well, Joe, the thing is, it has, and you made it happen. D'ye understand me? He was calm, calming the anxious Seanie with his free hand; Joe, he said, look at me: we answer for what we do when we take a life, you see? Not to god or any of that malarkey, we answer to ourselves, ye see, every day of the rest of our lives, it makes us who we are. It needn't have happened, you might think it shouldn't have happened, not for me to say, but you pulled the trigger, Joe, now you have to be the man who did that. I wanted him to take me in his arms, like Granda would, and I think he saw that but he saw, too, that it wasn't his place. Come on he said, giving me a shake, and sure maybe the fucker isn't dead after all, hard to kill a bad thing. And we almost laughed, the three of us. The grace of rough humour.

And now where am I? Order, old man, keep order now if you please. Save what is what for where is where.

And of course, yes, but I know this, I have been standing at windows all my life. Here at this window now, and at so many other windows, here they come in a long procession, one after the other, at so many windows since that first window the night of the funeral, Mam and Dad gone, I was saying, over and over to myself, Mam and Dad gone and the rain falling and this is me, now, this is me here at the window. This is me.

Years later forming the phrase 'a pleasurable melancholia'

and feeling the quaint exact rightness of the words.

I should have known this would happen, for fuck's sake! Get out of here, old man, shake this off now, get out and, what's that the phrase is nowadays, get out and get a life!

No need to actually go out, I tell myself craftily, stirring the soup and chewing happily on day old bread. Sure it's wet out there; what you could do, though, is you could run a nice, hot bath for yourself in a while, and take yourself into bed with a good book.

Jasus, I'd completely forgotten the package from Amazon! What have we here now, yes, yes, hmm, ah! This fellow Tóibín.

Later, a good book this, putting it face down on the duvet, I get out of bed, noise on the street out front. I go through, crack the window, look down. A noisy gaggle of boys and girls, all bumping and banging off each other, green scarves, those ridiculous hats, all singing 'The Fields of Athenry'. Of course, and damn me for forgetting, Ireland vs. France today.

That day with Sam, his South County Dublin passion for rugby: will we go? Ah, I don't know. Then sure why not? And hearing that song for the first time, god alone knows why they sing it, and then the shock of the big gangly blue-eyed merry galoot beside me roaring *Allez les Verts*! *Allez les Verts*! Come on, you Cork bastard! And at the top of my own voice, roaring crying mind, all of a sudden and not giving a tuppenny damn, here's me and the master: *Allez les Verts! Allez les Verts! Allez les Verts!*

I lean out the window and in a voice I thought I had long since lost I bellow down happily: *Allez les Verts! Allez les Verts!* Their shocked, delighted, innocent up-turned faces.

19

Lehane switched off the hall light before opening the door. Mr Lehane, I never addressed him, never referred to him then or after, as other than mister. Tony took a half-step forward, we had been standing a way back from the door so's not to alarm the man, and when he'd beckoned us in, Mr Lehane stepped out himself, for all the world looking to see when the rain might ease.

No woman or child in the house, he said, showing us to chairs around a low fire, you can be at your ease. Now then, who's this, lean forward boy; ah, Mick's lad. You in trouble, then? And before I could answer, to Tony: what's he gone and done, not one of your glory boys, is he? A wink to mollify Seanie, who relaxed. Cassady, he said. Oh that gentleman, giving the boy a hard time, is he? He shot him, Seanie butted in. Not long ago, he added inconsequentially. Mr Lehane looked at me thoughtfully, peering over his glasses, you felt he had perfected that look over the years. Is he dead, by any chance, lad? You don't know, I see.

Well, with an offhand brutality that shocked me, even in the state I was in: he wouldn't be any loss, anyway, what I hear. Tea, lads? No, we'd better get back, Tony said. Mick'll give you a shout. Probably tomorrow, but ... I know, I know, sending him away, is he? What I'd do anyway, be for the best.

He went through to the back, returned with blankets, swept cushions to one end of the sofa. You won't want to talk much, lad, I expect. Try to get some sleep. We've dealt with worse, believe you me, and there's no beating Mick when it comes to organising things. I'm out early in the morning, school you know? Help yourself to anything you need. Don't make any noise, OK? And don't be seen. Toilet's out back, don't flush. There's hot water ...

He was putting off leaving even though he was keen to be gone, even though it was clear he'd been settled by the fire for the night. Ask me, I said, sitting up straight, ask me.

All right, did you mean to kill him? No, I said, I was aiming for his legs. And the gun kicked, yeah? Dear, dear. Well you don't look the type, lad, if you don't mind me saying so, and I'm glad for you. He was telling me something about himself, something real, and he wanted me to see it, to understand, and he could see that I did; I had the strange feeling he wanted me to forgive him for something but he knew, and I had just learned, that's not how it works.

He turned the light off, the light he'd been reading by, and he didn't look back as he went out. I listened to his footsteps going away down the hall. I lay down, not feeling the cold at all, and pulled the blankets up to my chin anyway, and slept. I slept.

I woke to an empty house, dressed except for my boots, didn't know what to do then, I just sort of ... stood. I padded about in my socks. I nibbled some dry bread, I drank gallons of water, running the tap very quietly. The air felt thick, even though the rain had cleared and it wasn't warm. Everything felt ... absent? Yes, there was a kind of, a sense of, absence. Mr Lehane had a library that would give Bishop Lucey a heart attack. They don't, I remember thinking, they don't call him Red Lehane for nothing. But I couldn't read. I just ... sat there, looking into the dead fire.

They'll be here about eight, he said, letting himself in quietly, tucking his leather bag under the hallstand. In a van, Tommy Mac, you understand? I nodded; Tommy worked in the railways, would have managed to get hold of a CIE van. I don't expect you were able to eat, were you? I thought not. I'll make tea, ham sandwiches, you have to eat.

The afternoon passed, somehow. We tried to make conversation, but we hadn't the hang of it. The dark came on. A double tap on the front door came as a relief to us both. The sliding door in the side of the van was open. Good luck, lad, you'll be fine, Mr Lehane said, ushering me out with a hand in the small of my back; and when I half stopped, meaning to thank him, he pushed me harder. Get in, he said, and get going. He shoved my case, Michael John's old case, in behind me. I squatted, looking at it, dazed. Good luck to you ... and the door closed softly.

A garage on the Lower Road; we pulled in and while Tommy was filling the tank Granda slipped out of the attendant's dimly-lit booth, into the front seat. All right back there? I was kneeling on a pile of mail bags. I said that I was. Good, he said, good. The attendant wouldn't take any money from Tommy, waved him off, waved us off.

You can come up the front in a bit, lad, Granda said, unless you want a bit of a sleep? No? Comfortable back there? I managed a few grunts, but there was a big block in my throat still and, worse, a dim sense that I couldn't find words even if I was able to speak them. A fog with weight in it, that's the best I can do to describe it.

We're passing a pub here on the left, he said, it's the last pub in Cork going east and it's called The Oriental, good hah? He didn't seem bothered that I wasn't answering. Tommy muttered something I couldn't catch, then Granda turned and leaned in over the half-partition, so that I could see his face: you didn't plug him, anyway. Took his ear off, is all. They have him sedated in the North Infir. and they haven't a clue what happened. Not yet, anyway.

I heard him, and I could feel myself struggling to take it in. Down in my belly a turbulence of some kind that swelled up into my chest and burst out as a sob of relief. I thought, I said, I thought ... Aye, Granda said, still in that same matter-of-fact tone, well you thought you'd killed a man, of course you did.

No one said anything for a good while after that. Somewhere beyond Fermoy, Tommy slowed down so that I could clamber on to the bench seat in front without jogging his arm. Never liked Fermoy, Tommy said, glancing in his rearview mirror, nothing good ever came out of Fermoy. Garrison town. A bit harsh of you, Granda said mildly, but he had a small grin on his face all the same. Now lad, all brisk and Mick again, that fella is going to come round soon, and he'll be gunning for you, sure and certain. Even if he didn't think you had the balls or the means to do it, this is his chance. It's a mystery to me why he got so fixated on you but I've seen it happen, I've seen it happen. So ... I was thinking we'd lose you in Dublin for a while, but that won't do. Then I thought maybe England, but that won't do either. No chance of losing you in the building work, you'd stick out, you see, so I had a brainwave.

A long pause. Waiting for me. In what was almost a normal tone of voice I said: right, so what is it, this brainwave of yours? He's getting back to himself anyway, said Tommy, never taking his eyes off the road. So he is, Mick was smiling, but pushing ahead. You're going to France for a while, me lad, to a very good friend of mine. Mine and Tony's, you understand? Lehane's, too, he added, though Lehane might be more an acquaintance ... never mind, right then, what do you think?

France? I said. France? I haven't a word of the language, I know nobody, France! Back to himself all right, Tommy said, with no little satisfaction. Would you listen to him?

Ah for the love of god, Mick said, would you listen to yourself. First, nobody will dream of looking for you there. The branch are far too close to Scotland Yard since that fucking caper started up on the Border, so I wouldn't trust you in England. You won't keep your mouth shut, will you? You wouldn't be the best ever at keeping your head down and your opinions to yourself, now would you? And anyway, look at you, half the world's books read and you've hardly been out of Cork!

That last bit stung, but not half as much as it stung when he said: and it's about time you found something to do with yourself in the world. You can't drift forever, waiting for inspiration.

This he said softly, and not unkindly, but he was saying that childhood is over, and I heard what he was saying, and it made me cold inside, and sober, because all day, dulled and confused as I was, I had been struggling to say this to myself.

How long did I sleep for? I was snuggled into Granda's shoulder, his arm loose around me. Ah, he said, the dead awoke ... and spoke to many, Tommy finished the familiar saying for him. We're here, Granda said, straighten up now lad. Tommy was driving carefully down a suburban street, tall red brick houses on either side. Big heavy trees leaning in over the roadway, big wide footpaths. He stopped at a lighted house, I shrugged my wrist out of my sleeve, two o'clock in the morning, a lighted house. Right, I said briskly, what now? Would you look at him, Granda said, up and down, up and down ... like a whore's knickers, Tommy finished it for him. Switched off the engine. Right, men, Mick said, and slid out the door. He peeled off his coat, and took off his tie, opening his top shirt button, plumping his high white collar. He leaned towards the rearview mirror and sleeked back his hair. Would you look at him, I said to myself, fresh and sharp, nice suit, too, the Sunday best. Right, Tommy, he said, you'll be OK? I will he said, I'm expected, be good to get a kip. He, too, was out of the van, stretching, looking carefully up and down the street. I stood out onto the street beside him and tentatively offered him my hand. He looked at me for a second and then dragged me into his arms. You be good now, boy, keep your eyes open and, don't forget us now? Hear me? I was awfully close to breaking down myself.

You're a good man, Tommy, I said, you were always very good to me since, since ... ye were all very good to me, all of ye ... Aye, he said, prising my fingers off him, I'll be sure to tell 'em. Then, drily, they'll be thrilled I'm sure. Go on, get out of it. You better follow Mick now lad, everything will be all right, you'll see. Go on now.

I stood on the street, watching him drive away, watching until the tail lights vanished when he turned left at the end of the long road.

Behind me, a door opened; I heard it but I was lost in saying goodbye to myself. Then Mick whistled softly, just once, and I turned and walked up the steps to where a figure stood outlined in the doorway, Mick one step below and to one side.

20

Genevieve, not Vincent. She doesn't like me to throw the keys down to her; I'll have to buzz her in, and this irritates me, buzzing people in irritates me, I don't know why. I leave the door open and close down the laptop while she's climbing the stairs. A graceful girl, Genevieve, Gen, but for some reason she clumps when she climbs the stairs.

Ah here, old man, what's with the bad temper, eh? Stop it, now.

We touch cheeks, once, twice, and I sniff and say: now what is it? Don't know, she says, offhand, skipping past me; from a friend's place, thought I'd try it out.

As usual, she's pulling down books from the shelves, looking at them a second or two then shoving them back. Some kind of loose-woven coat she has on, long and shapeless, skinny black jeans, neat short boots with pencil-thin heels.

I like when you do that, she says. Do what? Look me up and down like that and then give that sniff of yours. Appreciative.

Sniff? Do I sniff? More like a wrinkle, I suppose, you know, with your nose?

With this one, conversation is often first cousin to unarmed combat, or, better, swordplay: parry, feint, thrust; parry, feint, thrust.

Usually, I find it exhilarating.

I'm tired today, I tell her, and I'm hungry all of a sudden. Me, too, she says, turning towards the door, me too I am hungry. Come on, then.

I like this hallway, she says, standing at the bottom of the stairs, her head craned back as she turns a full circle on her heel; makes me feel safe, somehow, you know. OK, where are we going then, same place you bring all your mysterious lady visitors? You do have mysterious lady visitors, Joseph, don't you? Besides me, I mean?

I score a point by ignoring this thrust.

As Gen leads the way towards the indicated table, the patron, Gaston, a man I have never warmed to, makes what he intends as a man-to-man gesture of appreciation behind her back. As he slides away to bring menus she says: ugh, nasty old lech. I am always impressed when someone shows signs of having eyes in the back of their head, and unfortunately she sees that I am impressed, so we're honours even again. Stop looking at me like that, she says, peering haughtily at the menu. One doesn't wish to be ungallant, I reply, and win a small complacent smile (and a point) for my troubles. Yes, she says, matter of factly, appraising them by peering down, not bad – and of course they're my own.

The tech children have a useful phrase, 'early adopter', and I was an early adopter of the more severe kind of feminism. I can still be wrong-footed by the casual and untroubled way in which so many French women seem content to appraise themselves as sexually desirable. It's the left puritan in me, I suppose, but it seems to me letting the side down. Which said, I have always loved that charge of excitement I feel in the company of a desirable woman. Nothing, alas, is simple.

Gen is amused, somehow intuiting at least part of what is passing through my mind: what do you do for sex, these, days, old man? Mocking? A little, perhaps, but also genuinely curious, and not unkind. Not too much, I admit ruefully, but ... there was a time ...

I'll bet there was, she says, and favours me with an admirably executed seductive smoulder. I make a little applause. *Adjani*? she asks. More ... *Bujold*, I think, but beautifully done, my dear, beautifully done. She hesitates, but decides to accept it as a compliment.

And now, I say, as the soup arrives, what brings you here? We're not going to play a little more, she asks, mock-plaintive, not even a little bit? Uh oh. All right then, serious, OK? Look, he spoke to his brother, half-brother, you know who I mean? Eh, bef! I told him, would he listen? No, he would not listen. Fellows like that ...

She breaks off, staring out the window at god alone knows what, then says: OK, look, I don't know what you did or how you did it but those two fuckers, the cops right, that were hassling him. They came to his place last night and, you won't believe me, they apologised for the misunderstanding! Can you believe that? Of course you can, Joseph, you very mysterious man, I am quite sure you can believe that. Joseph, I may be serious? I ask myself how this quiet old man can make such a thing happen, you understand? And, frankly, I don't like this, it makes me nervous.

I can't quite work out if she's attacking me, goading me, thinking out loud or thanking me – so many inflections flitting through her light, pleasant voice, so many changes of expression on that mercurial face. Rushing her words now, she continues: but, why is it me who comes to talk to you of this? Because he doesn't know if he can trust his brother to keep to his word – he says he will break with those people but ... we are not sure. So, brief, he is ashamed to see you.

I am processing what she is telling me (the thought that the half-brother might be unreliable had, naturally, occurred to me before now), but most of my attention is engaged in tracking, as much as I can, all of the conversations about Vincent that I have had with Gen. I am pretty certain, completing the tally, not large, that never once has she mentioned him by name – and certainly not by the name he assumed to amuse me and to send me a signal that first night by the Panthéon.

If the brother's not going to keep his end of the bargain, there are consequences to that, and Vincent can surely figure that out for himself. And, why should he be 'ashamed' to see me?

Nothing is more dangerous than idle curiosity – no, not curiosity, inquisitiveness driven by a sense of entitlement. She feels entitled to know what's going on, and what she really wants to know, she wants to know two things: how I am able to, as she sees it, wield so much influence, and – why should I trouble to exercise so much influence on her man's behalf? In some strange, half-thought out way she worries that I may be a threat to her. What? Her power over him?

In any case, there are things going on, in and around her life, that she does not understand, and clearly she hopes to inveigle some at least of the missing information out of me.

In such situations, of course, the solution is always a simple lie, told brazenly and with maximum sincerity. I take her hand between my two hands, I become the kind, understanding uncle. Gen, you're looking at this the wrong way, you see? Your head is full of Islamic terrorists, undercover policemen, a mysterious old man with secret powers?

I am hamming this up, but carefully, and she gives me a tentative smile.

It's really very simple, I say, listen: I have a pupil whom I have come to like, yes? A bright young man who is friendly to me, who brings round his beautiful, witty girlfriend from time to time, to cheer me up in my loneliness, yes? And my young friend has a brother, excuse me, a half-brother, who's having a spot of trouble, yes? OK, so, it's family – but I, too, have a family, I happen to have a cousin, not a first cousin, I don't see him very often, we have such different lives, but my cousin, how do I put this, is a man not without some influence, yes? Lucky for us, eh? So, naturally I ask him for some assistance, eh? You see? Family,

Gen, the family is the foundation of the state – where would we be without family?

It makes me sad, and a little ashamed of myself, to see her face brighten with relief. Oh Joseph, of course, of course! And I look modest, pleased, even a little grateful that my humble efforts to be helpful should elicit such warmth, such gratitude.

Actually, I think, summoning Gaston who has been keeping a nauseatingly tactful distance, I despise myself. I order brandies to finish, taking mine in one mouthful.

She treats me to a long embrace in full view of the window as we part. And we won't say a word about this, will we? I mean ... well, he might be embarrassed that I came to see you. I'm sure he'll tell you himself ...

I make the appropriate soothing noises, the half-pats on the arm, all that palaver, but by now I am so angry with myself that I'm relieved to get away.

So, old man, I settle in my window seat, face to the night sky, the sodium glow on the mansards across the street, I ask myself: why so angry?

Not easily answered. Writing this life of mine I am all the time choosing, I am ordering, setting things down in linear order, the way we think the world proceeds, or should. But of course, I think it was Bergson said this, or something like it, time is experienced duration, no? Something like that. The station you've left behind coming up again, and perhaps again, perhaps many stations in different kinds of order, yes? Out of sequence, simultaneously, that sort of thing. And then there is fat time, and thin time ... Anyway ... anyway, yes, it isn't of course Genevieve you're cross with, well perhaps just a little, but, come on then, face it: yourself. Myself, indeed. More exactly, in fact very exactly: the man I have allowed myself to become.

And Thérèse was beautiful in much the same way Gen is,

had the same kind of unease in her long bones, was constantly setting and unsetting herself, that radiance in her eyes and in the ways she moved. Ah yes, the ghost in the corner, Thérèse; even the vigilant Gaston missed her smoky presence, Gaston sitting there avidly watching our little comedy, half amused and more than half pitying. Pitying you, you mean? But exactly. Pitying me.

Had I her number, I would ring Gen now: I could apologise for that cousin, I could apologise for patronising her, for my puritan devotion to secrecies, discretions, the life lived in shadows, but ... what then?

But, what then?

Going nowhere, old man; better hope you sleep now, disturber of ghosts, spark-setter of useless regrets.

I will not speak of this to Vincent. I will ask him his real name.

21

What have you brought me, Miguel? A handsome young man! How very kind to me you are! Come here, young one, step up into the light. And you too, you blackguard, you skulker in shadows, step up so that I may see what you have suffered, so long since you saw me! Let me see that face of yours.

Commanding, yes, and comforting, that too. She was a black shape in a brightly-lit doorway, and all of a sudden I wanted to walk into that deep dark space and be safe – safe, reassured, comforted and ... protected. Yes. I felt ... drawn. A new feeling for me, and yet somehow familiar. I expected, why I do not know, such a fleeting thought, that Mick would put his arm round my shoulders, would bring me forward with him, a gift, and offering; the occasion, if I may put it like this, seemed to demand some such thing. You see, I had come so far forward in myself, I who had been numb for days now, unfeeling (I thought), unthinking (I would have said), I had come so far forward in myself, just there, on the steps, that I was quite clear, sure in myself, that this was an occasion.

So few occasions in a life!

Behave yourself, woman, Mick said, and there was an ease between them, a drawl in his voice I had not heard before, a different kind of authority, something earned and agreed between them, that made me look at him very sharply as he came forward into the light. That, I thought, seeing the litheness in him, the faint hint of playful insolence, that is one very confident man. Would you look at the step of him!

I waited for them to embrace, there was such a charge between them, but the old Mick said, gruff as he could be: don't be standing there like a gom, did I never teach you manners?

Come up here. I stumbled forward, stopped. The top step was broad enough for us all. Eleni, he said, quite formal, this is my grandson, Joseph. Joseph, I wish you to meet Eleni. Playful but serious, both at the same time. She had shoulder-length hair, very black, parted severely in the middle. A prominent nose, and such deep, dark liquid eyes, such a shrewd, unwavering regard! I couldn't find words, I just stood and stared at her, it had never occurred to me in my youthful cockiness that a woman her age could be so unmistakably sexy. All that authority, all that presence, so formidable a woman, I felt all this but, god help me, what rushed over me was a powerful, confusing shock of desire!

Then they were laughing at me, frankly and unabashedly mocking me, my confusion, my stammering and blushing. I felt a sudden surge of rage, and they both saw it and then Mick did put his arm around me, and he was still laughing, but maybe more gently now, and he even ruffled my hair like he used to do when I was a boy.

Such a compliment! Ah Miguel, it comes down in the blood, you see! She, Eleni, she took my face in both her hands and she looked at me a moment and I felt I was very close to something, not someone, something ... she took my face in both her hands and, very gently, she kissed me on the lips; she drew us both in to her and, hesitantly at first then fiercely I put one arm around her and then, one last tiny hesitation, my other arm firmly around that astonishing man, my grandfather Miguel.

I glimpsed a luxurious high-ceilinged room to the right, a dark room that I sensed was book-lined, that smelled of cigarette smoke, then she shut the front door firmly behind us and walked to the stairs. When she saw that I had not followed, she turned and beckoned me rudely: come, boy, bring your case, you need to sleep.

The room was lit by a red-shaded bedside lamp, the coverlet

turned back on the wide bed. She picked up a pillow, sniffed it, tossed it to me, indicated. I bent my head to the clean white cotton, inhaled – some subtle perfume, faint and elusive. You see, boy, you shall have good dreams tonight, I think. My daughter's she said, with a vague wave at the room. She is in Rome presently. She makes a good aura, no? I did not understand what she meant. She smiled to herself. Bathroom, here. A bedroom with its own bathroom, I thought. And now, goodnight boy. I wanted her to stop calling me boy, and I almost said so, but then, somehow, I understood, all at once, that by 'boy' she meant something not quite the same as what, up to that very second, I had taken 'boy' to mean. She closed the door softly; I registered the click even as, too late to say thank you, good night, whatever, I came to myself.

I woke in a woman's bed for the first time in my life and the light in the room told me it was late morning. So powerful was the sense of feminine presence that I did not want to open my eyes for a long while; I just lay there, luxuriating, taking long, slow deep breaths, feeling my ribs rise and fall, feeling myself in my body.

I felt a lazy urge to masturbate, but decided against it. Hunger drove me out of bed, the smell of rashers coming up through the house, the drowsy murmur of voices, short sudden bursts of laughter. I listened in wonder to Michael John laughing. I had never taken a shower before, I enjoyed it for the sense of sophistication it gave me. Heroes in American books are always taking cold, hard showers to prepare for the day; I tried it, eventually, and decided, spluttering and shivering, that they were mad.

I went barefoot down the stairs, had found no fresh socks in my case, rummaging through. I stood in the double-height hallway, the sun warming the faded green tiles underfoot, and I felt, very simply, comfortable; when I say that I felt at my ease, I mean that this sense of comfort was also a sense that, somehow, I fitted in here.

Boy! Breakfast! Beckoning me, both hands. Come, come before that impossible man incinerates everything! Ah but, always I say this, Cork brings me nothing but trouble and confusion!

She was tall, Eleni, and solid, a certain articulation to her hips as she strolled down the passageway. *Arretez*! she said, without looking around, and Mick, when I came through into the bright kitchen, was chuckling, his back to us both, attending to a frying pan, toast, kettle. That was the first time in my life I heard French spoken, and often in the decades to come, often in the most incongruous circumstances, when I would hear *arretez* I would always be hearing the echo, the antiphon, in that deep throaty voice.

We were all barefoot, I saw, circling the laid table, and the kitchen was warm, the tiles underfoot were warm. We didn't have radiators in our house, and I approved of them at once. You should be warm when possible, I agreed with myself. I sat, and if I expected this gentle freefall to continue, this soft landing in comfort and reassurance, Mick knocked that out of me right away.

Right, lad, he said, smarten up now. He laid down the filled plates, poured tea, tossed his tea cloth apron towards the sink, and shrugged when it fell to the floor. He's minding the suit trousers anyway, I thought sourly, not wanting to come fully awake, not yet, knowing that I had to.

This fella here, he said, shot a cop. Not politics, he's not involved, right lad? I nodded. So, this cop, you know the type, he was making life a misery for Joe here. Fixated on him, he was. A few weeks ago, he beat up a pal o' Joe's, assaulted the pal's sister, *tu comprends*? Eleni with her eyes, said, yes, continue. He didn't rape her, you understand, but it was ugly and the girl's not the better of it. This was to get to Joe, you understand? *Bien*, Joe here takes it into his head to shoot the bastard. I don't blame him, but it was stupid and reckless.

I wasn't even offended, amazed to hear Granda speaking French, then cursing myself for a fool – what else would have he have spoken, France, the Maquis, during the war? – but also struck dumb because I had just intuited, having nothing to go on but a certain feline quality to what was passing back and forth between them, that this pair had spent the night together as lovers.

Joe, it would be good if you'd pay attention here? You don't mind? The officer's whiplash in his voice.

Doucement, Miguel, gently now.

Ach, he said, but relenting all the same, he's heard worse from me, haven't you? He knows that I mean nothing by it.

Ye fecker, I thought, aren't you the man that's pleased with himself?

Not England? she asked, then answered herself: no, not, perhaps not after all. So, Henri then?

Henri, Mick nodded. Far and away the best thing for it. Be good for the lad, too, Broaden his horizons, you know yourself.

Excuse me, I heard myself say, and I didn't recognise the tone of voice in myself but I took a liking to it immediately. Excuse me, but would it be out of order here if I were to have a say in all this? I'm not a fucking parcel!

He was amused, just a flicker in his eyes, but he glared at me, genuinely indignant too. Well of all the fucking ... listen mister me lad, do you know the trouble you've caused, the trouble you've put people to! Do you? Both of us glaring at each other now, and I didn't like it, in him or in me, but I wasn't going to back down, I was ready to get stuck into him, but his eyes went sideways, and so did mine, following, and Eleni had her eyes downcast, staying out of all this, a small complacent smile twitching the corners of her mouth.

Well fuck it, I've seen it all now, Mick said, struggling not to laugh, and I got up and said: I'll make more tea, so. And Granda said, good lad, the kettle's near boiled.

Two days I spent in that house, Mick in and out, always 'going to see a man'.

Dictionaries, phrase books, picture books – a crash course on France from Eleni. My head was reeling, to tell the truth, but she would say: Never mind, boy, never mind, you think nothing is going in but everything is going in, believe me, and it will come out again after a while, when you're ready to fit it all into place. I had no idea what she meant by this, but if Eleni had told me the moon was a satellite of Russia I would have believed her. I tried to imagine myself as a hole in the ground into which everything was pouring, and if there was a certain grim irony to the metaphor I chose for myself – well, it passed me by at the time.

Mick said you only wounded that policeman she said, sometime that first afternoon. Yes, I said, and if she heard the relief in my voice, she paid it no heed. Would you have preferred it, to have killed him? I saw at once she meant it as no more than a bald question. I'm trying not to think about that, I said, feeling awkward and evasive, but the answer pleased her, for some reason, and she merely grunted: probably better, all things considered, that you didn't, eh? But that wasn't a question.

Late in the afternoon, she picked up on something, a niggle that had been growing quietly in the back of my mind. She sighed, put down the book from which she was taking notes, said: oh very well, very well then. I suppose ... Better me than Mick, anyway, who knows what he might tell you? So much he has spared you!

She saw she had disconcerted me. Ah boy, boy, you must relax, there is nothing bad to know. Then, composing herself as if to give a deposition: Mick and I, you must know, we met as comrades in the Brigada, you know the Brigada? *Eh bien*, good. Has he told you much? No, then this I leave to him. He tells me you are a reader, yes? Then if I am a judge, and I am a judge, you may believe me, when he told you the bare bones (that is all he told you he says, I asked him of course) then, if I am not mistaken, after he told you whatever he told you then you went to the books, yes? I nodded, I said yes I'd read a bit, I did not tell her that I had devoured everything I could get my hands on, including Mick's own modest library.

Well, then, we were comrades and lovers; first I was his commanding officer and then he was mine. The commissars, you see, they did not feel safe with women in charge. They did not feel safe with women in charge, you understand me?

I didn't, not then, but later I did, I came to understand all too well, and I saw why she had repeated this phrase, and I would feel ... honoured, that she had seen something in me, that she had foreseen that this would become important information in my life.

Battle stories, young man? I do not think you want battle stories. I will tell you this, your grandfather Joseph Lyons, my Miguel, they made a pun on his name, they called him El Léon, the lion, yes? He was a lion, that man. He still is, I blurted out, and she had shadows in her eyes suddenly, but she did not move out of her chair, she looked across at me and I saw pride in her look, and gratitude, and I saw love.

She answered my unspoken question: Ah, you must play the cards you're dealt, my new young comrade, you must play the cards you are dealt, eh? Not so? And I agreed that it was so, thinking I understood. She shook her head, and she wasn't being unkind when she said: no, you don't understand. I will put it in words for you, but only time will give you to understand.

You see my library, you see where I live, yes? Well, no, better you don't go outside but you see my house, how I live, OK? Is this like your house, in Cork, is it? No, I don't think so. Here in Dublin I am a professor in Modern Languages; in Athens by 1934, oh impossibly young, I am already in the Polytechnic, teaching politics.

Athens? I thought, stupidly.

Ah but you thought I was French, of course, of course. Well, never mind all this, OK? Miguel, Mick, now that man was born a soldier. What we called, a soldier of the proletariat. A good soldier, and yes he had good politics, very good politics, my Miguel. Your Mick, he says you call him sometimes Michael John, sometimes grandfather? Granda, I said. Yes well, never mind, he still has the best politics of all, the politics of his big, strong heart. He has a very clear mind, you agree? But, he will say this himself perhaps, of course not in my words, only in war can intellectuals and soldiers fight side by side. Never mind if you do not understand now what I am telling you. After the war, intellectuals go back to being intellectuals, soldiers go back to being soldiers or carpenters or peasants, you see?

I told her that in Ireland, as far as I could see, we had no intellectuals at all, and probably far too many soldiers, or people pretending to be or to have been soldiers. I told her that I had met a handful of real soldiers, I meant Mick and the men, and that they seemed to me sad but decent people. She laughed, my god how she laughed, but I didn't mind, and when she told Mick later that night what I had said, word for word almost, Mick laughed too, but a bit ruefully maybe, and he gave me a long speculative look and said: well at least you were paying attention anyway. We must have been doing something right.

My last thought, falling asleep: Cassady, you bastard, if you only knew the favour you did me. Still, and I meant this casually, so to speak, but genuinely: I hope you rot in hell.

All next day at the books again, the both of us, and when Mick came home it was with a rake of new clothes for me. You can pack those later, he said, Eleni will give you a case, I'm kind of attached to mine, you don't mind? I shook my head.

Sit down, then, he said, there are things you need to know. We're sending you to a very good friend of ours, a very good man, you understand me? A man you can trust your life to, yes? Henri, I said, the famous Henri. He looked at me sharply, but saw that I meant no offence. What's Tony always telling you, he said nevertheless. To mind my mouth I said, I know, I'm sorry. Ah ye meant nothing by it, lad, it's grand, it's grand. I told you, remember, I got out of Spain with Henri? I looked at Eleni. Me, she said, I got out, I was sent out, a year earlier. A flash of bitterness there. Mick laid his hand on hers. Ah Eleni, Eleni ... She sighed, then brightened, patted her behind: shot in the rump, boy, would you believe it? Shot in the rump, rump is a much better word than ass, isn't it? Don't you think? A rump is plump, when I hear ass, I think of those skinny little donkeys ...

Mick, away somewhere else for a moment, said half to himself: Valencia, remember? The hospital ship? I had to threaten to shoot you meself unless you'd go?

Something of an ancient quarrel turning over in the depths, subsiding.

So, where was I? Henri, OK. The war, you know this, I spent with Henri, I mean the second war. Henri, lad, is two birds with one stone, you get me?

I didn't, I hadn't an idea what he was talking about.

Jesus and I thought you were quick, he said, and the exasperation was only half feigned. I had a sudden insight into the strain and worry I'd brought into his life, and he saw it in my eyes, so very quick always himself, and something flashed through him that came close to frightening me.

Tell me, he said then, very gently, tell me why it is, why do you think it is, that you have no idea what to do with your life?

I hadn't expected this, but then Mick was always a master of tactics.

Off guard, wrung out and still in the aftershock of what had happened, what I'd done, I corrected myself immediately, I shook my head. I don't really know, I said.

I was conscious of Eleni leaning forward, watching us. I looked Mick in the face. I don't know, I said, and there was a relief in saying it, I don't know, Granda, I really don't know.

Ah Joe, Joe, he said, there's nothing for you here. That's what we've made of this country, boy, nothing. Nothing for you, anyway. Not for the likes of you.

Away back inside myself, a small voice was asking: what exactly does that mean, though, 'the likes of you'?

This country's fucked, I said, surprising the both of us with my vehemence. It is, he said, but sure nothing is forever boy.

D'ye remember Seanie ... I said, but he was there ahead of me, his answer coming before I'd finished the question. Remember that night in the kitchen, he said, when Seanie came home half cut? Not like him at all, I said inconsequentially; not like him at all, Granda agreed. And, he went on, overriding me, he looked at you, head down over the books as per usual and he said 'Mick, Mick, would you ever tell me, is all this all we have to offer this boy here?'

Meaning Ireland, I said. Meaning Ireland, he agreed. And more than that, I said, and he nodded agreement, looking me cold and straight in the eye.

For a moment, a long moment, everything hung in the balance; I caught a glimpse of a dizzying void, saw that all the good humour and patience, all the civility of our life there in Blackpool was true and genuine but also both willed and desperate, an agreed story the men and Mick had built up to sustain themselves, to sustain me. Out there behind and beyond that little world …

Miguel, Eleni said, soft but clear, looking up at the clock. I felt a stab of alarm.

Well, lookit boy, I had it in mind, well to tell you the truth I'd even discussed it with Eleni (ah, I thought, all those random weekends away), stop that now, listen to me; I had it in mind for a while now that it might be good for you to get away. I mean really away, not just to England like the Dagenham Yanks, you understand me? Somewhere that would stretch you, you get me?

A pity it took all this to galvanise me, haw?

He brushed my gaucheness aside.

So, there'll be a car here in an hour or so, we better get something to eat, eh? An hour? I squawked, and I was too shocked to be embarrassed at the sound of myself. An hour?

Eleni looked at me coldly: what did you think, boy, that you come here on holiday for life?

Mick, matter of fact, put an envelope on the deal table: money, a seaman's Union card, a grubby envelope addressed to someone called Seanie Lamb, a Dublin City Library reader's ticket, some crumpled bus tickets, a holy medal of some sort, a ticket for some match in Croke Park ... I saw that the Union card and the reader's ticket also bore the name Seanie Lamb. Mick watched me sift through all this: the Lambs are a sound family, he said, Seanie's gone missing for a few days, as far as his mother knows he got a bit of casual work on the Liverpool cattle boat. Liverpool, I said? Is where you're going, Mick said. Liverpool first. Brisk again now. You'll be met, he said, don't worry, they'll know you. How, I asked, thinking I was asking a very reasonable question. Eleni looked from me to Mick, from Mick to me. I got up and went to look in the mirror over the sink.

I suppose that I had never really looked at myself before, I mean really looked, I mean gazed at myself dispassionately, as if trying to commit what I saw to memory.

When I had composed myself, when I'd sat down at the table again, when I'd gathered in all the papers, the money, the bric-a-brac, Eleni said: the very image, eh Miguel? You know, it is a good job he is going, really. We looked at her, surprised. She waved her hand across her face, airy, dismissive. You see, so much he reminds me ...

We were still laughing when the car came to collect me, still laughing at one thing or another, when Eleni turned off the light in the hall, looked out to check that it was indeed the expected friend at the wheel, leaning out into the pool of street-light to show his face. You have my address? she asked. I recited it. Good, she said, always put professor, it makes them so much less likely to ... And the letters to Mick, no stamp, inside my envelope? I nodded again. She took my face in her hands, and she looked into my eyes, it seemed like for a long time, and then she gave a little sigh, not unhappy, and said: remember, boy, always, that nothing is forever. Play the cards you're dealt, eh? And she turned away and walked back the dark passageway into the kitchen and closed the door.

I was bracing myself inside to take leave of Mick, of Granda, when I noticed he was already halfway out the door in his stockinged feet, swinging my case as it if were empty. I hurried after him. Jesus' sake, boy, close the door will ya? And then, did you think I wouldn't make sure I'd seen the back of you?

Opening the back, door, shoving the case in after me, roughly enough I thought. He introduced us brusquely: Joe, Eddie.

Howya, said Eddie, the one word I ever heard this Eddie say.

Mick went back up the steps for his shoes, called something down the dark hall to Eleni. I thought she might have come out to wave me off, but no. We drove through the streets of the capital city and I had my eyes firmly shut, I didn't want to see anything. I wanted there to be nothing only the night, and driving, and the proud head of my grandfather in the seat in front of me. We came to the docks, and Eddie switched off his lights, the car's engine sounding no louder than a sewing machine, and then he stopped by some dim stacks of crates, and Mick patted him on the shoulder once, and said thanks, and we got out. I glanced back at Eddie, but he just sat on, not looking at me.

We stood in the dark for a while, saying nothing, and then two men came by, slowly, all the time in the world, and they were whistling in unison what in my innocence I thought was 'Tannenbaum', an old favourite of quiet Tommy Owens. I was startled when Mick joined in, and the two men stopped, a few yards away, still whistling but looking carefully all around them.

Mick gripped my two shoulders, turned me around roughly. He said, listen boy, tell me now, didn't I look after you? Wasn't I always there for you, wasn't I? Did I ever let you down, did I? Answer me now, answer me Joey, for the love of god!

Nothing, nothing is more naked than the human soul in its extremity of need.

If I ever did one thing right in my life, anything, if I ever did one thing right in my life I did it then when I took his face in my two hands and I said Granda, you were mother and father to me, you were night and day there for me. Always and ever. You did a good job on me, Granda, you always did right by me, you're the heart and soul of me, you are. And then I said, and it came up out of the soles of my feet, ah Granda ... and he looked away down into my eyes in the dim light and I looked away down into his eyes and we knew there was no more to be said.

One of the men coughed, quick and soft. Right, said Mick, out with you.

I stood in between the two men where they'd parted to make room for me, and one of them took my case in a big fist. I couldn't see their faces. Nothing was said; the two men gave Mick a sideways look, and we straightened, the three of us, eyes front. Good men, he said, and he meant the three of us, then he jutted his chin and we moved away, falling into a marching step after a couple of shuffling paces, the stocky smaller man counting cadence – *clé, clé, clé deas clé* ... and then with a short laugh, giving that up.

I looked back only once, when we came into the light from the ship and it seemed more sensible to the three of us, no need to say it, to give over the play-acting.

He was standing out where the moon just barely touched him. I saw he had taken off his hat, because the faint light caught the silver in his hair. He raised his arm once in abrupt farewell, and then, somehow, he was gone.

Good man yourself, Mick, I said softly, speaking but to myself, good man, Mick. I'll be seeing you.

Part 2

22

Rain, great slanting sheets of cold rain, blue-black in the weak harbour lights. I think I must stink of fish, stepping carefully up from the deck of the trawler and onto the uncertain pier. The tall man steadies me from behind, pushing; the short one, the heavy-set skipper, has me by the wrist. I shrink down into the heavy coat they have given me, let my weight fall down through me to my feet. When the skipper is satisfied that I am steady enough, he lets go of me, reaches past me for my suitcase, puts it into my hand with a gesture that is surprisingly gentle and paternal. I don't know their names, they do not know mine.

It was a rough crossing from Cornwall. I have not been sick, a fact that just now, standing here, taking it all in, surprises me. A hand in the small of my back – I had not seen the car, had been looking out over the broad dark harbour, but there is indeed a car, the exhaust telling me that the engine is running but there is no engine noise – perhaps it's masked by the deep rumble of the trawler's engine, the high constant wind, the noise the rain is making as it beats down on the broad granite pier, the sea wall twice the height of a man.

The back door of the car is held open by the driver, who's leaning back from the inside, steadying the door in the gusting wind. The skipper pushes me again, so that I am stooping to enter the car, craning back to look at him, meaning, I suppose, to say thanks, to say something, and a hand from inside the car grabs me, pulls me in. My suitcase lands on my lap and the car is already moving away before the door is slammed in on me.

Treachery, the police, betrayal? No. As fast as I process the thought I discount it – why here, after all, why not in Dublin, in Liverpool, on that long drive down from the Liverpool docks to a small fishing port in Cornwall? I have slept, if at all, in a kind of low fever, I've been at sea for two days, locked down in an empty fish hold, unspeaking, unspoken to, fed tea and sandwiches in silnce, but some part of my mind is quick and efficient at processing thought, something that seems to have woken in me between taking leave of my grandfather and being here now, in this small fast car, bucketing down the length of a pier in France in the rain in the middle of the night.

I make no attempt to speak, nor do these two men. At the pier's root, in front of a dark mass of buildings, the car stops. I am ushered out, across the rainslick granite slabs and in through a heavy dark door. Inside the door, a steep, rough wood stairs, dimly lit. The driver climbs swiftly ahead of me, the man behind me closes the door softly to, without quite closing it, I notice this, notice myself noticing, and then he nudges me with my suitcase, not roughly. I climb, I follow a short corridor, also dimly lit, and a door before me opens just as I am about to stop. I walk in, I halt. It's warm, a large square room, benches and desks of different sizes scattered it seems haphazardly around. Dim here at the entrance, but at some kind of dais on the far side of the room there is a pool of intense light and there is a man sitting behind a heavy bare desk, smoking, looking steadily at me.

Square, heavy, thoughtful, dark and squat, this is the first impression he makes on me, this Henri. I walk towards him, already unbuttoning my heavy borrowed coat, but when I reach out a hand to offer him a handshake he merely grunts, indicates the chair placed facing him across the desk. When he stubs out the cigarette with a single stab, when he leans forward into the light, his eyes are not particularly friendly. He reaches a hand towards me, flicking his fingers against his thumb, a gesture I take to mean: papers, quick. I reach into my jacket pocket, fumbling to reach it inside all these layers of cloth, and Henri, the small man standing beside him and the big one who is now almost directly behind me, I feel his breath, they all three of them tense. I hand over the papers Mick had given me in the kitchen, in Dublin, and Henri reaches for the long arm of the lamp, brings the light down closer the better to examine the bits and scraps of paper he has laid out before him. He looks up at me, he looks at me for a long moment, weighing me up. He gathers the papers up, patting them into a neat pile, then hands them across the desk to me with a brief nod. Then, changing his mind, beckoning impatiently that I should hand them back.

I am, I realise, disconcerted. From Mick's old comrade, his dear friend, I had expected more warmth – not this suspicion, this brusque, offhand attitude.

Very good, he says suddenly, gently, in English, very good. May I please put to you a question? Of course, I say, but I haven't spoken for some time, my voice sounds embarrassing to me, squeaky. From Liverpool, how did you get to the fishing boat? I was met, I tell him, a small man and a tall man, the tall one had a very refined accent, the small man sounded to me like one of those Cockneys we used to see in newsreels. The tall one, he had a car, big old fashioned powerful car. We drove. I mean, he drove, we drove to Cornwall. Could you say, the voice still gentle, could you say what kind of car it was? Yes, yes of course, it was one of those big Bentleys, a big green open thing, one of those cars we used to dream about when we were boys!

I had been tremendously excited by that car, and half-ashamed at myself for being so juvenile. That shame came back to me, sitting there, and I'm sure I must have blushed. You make it sound like something from one of those English comedy films, Henri said, the officer and his servant? Oh no, I said quickly, not like that at all. The Cockney one? He was the one in charge, no mistake. Tough guy, too.

Footsteps crossed the room behind me, I turned and watched a man walk out of the shadows, heard him laugh: oh yes, you are quite right dear Joseph, a tough guy indeed, but I hope you had time to notice that they are both tough guys? And you are right, also, that this Cockney one as you call him, that he was in charge. We remember him well, eh, René?

I'm confused. This new man, this stocky, humorous shrewd-looking man, he calls my interrogator René. He's enjoying my confusion, I look around and they are all enjoying my confusion when the new man raises me gently by the elbows, out of the chair; he turns me to face him, a hand on each of my shoulders now, he looks me up and down and then he embraces me, a hand coming to the back of my neck.

So, he says, releasing me, taking me by the hand now, almost formal, so, Joseph, I am very pleased to meet you. I am, of course, Henri. You assumed ...

Yes, I did, I say.

Ah Joseph, Joseph, were you not taught not to make assumptions? Tsk, tsk, I would have thought Miguel ... ah don't look so angry, young man, not so angry, eh? What do you think, René, was he going to hit me there, do you think, perhaps for disrespecting his grandfather? I know, of course, he's hungry, I bet you the young man is hungry! All young men become irritable if not fed at regular intervals. Would you like to come eat with us, Joseph? Hungry?

Now everyone's smiling at me, this René has me by the arm, he's saying ah you understand, my boy, we have to be careful, heh? You never know ...

And the driver and the muscle from the back seat are shaking me by the hand now, real smiles on their faces, not polite, real smiles, and inexplicably I feel a great wave of sadness pass through me. There is something about the way these men are with each other, a sense that quite complex things can be said, or not said, in any case be understood between them, that no outsider could hope to grasp. Soaking in this matter-of-fact welcome, I am nevertheless very precisely and exactly aware that I do not belong here. These, and I feel it strongly, are not my people, and this is not my place, and yet … Months, years later I will understand that it was at this precise moment that I left home forever.

While the men conferred, feeling suddenly a deep weariness overtake me, I walked to one of the long windows of this loft and looked out into the rain. Great sheets of it still, coming and going, and in the gaps between each drenching sheet a wide empty harbour, a few lone buildings under or near lights on the far side of the choppy, open expanse. I might, it occurred to me, be anywhere at all, and the thought made me shrink into myself, hunch my shoulders, notice my breathing. That was the first time as a grown man that I felt absolutely alone in the world – and I found that the thought, while it made me indefinably sad, did not make me feel vulnerable. Instead, and I observed this with some surprise, I felt that I might have some strength in myself that would carry me through my life, I had a faint sense, no more than a faint sense, that my life had at last been put into my own hands, and that I had somehow, somewhere in the recent past, accepted the responsibility.

Come! Henri was jovial now, and peremptory. We should eat. He reached an arm towards me, and I fitted myself to the curve of it, feeling weight on my shoulders as he led me to a door behind the dais, down a broad stairs into a dimly-lit kitchen.

René sat, fitting my papers into a large brown envelope, sealing it, pushing it across to me. These will be needed, no? So, if you please, write the address to which it must be sent. I took the pen, wrote Eleni's name and address on the envelope, pushed it back.

A big, broad smile from René, he showed the envelope around. Ah Eleni, Eleni, what a magnificent woman, eh? Tell me lad, her *derrière*, it has recovered, eh? Everyone laughed, and when they saw me blush they laughed even louder. Henri lowered a big steaming bowl of shellfish onto the table; the muscle, with surprising delicacy, was busy laying out bowls, spoons, napkins, a plate of chopped lemon. The driver was sawing off big chunks of bread. I had never eaten *moules* before, but I watched and saw how it was done and when we had finished eating, when the bottles of rough white wine had been drained and I caught a whiff of coffee brewing, I found myself feeling ... content. At ease. Among friends.

Henri was watching me shrewdly. Good, he said, good. You understand. He poured a measure of cognac into each coffee cup then, and we raised our cups when he proposed: to absent friends, to absent comrades. A quick stab of grief shook me. I shrugged it off, but not before Henri had noticed. He raised his cup again: to our new friend Joseph, and to Miguel, to El Leon! Fists crashed on the table: El Leon!

My friends, Henri said, softly, my friends our young Joseph is overwhelmed, and one is not surprised, to find himself in such rough company. Before long we will reduce him to tears! Come, Joseph, you can sleep in the car.

They gathered around me in my bewilderment; I had thought I would be staying here for the night, but amid hugs, handshakes and slaps on the back I found myself ushered outside into the night again, and into a different car, a big black touring car, high roof, long bonnet, the engine already ticking over, a stranger at the wheel. There was room to stretch out in the back, even when first my suitcase and then Henri followed me in. Doors closed, softly, no slamming here, and the car rocked gently in a strong gust before the driver engaged gear and we moved off. I twisted in my seat, meaning I suppose to wave farewell, but the shadowy bulk of the building behind me was already dark and there was no one to be seen.

Where are we going, I asked Henri, after a few minutes had passed. He settled himself a little more, wriggling his broad shoulders. Paris, he said, you should try to sleep. It is a long way. Paris. You should sleep.

23

These past two days have been difficult; I find myself fighting off some kind of lethargy, some reluctance, perhaps an impatience to be done with this sieving and sifting. No word from Vincent, and this, I acknowledge, is contributing to my sense of unease. It's late afternoon, I tell myself, warm outside, sunny, the streets are quiet, what you should do, old man, is take a grip of yourself, take a long walk somewhere. Right, then! I strip, shower, shave, making the business of getting out into the world a series of small definite tasks. Vest, mauve shirt, black sweater, a dark jacket, black corduroys, stout shoes. Hah! Better already! A light Mac over the arm, a cane from the hall and I'm out! What now? A drink, by god, why not!

The outside tables are in shade by now, but it's still, just, warm enough to sit outside without drawing unnecessary attention to myself. The Basque lad is quick off the mark, dusting the table with a flick of his cloth, smiling to himself when I order a cognac. Surprising us both, an afterthought as he's turning away, I ask him to bring me a cigar, a good one if possible.

And now I set myself a test. That young man I was, arriving into Paris for the first time, what if anything would he make of me, were he to amble by just now? In the way of such things, as soon as I formulate the question I realise that I have a different question entirely in mind: how did it happen that I fitted myself with such brutal quickness to the ways and mores of this alien city? For, the fact is, in less than a month after landing here I knew, I knew I would make my life here.

I leave the money under the drained glass and, puffing occasionally at my Cohiba, I follow Rue de l'Estrapade to where it meets Rue St Jacques, turn right, cross Soufflot carefully, and so on down to the river. Almost I go to salute the porter at the Sorbonne steps, but I catch myself in time. Fool, that was a long time ago.

There are so many different kinds of time, I'm thinking, and lately I find myself drifting in and out of the orderly march of days. Well, naturally, immersed as I am in writing this narrative, no, these narratives of mine, I might expect that my attention would be pulled in different directions, no? But, that isn't quite right either. Now, for instance, as I drift along the quay, its river of traffic an ugly noisy repeat of the Seine across the way, it isn't so much that I am following in my own footsteps, it's more that I feel inside myself twice, that I am walking then, in those early days, and now.

A phrase comes: both of me.

That stops me in my tracks, all right. Not the concept, I am too muzzy-headed to zero in on that; no, the phrase. It shocks me, because I realise that I cannot find an equivalent phrase in French. I feel dizzy, and it must show, because a young woman, passing by, comes suddenly to the edge of the pavement, takes me by the elbow, asks if I'm all right. I am, I assure her, I just now remembered something I neglected to take care of earlier. She's not, perhaps, convinced, but goes on her way with a shrug, looking back once over her shoulder. Unusual, that, to notice, to intervene. Almost certainly not a Parisienne. Where was ... ?

Ah yes, isn't that strange, now, that I'm stumped by this? It's been many years since I noticed whether I'm thinking in English or French. I assume that it's a question of milieu, the press of circumstance. Of course, most of the time, when I'm not teaching, I'm speaking in French, and therefore speaking to myself in French. Now, these past days, writing in English, it's as if, this occurs to me as I find a gap in the traffic at last and cross, it's as if English has elbowed my French aside, or at least knocked it off balance.

I learned French fast, when I came here first, because ruthless Henri, that shrewd man, arranged for me to live with people who point-blank, on his instructions, refused to speak English to me. Do not think that I rebelled, do not imagine me furtively sidling up to tourists in bars for the temporary relief of speaking my own language. This is the point, you see, I had no particular attachment to the idea of my own language.

This morning, struggling to recapture that first night, in that loft in a fishing port somewhere, I assume, I never asked, in Brittany – this morning I remembered something I've never thought of since that long-ago night: I knew, immediately and absolutely, that I would make my life here, in this country not my own.

Well then, I must have decided, I shall speak their language. I do not recall thinking this, but I know how my mind works; I say then with confidence that I decided to live not just in another country, but in another language.

I don't like these damn restaurant barges. Parisians never eat in them, unless, wearily, to humour some country cousin, some visiting business acquaintance who thinks them typical. They belong in that tourist miasma that has settled like a thin fog over so much of the city, a kind of enormous hologram that subsumes the solidity of church, court, apartment block, theatre, what have you. Bad enough, and in fact I can live with it, that decent restaurants must compete with those garish establishments that advertise their 'food' by means of coloured pictures – I don't really mind this, it's practical, and I don't really mind tourists or tourism, though I'm happy to join in the endemic Parisian snobbery about such things. No, it's the way in which things that have a perfectly decent and plain role in the order of things are hijacked to other, more venal purposes that grates on my nerves. There, for example, directly across the river, is a glaring example. I am a lifelong agnostic, and I mean lifelong, since I was a schoolboy, but there's something sordid about the way Notre Dame has become what they call a tourist attraction. Off-season I like to walk down and immerse myself in its soaring silences, its caves and pools of quiet; I like to look up at the windows while absentmindedly inhaling incense, relatively unbothered by the rote chatter of the mass, should there be one going on. Nothing religious about this, nothing a person might call spiritual, either; I simply like to immerse myself in the layers of time, to inscribe myself in those millions who have walked, sat, wept or been rapt here. No more than that.

And you just can't do that in a fucking tourist attraction.

I don't care if that fucking barge serves good food, either, it just annoys me.

Whoa, old man, it looks as if you're going to explode here – Vincent appears beside me, beaming. What are you so angry about, eh?

Nothing, I say, nothing, an old man's fancies, eh? Where have you been? He looks at me in surprise? Where have I been? Holds out his shoulder bag, I read 'Institut du Monde Arabe'. That's not what I mean, I say, and I hear something querulous in my voice that makes me flush. Now he's concerned again, mistaking the import of my sudden colour: hey, Joseph, seriously, is everything OK?

I shake off his solicitous hand, set off across the bridge. He stands there for a few seconds, then hurries after me. I halt at the Memorial of the Deportation, as I always do when I come this way. My breathing slows, my irritations ebb away.

A pair of CRS troopers saunter by, the older one tipping me a vague salute, the younger one, head shaved, mirror sunglasses, giving Vincent a calculating, faintly insolent look up and down. Steady, I murmur, steady, and this time it is I who lay a hand on his arm, concerned that what I feel from him may be showing in his face.

It's OK, he says, it's OK. Let the fucker figure it out if he can, the old Jew and the *beur*.

What, I ask, startled, you think I look like a Jew? Vincent steps back a pace, a mocking grin on his face: well you surely don't look like a *beur*. No more do you, I retort, obscurely stung but beginning to find his amusement infectious. Vincent flicks imaginary lint off the lapels of his silk suit: oh dress him how you will, he says, an Arab is an Arab. But, he's laughing now, and after a second or two, so am I. Waiting to cross the quay behind us, the younger trooper is looking back at us now with frank, somewhat menacing, curiosity. Come, I say, leading the way, let's confuse the bastard entirely, let's go say a prayer in the cathedral.

We perch on the low wall near the statue of Charlemagne. We sit side by side, neither of us inclined much to talk until Vincent says: they came to visit my half-brother, at home. Ah, I say, deciding that I don't know this, did they? He gives me a level, speculative look. Yes, he says, they did. Those cops. They apologised, they assured him they would be leaving him alone. Ah, I say, and this was when? A few days ago, I should have told you, perhaps? I should have called to thank you?

An edge of what, there, truculence? Some kind of challenge, some kind of discomfort anyway. I let him be. So useful, silence, when you wish that someone should declare himself.

Vincent has his head down, a familiar posture among the young when they're trying to choose their words – I wonder why that is? For myself, when I am in such a situation I seem to recall that I raise my chin, swallow my upper lip, tilt my head to one side, cup one hand in the other. What? I'm drifting again, I've missed something Vincent said. Patiently, he repeats himself: I do not know that I can trust my half-brother, you see? Of course I am grateful for your ... intervention. I do not wish you to feel discomfort, I mean the discomfort of fearing I shall be obliged to you, but there is a chance that Hamid will not learn from this.

Genevieve, I realise, has this all wrong. Vincent is not ashamed, and now that I think of it, that was an absurd reason to offer for his not coming to see me.

Tone, I learned that early; tone is all important, tone is the giveaway. Vincent is calm, reflective and inward – he is sharing his thoughts with me, not pushing some responsibility my way, not apologising for involving me in this business.

You might say he is thinking out loud, but I see, rather I hear, that he is curious to know what I think. There is a chance Hamid will not take this way out he has been offered, he says. Therefore there is a chance that Hamid will be killed by these Jihadists, you see? Either he says nothing, and they find out he was talking to the cops, they kill him, or he does something really stupid like he goes to them and tells them everything, and then they kill him. Or, say, at some point, perhaps to shield someone else on whom suspicion has fallen, the cops give him up to these people – you see why I say this also is a possibility? Because they came to see him in his home, you see? Word gets around. Maybe the bastard cops meant for word to get around, eh? Maybe they did not like being warned off by ... your friend? And, you know, maybe also I am being, dramatic? Why do I think this, that they will kill him, eh? All this in the dispassionate voice of someone calmly weighing up options, but there is more to it than this. Vincent is rehearsing his options because he is deciding what to do. Rightly or wrongly, he is assuming responsibility for his half-brother, and he is not consulting me here, I understand this, he is rehearsing his options in front of me in order to demonstrate to me a seriousness he believes is essential to him, a seriousness perhaps that he fears I may have missed. Perhaps also, he would like to consider what I think. Nothing is quite clear yet, so I decide to push things, see where we end up.

You could frame him for something relatively minor, I suggest. Vincent looks at me, startled. He'd maybe cool down a bit behind bars, I explain, and his being away might also mean these headcases would forget about him. Or you could have some people take him for a walk in the country, explain the facts of life to him. Or, you could have him emigrate. Or, if what's worrying you is that he will drag the whole family into this, you could shoot him. Or, if you don't feel up to doing it yourself, simply have him shot.

I am trying to provoke him, not really sure why, just following my instinct, but Vincent's not falling for this.

A big lazy smile is what I get for my troubles. Oh no, old man, he says, no, no, no, you're not getting away with that. And as suddenly, serious again, he looks me in the eye and asks: what should I do?

I hadn't expected that, a direct request for advice. I don't like giving advice, as a rule. You advise someone, say, to leave her abusive husband, and next thing you know they're both ganging up on you. It's happened to me. You advise someone ... well, we all know what this is like. I don't mind intervening in situations, I should say, but ideally on my own terms and with no one but me knowing exactly and to what extent and effect I am intervening.

I am ... disconcerted. I don't like that, I'm not used to that, and of course this makes me irritated with Vincent. I had forgotten how quick he is, how perceptive. His face closes down, he stands up, he says he is sorry, he should not involve me in this any further ... and I feel shame again, today has turned into a day of small shamings, I rise and take both his arms in my grip: my friend, I say, and he sees at once that I mean this, just this; my friend. We need to consider very carefully what is best here, yes? He holds my look, I see need there, doubt, too, and then reassurance. That beaming smile again. We set off walking, across the open square, on again by the *Préfecture de la Police*, on the river side. You know what happened here, he asks, and I tell him that I do. My father was a *Harki*, he says, studying my face, satisfied with my nod in response, and then he asks: why did you not ask me back there what a *beur* is? And answers himself when I say nothing: because you know, of course you know, I should not be surprised. You do not mind that I am not surprised? No, I say, I don't mind.

We walk in silence on into the twilight, we walk as far as Pei's glass pyramid, a long walk for me but I am not tired, although I'm resolved to take a taxi home.

What seems likeliest to me, I finally say, if you are right and your half-brother is indeed a true believer, what seems likeliest to me, if he's not a fool, is that he will consider himself free of the police now, he will have no wish to put himself in danger with his colleagues, so he will stay silent. Agreed? Which leaves him free to continue in this business. Yes. So, he continues to be a dangerous man.

Vincent is looking at me intently now, willing me to continue this train of thought.

So, if he is dangerous, you wish to know if I intend to do something about it, yes? If perhaps I intend to go to ... whoever I spoke to, to say, this has not worked, I hand this man over to you?

I have hit home, I see, but then I know Vincent is quick.

No, I say, I will not do that. I do not tell Vincent that my friend, my acquaintance, will certainly have made his own arrangements to have this Hamid kept under surveillance; I take this for granted, but I feel sure that this will not have occurred to Vincent.

And still he waits, what is he waiting for? Ah, now I get it. Strange that it should have taken me so long. Vincent is, I am sure of it, genuinely concerned for his half-brother, but he is also concerned for himself. More precisely, he is weighing up the consequences for himself of being drawn down into some confusion by his brother's actions, his brother's politics. The thought had occurred to me, that he feared for his own safety, or at least his own liberty, should his brother end up being arrested in connection with Jihadism, but that would not be a problem for a law student at the Sorbonne, certainly not a problem for someone as cool and level-headed as Vincent.

No. Vincent, and he sees me seeing this, he sees the realisation take form in my regard, Vincent has political ambitions; what he fears most is the taint of scandal, the possibility that some transgression of his half-brother's can be, could be, will be used to derail his own ambitions.

Ah Genevieve, Genevieve, I see that I have misjudged you. I find myself wondering if Vincent realises that she means to marry him, is already in training to be that very French phenomenon, the managing wife of a rising political star.

And still he says nothing.

PS, I say, a question, meaning *Parti Socialiste*. His hand gesture is eloquent, it says: of course, what else, bad as they are, one makes the best of a poor choice. He says: ah Joseph, Joseph, always straight to the point.

Tell me, I say then, meaning to provoke, but not unkindly, tell me what you propose to do. Good, he says, this is what I think: he will grow out of this and nothing will be affected – or he will get deeper into this and become involved in some atrocity perhaps, or at least be identified with those who condone, if they do not perpetrate, atrocities. Yes? I have tried to protect him, and I am very grateful to you for whatever it is that you have done. I, we, have bought him some time for reflection, that is fair to say, yes? Good. Well, if he does not seize this opportunity, too bad, eh? In any case, it is not so easy to escape the attentions of the police when you have drawn it upon yourself, I imagine he will be under some kind of surveillance. For myself, it is necessary that soon now I take a public position that separates me once and for all from such primitive politics.

There is something very wearying about young politicians, the inwardness and self-regard of their ambitions, the utterly unconscious way in which they slide into dead language.

Something of the faint disgust that I feel must be showing in my face because I see, to my horror, that I have hurt my young friend. He has sufficient tact to turn his face away, whether to spare himself or me I do not know, but the hurt is genuine.

I feel slightly faint, somehow I have forgotten to eat tonight, and then I feel panicky because of forgetting and because this conversation is slipping beyond my control, my understanding.

I look around for somewhere to sit down, and then Vincent has his arm around me, he is asking when I last ate, tutting when I shrug. Listen, he says, that time we met, when I was stealing that car? Yes, I say, confused. Well, he says, you see that was an experiment, you see? He is leading me towards the river again, shepherding me across the road, an arm around my shoulder. There's a nice restaurant I know, he is saying, just across the bridge. An experiment, he resumes. Some young guys I work with, from beyond the *Périphérique*, yes? They showed me how it's done. I wanted to see if I could do it, that's all.

No, I say, instinct kicking in suddenly, that's not all. No, he agrees, you're feeling better aren't you? No, that's not all. I wanted to see what would happen to a young Algerian driving a clean new car, I wanted to see what would happen if I were stopped ... and they saw they had stopped a young bourgeois, a law student.

Your father was a *Harki*, I say. So quick, Joseph, so quick you are! Yes, a loyal policeman, a loyal Algerian French policeman. You know what happened, yes, when France finally let Algeria go? How many *Harki*s who stayed were butchered? How many who came home to France found themselves cast out, cast aside, dirty Arabs?

And now you are thinking, perhaps, here is a conflicted son, seeking to rise in the country that betrayed his father? No, I say, pulling back from the kerb, he'd been going to walk us out under the traffic, no, I say, that's not what I think.

We're across, he is slightly ahead of me now, intent on this restaurant he has in mind. Tell me, Joseph, is this your country? The question stuns me. I can't answer, not immediately. We walk on in silence until we come to the restaurant, enter, are shown to our table. Vincent calls for the wine list, we order food, it comes reasonably quickly, a bad sign; the waiter retreats to the back of the small, dimly-lit room.

Now come on, Joseph, I see the books in your library, I am not, we are agreed, a fool, eh? What is your answer? Eventually, the words feeling heavy in my mouth, I say: this is my place, Paris. I have no country.

And Ireland, he asks, very quietly?

Ireland, I say, Ireland is where I am from.

We address ourselves to the food after that, the fish unremarkable as I'd expected; at least the Chablis is passable.

Over coffee, surprisingly good, Vincent picks up the thread. One does not wish to be ... grandiose, you see, but the thing is, I do have a people, even perhaps a country. Can you imagine my father's life here, after all that had happened? He did well, mind you, as these things go. Some stubborn streak in him, I expect. Opened a café, saved, was shrewd, opened another, another. We are, you might say, comfortably off, that is the correct English phrase, is it not? I am startled, had not noticed he was speaking English. But always, you see (back to French now), always, to them, an Arab. Never mind that not all Algerians are Arabs.

And as with the father, so with the son, naturally. When I was, what, fifteen? Yes, fifteen. Somebody left a book in our house, Aimé Césaire, you have heard of him? Ah, forgive me, of course you have. And after Césaire, well Fanon, of course, the usual. You understand? So, here is the bright son of a conflicted father, a son of the Republic, son of a betrayed father, but this is the only place I know, you see? You see what I am getting at here, dear Joseph? Yes. A good school, you see, liberal, oh so liberal, and ... something in me turns stubborn, you see, something that sees the lie underneath it all. To myself, I am French, evidently, obviously. But to them, to them I am always first Algerian, then, provisionally so to speak, I am French. So, like this: I have a people because I choose it, a people inside a people.

You are perhaps a little disenchanted with me, Joseph? Perhaps you are right; your generation, after all, you have seen too much of what you call politics. Well, we know each other a little by now, yes, you will not mind that I speak freely?

Then, leaning across the table, holding me with his eyes: you do not mind that I disappoint you, that I am not how you have constructed me?

Genevieve came to see me, I say. I know, he says, you under-estimate her, I think. He lets this hang in the air and then, thoughtfully: no, perhaps it is I who under-estimate her. And, straightening in his seat, a shadow passing over his mobile face: perhaps I under-estimate you, also, dear Joseph.

Now, listening to his own words, following some train of thought I can only guess at, he seems sad, a little lost.

I ask myself why it is that I, too, am sad, but I am playing with my own mind, playing with time, because I know, we both know, we have somehow passed through that moment where people become real to each other. If it pleased Vincent to amuse himself by befriending this mysterious old man, if it pleased me to befriend this lively, surprising young man, it is also true that we have been making fictions for ourselves, keeping each other as deliberate, no, cultivated mysteries in each other's lives.

There's a taste of copper in my mouth, and it doesn't come from the food or from the wine. It's a familiar taste, as if my body chemistry has its own way of signalling its disgust with my shallow dishonesty.

I have no real gift for getting on with people once intimacy passes a certain point. My chosen solitariness is precious to me; perhaps imperceptibly, over the years, I have come to guard it more and more, as if everything threatens it, as if it can somehow be worn away, eroded, by letting people get too close to me.

No, not quite that, by letting myself take too much of an interest in other people's unknowable lives. I do not propose myself here as some kind of monster, it isn't at all that I am a misanthrope, perhaps quite the opposite is true, perhaps the difficulty is that I empathise too much, and I have so little energy left now for that, I cannot afford that drain on my time, my attention, my affections. A sudden dart of a thought: was I always like this?

But, I have allowed Vincent to assume my friendship, perhaps unknown to myself I have been signalling to him warmth and interest I would have done better to conceal. And Genevieve, too, she came to see me because she sees my fondness for Vincent.

I do not want a son, nor a surrogate for the son I never had. I have not perhaps, made this as plain as it would have been decent to do.

And so ... this taste in my mouth, this ugly debilitating sense that I have been dishonest, somehow, misleading at best.

I startle back, suddenly aware that I have been silent for some time. Vincent is sitting on his hands, leaning slightly towards me. What? I say.

He laughs, low and somehow indulgent. Ah Joseph, he says, the things that must go through your mind! I watch you having some kind of quarrel with yourself, and I am very glad that I am a simple poor law student. And one-off car thief of course, he adds, delighted when this provokes an indignant snort out of me, Hah! he says, you see, at least I can make you laugh.

He waves off my offer to share a taxi. No, no, I have some things to do. Then: there is something you have been meaning to ask me, is there not? Yes, I say, what is your name? He looks about him, a comic conspirator, leans in to whisper in my ear: Vincent. And when I recoil, thinking he's mocking me, I see from the expression on his face that this is indeed his real name. He makes a *moue*, hands together, palms upward: it's true, alas, my father really did try to integrate, you see? That, I'm afraid, was his tragedy. And now I am cursed with a perpetual urge, when things in my life get complicated, to cut off my ear.

He looks so doleful I burst out laughing, and laughing we flag down a cab; he instals me in it with all the *punctilio* of a dutiful son sending a tipsy father home. The driver is monumentally bored, a young Somalian festooned with gold chains. We do not speak on the journey, and I have scarcely closed the door having got out when he is accelerating away down the echoing street, a slight screech of dismissal as he rounds the corner a fraction too fast.

Lying between sheets but scarcely feeling the touch of them on my body, I fear that I will not sleep. Today has been too confusing, I do not know if I'll have the will to begin again in the morning to take up the thread of this self-imposed task.

24

The first time I woke we were travelling at speed on a sunken road, the high hedges arching over us, so that the brilliant headlights lit a white dusty surface speeding towards us in a dark tunnel. I'd fall asleep again, wake now and then to a patched wall, a roof at a crazy angle, a line of telegraph poles machine-gunning past, bright-lit fragments spinning in and out of vision.

I think that a deep exhaustion was trying to drag me down, was reaching for me, but I stayed near the surface of whatever was going on, in a deep comfortable fug of leather and cigarette smoke and human bodies, in a capsule hurtling through the night.

We came out of the journey and out of the dark as Paris began to solidify around me. I had been, as I'm sure I've said, a bookish child, and all omnivorous readers know the sensation – of arriving into a city that has already occupied a space in your mind. That morning, for the first time, I felt the dislocation that comes when the concrete actuality of the city itself displaces the wispiness, the fragments and tatters of the imagined place.

I had not expected Paris to be grey and drab, I had not expected the peeling posters, the faint scent of rotting fruit and vegetables threaded through the rich exhaust fumes of trucks and buses, I had not expected the busyness of the people, dawn scarcely broken, as they bustled in all directions with fixed intent.

I had not expected such density of high solid buildings, crowding in around me.

I went immediately to sleep again, and when Henri nudged me awake, a switch had tripped inside me, the sense of vertigo that had rattled me replaced by a calm, boundless, watchful curiosity. I say this because I felt, stepping out of the car, unsteady on my feet, as I was, a sense of well-being starting to flush through me, a vast willingness to engage with the world.

We stopped outside a great cinema, its walls all of mosaic, a place at once mundane and impossibly exotic – like the people flooding past, people it seemed to me from the four corners of the earth. In this cinema, the Louxor, years later, I would sit silent, overwhelmed by grief and anger in a huge audience gripped by the same emotions when at last it was considered safe to screen Pontecorvo's *The Battle of Algiers*. Then, that morning, I stood on the pavement and could not have felt more alien had I been standing, jostled and bustled, in the great souk of Algiers.

Indeed, leaning into the car to accept a lit cigarette from Henri, I was impressed, and a little afraid perhaps, to see so many Africans and Arabs in the crowds around me. Not afraid of these people, afraid that much and all as I was prepared to try to understand, to grasp, the French, I would never succeed in reaching beneath the surface of all that it meant to be African, Arab, or for that matter Russian, Polish or Jewish Parisians.

We stopped there until the driver, Pascal, came striding towards us, swivelling through the throngs, a great paper bag of bread and pastries held aloft for safety. Overhead on the massive metal bridge the Metro screeched, and all around us the traffic roared until in that confined place I began to feel the noise as a great intolerable weight. I ducked into the car with relief, stomach twisting in anticipation at the aroma of fresh baking, and Pascal, gunning the great smooth motor, slid us out into the traffic and threaded us through a succession of side streets until we passed slowly through a square that I saw was called Place Léon, and turned onto the street that would be my home for years to come. The Rue Cavé.

Pascal, without a word, climbed out of the car, took my suitcase from the boot and disappeared through a dark doorway. I went to follow but Henri stopped me, his hand on my thigh. This will be strange for you, he said. What you have done, I see in you that you have not yet absorbed it. This is natural, this we all understand, we have all ... well, no need to speak of this, I think. You do not know how long you propose to stay here, to stay in France, is this not so? Yes. But Miguel, he says to me that you have been in a dream for some time now, that he thinks you do not know what to do with your life, this is so? You say nothing, OK. Well, here, in this house, you will be among friends, you will find it strange of course, but that is perhaps a good thing for a young man. A number of comrades live here, some will move on, others will come, it is that kind of house. You have a room, of course; everyone shares what is to be done, you will fit yourself to this. But, you will need to work, yes? To earn a living. I will come in with you, I will introduce you to the comrades and they will help you to settle. In one week I return, and then we will discuss what it is you wish to do. Now, come.

A store of some kind on the ground floor, disused, shuttered and padlocked. A steep, narrow staircase inside a separate entrance to the side, then up to a short hall opening into a light-flooded kitchen, the side to my right all glass from the tabletop up, small squares, iron-framed windows. A high, high ceiling, tall presses and cupboards, an overwhelming smell of coffee.

And, the people who would, over the next ten years, become what family I was to have here. How gauche I was. I took in the two women regarding me gravely, unmoving, and scanned past them looking for a man in this place. I never knew with Henri, what he really saw, how much he understood of what the world pressed in on him, but he burst out laughing now, slapped me on the back, said to the women: you see how you frighten my poor shy Irishman!

Introductions, then. Marie Louise, a cigarette vertical between the fingers of her left hand; her right hand, extended to me as she stood, bony and cool. A thin woman, dark short hair, a sense of contained and focused energy, pale green eyes unwavering, unreadable.

And, reaching a hand to me but not rising, her face half averted but her eyes direct, expressionless, Thérèse.

A charge in the air, in the room, the light more intense, a whiff of sweat from Henri beside me, my breathing sharper, the brown-black tang of the coffee almost overwhelming. All tiredness vanished, and then that curious change in focus, an aura around her while everything else became fuzzy around us. The pin-sharp glint in her black eyes. She looked away, still expressionless, looked down.

Marie Louise jabbed me, a bony forefinger, once, twice. In English she said, let me show you to your room. That enigmatic smile I would come to know so well.

A small attic room, the ceiling sloping down to a window whose bottom edge was an inch or two from the board floor. A faded rug by the wooden bed that took up most of the space. A small table to one side, under the wall light, dictionaries, newspapers and magazines heaped to one side. A narrow, tall cupboard. My new world. Pascal came huffing in behind us, dumped my suitcase on the floor, left without a word, followed by Marie Louise.

I took my jacket off, reflexively sniffing my armpits. Rank. Thérèse. Long dark hair, pulled back in a soft ponytail. Lean, a green sweater. My neck-hairs bristling. Some certainty making me stand there, stand there ... I went to the window, knelt to look out and down. The street far below, greyblack rooftops and high chimneys all around me at this level, a pale blue sky. Down the bare stairs again.

We drank coffee, standing around, all except Thérèse who stayed sitting, gazing out the window across the narrow air shaft, the cup in both hands, a slight steam rising to her sharp nose. Everyone talking quietly, me standing there looking down at the floor, not quite uncomfortable, not quite at ease.

Leaving, Henri beckoned me to follow him down to the street. Listen, he said, these are serious people, you understand? There will be work to do, but they are friendly. You will make your own way with them. But, I ask you to pay attention to one in particular, OK?

You mean, Marie Louise is in charge, I said. An enigmatic look. Well, OK, if you wish to put it like this, she is as you say in charge.

Pascal gunning the engine, impatient to be off, but a relaxed wave from him as Henri settled in beside him. A smile.

I went back in and there was only Marie Louise in the kitchen. Sit down, she said. I sat down. She pushed a note pad towards me, a couple of pencils. I was puzzled by the graph paper, I associated it with geometry, arithmetic, but said nothing. Very well, she said, relaxing, slouching back in her chair. Henri says you do not know how long you will stay. I knew she did not necessarily mean in this house. Suddenly, I wanted to be told I could stay here as long as I liked. Well, she said, you need to learn the language, yes? Yes, I said. Good, now what we will do here, we will speak to you in French only. Do not worry, we will be sensible. Small things, then bigger things, you understand?

Does everyone here speak English, I asked. Yes, she said, but Thérèse perhaps a little less than me. I lived in London, she offered. For two years. During the war. During? Yes, she said, and perhaps she was pleased that I saw her point because she got up then and brought us both more coffee, lit up a cigarette, offered me one. I came back here, you understand? Yes, I said, I see.

Start with the magazines, she said, try to make sense of them. Only try to decipher the things you think might be interesting. To be interested, that is the key. Ask us about things you do not understand. Someone will always have time to explain, you know, but better you puzzle things out for yourself. Now I, too, must go to work.

She handed me a set of keys, explained which one fitted which lock.

I slept then, I slept all day, exhausted without having known I was, and when I woke my new life had begun.

25

I woke this morning feeling good, spry. I woke in a curious moment of double-mindedness, flinching inside myself at the idea that all yesterday's confusions would be waiting for me, dreading that I would be muzzy-headed, out of sorts – and at almost the same instant, perhaps a microsecond later, registering clarity, sureness, anticipation of the day.

A bath instead of my usual shower, because I wanted to ponder this: how one sometimes catches oneself being two kinds of attention at once.

No doubt there are whole libraries devoted to the phenomenon, and somebody less intellectually lazy, somebody more coherent, would be able to puzzle it out, but I have always preferred to puzzle things over rather than puzzle things out.

Clear air this morning, a sense somehow of steady order in things. As if the tops of the buildings have eased back and away from each other, to let in air and light.

As I pull the street door shut behind me, Mme Frenaud, her batons peeping from a worn leather shopping bag, greets me courteously, a hint of incipient warmth in the inclination of her head. Well now! Passing the college, a young woman emerging from the archway stands back a moment to let me pass, light in her eyes, another smile, a kind of benediction. Goodness! I take a table outside Bar Delmas on the Place de Contrescarpe, surrounded by pensive older men singly at tables, by gaggles of youngsters more subdued, thank god, than usual, but as I fumble at my *pain au chocolat*, take a good hefty belt of my Americano, I realise that I wouldn't at all mind if the place was booming and buzzing.

All this good humour! I am, I suppose, buoyed up by having

so vividly in my mind the sense of ease I felt, all those years ago, coming to terms with the city.

And then, my small bit of shopping done – a few lamb gigots, fruit, unseasonal lettuce (god knows where from), a random assortment of vegetables – I headed home to spend the day writing as, batteries charged by a fresh pot of coffee, I settled to make my notes.

My retrievals. All my life I have had this sense that moment by moment I have been storing up my life, having it always in mind that someday I would embark on a process of retrieval. The inner voice admonishing me, even in the midst of confusion (and there has been so much confusion): remember this, pay attention now, you will need to remember this.

I went out again this evening for no particular reason, simply to enjoy the sensation of walking around; an uneventful walk, to be sure, but opening the front door again, listening for a moment to the silence of the house piled over me, I remembered, as if it explained something, that I have always been a walker.

Something came back to me of those walks around Cork in my adolescence, that sense of agreeable melancholy that gave those years their particular savour. And something else pushed through more forcibly, a kind of multi-layered impression of the long walks I embarked on when I began to settle in, to settle to, this city. I walked everywhere in those early days, making the map real, adding street to square to avenue, outwards in a rough spiral from what had become, so very quickly accepted, my new home. They had put me in charge of shopping, Marie Louise reasoning that working out my vocabulary from a shopping list would help me become proficient. They'd specify shops where this or that was to be found, colluding to send me further and further from the house so that I would have to learn the quartier, learn how to ask for and understand directions. And in the evenings, depending on who was home for the night, we would talk and talk and talk.

I discovered that I, who had grown up almost entirely among men, had a natural sympathy with these women. I did not understand, of course, at the time, how artfully they built that sense of ease in me, how they took my shyness, my otherness, and remoulded it, remade me.

There was a constant undercurrent of the erotic in that house: nobody much cared one way or the other, for instance, if they were seen walking naked or part-clothed from bathroom to bedroom, and as my proficiency in the language grew – perhaps faster than they sometimes realised – I found myself privy to their amours, their sudden adventures, their disillusions, their yearning. Their final judgements, too, as some unfortunate man friend found himself cast into exterior darkness.

Standing here in the hall, in the dark, I shake my head vigorously; too vigorously perhaps, it brings on momentary dizziness. I switch on the light and climb the stairs, let myself in. Pause to collect myself.

All day I have been sitting at my desk, head up in reverie, snared by some insight, some long-buried memory lifted up into the light, doubled with, strengthened somehow by, this younger self in the first flush of claiming his life as his own.

Now, in this comfortable twilight, I feel the day's strength begin to ebb away.

I should be thinking about Vincent, of course; I am conscious that I have been keeping this at bay, but the thought makes me suddenly irritable. Yesterday was terribly confusing in some way; it is as if, without meaning to, I have incurred some obligation here – the thought brings on a mild nausea, something disagreeably close to panic.

I go through and splash water on my face, retrieve what I'll need for cooking from shelves and cupboards, am trimming fat from the lamb gigots when I hear myself tell myself: 'for god's sake, man, get a grip'.

Like that. As if a voice had spoken. When this began to happen to me, oh years ago now, it worried me. I did not like to consider the implications of what is called hearing voices. I worried about it, frankly, but never spoke of it to anyone. Then one day, so simply, I just answered back – and never worried about it again.

So, I got a grip. Cooked, ate, lit the standard lamp by the window and settled with a book. Montague's *Tides*, a gentle book with a spine of something solid and sure behind its impressions and evocations. A touch of vanity there, too, but little harm in that.

The day settled until I found myself composed enough to jot down these present notes, and now I find myself ready for bed, calm enough at the prospect of tomorrow and its unburyings, and perhaps a little out of sorts with Vincent. He should have rung today, no?

26

The Rue Cavé. I came back from shopping one mid-morning, pleased with myself that I had managed to make a weak joke with the greengrocer's young wife, and found Thérèse in the kitchen, papers spread out on the table before her, a lit cigarette in the ashtray, a mug of our bitter black coffee in one hand, a pen in the other. She looked up, startled, but I knew I could not have surprised her, climbing the stairs heavily laden; even so, I was prepared to go along with the act but she straightened, looked me directly in the eye and shrugged humorously: what can I say, dear Joseph? I was waiting for you.

I had seen very little of Thérèse in the weeks since I landed into this house. Marie Louise had me in charge, but Thérèse, serious, distant and severe, had been coming and going all that time, travelling the length and breadth of the country as far as I could make out. But for all that I hardly saw her, for all that we'd barely, in any meaningful sense, spoken to each other, I had been acutely conscious of her existence since the first moment I'd stood in this kitchen.

I knew when she was in. I knew when she was out. I would ask after her on days when she wasn't present, and once or twice I caught a look in Marie Louise's eyes that made me curse myself for my awkwardness, my obviousness.

Now, in the silence that stood between us, I had a sudden piercing memory of what I'd felt walking upstairs that first day to view my room. That cold hand of fate on my neck, the certainty that she and I would have something between us that would shake, shape and somehow confirm me.

With her eyes she led my eyes down to her full, unsupported breasts beneath the black ribbed polo neck sweater she wore. I saw her register that I understood she was naked beneath it, as I guessed she was naked under the knee-length corduroy skirt. When my breath shallowed in a catch of desire she smiled; I thought it a shy smile, but I did not know her yet.

With a confidence I did not feel, but understood I must show, I took her hand in mine. She dipped away to crush out the cigarette, drained the coffee and followed me barefooted up the narrow stairs.

I learned what it is to be absolutely alive all the way into the depths of and out to the very electron shield edges of my own body.

I learned what it is to be luminously competent in my own body.

I learned what it is to give and take pleasure in the body, and not to be afraid when I could no longer tell which was my body, which was hers.

For the first time in my life, I learned in the blood what it is not to be alone.

I had not realised how absolutely alone in the world I had been until then.

I should be accurate here: this last is the only realisation I came to in the living moment – the rest I intuited, felt but did not understand. Late that afternoon, when the first delirium had passed, the rage and the fury and then the smooth supple passages of gesture and caress, the gradual carnal quietening, I was overcome by that exquisite understanding, and I wept without caring to know why.

Nor did it seem to me that she was disquieted by this, only she held me until I grew calm and then gradually, carefully, she set me on fire again.

Tell me, she asked, as we lay side by side, our heads on our folded arms, our faces towards each other, tell me she asked, why did you shoot that policeman?

She put the flat of her hand between my shoulder blades, pressing me down as I went to rise. Ssh, ssh, she said, gently, gently. Why did you do it?

It came to me then that I had not stopped from asking this question since that night in the rain on the Watercourse Road when, for a fraction of a second, I had thought of not doing it, the trigger already pressured, his moon face already turning towards me. It was a kind of wonder to realise, lying there as her sweat cooled on me, as mine on her, that I had been thinking about this all the time since, and entirely unaware that I had been thinking of it at all.

I heard myself say, very simply: he asked for it.

A phrase from my childhood, a catch-all explanation men would reach for when a dirty hurler got a dig in the mouth from someone he'd pushed too far with his niggling, when a schoolboy had taunted another beyond endurance. He asked for it.

I felt a hot flush of shame, to have offered her such a banal explanation. I started spluttering, but she put a finger on my lips and said, yes, it's true, there are such men. But, you didn't kill him? No. Perhaps, after all, this is for the best.

It would be years before I understood that behind the obvious meaning of those words lurked a wise and somehow instructed judgement of my character.

She slid out from under the sheet, she gathered her things, and I had the sense to make nothing of this, one way or the other.

Perhaps I was in shock.

I must go to Bordeaux tonight, she said, Pascal is collecting me.

Come on, I'm hungry, aren't you hungry? They'll be home soon, we should make the dinner.

It was early evening, I had registered but not remarked the light fading, the sounds in the street below of people returning from work.

We were four to dinner, Marie Louise and Claire, an older comrade whom I liked a lot, Thérèse and myself. After dinner, when Thérèse went to pack, I ventured to make conversation with Marie Louise and Claire, to act as if it had been a normal day, but they laughed in my face, they rattled back and forth to each other, pausing only to look at me, and I felt a kind of fury at first, that I could not understand their words but they would not stop laughing, nor make any allowance for my demands that they explain themselves. Eventually, I had to concede that I understood perfectly well what they were at. I was doing my best not to look smug, I who had been a virgin until that afternoon, but I lost my composure entirely when Thérèse walked back into the kitchen and I saw in her body what they must have registered instantly, her languid catlike grace of movement, the light and the ease of gratified desire.

She shrugged into her duffle coat, rattled off what sounded like instructions to Marie Louise, picked up her bag, kissed me roughly on the cheek and was halfway down the stairs to the street when the car horn sounded outside. I heard the door bang, hung my head in confusion and when I looked up the women had gone.

Thérèse was away for a week, and I knew better than to ask where she'd been when she blew into the kitchen on a rainy night. You might expect that I had passed the week aching for her return? Not at all. I wouldn't have minded had she stayed away for longer. My body was singing to me for days after she left, but my mind was asking hard questions of me, and I was hard put to answer.

There was, too, a certain tension in the house. Henri had

promised to call back in a week when he'd landed me in here, but he didn't. Indeed, months had gone by and there had been no sign of him. When I ventured tentatively to inquire, I was brusquely shut down by Marie Louise, given clearly to understand that none of them wished to discuss his absence.

The day after Thérèse had left for Bordeaux, Henri appeared in the house just after dawn. He was burned by the sun, deeply burned, and under what should have been a healthy tan I saw a greyness that went with the deep lines scored on his cheeks, the deep furrows on either side of his mouth. I felt terrible for him when he tried to smile, meaning to reassure me, and he saw me recoil and thanked me with his eyes for my frankness.

I knew without asking myself how I knew that his absence, and now his appearance, had to do with this terrible business of Algeria. I had understood by then that Henri, that all of them, were of, or somehow affiliated with, the Communist Party.

The FLN had begun setting off bombs in Paris, and there was much talk in the shops and in the streets of what was to be done. I assumed that the Party, being objectively anti-imperialist, was in favour of Algerian independence, but by keeping up my studies and by keeping my mouth shut, I had picked up enough from the women of the house and from the steady stream of visitors to realise that the Party was far from being a monolith, that it contained various factions with different points of view, and that what I called to myself in my new smug French the *Faction Henri* had a particularly nuanced view.

Well, said Henri, my Irishman, I fear I have let you down. Did I not promise to find work for you, eh? Unconsciously I made the hand signal for 'it's nothing, don't mention it, don't worry yourself', and he laughed when he saw that; in appreciation, I think, but also because he needed to laugh. More, he needed to be reassured that I was not yet one more problem for him to solve.

Young Joseph, do you understand what is happening here, now? What it will mean when Le Grand Charles finally realises that he must master the army? Ah, I am sorry, you can have no idea what I mean, eh? Let us leave this, and perhaps when times are more tranquil we can think about your political education. If you wish, if you wish ...

I had the uncomfortable sense that he was wondering what to do with me, perhaps even I feared that he might be thinking of sending me home, but I was not prepared for him when he leaned across the table took one of my hands in both of his and said: listen, my boy, it is not for me to interfere but with Thérèse, with Thérèse you must take care. I drew back, stiffened, and he patted my hand, soothing me as Mick used to do when I'd come in from the street or home from school angry about something. No, no, I do not disrespect you, I do not disrespect my friend and comrade either, no, no, but you are, you must understand this, you are of different worlds.

Like this, eh? You are still in the dream, you are perhaps ready to exchange one dream for another, the dream of a young man discovering his body, the body of another, all that this means, eh? But Thérèse, you must understand that for Thérèse all this happened long ago.

Will you understand me if I say that she is a fully awake person? No? No. But you will, Joseph, you will.

Ah, I am becoming an old fool. Pulling away from me, rising to his feet, buttoning up his jacket. Miguel had a saying ... ah yes, do not be rushing your fences, do not be rushing your fences. Perhaps I am rushing you at your fences, eh? You think so?

I did not know what to think, and still less could I think of how to answer him.

My friend, have you written to your grandfather? No, I see you have not. Well, that is OK, he would understand. But perhaps you should tell him you are convinced to make your life here, for a while at least? Perhaps you will tell him you are well, that I am well also? That would be good, I think. And, yes, yes you can tell him that you have found a job! I almost forgot!

My dear Marie Louise! Perfect, such timing!

She had come silently up the stairs and was unwinding her scarf, looking at us thoughtfully. Marie Louise, tell our young friend the news.

Ah Henri, you are well I hope. I see you have been ... she stumbled in her words, blushed, then looked stricken. Affable Henri soothing her, ah my dear, you must know by now how quick our Joseph is, I think you will find he understands more than you might think, eh boy? I am quite sure that Comrade Joseph has a very good idea of where Henri has been, perhaps even a shrewd guess or two at what Henri has been up to, eh boy? Modestly, making a deprecating gesture, I allowed that perhaps ... and then stopped in my tracks, realising that he had been speaking to me in French. Delighted, he hugged Marie Louise to him: you see my dear! And I wager, I do, that you had no idea he was picking up the language so well? No, she said, part-amused, part-accusing, I had no idea. For a moment I saw behind the cool amiable mask she invariably presented to me, saw, I mean, that it had been a mask. I saw the face of power, before she laughed and turned away. Not, though, before I had noticed myself noticing and filed that thought, too, away for future consideration.

Yes, yes, the job, she said. I have given this matter some thought, you understand? Henri nodding encouragement. On Monday next, dear Joseph, you start a new life as ... a library porter.

Did she expect me to be happy with this news? I was not terribly impressed.

Oh Marie Louise, look at him, do you think our young Irish friend is some kind of snob, heh? And now he is embarrassed. Explain, please.

Silly boy, do you think this is to be a real job? You will be employed by the University of the Sorbonne, to work in the library. The comrades in the library will take great care of you, never fear. From time to time, for the sake of appearances, you will be expected to shift some books, push a trolley, be seen to be busy – but never so much as to distract you from your reading, your studies. You see, do you see what a perfect opportunity ... Henri, do you think after all he is a bit simple, that he does not understand ...

I do, I said, jumping to my feet, suddenly seeing the vista opening before me. I do, I see it, it's perfect, thank you, thank you so much!

I think I began to laugh at myself just before they, in their turn, began to laugh at me.

Ah yes, said Henri drily, I seem to remember that I, too, was once enthusiastic. Good night, friends, I will call by soon again. Marie Louise, that other matter? Yes, yes, she waved him away down the stairs, it is taken care of.

I put the kettle on to make her a tisane, ginger with lemon, her preferred nightcap. Was he warning you about our Thérèse? Her directness startled me. Yes, I said, not daring to say more. Well, she said, looking directly at me, I suggest you think carefully about whatever he said, and then make your own decisions. You hear? Your own decisions. Do you know what a decision is, young Joseph? No, you don't. A decision is a fork in the road you can never revisit. It's always downhill from a decision. Now, good night.

I have a job, it seems. Well, it sounds interesting enough, even if it's not a real job. Back there in my other life, as the end of school days drew nearer and nearer, I often asked myself what it was I wanted to do with my life. Never with any real seriousness, it suddenly occurs to me, I would lie there in my bed, drifting, considering this possibility and that, but nothing drew me, and I was perfectly content to let it be so. I had my grandfather, the men, a home, and nobody was forcing or urging me in any particular direction. My teachers had no interest, it seemed to me I had no particular skill, and the thought of university scarcely even occurred to me. In a rare romantic moment, I told myself I was a small boat, well-found, content to let the wind and current take me. And now, here, after that short and hectic drama, that abrupt transition from one word to another, held up and cossetted by these good people, it seemed to me that nothing had changed. Henri had found me a place, it would do as well as anything. It would be novel, add to the daily novelty, and that would do me. There was nothing I particularly wanted to do, so I would do this. Wait and see.

27

I woke this morning with a decision already formed in my mind. It spoke itself to me as I was waiting for the coffee to come to the boil. I texted Vincent: write me 800 words. Just that, I knew he would need no further explanation. I wasn't ready to talk to him, too early in the morning, too many other things crowding my mind, but I've always believed in keeping the momentum going – and, I suppose, though it does me no credit, I've always had a perverse pride in my ability to keep all kinds of different things in motion at the same time. A kind of vanity.

Thérèse once made the opposite point: that I had a certain ability to keep all kinds of things hidden from myself, to live as if it was always the here and now but switching between different personalities, different predicaments. Different tenses.

There is a certain logic unfolding at the moment in this business between myself and Vincent, and clearly he is aware of it, too. He texted back almost immediately: may I call by this evening?

But certainly, I answered; and switched off the mobile.

I sipped my coffee, considered my options for the day.

The young man that I once was needed me to sit down and continue his story, but I went to bed a bit fed up with him last night, and truth to tell I feel a bit petulant about him at the moment. So, decision made it seems.

I remember very clearly when *Libération* was founded, by Sartre and others, in the aftermath of 1968. Sartre was going through his idiotic fascination with Mao's so-called Cultural Revolution, and it seemed to him and his co-founders that a 'counterpower' newspaper was needed. I remember Marie Louise predicting, correctly, that its flat management structure – editor, journalist and cleaner being paid the same wage, wouldn't last. I remember Henri being pleased with a left-wing paper prepared to criticise the Left from the left, though he, too, considered Sartre an idiot. Until five years ago, when Edouard de Rothschild invested heavily in the paper (followed by the departure of the editor and a revolt by journalists), it had maintained a leftist slant, but lately it had drifted rightward. Nevertheless, a number of good men and women remained at the paper, and I needed to talk to one of those now.

Good, a morning's escape from the tyranny of the past, I thought – and winced at the formulation. So that's how it is, old man, I scolded myself, feeling sorry for yourself, eh? And look what it does to your language. You need a break, that's all. When I lived here first, the Marais was deeply unfashionable. Now, alas, it is all too fashionable, and as I sat in a little café near the Rue Béranger headquarters of the paper, waiting for my friend, I was thinking gloomy thoughts about fashion, gentrification, the ludicrous price of coffee and the erosion of politics. My friend is a robust, heavily-built woman, and when she laughs, by some kind of contagion, everyone in the vicinity laughs too. She laughed when she saw me sitting there, told me I looked like someone who had discovered a bad smell in his own coffin, ordered us two large armagnacs, drained hers in a gulp and asked: well, you walking corpse, what can I do for you?

I should have married someone like you, I said in reply, surprising us both. I should have married you, maybe? Eh? This set her off again. What, she eventually asked, marry you? I'd have slit my wrists on the honeymoon. Now the whole café was chuckling, it was a small place after all, and when she leaned forward suddenly, took my head between her two strong hands and kissed me on the forehead, some of the customers gave a subdued cheer – and suddenly I felt, yes, cheered. And disoriented a moment, catching myself in the null zone between two languages, feeling the doubled meaning of things, my two worlds, kiss my attention and slide away.

Hello, hello? Joseph? What can I do for you, eh? So I told her, lowering my voice, about Vincent; I mean, I told her I had a young acquaintance who had some interesting thoughts on what was happening among his young Algerian compatriots ... spare me, she said, interrupting, a young man with political ambitions, yes, am I right? Now it was my turn to laugh, people who are quick on the uptake have always delighted me. OK, OK, she said, and I couldn't tell if the weariness was feigned or not, which of course told me something of her current predicament, OK, send him to see me.

On the Metro, on the way home, I tried to imagine myself a stranger in this city but the effort began to irritate me, so I gave up.

I brought home a sandwich from the minimarket opposite the wine shop, ate it standing up in the kitchen, washed it down with tap water.

Sat down to catch up on the day's writing and could not remember what the filling had been. In the sandwich.

Some kind of unease is stirring deep down in there, I told myself. Be careful now.

Twilight was coming on when I looked up from the screen at last, and there was a kind of twilight in my head, too. More exactly, in my understanding.

There have been days when, faced with this fog in the brain, this dull ache of incomprehension, the sense that the world is out of focus and that I have, moreover, no place in it, I have had the luxury of walking away from it, so to speak, and taking to my bed with a good thriller.

To be honest, this is exactly what I was considering, not caring that this would mean letting dinner go by, when I remembered that Vincent was due to call – and just then the doorbell rang.

I let them in by the usual means, Vincent and Genevieve, amused and a little perplexed to find them identically dressed – by which I mean each in a soft black leather jacket, white tee shirt, blue denim jeans. A signal of some kind? But, how to decipher this?

Gen saw my perplexity, understood, smiled. Joseph, relax OK? Pure, simple coincidence. You think we look good? I do, I said, you look good, both of you. She seemed genuinely pleased, which for some reason made me feel a flicker of dislike for her, but Vincent, I could see, was impatient to let me see what he had written. Here, I said, taking folded euros out of my back pocket, you two go and get Chinese for three, no, better still, something from the Tibetan. Go on, go. Take the key. I beckoned Gen towards me, gave her a hug, whispered in her ear that, really, they did look good, and shushed them out the door.

Interesting, that. She understood exactly what had flashed through my mind, the unfairness of it, my quick impulse to undo the injustice of it.

Vincent, I thought, leafing through the pages before settling to read his article, I hope you understand what you've got in Gen.

It was a good enough piece, I saw at once that it could run more or less unchanged, and I saw too, before long, that he had guessed correctly where I meant for him to place it: in fact, viewed from a certain angle, it read almost like a delicate parody of the current milk-and-water *Libé* house style.

Well, he asked, barely able to rein in his author's demons of diffident pride and doubt, what do you think? I think, I said, deliberately slow, you should help Genevieve dry the plates she has steeping in hot water to warm them, then we should lay out the food and talk over dinner.

Of course I was torturing him, and I was enjoying not so much his discomfiture but Gen's quiet satisfaction at seeing him checked. How many times has he read it to you, I whispered, passing into the kitchen. She showed me four fingers behind her back, walking on through to where Vincent, with a fine clatter, was spraying cutlery and china on to the table.

Well, I said presently, touching a napkin to my lips, it's good, you know?

You like it, you think it's OK then? Trying not to sound eager.

I meant the rice, I said – and immediately regretted my infantile cruelties. Ah Vincent it's good, your piece, careful, considered, measured, expressed with clarity, you understand?

Ah, he said, expression unreadable. Then please tell me what's wrong with it.

Gen frowned at him, made as if to say something, didn't.

Then, he laughed, and I laughed with him. OK Joseph, OK, I get it, I get it.

I was pleased he did. Of course his piece was written in young lawyer prose, I'd expected that. What I hadn't expected, perhaps, was the carefully-weighted balance between analysis and warning, the skill with which he had skewed the piece to perhaps a small handful of people, those powers in the Socialist Party who understood what was really happening out there beyond the *Periphérique*. As an audition, I told him frankly, it couldn't be bettered.

It might or it might not have been a coincidence that they turned up tonight dressed identically, but I saw at once, from the way they looked at each other, that Genevieve had contributed more than a sympathetic ear to this debut. In the space of a few days I had revised my opinion of Gen twice. Now, ruefully, I understood that I might have to revise it again, for I saw, though I'm not sure Vincent did, that he had found a partner in his ambitions, but one who likely had serious ambitions of her own.

I thought with a pang of Thérèse, that serious-minded Party organiser, so stern in denial of her own ambitions, so properly dismissive of my disengagement from what she was pleased to call the real world. More exactly, and it was as if she were speaking in the room, I heard her say: 'but, you didn't kill him? No? Perhaps after all this is for the best.'

How many times in the decades since that morning had I marvelled at her acuity, marvelled at how directly and simply she had read in me my stubborn refusal to fully engage with that famous, that over-valued, real world.

They are looking at me oddly. Have I spoken these things aloud? Joseph, everything is well? You are OK? and Gen chiming in: you were very far away for a moment ... her voice tailing off at my warning look. I know she was about to say something tactless about age and health but I channel my sudden fury into a burst of activity. (No, not fury, fear more like. Yes, fear.)

We clear the table, we wash as we clear, we dry, we store things away, we get out some glasses, I pour three liberal cognacs, we toast Vincent's formal declaration of political intent – for we all three understand that this is what it is.

I suddenly realise that I haven't told him, told them, what I have in mind for the article. What I have arranged.

She will expect you tomorrow, I say, and am about to ask if that's convenient when I realise how absurd the question would be. Genevieve is elated, of course, and I am sure that Vincent is, too, but he is wondering, I know he is, just exactly what is going on here. First the mysterious intervention in the case of his half-brother, now this old man has arranged for his debut on what is still, after all, a considerable stage in the politics of our time.

Who, he is asking, is this old man; what is he? Perhaps unknown to himself as yet, he has begun to consider the possibility that a friend with this kind of access has the power to become also a threat.

I am not a fool, I am not unaware of the dangerous games I play with my own vanities, and I see that I am becoming for Vincent, for no particular reason, what Henri was to me.

But, no, not exactly, so therefore not at all.

Henri was bound to me first by obligation to my grandfather. Later, we forged our own alliance, on mutually advantageous terms. But, I was willed on Henri (albeit he accepted of his own accord) and Vincent, well Vincent I acquired on a whim, by chance, perhaps also by some mysterious intuition of elective affinity.

And now, suddenly, I feel sad. Some part of me would prefer that he was, in fact, a car thief. I have seen, all too often, what happens to bright young men and, less frequently, women when they engage with politics, more precisely when they conceive a personal political ambition. The slow death of the moral sense, of the animal appetite for life as a thing of surprises, in a thousand toxic increments.

The chances that Vincent, or Genevieve for that matter, will escape this hollowing-out are, I fear, remote.

Then, very deliberately, I say it out loud so that some day they will remember the moment, perhaps understand what I meant: well, fuck it anyway, I'll be dead, I won't be around to see it.

See what, Joseph, they ask in unison, and for our own peculiarly different reasons we all three of us find this very, very funny.

They do not expect, and they do not get, an answer.

28

I remember asking: how will she recognise me, my contact? The Sunday before I was to start work at the Sorbonne. The derisory laughter my innocent question provoked, my fury at being mocked, not just by their laughter but by their refusal to let me in on the joke. Thérèse and Marie Louise eventually left the kitchen, still spluttering, and I thought that perhaps Thérèse would explain when we climbed the stairs to bed. I thought it would be safe to sulk until then, having some vague notion of dissolving my anger in some erotic glow, but she wrongfooted me, pulling on her coat, saying she had to go out and wouldn't be back before morning but I was not to worry, that I should be in the café appointed in good time tomorrow morning and all would go on from there. If she noticed my helpless flare of jealousy, submitting to her cool lips on my forehead as she went out the door, she gave no sign.

I thought of course I had mastered myself, could accept such weakness in myself and then overcome it. In truth, and it would be some time before I understood this, I was simply intimidated by her.

What I did understand, finally, sipping cold coffee after the house had settled for the night, idly scanning some magazine or other, was why they'd laughed at my assumption that I was being passed into the care of yet another woman. Not at the assumption itself, you understand, rather at my complacent ease with being looked after by women.

Next morning I sat as instructed at the zinc-topped bar of a café near the Rue Gay Lussac, nursing a thin black coffee. Given my innocence, my naivety even, it would have been reasonable had I shown surprise when a heavy-set middle-aged Algerian man appeared before me, looked me frankly up and down then gestured that I was to follow and marched out the door.

I put my lack of surprise down to this, the omnipresence in the city, in the narrow circle I lived in, of the Algerian question at the time; part of me was, you might think of it in this way, prepared for Nabile or someone like Nabile, to enter my life.

Nabile Djebar. He introduced himself over his shoulder as he set off at a fine pace, waving me to silence when I tried to tell him my name, his gesture telling me he knew, he knew, no need to be wasting time. They tell me you're not a comrade, he said. No, I said, not a party member, no. But yet that you are a comrade? I thought that perhaps he was confused, but halfway across the street he gave me a smile of such brilliance that I was encouraged to look him in the eye, and I saw then that, somehow, and not just because he'd been briefed, he understood my situation. As we approached the college, I saw him gradually, subtly, settle into himself, becoming it seemed to me slower inside, heavier, more square in the shoulder, and I saw the respect he accepted from all kinds of people as he moved through the building, a making of room to pass here, a nod there, a brief handshake from some suited functionary. When he put on his porter's dustcoat he glanced at me sideways, so obviously searching to see if I understood what all this meant; without forethought, I bowed my head to him, a gesture I had never before made to any person, and I saw by his dignified acknowledgement, a slight tilt of the head, a smile, my look held for a long moment, that he would be my teacher and would in time become my friend.

We were a very mixed crew, I thought at first, we porters. There was another Algerian, a thin, nervous man of about my own age who seemed to be permanently making and serving coffee in the comfortable underground room which was our unofficial headquarters. (I would see rooms like this again, in hotels, hospitals, railway stations, Ministries and the like, little independent republics carved out by men, and sometimes women, who served as they pleased, by their own unwritten rules, those who presumed to command them. A few comfortable armchairs, rejects from some status-conscious office, a large table, a miscellany of office furniture converted in some way or another to serve particular needs, the means to cook or at least reheat food – in short an oasis of hidden comfort.) A considerable number of men kept coming and going, so that it took me some days to form a picture of these new workmates of mine, but they seemed in the main to be middle-aged men of a certain stamp – quiet and unassuming to a casual glance, but a better eye, and in my case time, would show that these were not men to be trifled with.

They made me welcome, though the young Algerian, Hakim, seemed shy of me, and even a little afraid. Nabile had carved me out a space in this room of theirs, a small battered table, a wooden chair, a lamp; here over the next few years, under his benevolent rule (exercised, he made it plain, in constant consultation with Marie Louise) I would provide myself with a superb education.

The men became proud of me, little by little, 'our scholar' as they called me, making time for me when they could within their own Byzantine system of allocating work, but seeing to it, too, that I did a fair share – as Marie Louise put it one night, asking if it were so, you see my young Joseph, these men work on their own terms, but they work. They want you to know that work is a good thing when properly and willingly done.

That first day, though, as Nabile took me on the grand tour of the library, I was thoroughly intimidated at the prospect of ever making myself at home in a world of learning. So many books, such formidably disciplined minds at the polished tables and so many of them, such an impenetrable language! Nabile understood my disquiet, perhaps even better than I did, had even foreseen it and clearly he had explained my predicament to our colleagues for when at last we retreated to our little hidden world, I found a copy of a child's book, *Babar the Elephant*, and a giant Larousse dictionary lined up primly on my table. Everyone was watching discreetly to see how I would react. I stood for a long time looking down at the books with a vacant expression on my face and then, when the strain was almost too much for them to bear, I pointed at the elephant with a forefinger and solemnly mouthed: Ba! Bar! Letting on to be delighted with myself.

Their laughter was my acceptance, cemented immediately when Jean 'Maquis' baptised me 'elephant', making the sign of the cross over my bowed head only when I reassured him that though I was indeed Irish, I had long since (long since!) ceased to be a Catholic.

Incidentally, in all the years I worked there, that was the only time anyone ever referred to my being Irish, and at that 'Maquis' earned himself a reproving scowl from Nabile.

All, of course, with the exception of young Hakim, were Party members, disciplined even when wayward, but would speak of the Party brass in disparaging terms scarcely to be distinguished from the terms in which they spoke of their more obvious enemies. I had begun to grasp that in some way the Party was omnipresent in French life, and enjoyed a particular mix of lenience and disapproval from the state, deriving I suppose from its role in the Resistance. In day-to-day terms, this pervasive presence of comrades in the university would manifest in an unexpected conversation with a high functionary, a covert salute from a cleaner, a mysterious melting away of difficulties of all sorts with paperwork, tax and pay affairs, holiday entitlements, the thousand and one bureaucratic snares with which French life is beset.

Sometimes, in the ensuing months and years, I would have the vertiginous feeling that my life of clandestine study was in some way a common project, that whole battalions of strangers had somehow committed to my education and support.

In fact, of course, they had, but for the most part in the unthinking way of those committed to a project unfolding on a multitude of fronts.

Perversely, I drew most comfort from the very impersonality of it all – it gave me the vaguely oceanic feeling that somehow my life was being and would be borne up on a tide of general goodwill.

That night, after dinner, when I was washing up, sad that Thérèse had not returned, I was thinking back over the day I'd spent, already looking forward to seeing Nabile again, when Marie Louise said suddenly, you know reverie has become your way of life, young Joseph?

I turned to look at her. The stillness around her, the light from the tin-shaded bulb above her accentuating the thin bones of her cheeks. She had a black cardigan draped over her shoulders. Her hands lay flat on the table, pinning down a sheaf of typewritten pages.

Sit down, she said, and listen to me now. You have not written to your grandfather since you arrived here among us. You have done exactly what you have been told, you have given yourself over, do you understand? To us, to Henri, to Thérèse and now to your new work. You are like a boat launched on a river, do you understand me? A person without will. I have been trying to understand this.

I fumbled for the kettle, lit the gas.

The stillness of night through the big window. The deep airshaft a well of blackness.

Joseph, she said then, I want you to tell me, take your time, I want you to tell me what you think now, about shooting that policeman.

I felt a flash of resentment, of angry impatience, oddly akin to what I'd felt, was it only the night before, when Thérèse announced without warning that she was going out, would not be back. What I mean is, I felt this stab of resentment, saw how it resembled that stab of jealousy, saw that what they had in common was ... disturbance.

Marie Louise, following this impassively, nodded, as if to say, yes, keep going.

I thought about what she'd said, realised that I had indeed become almost wholly passive. I could feel it crowding in on me then, the weight of all the time that had passed since that gunshot echoed on Watercourse Road, time like a great wall of blank softness, looming up behind me. Pushing me on, day to day, away from ... from the last time I had felt in charge of my life.

I sat down suddenly, my legs unable to support me.

I felt, how to say this, that the blood inside me had ceased to circulate, that the movie camera behind my eyes had frozen on a single image. Cassady, his face as he turned, the moon blankness of it. And the shot, so much louder than I'd anticipated, echoing and echoing off the buildings.

And now I remembered, simply and without fuss, the thought in my mind as I stood there between the clashing echoes and my dash for home: I should not have done that.

I should not have done that.

The kettle began to whistle. I rose, shut off the gas, I made the tisane in a small china pot, set two cups in their saucers on the table, fetched the honey from the shelves – she likes honey, Marie Louise likes honey in her tisane, spoon ...

And all the time like a metronome: I should not have done that, I should not have done that.

Content that she had got through to me, uninvested in my answer – my silence her satisfaction – Marie Louise patted the papers on the table. You see, comrade, I have prepared you a reading list. The library will defeat you if you go around gawping like some bewildered peasant, yes? You must have a direction. Here I have for you suggestions only, I have no doubt but that soon you will formulate your own plan. Once you have begun. Here I have put the books a French schoolboy will have read, then some grammars, some politics, poetry, novels, histories. Henri, he will not mind my saying this, Henri says we should do this to fit you for life in France, we should assume you will not go home.

This last with a note of challenge in her voice, but I chose to ignore it, spellbound by the flooding realisation that right now, here, tonight, in this room, under the shaded light, under the gaze of this woman, I had come back to myself.

I said, very clearly, in a voice I recognised, in English: Marie Louise, I am grateful for this, more than I can say. Thank you.

I will write to my grandfather tonight. I thank you for this list.

I am at home here.

She smiled, a sudden surprising shyness in her expression. Really? Oh yes, really. Well, that is good, she said, and she came around the table, I stood, she embraced me, took my face between her hands. I thought she was going to kiss me then, felt a sudden intoxication, felt myself go suddenly hard. I went to back off but she pressed against me for a moment, then laughing pushed me away. Joseph, she said, I know you are only an idiot like all young men but I am flattered. Not that much, don't be full of yourself, but yes, a bit. She patted the pages on the table, went laughing out the door. I watched her climb the stairs; I laughed myself when she called back, stop looking at me like that. Write your letter.

I went out for a long walk, hoping I suppose that Thérèse would be there when I got back, but she wasn't so I wrote that letter. I wrote long into the night, and when I had finished I folded the wad of pages without re-reading them and I addressed the envelope to Eleni in Dublin, left it on the kitchen table and went to sleep feeling as if all the blood and life and breath had been drained out of me but for all that relaxed, confident and at ease in myself in a way I knew I would never be able to explain.

29

We don't have memory, these days, we buy it. I can scarcely remember now, all these years later, what I wrote to Mick in that first letter, the first of so many, and of course I don't have copies of what I wrote in those letters, though I have kept all of his. Today, recalling as best I could how I came to resume my long conversation with him, I began to think how fallible the record is, how easily our words and thoughts, our lives in fact, go spinning off into the dark and the silence.

I missed lunch today, writing on haltingly into the mid-afternoon. Before I went out to get myself perhaps a sandwich, feeling disinclined for anything but minimal contact with people, I automatically saved the work to date on the memory stick – and found myself thinking, not for the first time, how extraordinary our technology has become. Imagine, so much information stored on such a small object!

I have all Mick's letters to me, in a file box tucked away in the back room. I haven't read them since I came back from his funeral, years ago. I could go in now, I suppose, take down the box, untie the brittle tapes, I could go through them one by one, checking what I can learn of myself from studying his replies – always and only replies, never once did he write to me except in reply to one of my letters to him. It would be, I see I am entertaining the thought, a way of cross-checking this pursuit of myself that I am engaged in – but I don't want to do that.

I don't want to confuse myself.

I don't want to second-guess myself.

When they came to publish Henri's obituary in *l'Humanité*, I remember being appalled. Such a complex life reduced to a straight line version, yes, a version, to a single monotonous narrative line, a bare and almost contemptuous disposal. More than appalled, I was angry, and also bewildered: not, of course, at the obituary in itself, after all what else could they have written, what else in their eyes had Henri been but a useful cadre? What would have been served if they had tried even to hint at the complexity of his relationship with the Party, the complexity of his life? No, that wasn't it, they wrote what seemed to them appropriate – no more, no less.

I suppose what bothered me about that was the thought that this might be the only record remaining of that troubled, vibrant, sceptical man who had loved every second of being alive. There would be no other record. We who knew him, we too would go down into the dark, and our memories with us, our memories of all that we had felt and been and thought, our memories of all with whom we had shared this life. Gone. All gone. As if they, we, had never been.

Ah for fuck's sake! Would you get a grip? I know what all this is about.

In the post last week, a book on the Irish War of Independence. Billed as the most thorough study yet of that peculiar struggle. I went to the index and found Mick there, three references to his role as a Flying Column commander. You might say three footnotes. Save for those who knew him, no sense whatever of the man so animated by a passion for liberty that he would fight in three wars for it. No sense of the man who walked away from the Civil War, refusing, as he put it to shoot the people for whom he had fought. I've sought him in books on the Spanish War – two references, his name merely, two of the battles in which he fought. I can't pretend to have read everything written on the French Resistance (who can?) but I found him nowhere in the many books I've read, and I believe Henri when he says that nobody outside their unit ever knew Mick was Irish, that he vanished from the region as mysteriously as he'd appeared; a friend of Henri's from Spain, no more, no less.

A soldier of liberty. Unknown to history.

Now Mick never minded his invisibility, he made that clear to me when I was a boy, and I understand that he chose this invisibility, never put himself forward as a veteran, would scarcely comment on, much less lend himself to, any subsequent reiteration or version of the Republican struggle. We touched on the subject in letters from time to time; he knew I was angry, but try as he might he never could understand why I was angry. There were times, when I was younger, when he thought I was trying to make some kind of name for him, he could be cutting about that. But that wasn't it, no, what moved me then and moves me now is a kind of incomprehension: how can it be that such a man can fall out of the record?

There, that's it: the record.

Nabile used to call me 'our record keeper'. In all the years I spent in the Library, I took notes obsessively. I have them still, the tall black notebooks in which I tracked every book I read, tracked every thought those books provoked. But there are the red notebooks, too, the ones I kept as a kind of diary, though sporadically; observations on our work life, on what I saw and felt in the university, on the streets, random jottings on the larger political life of our times. These, too, I have kept, but I have not read them in decades now.

It is enough that they exist, that some kind of evidence, some kind of witness, is available.

Naturally, I am unable to say for whom this record is necessary – any more than I can say for whom I am writing this record of my own insignificant life.

But, stupid to say I am writing it for myself. At least, to say I am writing it for myself only.

Nights like this in Cork, the same cold pungency in the air, the drift of woodsmoke, the street-lights each with its blue-grey aureole, sounds in the street muffled and sharp at the same time, I might get Mick to speak of his parents, his brother and sister whom I never did meet, both away in America all their lives, of his grandparents, uncles and aunts, great-grandparents ... he had an extraordinary grasp of his own genealogies, those complex ramifications back into time, back out across the country as it had been. And yet, his only child dead, his only grandchild gone into what would prove a permanent exile, he did not grieve, he did not feel bereft – or so, at least, he assured me. He was content, it seems to me, to exist for as long as he could, to live as well as he was able, and to leave no posterity, no mark, no trace on what Mandelstam calls 'the windowpane of eternity' except the fact, by few remarked, of his having been.

For a very long time, the last of the last myself, I thought that I, too, shared his indifference to the future – and I think that perhaps I do share it, but this business of excavation, this business of making a record, it makes me uneasy; I sense a question looming that I fear I may be unable to answer.

This I know: Mick was a soldier, a born soldier, a type that perhaps has vanished from the world. I do not mean that he lacked a political sense; he soldiered for a politics he believed in, but it is as if he was born in full possession of his own temperament, incapable of accommodating himself to the nuanced life of those whose dealings with power are accomplished in the language of politics, its slippery compromises, its shifts and shapings and stratagems.

This also I know: that I never was, could never have been, a soldier.

These past few days, struggling to hold that younger self of mine in view, I note that Thérèse and Marie Louise, most likely without conferring or discussing, had homed in on the essential question: what did it mean to me, that I shot that guard?

Even now, a lifetime away, to all intents a different person, I sense myself slacken here, go vague, begin to cast about for something, some other question, that might distract me, might get me off the hook.

I know that Mick shot people, shot and killed. At a distance, mostly, in Spain; close up in Ireland, sometimes almost face to face in France. He had no sense of guilt about it that I could see, no anguish, none of the night sweats one reads of, no need to make reparation, expiation. He was not a cold man: on the contrary he was warm-hearted, generous, a good man. Just, he was a man who, called upon to soldier for something he believed in, picked up his weapon and went. Important to say he went with his own full consent, aware of, responsible to, the consequences.

Ach, and here I am again, jinking off after Mick ...

Very well. A drink, a whiskey. It's going to rain, I can smell it.

Like this, then: I knew when I pulled the trigger on Cassady that I was making a mistake. Better to say, that I was making the wrong choice. All the preceding summer I had been in a close fog of doubt, unsure, as I thought, of what I wanted. I could have gone to the university, but I hesitated. I could have walked into any number of jobs, I was intelligent, I knew this, and could count on a myriad connections as Mick's grandson, but I hesitated. I knew what I didn't want, or thought I knew, but I had no idea what I wanted. Was I in love with Theresa? No. I think I knew that even then. I had been infatuated, englamoured, but that was already waning; I was beginning, though I didn't realise it, to be bored with her, bored with what I had felt for her – or thought I'd felt. And my friendship with her brother? That, too, was turning towards disappointment. I had a sense, no more than a glimmer, that they were preparing themselves for a foreordained life, that they had already consented to live out their lives, incurious and uncomplaining, in our provincial city. They were good people, I knew that, I still think of them as good people, and it is in its own way a good city, but I felt, though I had not the words or wit to properly frame the thought at the time, that they had already surrendered.

Cassady, the ignorant young brute, put it up to me. I think I felt it in my bones, in my blood, that his hatred for me was ancient, unthinking and absolute, had nothing to do with his work or his antipathy for what he might have thought my politics were; I think it was a primordial clash of types. Somewhere deep down, down deep in the cells it might even be, his type has always hated mine.

Her father, describing Cassady's assault on Theresa, told Mick, told me, the policeman had grabbed her between the legs. His polite phrase was a kind of editing, masking the brute directness of what was intended. I knew different: Cassady's message to me was as crude as he could make it: I mauled your girlfriend's cunt, I hurt her in the cunt, what do you think about that boy?

I think the moron imagined I would come after him, would try to fight him. I'm sure he was salivating at the prospect of beating the shit out of me.

I shot him to make it clear that he had misjudged me very badly. I wanted him to know in his bones it had been me, I wanted him to be absolutely astonished at how badly he had misread me. I shot him because I was an arrogant son of a bitch, infinitely more arrogant than he was. I shot him because I could, and because I wanted to, and because I was done entirely with my life in that little city and needed some absolute way out.

There was nothing I wanted to do with my life there.

I did not want to grow old there, Mick's grandson, looking

after Mick as he declined; married or not married, a good job or not, an alcoholic or not, liked or disliked, getting fat or staying thin, eating the same food year after year, hearing and telling the same old stories year after year and mixing with the same people year after year, walking the same over-familiar streets year after year – I did not want that predestined nightmare.

Do not misunderstand me, I knew none of this when I cleaned and oiled Mick's old revolver, I knew none of this when I stood in the shadows, in the rain, waiting for that fucker to walk into my sights.

Or rather, I knew it, I knew it all, I knew even more than I am recording here, but it was all packed in a small ball as dense as a lump of coal, all packed in my skull in a knot it has taken me years to unravel.

I feel my finger take up the pressure on the trigger; there is a moment when I realise why I am really doing this, an intense moment when all of my motives are present to me, and immediately after there is a moment when I realise I am making a terrible mistake, and the moment after that when I increase the pressure past the tipping point and the gun bangs as he half turns towards me and the echoes go booming off the walls.

I told Marie Louise that I had shot the man because he had assaulted my girlfriend, that he had been persecuting me, that I feared he would kill me. She said she believed me. I do not think she did, but she never mentioned it again.

I told Thérèse the same things, but I added that I feared he would attack my girlfriend again, that he would rape her, that I feared for my grandfather's safety. She looked at me a long time, and then she said, flat and final: I do not believe you ...

Ah but I am tired, and this is taking too much out of me. I mean to go out for a long walk now. It has come on to rain, the light rain that I love so much; night walking in light rain, the pockets of dryness here and there in the narrow streets, the soft gusts of wind. I walk with my face towards the sky, seeing and not seeing what goes on in the apartments above me, in a null comfort, in a silence that pays no heed to shouts, the occasional traffic, the undying and ever-present hum of the city.

And then a long bath, a long deep bath; to go through to my bed in the dark, no, in the faint glow of the night carried down the courtyard well. Sleep then, sleep. But first, now, I must go out.

30

Thérèse. There was a morning, a Saturday, long after I had begun my work in the library. I had become fluent in French, we had long since ceased speaking in English. We were lying at an angle across her wide bed, striped light in the room, heat in the sun. Spent. In that place where two people can lie side by side, each in a separate quiet of thought, at ease. That place where things surface that have been a long time coming to ripeness.

I felt her shift, prop herself on an elbow. I felt her gaze on me, I was in no hurry to open my eyes, feeling the weight, the gathering force and point of whatever it was she might be about to say.

You've changed, she said, flat and uninflected. I said nothing.

Shall I tell you how you have changed, she asked. I said nothing.

When you came here first you were numb. Passive. Whatever we put before you, you accepted. Whatever we asked, you did. You listened, you learned, you took everything in. You volunteered nothing, you had nothing to give. This is true, no?

Please answer, she said. All that you say is true, I said.

You see? She sighed, not impatient. You see, now you are mimicking yourself. But I say again, you have changed.

I opened my eyes. I watched the lights dance on the roughly plastered ceiling, I thought about what I might say. I knew perfectly well where she was going with this.

I sat up, knocking her off balance, then gathered her into my arms, settled her, my arms loosely cradling her head.

Yes, I said, I have changed. Of course I have. To live in another language is to change your world. Somehow she managed to elbow me, a sharp jab that hurt. Do not dare to quote at me things you have read in books, she said. I looked down at her, she looked up and we smiled, a lazy smile, one of those that goes back and forth between people at ease with one another.

OK, I said. I'll try again. Yes I have changed. I have changed my world. I have decided to change my world.

That's it, she said; more or less; you have decided. Now you decide, you make decisions.

It was true. Not only that, not only had I become accustomed to making decisions in big things and small, I had come to have a positive appetite for making decisions.

Often now, when we'd all sit down to eat together, it would be to a meal I had made, a menu of my choice. I had set up a rota for housekeeping, a rota for shopping. Each day on my way to work I would vary my route according to a plan I had carefully drawn up, a plan designed to give me maximum familiarity with the city. On weekends I would mark out an area where I had not been before and walk it down thoroughly. I knew the restaurants and cafés where I liked to eat in accord with my moods. I would arrange my workday to suit my study plans; every three months I would review and re-design my work plans.

I must have drifted off, thinking about all this, when Thérèse asked: so, have you decided what you want of me? Where I fit in your Napoleonic plan?

Careful now, I thought, neck hairs bristling suddenly, breathing sharpening; careful now Joseph. Napoleonic.

I held her away from me, the better to read her face, but she pushed back against me, sat up, turned sideways on the edge of the bed so as to look straight into my eyes.

Do you love me, Thérèse? Counterstrike.

If I knew what love was, she said evenly, turning my point.

Perhaps you don't, I said, perhaps you have never loved.

I thought I was being witty, I thought I was being worldly, I thought I was matching her tone.

I thought we were playing.

She hit me so hard I almost blacked out, not a slap, a fist in my eye. I was outraged, in shock, absolutely in confusion.

Get out, she said. Get out, now. Standing there like somebody being pulled in all directions at once, like someone about to explode. Get out, she roared, get out before I, before I …

I scrambled out, lurched back to my room. I was standing there, still in shock, completely at a loss, when Marie Louise appeared in the doorway. Icy. Get dressed, she said, get a jacket. Come down.

In the kitchen, buttoning her coat, she looked me up and down with contempt. You are a fool, she said, such a fool. Did I not tell you to be careful with Thérèse? Did I not say?

I couldn't find words, I couldn't even understand what any of this was to do with her.

Come on, she said, and turned for the stairs.

It was raining, a soft chill rain. Fool that I was, I almost said something about going back for my cap, but she gave me such a look of contempt that all I could do was follow her as she marched off down the street.

She dived into a bar, ordering cognac for us both as she swept past the barman. She shook off her coat, sat me down with an imperious look. I hunched there, still in shock I suppose, feeling the heat and pain gather around my eye. The barman brought the drinks, glanced at me, was maybe going to say something but recoiled when Marie Louise glared at him.

But there was something of resignation in her voice when after a long silence, her eyes downcast, she spoke to me. Joseph, how old do you think Thérèse is?

I don't know, I never gave it much thought, twenties, maybe? late twenties?

Thérèse is thirty-four, Joseph. Ah you young men. You remember, I told you to be careful with her, with Thérèse, yes? What did you think, that I was perhaps warning you not to fall in love, eh? Well, that too, but you did not hear, perhaps it is my fault too, you did not hear what I meant. Not all that I meant, to be exact. So. I meant – drink that, it will help – I meant be careful how you treat her, what you say to her.

I spread my hands helplessly, winced, my eye was beginning to close up, it hurt like hell.

Charles! she called, tapping her cheek under her eye. Charles, with only a slightly reproachful look at Marie Louise brought a bowl of ice cubes, a bar towel. She smiled at him, said, not me Charles, it was not I who did that to him. He laid a hand gently on her shoulder, turned away back to his place behind the bar.

Some part of me registered that he was on guard. Registered that gentle touch.

Oh Joseph, how much do I have to explain in order to explain, eh? Vichy, you know Vichy?

Yes, I said, I've read ...

Enough, she said, that will do. A particularly nasty police, the Milice, the police of Vichy. Frenchmen preying on Frenchmen, animals, the scum of France. OK, OK, I will calm down. You will not be surprised that Thérèse, her parents, were *Resistants*, no? Careful, oh careful indeed but not careful enough. Perhaps somebody talked, perhaps only these animals they made a guess. One night, this was early in 1944, to their small house in the mountains, OK, one night there came four of these *canaille* in a car.

They heard the car coming, coming up the hill. Thérèse, their only daughter, they made her leave the house, they would say she was in Clermont, visiting a schoolfriend. I make this short now. Her mother and father, they met them at the door. They knew these men, these Milice, Thérèse knew these men. What they expected, her parents, who can say? An argument, maybe? Maybe even an arrest. She says, there was something lazy about them, these men. No hurry. Something was said, her father, his arm around her mother's shoulders, answered them. Silence, then something else was said, her parents they moved a little to one side of the door, as if you would say the men wished to enter. Then the leader, Guéant, he walked up to them and with a revolver he had been holding by his side, he shot her mother in the throat. In the throat, you understand. Where she was hiding in the trees, Thérèse could hear the blood gurgling from the wound. This, this bastard, he waited, the husband desperately trying to stop the blood, hearing his wife's last desperate breaths, he waited until she had breathed her last and then, casually says Thérèse, he was so casual, this Guéant, he shot her father in the back of the neck.

Then they drove away. They drove away. Back down the hill, all of the mountain country around them dark, no moon, not a light in any house.

And Thérèse, my poor dear Joseph, what was she to do? You see?

No, I said, it's horrible, I can't even imagine ... but what do you mean, what was she to do?

Truly you do not understand our world. They have been told she is away, they will watch for her return – but they will not see her return. Suppose she buries them, her parents, what will this mean? It will mean she was present, that she was a witness, yes? Of course. So she does what has to be done. She gathers some clothes, some but not all of the money her mother keeps hidden; she leaves the lights on. The shots will have been heard, somebody will come, eventually, to see what has happened. A courageous neighbour, a comrade, it does not matter who. They will have their burial.

Thérèse, it is clear to her that all she can do for her beloved mother and father now, all she can do is survive.

I sat there numb. Marie Louise signalled for two more drinks.

She went on: I was passing down the stairs when you said what you said, you understand me, when she struck you. 'Perhaps you have never loved', those were your words, I am right?

I raised both my hands to show I had understood. She was going to go on but stopped. We sat on in silence for what seemed a long time. We had forgotten the ice, until Charles with a reproachful look at Marie Louise came with a fresh bowl, took away what had melted. She wrapped some ice cubes in the bar towel and very tenderly, leaning awkwardly across the table, she dabbed at my swollen eye.

It still wasn't me, she said again over her shoulder, getting a laugh from Charles, a shake of that massive head.

Where was this, I asked. Where? I will not tell you where, to you it does not matter, OK?

What did she do? I could put no force in my voice. Almost it was a whisper.

She walked, said Marie Louise, she walked. For a long time. She walked out over the mountains in the night, sleeping by day, scavenging what food she could, sleeping in woods, wherever. A scout found her, a *Maquisard*. So thin, so feverish she was like a burning skeleton. You know whose words these are?

I shook my head, said no.

These are the words of Henri, my child. She found Henri, Henri found her, what does it matter. It happens, this scout he was what you might call one of Henri's bodyguards, one of Henri's young men.

Henri, I said, then Thérèse, my grandfather ... ?

No, no, they never met. This was not Henri's region, you understand? He had come for a meeting, a conference of organisation. So, Thérèse. The young man brought her to Henri, Henri passed her into the care of a comrade from her own region. When all was over, when war was over, he remembered her, he had her sent here to him. So that he could care for her – why not?

There was a question I did and did not want to ask. In truth I was almost afraid to say anything at all, afraid that I might say the wrong thing.

She sensed what was on my mind, sighed.

This, this Guéant, you wish to know, yes?

I nodded.

Well of course we found him. (I heard: we). After Normandy, when the Germans began to retreat from our area, we sent a squad for them, this bastard and his vermin accomplices.

Such a coldness in her voice. Steel now, ice. We liquidated them, of course.

Marie Louise, I said, very softly, Marie Louise, you spent the war in London, yes? You told me.

I told you I spent two years of the war in London. I did not tell you of my return. Why do you ask?

I folded my hands before me on the small round table. I said nothing, I looked at her, calm now. Myself again.

So, she was almost smiling, but it was a sad kind of smile; so, Joseph, you are becoming attuned. Yes, and like all men you want to know things, you must know. Yes, we found them, I say we liquidated them, I mean me, I did, that was my area, it was on my orders. Do I shock you? Eh?

What should I do, I asked, about, you know, about Thérèse?

Nothing, there is nothing you can do. One never knows what will strike her like this. We have learned to wait. She comes back. For now, it is better to let her be. Honestly? I think she is very likely already gone, she has places she goes to, you know?

Marie Louise, I said, this is not my world. And she said, now it is, now it is my poor one. Don't you remember choosing it?

Go for a walk now, Joseph, it is always good to walk. Go for a walk and come home when you have settled.

Home, I said. Yes home, she said, and she held the towel full of ice cubes for a moment to my cheek. Home, she said again, what other home do you have?

I set off walking aimlessly, making a long spiral out from the bar, knowing that by winding back again I would not get lost. God knows what I thought about, god alone knows because when I got back to the house near midnight the news that awaited me knocked everything else out of my head. As I turned into the Rue Cavé, two men stepped out of a darkened doorway, evidently meaning to detain me, but one of them, though I did not know him, gave me a nod of recognition, waved me on. I could see a van outside our front door, its exhaust trailing upward in the still air. As I got closer, two men emerged, carrying a long heavy box between them, loaded it into the van, turned and went back inside again. I leaned over to look at the driver, Pascal nodded at me, gestured with his thumb that I should go in. The side door off the hall, the one I had thought seized up, stood ajar, a grainy yellow light spilling out onto the muddy tiles. I went to look inside, but someone blocked my way, not roughly. There was a smell of must, dust, damp and machine oil.

I went upstairs. At the kitchen table, unspeaking, Marie Louise, Henri, a gaunt feverish older man I had never met before, and Thérèse. Henri motioned me to sit. Fearful, a bit abashed, I sat down opposite Thérèse, not daring to meet her eyes. When she laid her hand on mine, when I looked up at her and she gave me a half smile I came close to weeping. Then Marie Louise put her hand on Thérèse's hand and Henri said, very simply, Joseph, something terrible has happened, terrible, terrible. He looked ... stricken. As if he had aged five years since last I saw him. Grey in the face, exactly as the cliché has it. I remember being surprised at that. I was young, remember, I knew nothing of the real nature of clichés.

Whatever was going on, I was trying not to be part of it, trying to refuse it, to block it out. I must have known it was bad.

The gaunt man spoke, looking down at the scrubbed table, the lamp with its tin shade swaying slightly in the breeze from the open door down below. There was a demonstration, he said. Algerians, maybe 20,000, maybe 30,000, we do not know. It is OK, Henri? (Meaning, is this one to be trusted, are you sure?) Henri waved him on. OK, the police they went crazy, I mean you to understand really crazy. Beating people over the head, beating them hard. And then they started throwing them in the river, in the canal. They commandeered buses, they drove them, prisoners, to the courtyard of the police headquarters, the buses were running with blood; in the courtyard, no numbers, they had taken off their numbers, the police beat maybe fifty people to death. Some brave police tried to stop them. No good. On the Pont Saint Michel, a young man being beaten, beaten, he climbed over the railing to escape, clinging to the parapet, they beat him on the hands until he fell in the river.

In a flat monotone. Looking down at his hands. Everyone looking down at their hands.

A loud crash from downstairs, someone had dropped something a wooden crate by the sound of it. Henri on his feet, roaring down, imbeciles, idiots, were you not warned, were you not told to be careful. Rage, vein-bursting rage. A silence, then a calm voice from downstairs: Sorry *Patron*, nothing broke. Sorry.

Marie Louise in a low voice said, simply, Henri. He slumped in the doorway, indicated me with the back of his head. Tell him, he said. Marie Louise said, Joseph, we are sending you away for a little while. It is not clear what will happen right now. This thing tonight, the police, it could not have happened without permission, you understand? Without planning? So – and she gestured towards the stairs – one must take certain precautions. You understand? We just do not know what is going to happen. Tell me you understand, please.

I understood all right. I understood they were moving weapons, but whether to keep them safe or because they expected to have to use them I could not tell. I understood that these murders could not have been spontaneous. I understood that all kinds of thing were possible now, up to and including a full-scale army revolt. I understood that France had been nursing an incipient fascism since the Algerian business had begun. I was Mick's grandson, there were many things that I did not need explained.

But I was fucked if I was going to be moved on like a crate of rifles, grenades, explosives whatever the hell had been stored down there all this time.

No, I said.

No what, no meaning you don't understand? Marie Louise looked at me as if I had somehow disappointed her in front of this stranger.

No, I said, meaning no I am not being fucking *moved on,* or out, or anywhere. You think this place is compromised? Fine. I'll go somewhere else. But I am not being moved. I will find somewhere myself. Answer me, do you think I will be safe at my work? She looked at Henri, at the gaunt stranger, she did not look at Thérèse. She said, I think that would be OK. We hear good things ...

Meaning, they would not give me up there.

So, I said again, you think perhaps this house is compromised?

Perhaps, she said. It is best to assume so, myself I am leaving for a little while, you know you can come with me …

No, I will find another house, I said, and Henri was about to intervene when Thérèse said, I have a place, a place nobody knows about. He will stay with me.

A long silence. Then she added, not looking at me yet, that is if he wants to.

Marie Louise was the first to recover. Is there a telephone? she asked. Thérèse nodded. Marie Louise looked at Henri, I saw permission pass between them, but who was asking and who was granting I could not say.

A motorcycle engine throbbing softly down below, switched off. Somebody called up softly. Henri went down, and when he came back he looked, if it were possible, even grimmer.

Papon, he said. Papon gave permission.

Ice in the air now, a low, building charge of anger. The gaunt man suddenly banged a fist on the table. We should have dealt with him in 1945 he said, and there was a charge in his words, a bitter accusation. I thought it was directed at Henri, or even at Marie Louise, I remember thinking that I was nearest to him if ... but then I saw in their faces agreement, regret, the unresolved truculence of those who have been bested in an argument and remain unconvinced, and I understood.

Now it was all movement, Marie Louise and Thérèse vanishing upstairs, Henri and the gaunt man (why had he not been introduced?) going shoulder bumping shoulder down into the street, murmuring. I heard the van doors slam, I heard it pull away, and moments later the motorcycle engine coughed back into life. Escort, I thought, with some faraway part of my mind, but I was back in Blackpool by now, hurrying in the door, rain in my hair, the gun still warm in my pocket and the men gathering into action, Mick as grim and focused as I had ever seen him.

For just that moment I felt and saw, or thought I saw, my two worlds merge – but Thérèse came into the kitchen, followed by Marie Louise, and they told me gently to go pack a bag, not to worry, that this was no more than precaution, but to hurry. Hurry now.

And presently I went away into the night, arm in arm with the woman I thought I loved, and after that everything changed.

31

I haven't shaved for days now, always a bad sign. I woke this morning stiff and sore, a sour reek from my pyjamas when I lifted my arm to check the time. Also, I am starving, ravenous. This is good and bad. Bad, because yesterday I took no meals, merely snacked my way through; pacing and writing and pacing and snacking, making weak tea because I couldn't spare the concentration to make coffee. Good because when I wake hungry it spurs me to take charge of myself again. A long pattern this, stretching back as far as ... never mind.

So: a crisp day out there, hard bright sun, a slight chill, not really cold. Excellent. I stand at the bedroom window, strip, fold my pyjamas neatly even though they are going into the wash. Bathroom, long piss, check face in mirror. OK, not dead yet. Long hot shower, cedarwood bath gel, lemon and tea tree shampoo. Good smells. Shave carefully, lemon and tea tree moisturising cream. Lovely.

Somewhere along the line here I start laughing at myself, self-pampering old fool. Why not, I answer, why not! Now. Underwear from the hot press, soft cotton faded pink shirt, black cashmere wool pants, black sweater ditto, cotton socks, black desert boots. Well natty old me! And whistling, too! Oh out for breakfast, I think, the school run just over, the streets calming down this fine October morning. So, scarf in the shoulder bag in case it's colder than it seems, which one, the grey, yes, so the dark grey tweed jacket, yes. Now, where to? Still whistling, jaunty. Café Delmas, I think, indifferent omelettes, decent enough coffee but best of all, this time of morning, sun in the face.

Lavender polish on the oak stairs, something fresh and floral in the hall; Malacca I think, for twirling if the humour should strike me. Out.

Somebody's little dog has shat on the pavement, just outside the door. Lovely. Ah well.

Mornings like this, I think suddenly, leaving Thérèse's little hidey-hole, her *chambre de bonne* on the Rue Rollin, the short brisk walk to the library, Christ but it was good to be alive. For a while.

Won't think about this just yet, I decide, feeling myself purse my lips, acting 'judicious' to the permanent audience, looking sage, a man who has come to a wise decision, approves of himself with a nod.

A boy towards me, late for school. What, eight, nine? A sparrow boy, grave and alert, thumbs in the shoulder straps of his heavy bag. Looking up, down, around, brisk but at ease with himself. One imagines he will give a good and acceptable account of his lateness, that his account will be accepted.

I should like to have been such a boy.

Perhaps I was.

My cane takes his attention, he fixes it with a look, not breaking stride, looks up at me as he approaches. Looks into me. Nods. Recognition. One of ours. I turn to look after him. Without looking back he raises a hand in salute, then resettles his bag. A small soldier on the march.

The omelette was better than I'd expected, the coffee agreeably bitter.

Back in the apartment I busy myself for a while with small domestic matters. A motorcycle comes down the street, stops. Fires up again, moves away. I know he has stopped at my door, but for a moment, sweeping brush in my hands, I hesitate to accept it.

There is a wire cage fixed to the door behind the letter box. In the cage, unstamped, a heavy cream envelope.

This is not good, I think, feeling a weight in my gut, feeling my shoulders slump. This is not good.

Ah well.

The stairs creaking as I climb. The sun now on a corner of my work table, the grain in the polished wood, the laptop front and centre. I sit in an easy chair, with a thumb I slit the envelope. A single sheet, a single sentence. Unsigned, as I'd expect. 'Regrettably, it has become necessary to detain our friend.'

At moments like this one must think with precision, one lines up the questions and perceptions, one lets them sit for a moment, then one proceeds. I am disappointed that he knows where I live, but then that is absurd. It is his business to know. Nevertheless, a crack in the wall. Next, which friend? A moment's thought and I decide: not Vincent, no. The half-brother, of course.

'Detain', a curious word in the circumstances. Arrested? No, more ominous than that. 'It has become necessary'? Yes, that's the troubling phrase. I am invited to follow this up. Which means that my subtle friend wishes to discuss another, most likely related, matter.

Which means I must postpone what I acknowledge now were my hopes for the day.

The once-and-for-all closing over of this business with Thérèse.

This conversation that I am obliged to have first, I do not wish it to take place in the apartment. My ghosts are settled here, I do not wish to disturb them, I do not wish to disturb this uneasy but settled communion. Nor do I think it wise that I meet with Vincent in a café, a restaurant. The situation has become ... delicate.

Where, then? Somewhere nearby, convenient for him, somewhere ... of course, the Irish college.

I text him, must talk to you. Half an hour later I am sitting under the pollarded chestnuts at the far end of the courtyard, waiting. Some aversion has kept me from making more use of this quiet place, some absurd anxiety that I might be recognised by an Irish visitor. And now, twice in so short a time. Recognised? The older I get, the more unlikely that becomes, but there, some things we go along with no matter how ridiculous. Vincent comes through the arch, the heavy door banging to behind him, looking to left and right as he crunches across the gravel courtyard. He pulls one of the light red metal chairs around so that we are sitting side by side in the sun, his right hand reaching to press mine. Half-moon glasses pushed to the end of his nose, he smacks a bundle of books and papers down on the rickety red table. The old professor and his pupil. Nobody takes any notice of us.

So, he says, there is a problem with the piece? The newspaper? No, I say, not that I know of. He looks at me over the glasses, a considered effect. I suppress a smile, the boy can be so transparent. Hamid, I say, it's Hamid. When did you last speak to him?

He adjusts the glasses with both hands, shielding his eyes from me for a moment. I am both irritated and, faintly, amused. What's happened, he asks, what have you heard?

I have thought about what I will say and do here. I could simply tell him what I know, ask him to leave it with me, simply advise him to be cautious, to await developments.

Instead, I reach into my inside pocket, hand him the note, sit back to watch him read.

He takes his time, letting the implications sink in. Good.

So? What do you think it means? What means this 'detain'? Will he be safe?

I approve of these questions, but I tell him I do not know the answer, to this or to any other question he may have. I do not have answers, but I have a proposition.

He considers, he takes his time, assessing the implications.

He cannot possibly know this, but if he does not agree it is likely, very likely, that I will conclude I have made a mistake with this one. To my surprise, I find myself willing him to agree, and when he does, I exhale perhaps too sharply and he looks at me searchingly. And smiles.

If I had said no, dear Joseph? Ah if I had said no ... and he opens his hands to whatever the empty world might have brought him.

Yes? He asks the question with his eyes. You said yes, I say. Good. I must make a call now.

Most happily, my friend is free for lunch. I tell him I will be meeting a young friend later. Somewhere convenient, he asks? Somewhere convenient, I agree. He hangs up.

Vincent is looking pointedly at his watch. He's right, we haven't much time. Luck is with us, we pick up a taxi at the Panthéon, Vincent shuffling impatiently while some tourist laboriously counts out his fare.

Do you go there often, the collège, Vincent asks as we settle in. No, I say. Very rarely, as it happens. Too reminiscent of home, perhaps? Not at all, I say. And, this is home. He looks at me sceptically, asks: are you so sure? Well, perhaps so, perhaps so.

He scans the streets as we race and halt, race and halt through the building traffic. He is about to lose another layer of innocence, is beginning perhaps to intuit how many layers of innocence he has to lose.

I leave him in a café, no need to tell him to wait. I go to meet my friend. Is it unusual that he has brought some security? I do not remember him doing so before, at least not recently. As he rises to greet me, I glance back over my shoulder at the young man near the door, elaborately not watching me. A sigh from my lunch companion, a raising of the shoulders that says, what can you do, someone insisted.

A light salad, a navarin of lamb for me, calf's liver for him, a bottle of decent Sancerre. So, I raise an eyebrow at him. So, he sighs, some men it seems simply do not want to be helped. He went to those people, he told them we had tried to recruit him as an informer, he offered to play the usual double game ... ah, television, such a prompt to the foolish. Let me guess, I said, the one to whom he confessed ... a flip of the hand confirms my guess. So, I say, you brought him in. Yes, not that he's of any use to us. Now we have to think what to do with the poor idiot.

My young friend, I prompt. Ah yes, he says, poor Hamid already tucked away out of sight and out of mind, I believe he is to have an article in *Libé*, next week? It's not a question, so I just nod. Tell me, Joseph, does he have the long-distance in him?

I think so, I said. I don't really know him, of course, but I think so.

Is he sincere? he asks. Yes, I say, very. But also a realist.

Would he be, do you think, offended to have a small conversation with me?

No. He came of his own will, he took some time to think about it. I believe he understands.

What have you told him?

About you? Nothing. He isn't stupid, you must understand. He has some idea of how high one must go to do what was done for Hamid. He understands that I am making a connection for him, he understands, I think, that it is at your request, that you are curious to see ...

Yes, yes, he interrupts me, no need to say more. Tell me, your health is good?

I feel the tiniest possible flicker of alarm, and when he sees it he bursts out laughing. Ah Joseph, Joseph, we veterans, eh? Come, my friend, be honest with yourself, how many years now has it been since anything might have come of threatening you, eh?

You know, I reply, slowly, the thought forming with the words, you know I have only just realised, after all these years, that you are in all likelihood not entirely a bad man.

And at that both of us burst out laughing, so loudly, so boisterously that his bodyguard, alarmed, is on the verge of approaching us. Earning himself a vicious look from his master that sobers both him and me very quickly.

As we stroll towards the café where I have parked Vincent, I have a momentary qualm: I hope the boy has the wit to realise how dangerous this one is. And then I think, well, he asked to play with the big boys, didn't he? And besides, he has the mark on him. Let them find each the other's measure, it will be nothing to me.

Metro to Luxembourg, the chestnut leaves scuttling brittle and brisk around my feet as I cross on to Soufflot. On the Rue St Jacques, as I turn, wondering whether or not to call into the wine shop, that man again, the one who some time back made me think of Sam. He is standing outside the little grocery shop across the road, a small bottle of water tilted to the sky, the water bubbling in a shaft of light as he swallows. He brings his head down, shakes it, regards the now empty bottle and scans about for a bin. I do not know why I have stopped to look at him, and when he catches me looking, for a second he seems as if he's about to get angry. But, he just smiles, unconcerned, straightens his shoulders, marches away. I am obscurely pleased that he's lost his defeated hunch, it is as if a friend had regained my confidence.

I anticipate a visit tonight from Vincent, of course, and in the circumstances Gen will, no doubt, insist on accompanying him; they will be urgent, I anticipate this, and I expect they will have spent the afternoon discussing the implications of what is unfolding around them now. A little management is called for, I think; I make a booking in Au Port du Salut for half-past eight. Good traditional cooking, solid. I don't want to deal with this on my home ground. I will have a nap this afternoon, no harm to be husbanding my energies.

But, I find that I cannot sleep. I lie there, prey to unformed anxieties, fretful until I master my breathing and line up what's worrying me. First, I have left Thérèse, my life back then, that unfolding story, hanging there in space. For all that it costs me, I am immersed in this record of mine, increasingly under its spell. Today started out as a kind of undeclared holiday, but descended, deteriorated, into this anxiety. There is no obvious reason for it, no health problems, no sense of time's winged chariot crowding at my heels. And then, I ferret about until I find it, then there is this business of *Le Grand Sam*.

Of course his doppelganger earlier today, but those revenant memories these past few weeks, too. An insistence there.

Very well, old fool, choose: my younger self or the long fella.

Get up, get dressed again, coffee, open that damned machine. Sam it is.

I cannot, I must not, suggest we were friends. Easy to say, you might think, that we were acquaintances, chance acquaintances as the quaint saying has it. I am temporising, I know. When we first spoke, it was to acknowledge that we had seen each other often in the *quartier*. He was by then on the brink of becoming a famous man, but he had a way of blending in, the abstracted air, the leatherette shopping bag, the slow gait – all the same, I knew who he was. My own innate reticence, my knowing that he was by choice reclusive, these things inhibited me from acknowledging him in any way. I had sympathised with, understood immediately, his wife's response to the news of the Nobel: *Quelle désastre*!

On the other hand ... I had you spotted from day one, he said to me. It puts a mark on you, Ireland. What had happened was, him coming down the street on one side, me going up the street on the other, we had looked at each other, went to pass on as usual and then, somehow, both decided sure we might as well give over this pretended lack of curiosity. I was touched that he crossed over to my side, offered his hand. That was noble, he was not obliged to do that. Sam, he said. Joseph, I said, letting my boyhood accent shoulder its way through. A little. Jasus, he said, I might have known, Cork.

We stepped in somewhere, ordered two Jamesons. A bit early, he said. Ah sure ... I said. Exactly, he said. And we sat there for a while. I don't know should I ask, he said. I shrugged, only because I didn't know where to start. Fair enough, he said.

We sat in the cave, we watched our world go by. That fella there now, he said, a tip of his glass indicating a small stooped man going by, a shopping bag banging off his bony knee. What it is, he bristles every time he goes past me. Ah, I said, he was pointed out to me once by ... someone I know. *Action Francaise*, perhaps more, he'd know about you in the war d'ye see?

A thoughtful nod, a grunt. Tell me, he said then, and I hope I'm not being inquisitive, do you ever go back? No, I said, no. I was never minded to. Never minded to, he repeated thoughtfully, and he turned to look at me. Yes. Well, gathering himself up, I enjoyed the chat. I looked up at him deadpan, and we started laughing. We might do it again, he suggested, his tone somewhere between diffident and indifferent. Now and again. We might, I said, matching his tone, and offered him my hand. We shook, and he went out laughing quietly to himself.

All those years after, when we might share a quick word on the street, sometimes if he was unusually preoccupied only a half wave, or when we might very occasionally take in a match, take a day off to go drinking and wandering, we had that same ease with each other. It was nothing and everything to do with our being Irish by birth and French by choice, as a mutual acquaintance once proposed. I think now it was because we both lived in the after of a before-and-after decision. We had been given a country, a matrix, and then given another; we had accepted first one, then the other, with the same engaged indifference.

I didn't ask to be born, you know, he said to me once, well on in drink.

Well do you know what, none of us did, I replied, a bit lost in myself that night.

No, he said, there's that. And I'm all right here, he said, as far as it goes.

It suits us, I agreed.

Yes, he said, there's that, it suits us. Would you have another?

You've lost me now, I said, another what, another go 'round?

Jasus no, he said, another drink.

I thought you meant another option, I said, another life like.

He recoiled. You wouldn't take another shot at it, would you? He seemed genuinely to want to know.

Ah no, I said, twice is enough.

He squinted at me, trying to keep me in focus, the lights glinting off the opaque discs of his spectacles. Ah now, he said, you're getting deep now. I think I'd better go home. And he got up and walked out.

Ran into him again a week later and we shared a pizza for lunch. Talked about horses.

He never once asked what I did for a living. He never once asked what brought me to Paris in the first place, never asked how long I had been here, never spoke English to me if there was anyone else present, would switch to French if even a barman or waiter came near. How it is, he saw and he somehow understood how and why I carried myself in the world, and he consented to that. He never spoke of his work, his home, his worries or troubles, and certainly not of his successes. He never invited me to see a play, never gave me a present of one of his books. I returned his magnificent courtesy by never going to see one of his plays, taking care never to read any of his books.

And now here comes Vincent and, yes, Gen, looking up at me from the street, the doorbell still echoing through the apartment, the noise of the world come back as it always does until one day it will stop. Just. Like. This.

32

The morning after the police massacre, the morning after the collection and distribution of weapons, the evacuation of what had been for so long my home, there was a deathly silence all through the Sorbonne. Down in our little Republic, nobody moved, nobody spoke, each of us blank in his own thoughts we sat there as if dread and horror had stopped all the clocks inside us. All morning we waited for Hakim to come into work, Nabile constantly vanishing to make this call or that from the phone in a discreet nearby bar. Towards mid-afternoon a pale young man walked in, asked for the *Patron*. He opened his coat, we saw he was wearing a hospital uniform underneath; he took out some papers, selected a *carte d'identité*, handed it to Nabile. The young man looked sad. I'm sorry, he said, I took these from his pocket when nobody was looking. Nabile embraced him, shook his hand. We watched him leave, grateful for his awkward decency, and for a long time we stood there until Nabile walked out the back door without saying a word and we, also unable to find words, we went home too. We simply could not bear to speak of Hakim.

Home for the next couple of years was to be with Thérèse. She told me, when I got back to her place, that I was welcome, told me the decision had been taken to remove from the house in Rue de Cavé, in fact to dispose of the house entirely. I didn't mind, I was happy to move in with her, happy that she seemed willing to make our undeclared relationship something more concrete, more avowed.

We were content enough, in our way. Our bodies liked each other, and sometimes, without quite meaning to, we would manage to reach a place where some small unspoken wound might heal, a little, some nameless unease might soothe into peace. She continued to come and go, and after a while I became, perhaps not indifferent, no, I might say inured to these disappearances, the silences after, her unbroken refusal to explain. Marie Louise would come by, sometimes on business I was not made privy to, sometimes simply to eat with us. She seemed never to call when I might be on my own, and if at times I was inclined to read something into this, it never occurred to me to challenge her on it; even less was I inclined to mention it to Thérèse.

Henri I saw when he came to the library – on Party business I presumed, though of course I never asked. In any case, without being told to or asked to, I would absent myself from my by-now permanent study in a remote corner while he was there; I took it upon myself to cover for the comrades who would drift, one by one, down to our lair. I am quite sure the rest of the staff were aware that something was going on, but as it never seemed to bother them, I never allowed it to bother me.

I was immersed for the most part in my books, in my books and in the long solitary walks I would take, winter and summer, mostly by night. On weekends, especially if Thérèse was away, and she was often away on weekends, I might take a train out into the countryside, or to the Pas de Calais coast. We never once went on holiday, and Nabile contrived for me that my obligatory library holidays should be converted into overtime.

By now, in truth, my studies had become an end in themselves. Somewhere, in a succession of small, unnoticed moments, unregarded decisions, I had let go of the idea that I was studying towards some end that would conveniently reveal itself. I mean, I suppose, some vocational end that would, from a certain point of view, make valid the accommodations that had been made for me by Nabile and my fellow workers. This was never discussed, I am not sure that I ever seriously reflected on this gradual disengagement, but it was acknowledged, tacitly, by Nabile and others, and I had gradually become a full-time library porter. This not to say that I had ceased to be what is called an eternal student – it just meant that where others would make time to play cards, slip out on errands, take a nap or otherwise assert some autonomy inside the frame of the working day, I would continue to immerse myself in my books.

Thérèse would accept no contribution to the rent, and even though we shared household expenses – in this at least I had managed to have my way – I found I was accumulating considerable savings. I never touched them.

I kept up a correspondence with Mick, of course, and to a much lesser extent with Eleni. Reports on the day-to-day for the most part. Over the years it became clear to me that my interest in Ireland was waning, that the last vestigial thoughts of return had faded to nothing – but I did not make any connection, then, to the estranged way I was living with myself.

I did not realise that for Mick I had passed into another life, that our farewell on the docks of Dublin had been a real farewell for him, a soldier's farewell; if I thought about it at all no more than a parting for me. I did not realise how far and how comfortably I had drifted into a kind of living null.

A lull that lasted for all of seven years.

May 1968 came as no surprise to us in the library; we had been watching the tension build for months, listening on the fringes to the impassioned speeches, feeling the thunder build underground. There were days when I'd long for the lightning to spike up and out, for the great force to discharge itself in some shaking of the world.

The MAU, the University Action Movement, had occupied the Richelieu lecture theatre on 29 March. The Sorbonne workers had been ... unobstructive.

My co-workers felt that we were drifting towards the explosive days of 1945 again when the powerful left-wing elements of the Resistance had been outmanoeuvred by De Gaulle when the rolling revolution they had banked on had been skilfully, if only just, derailed. Indeed, as if to make the point that all De Gaulle's manoeuvrings had nonetheless left France with unfinished business, Petain's former lawyer, Tixier-Vignancourt, had established himself as a kind of godfather to a gang called Occident, right-wing students who regularly attacked leftist student demonstrations. Occident broke into the Sorbonne offices of the MAU on 2 May and wrecked the place. Next day, when Sorbonne students met in the great courtyard, joined by students from Nanterre, the Rector panicked and called in the police. I watched from a high window as the students left, peacefully enough, and thought things had calmed down until one of my colleagues came racing in to tell us that fighting had started in the streets outside and the students were being loaded into police vans.

I remember Nabile gripping me fiercely by the arm, a murderous look on his face. I knew he was thinking back to the night in 1961, to Papon's butchery; I had a sudden wild intuition where those weapons had been stored, the long wooden cases removed from the house on the Rue de Cavé. I wondered, I wondered ... that was powerful thunder beneath the city, and I thought that the lightning was about to lance out, to explode in all directions.

When it did come, when the streets erupted, my fellow porters, to my surprise, were censorious and negative at first. They thought the students lacked order, discipline, a programme. Not all of them, not Nabile at any rate.

Word continued to filter in. Some students had begun to rain down *pavés* on the police, who responded with unbridled rage, clubbing anyone in their path as they went on the rampage. When we heard that innocent commuters were being battered to the ground, patrons in nearby cafés being clubbed indiscriminately, I felt a cool surge of excitement – the police had overstepped, there would surely be a response.

Dispassionate excitement, if such a thing is possible. I know that if someone, Marie Louise, say, Henri, Nabile, had passed a weapon into my hands, a weapon and instructions, I would have gone calmly along with it. On the other hand, even though I was entirely in favour of the students, had followed with close interest and approval the development of their politics, I was clear in my own mind that all this had nothing particularly to do with me.

I must make myself clear. It is not that I felt or thought myself a stranger, it had nothing to do with being 'Irish' (or with not being 'French').

It was, as simply as I can explain it, nothing to do with me.

On the second day of the street battles, the university occupied, the city under a pall of drifting tear gas, Henri arrived in a car and abstracted Nabile and myself from the near chaos in the library.

Pascal, who else but, was at the wheel. When he saw me, he hopped out of the car, came around and embraced me with surprising warmth, holding me back by the shoulders to take a good look at me. Turning his head, he said to Henri: he's put on a bit of weight, don't you think? Bit o' muscle. He might come in handy yet. And even better, he doesn't stink of fish! I had never seen Pascal jovial before, but more than this, it was his evident fondness for me that I found disconcerting. Henri slapped him on the back, told him we needed to get moving, sat in and dragged me in after him. Nabile sat in the front.

We drove off at speed, Henri up front, full of good spirits, cracking jokes, his hands flying this way and that to support his non-stop chatter. It seemed to me he had shed years and cares, and then, with an awful simplicity, I understood that this was the Henri of battles, this was the man whom my grandfather had befriended in the fire and blood of youth and combat.

I felt suddenly very awake and very sober. For a crazy moment I thought that they planned to join those balletic youths on the barricades, that some sentimental idiocy had gripped them, but Henri, adept as ever at reading my thoughts, merely laughed at me: ah no, Joseph, come on, at our age? The others joined in the laughter, Pascal twisting around for a moment to let me see his amusement.

Somewhere near Bonne Nouvelles Metro we veered sharply into a cavernous warehouse and stopped. Two men shut the heavy wooden doors behind us and I was alarmed, a little, to see that each had a submachine gun on a sling around his neck, half-concealed under short open coats. A hand in the small of my back, Henri swept me into an open cage elevator and Nabile came in behind us, shutting the folding gates. Pascal turned the car around to face out again, sat there with the engine running.

On the top floor, organised mayhem. What seemed like dozens of men and women scurrying around or hunched over many telephones at an enormous table covered with notebooks, ledgers, piles of paper. Henri led me to a relatively quiet corner, sat down opposite me, his eyes dancing.

Well Joseph, now you can do me a favour. Beside us, next door as you say, beside us is a telephone exchange. Thanks to some friends, here we are accessing great possibilities of communication. Many people all over the world are endeavouring to get a clear picture of what is happening here, OK? I need you to sit here with your big clear brain and translate for us into English many, many messages. Some will be to foreign friends, you understand? Many will be used to explain to the Anglophones what is happening here. About verification, that kind of thing, you do not have to worry; Sylvie, you see Sylvie over there in the yellow dress? Sylvie will be the authority. Anything you see signed by her will be OK. They will bring you the text, you will translate, somebody will collect it from this box here, you see this box, eh? OK, do you have questions? No, I said.

No? Joseph, you are a strange young man but, good, no questions is the same as to say start work now, yes? Yes, I said. Sure.

He leaned forward and ruffled my hair, a gesture I suddenly remembered from years ago, that first time I stood in the kitchen of the Rue Cavé.

He got up to go to where Nabile, imperturbable as ever, stood at the head of the huge table, unruffled by the chaos swirling around him.

Henri, I said, perhaps one question? Yes, he said, over his shoulder, go ahead.

Who are we here?

He looked at me then, I mean really looked at me. A cold, long considering look. I had seen affection in that face, exhaustion, composure, merriment, determination. Now for the first time I saw respect, and it made me feel cold inside myself, not in a bad way, cold; and ... it was like that moment in a car when the driver changes gear, the momentary drop back before the drive train engages again, the speed moving smoothly up.

Ah Joseph, how you always know the right question to ask! Do you want your answer now, or ...

I'll wait, I said, but I had already understood.

The students had outflanked the Party, the Party would continue for some days to stay aloof from the growing battles, but all around me I saw, unmistakably, Party cadres I recognised mixed in with students and others more difficult to identify; I saw men and women I had met with Henri, with Nabile, and I saw older men too, and women in numbers, strangers, evident veterans of struggle, on whom history had laid a certain impress.

I ate and slept in this warehouse for days, and I worked day and night, translating at first, putting English on what was placed before me; then as I caught the spirit of the enterprise, editing, interpolating, improving and redacting – with Sylvie's tacit approval – unsupervised, unaccountable, unquestioned.

I could tell perfectly well what was going on outside, without ever leaving the building. At first the Party and its union the CGT opposed the students, fearing that De Gaulle would seize on the opportunity to repress them, inflict long-term damage. Then, as the days dragged on, and student delegations helped influence workers to occupy their workplaces (an aircraft factory in Nantes, the Renault works at Billancourt and so on), the chatter around me began to centre on the Popular Front of 1936. There was a sense among some that history was in some measure repeating itself. I could discern, from the messages flowing through my hand, obscure communiqués some of them, others appearing to be press releases from the Party leadership, two contradictory trends: factually, the old guard of the Party was deeply implicated with the government, trying in fact to stave off revolution. But the slant of what was coming across my desk suggested that this was a *pro forma* stance, that in fact (there were ten million people on strike by now, the students were bloody, exhausted, but still full of fight) there was a definite revolutionary strategy, a possibility working its way to the surface.

I could not have been, you might have thought, more deeply implicated in the historical moment.

The truth is, the more the pressure rose, the more frantic the atmosphere grew, the more arcane and pointed the messages flowing from my little desk in the corner to all parts of the Anglophone world, the more removed I began to feel.

I knew that what flowed out from me did not matter half so much as the echoes flowing back in response, and these echoes were all the more important since few knew of our presence here as the originating pulse. We believed, I still believe, that these echoes had a discernible, perhaps a considerable effect.

It was a dangerous game, but I didn't really mind. I was curious to see how it might play out. I felt I was discharging a debt. I was unemotionally uninvolved, but ... interested.

I did not consider myself either implicated or in any way responsible – except as a matter of private honour, of private choice.

When De Gaulle left Paris on the morning of 29 May, I stopped Henri as he crossed to the lift. Well, he said, abrupt, well? Speak up.

He's gone for the army, hasn't he?

Despite his exhaustion, he smiled at me. Ah Joseph, soon you will be able to go home. Yes, he has gone for the army but, heh, we gave it a good shot, eh?

In Germany, on a French base, De Gaulle received from General Massu and other officers their assurance that the army would support him. Massu had conducted a brutal campaign of repression and torture in Algeria. He and the president had been, almost certainly still were, bitter enemies.

It was over, all bar the shouting. (On 14 June, De Gaulle would arrange for the release of prominent OAS leaders; on 14 July he announced a general amnesty for all who had been charged in relation to matters in Algeria. Those were the terms of the devil's bargain).

Within hours of De Gaulle's return, the warehouse was cleared, silently, speedily, an eerily matter-of-fact process that was in its own way stranger than anything that had happened there over the heady, hectic preceding weeks.

Bravo, was all Thérèse said, when Pascal had dropped me home, after Henri had said I should take a week off, and Nabile had agreed. Bravo, she said, and she kissed me very tenderly, and took me and bathed me, and put me to bed. I lay in the half-dark under the roof, and she stood at the door looking down at me, and she said it one more time as my eyes closed over in utter exhausted peace: Bravo, Joseph, and thank you. Sleep now. Sleep.

33

Last night with Vincent and Genevieve began awkwardly. They were surprised to see me appear at the door, dressed to go out. Disconcerted by this break from the normal. They seemed subdued, not quite ill at ease but certainly not comfortable. They'd had a great deal to talk about, and very likely had interrupted a long, tortuous conversation to come and meet me. They needed to talk to me, of course, I am trying to convey not a reluctance on their part to be in my company but a sense that as we walked to the restaurant they were in time differently, or in a different time to mine. There was a certain ... grumpiness.

I like linear time, I like sequence, sequentiality – the arrival of a new fact, a new sensation, displacing, sometimes annulling, the fact or sensation that has preceded it. I know that time is not really like that, that we live in many different times simultaneously, that there is thick time and thin time, time that loops away only to return in a kind of ambush. But one must have linear time for certain occasions, and this was one of those occasions.

Too much was happening for Vincent and Gen, not least because the future that had been an airy sketch for them was suddenly taking on an alarming materiality, a presence and weight in the living moment, and people, especially young people, tend to panic when this happens, tend to take refuge in what I might call vague time, hoping to keep what frightens them, no matter that they may in fact desire it, at arm's length for a little while more yet.

We were going to a restaurant because I wanted to impose linear time on them without seeming to do so.

One arrives, one is greeted, coats are taken, perhaps one

has an aperitif; one is shown to one's table, menus are handed around, the wine list is consulted. There is a settling, a settling in and a settling down. One orders, one tastes and (hopefully) commends the wine, then the dishes arrive in their proper sequence, and so on. Order, imposed from without, is accepted.

What I did not want: the pair of them sprawled or pacing in my familiar, comfortable apartment with familiar, comfortable Joseph, teasing things out, teasing things out ...

Of course I had not been in a position to deny my old friend, earlier that morning, his wish to have words with Vincent. That would have been outside the terms of our tacit unbreakable understanding. Still, I could have briefed Vincent to be minimal in his confidences, to say only enough to satisfy what curiosity my friend might have had in relation to the half-brother.

It was still possible that this might yet prove to be how Vincent had played his cards.

There are times, I have always acknowledged this, when I lack patience.

Watching Vincent play with his soup, lifting the croutons as if to peer under them, setting them bobbing again, not looking at me, not looking at Gen, I had a sudden urge to just stand up and walk out. Walk away from them, let what would be, be.

Gen, sensing this, put her hand on mine, said: Vincent, talk to Joseph, please.

Part request, part order. No, not an order, to be fair, a contribution of firmness. For a moment he looked at her hand, there on the table, laid on mine, then he looked up at me and there was a world of fondness in his regard. For me.

I was taken aback, why not say so, and pleased, more pleased than I would have believed. I may have flushed, certainly I felt warm.

Ah Joseph, he said, what have you done to me? Gen took

his free hand, held it down between their chairs, a gesture of tenderness, partnership, pride, a gesture mysteriously meant to convey to me that she shared in this fondness.

What have I done to you? Tell me, what did you talk about? Besides Hamid?

Ah Hamid, Hamid ... Joseph, such friends you have. Hamid has been, how shall I put it, extracted from a certain situation. His jihadist associates were rounded up today; they will, I think, vanish into something called administrative detention. One of them will be freed with suspicious speed. Attention will turn to him. Hamid, it will turn out, was on holiday in Marseilles, and as he is in any case still on the margins, he will be safe. I have seen his holiday photos, his hotel bill – no doubt by now Hamid will have seen them too. Hamid, I think, has learned his lesson. Finally.

He looks at me steadily. He knows, they both know, what the price of this will be for Hamid. I am looking for signs of bitterness, but Vincent forestalls me. Joseph, first *Libé*, now this, you understand that I do not know why you do these things for me.

Very simple, I say. Power is more complicated than you think taking care of the world is more complicated than you think. And, you want to be in power, you want to exercise power, yes?

(Am I being too blunt, I wondered for a fleeting second – there is always the possibility that I have read him, read them, wrong.)

A bit of bother then with the waiter, impatient that Vincent has not touched his soup, is interrupting the orderly progress of things. Vincent eats his soup hurriedly, and for a second I register something about this haste, his underlying fear that things may be taken away from him, all kinds of things, if he isn't quick.

OK, I'll put it another way. It seems you have chosen, for good reasons, to pursue a life in politics. Yes, you agree? Good. I am in a position to help you. I choose to do so. I have had a long life, I have observed that very few people are really interested in power, in closely observing who has it, how it is exercised, how it may be recruited to a purpose. I know people in positions of power, all kinds of people in all kinds of position. If you wish, I can make them known to you. This morning, my friend wished to meet you, he wished simply to have a look at you. You will decide between you whatever is to be between you, if anything. It is obvious to you what he does. He had made you a gift. You must understand that you owe him nothing. It really is a gift, to you and at a remove to me. Nothing is owed. He will be interested to see how you respond. Disinterestedly interested, you understand?

I am telling all this to Vincent, but it is Gen's response I am studying. I'm paying particular attention to the faint half smile she can't quite conceal.

I understand that she has already explained this, or something like this, to her chosen life partner.

They will be a formidable pair.

When we'd finished eating, when we were standing on the street outside, when it had become obvious that I was not inviting them back, Vincent said, blunt and serious: will we continue to be friends, Joseph?

We will, I said, certainly. He embraced me roughly. Go on then, he said, releasing me, draping a possessive arm over Gen's shoulders, no doubt you have mysterious affairs to attend to.

I was still chuckling to myself, watching them saunter away down Rue Saint Jacques, and unsurprised when, without looking back, after a while Genevieve gave a little backwards wave of the hand that was not tucked firmly into Vincent's armpit.

And so that's that.

I slept well.

This morning, my baton and croissants from the boulangerie on the table before me, the proprietor of my little café brought my *noisette*. He stood there for a moment, looking away, then said: they came for your little Basque friend, you know. What friend, I said. My tone disconcerted him. You know, the one who worked here? I thought he was Romanian, I said, or Italian. I took no notice, to be frank. A thief, was he? No, no, he said, uneasy now, it was not the police, you understand, I think a political matter. Then my friend, I said, no doubt they will have you now also under observation, that is how it is done, you see, in terrorist matters. He did not like my severity, nor the idea of being under observation. I did not mean him to like it. I got up and left abruptly, pointedly putting the coins on the table, not into his hand. Bastard.

When I finished my work today, I made a pot of tea and settled in a comfortable chair at the open front window. So much has been swirling through this room these past few weeks, I felt like airing it. A phrase, I suddenly remembered, that Seanie had been fond of using: open the back door and the front window for Jesus' sake, we need to air this place.

Dead now, of course, Seanie, the signer of execution orders, and Tony Driscoll dead, who'd fought in Catalonia, Tommy Mac in a nursing home, a widower without children, one of the two who had married, and Tommy Owens who had also wed, late enough, gone off, as Mick had put it, to the bogs of Offaly with a nurse and never heard from again.

A pigeon across the road was battering in the zinc gutter, making a fine splashing. The drainpipe must be blocked.

I held them a moment in my mind's eye, like characters from a book I had read many decades ago: the men. The men.

As the light began to fade, I began to be uneasy. Perhaps after all, I allowed myself a touch of the thought, perhaps after all I have misconceived the distance between indifference and detachment.

There was a burst of laughter from the street below, it shook me out of my mood. I leaned over the windowsill and looked down. Two teenage girls, gawky and skinny, dressed in black, both wearing those peculiar Australian fur boots, bent head-to-head scrutinising a mobile phone. A boy, no doubt, that particular near-hysteria is reserved for anything to do with boys.

They made me smile, for some reason, a slow easy smile, and I felt the better for that smile. I allowed myself to form the picture, a white-haired benevolent old man, smiling down from a great height on two young souls learning the world.

Well at least you're not a grumpy old fucker, I told myself, shutting the window. Why don't you go out now for yourself and have a drink in one of those bars where they're used to you. You could take a book. One of those bars down by the Sorbonne where it's easy to strike up a conversation if a few whiskeys put you in the mood.

But don't forget to save and back up today's file before you go. We don't want to start getting careless now, do we?

34

Things changed in the library after the May events. Of course things had changed in the world outside, too; the inevitable backlash, but there was a shift also in the bigger world, too, difficult to describe. Vietnam, and its consequence that the world was somehow more hooked into itself, more joined up.

I expected that Nabile, the men, the comrades, would be despondent, somehow, would feel they'd been through a defeat, but it wasn't like that at all. There was a deal of whistling now when we worked, often boisterous good humour. In some strange way, everyone seemed indefinably buoyed up.

Whatever it was, Henri began to appear more often in work, he'd pass me a sheaf of documents – a mix of things, position papers, communiqués, all kind of things to be translated. Nabile had come up with a small cupboard from somewhere, and when I'd finished translating stuff in my corner, he'd lock it in the cupboard until someone came around to collect the stuff.

To be honest, I wasn't really paying that much attention. Oh I was conscientious, but as soon as I'd finished putting English on something it would slide away out of my mind and be forgotten. I wasn't doing this deliberately, it just seemed to happen of its own accord.

I was still living with Thérèse, even though Henri and Marie Louise took me to lunch one day to say that a new apartment was available and that there was room for us both to move in with Marie Louise. If we wanted. Did you mention this to Thérèse yet, I asked. Weeks ago, Marie Louise said, has she not spoken of it to you? I was ashamed to say she hadn't, but at the same time, I was in no mood for disruption of any kind, so I wasn't too bothered.

I never said anything to Thérèse, but I started to insist on paying my share of the rent, and eventually she agreed.

Thérèse. Bony as ever, those long bones, that slender waist, dark hair still pulled back in a ponytail, small breasts still high and firm. She smelled of vanilla, rarely wore perfume, used plain shampoos, but somehow smelled always of vanilla. We were still lovers, in a perfunctory, hygienic sort of way, but I didn't mind that, I was erotically incurious, mercifully untortured by hormones. We might go through weeks, months, where we would cook slowly in the evenings, listening to jazz on the radio, telling each other stories of the day, or we might sit in the lamplight in our little sitting room, reading, then retire peacefully to sleep. We read so much. Then she'd vanish for a time, work, and I might start eating out in cheap places, calling into bars now and then, late at night. Mostly when she was away I'd do more or less what we'd do when we were together.

We were living in a narrow street off the Rue Lacépedé, and it became a habit, whether Thérèse was at home or not, that often after dinner I would walk down the short distance to the river, would stand there for hours on end, tucked in unobtrusively out of the way, smoking, simply watching the river, the play of night lights on the river, the people passing by. I could turn all kinds of things over in my head, those nights, all kinds of things.

I wondered about myself a great deal, during those night vigils, during those years – why I continued in the life we had, why I did not take other lovers, have affaires, why it bothered me so little that Thérèse would be, so to speak, sometimes present, at other times absent. I mean, sometimes present, sometimes absent when we would be sitting in the same room, lying on the same bed. I could form no conclusions then, can form none ever since.

And yet, for all that, I felt closer to Thérèse than I had ever felt to anyone in my life – or so it seemed to me then. We suited each other, if I might put it like that. We would finish sentences for each other. A politician might say something on the radio news and we would turn to find each other's eyes, exchange a sceptical look. Or, passing some lost soul on the street, I would feel Thérèse's hand tighten her grip on my arm even as my own heart contracted in concern, in recognition of, empathy with, some unspoken hurt in that soul's eyes.

I might wake in the morning with a rough cough, red eyes, one of those colds that comes on in one's sleep; she would slip out of the flat before going to work, come back with honey, oranges, make me a hot drink, telephone Nabile to say I would not be in that day. Or, when her periods were particularly heavy, I would run her deep hot baths laced with lavender or clary sage, massage her feet for her, make her blackberry tisanes. What I am trying to say here, we minded each other. We looked out for each other.

There would be weeks, months, when nothing in particular seemed to be happening in our lives. There would be sudden incandescent rages, storms out of nowhere, shouting and helpless roaring, the kind that, just, stops short of inconsolable animal despair.

There would be sweet times, too, of harmonies, small grace notes – of flowers brought home, a shirt bought for me or perhaps a fine wool sweater bought for her – something seen in a shop window that we knew would please the other.

I was aware that ours was not a normal, a usual, kind of relationship, but I was never very interested in testing myself against ideas of the normal. I had a great interest in how people lived, I was then, and I hope I am now, a compassionate man, I was never any kind of monster. It's just that it suited me to be exactly who I was, who I am, and it never occurred to me to be otherwise. I was very happy to be who I was when I was with Thérèse. I did not understand that until it was too late.

One morning, casually, as she was hefting her travel bag onto her shoulder, Thérèse told me she was pregnant. A Friday morning, a dry spring morning, enough of a breeze that the exhaust fumes from the passing traffic were being lifted away from us. I'm pregnant, she said, settling her scarf loosely around her long, pale neck. I'll be back mid-afternoon Sunday. We can talk then.

I watched her walk briskly away towards the Metro, the bag bouncing awkwardly on her bony hip, her knee-length, russet, bell-shaped coat, her black leggings, the dark flag of her hair.

I wondered what I should be feeling. I wondered if there was anyone I should tell. I wondered who else knew.

I remember nothing of going to work, nothing of Saturday, nothing of Sunday until she came home, travel-stained, dark circles under her eyes.

Sit down, I said, when she had been to wash her face, to change her clothes. A blue linen shift, I remember, a dark blue cardigan over her shoulders like a short cape.

Sit down, I said, and talk to me. I squatted on my heels, my hands gently on her shoulders. Where do you go when you go away?

You mean is the child yours? She was bristling, hurt and angry, trying to rise.

I pressed her down in the chair, gently. No, I said, look at me. No. All right? That isn't what I meant. Do you go for work? What work do you do, Thérèse? Tell me.

It's boring, she said. you know what I do, I don't speak of it because, frankly, you never seem all that interested. I thought you just weren't interested. I'm an organiser, that's all, a regional organiser for the Party. A bureaucrat, a convenor of meetings, a processor of papers, forms, membership. That's all. I thought you knew.

I wasn't sure that I didn't know; perhaps after all, in those early days, someone, even Thérèse herself, had told me the details and I had simply forgotten.

It's boring, she said. You know? Boring but necessary. Life. Duty.

The air in the room was heavy, a kind of blue-grey weight, thickening us, making us sluggish.

The baby, I said. What are we going to do? There was a look that Juliette Greco had made popular, a kind of grown-up pout. I saw it often on the faces of young girls in the library, a half-turning away and up of the face. I saw it now. Thérèse? Look at me, what are we going to do?

I meant: how are we going to live, will we need more space, how will we manage our domestic affairs, will you have to give up working – a whole host of practical questions. I was trying to find my way into this new complication, trying to see the shape ahead of us of what it would mean. To be parents.

She jumped up in a fury, the skin tightening across her cheekbones, her mouth drawing to a thin compressed line.

I rocked back on my heels, I did not want to stand up – I feared what might happen if I did.

I do not know, I will never know, what she meant to say then, if she meant to say anything at all, but I watched her as she struggled with some volcanic force deep down inside herself. Perhaps she could not find the words. She turned abruptly and went into the bedroom. She did not need to lock the door. I went out, taking a net bag off the hook on the back of the door, I went and bought meat, vegetables, wine, I don't know what else.

I remember coming back, I remember the clunk as I put the heavy bag down on the small scrubbed table. I remember the silence, the deep silence, and I knew she was gone again.

Perhaps I suspected even then that she was gone for good.

Marie Louise came to find me in the Library a day or two later. She appeared, conducted by Nabile, as I was heating soup. We went outside, into a small hidden courtyard where men would play cards in the afternoon when the weather permitted. She stood there and looked at me, then she gathered me into her arms, she pulled my head down until she could lay a cool palm on my neck, and I felt a great hopelessness sweep through me, something that started with my neck and flowed down through my bones into my feet and on down into the ground. Truly, it was a remarkable feeling, as if all the electricity in the lowering air around us was being sucked down through me, earthed and dispersed.

I had to sit down, I felt my frame could no longer support me.

Marie Louise helped me to the bench by the weather-worn long table, she sat me down, she gathered her black wool coat around her, sat in beside me, shoulder to shoulder. In some far away part of my mind I was looking down on us from one of the offices far above, at the small fierce woman, the big-boned man who was turning to stone.

I don't know how long we sat there. Eventually, Marie Louise, like a conjuror, produced two cigarettes and a lighter, a flick of a gesture that somehow startled me awake again. She sighed on her first exhale, settled back companionably against me.

She won't be back, Joseph, she said, matter of fact, low key. Probably she will have an abortion, that is I think the likely thing she will do. Thérèse ... for Thérèse life is discipline and endurance, a long march with no turning aside, you understand? Discipline and endurance. I warned you to be careful, all this time ago, remember? I shrugged, minimally, not wanting to disturb her, so comfortably leaned in against me. You probably thought I was being bossy, yes? Now don't deny it, you did, and maybe I was being bossy, a little, I know what I can be like. But no, I think not really. Some things, you see the whole shape from beginning to end as soon as it starts, you comprehend me? The whole shape, Joseph. This thing with Thérèse, it was over before it started.

I could feel myself growing rebellious, a kind of snarl, umbrage, taking root in me, way down in the belly, beginning to rumble up and out.

Ssh, ssh, she was soothing me, actually soothing me, stroking my thigh with her free hand. I am not judging you Joseph, do not be silly now, and I am not judging Thérèse you see; all it is, sometimes one sees the thing entire, start to finish, in a first look, a first kiss – do not tell me that you do not understand.

I did, but I didn't want to, because under and out there around this moment and out there ahead of me I had a sudden vision of my life entire, the whole shape of it, its particular arc from nothing to nothing, its particular emptiness. No, not a vision, more like a three-dimensional massive intuition.

Of course these words make it seem precise, articulate, weighted, and it was nothing like that. It was more like a felt presence that would fill in over the decades to come, a prophecy in wood, stone, air, flesh and blood that would come to fill and be my world, my one and only life.

It was a kind of exhilarated desolation, and it came with a powerful, entirely unexpected erotic charge, a flush of dizzying heat and desire. A contagion.

She dragged me inside, I pushed her inside before me, into the small room where we had a couch for when someone needed to sleep off a hangover. We practically tore each other's clothes off, pawing and pulling, unfastening, unbuttoning, and we fucked with pure impersonal energy, animal and unencumbered, graceful and powerful, giving and getting and giving again until we were panting and spent and peaceful and shook, and silent.

Never again. That was the first time and the last time, we knew this already in our delirium and we didn't mind, we didn't mind at all.

Leaving, she said: Joseph, never forget, the world is what it is. She did not need to say, I will be your friend always. I knew that, as surely as I knew that from this moment on I would have what I had always, knowingly or unknowingly, wanted: full charge of my one and only life, full charge of myself.

In the middle of the following week I walked out of work in the late afternoon, found myself a bar across the river, and started drinking. As far as I can tell I worked my way north and west across the city then back again for the best part of the next three days, drinking the whole time. I can remember none of this with confidence. Where I slept, if I slept at all, I do not know. Over the years since, I have sometimes passed by a bar or café that seems for a fleeting moment familiar, touches some dormant memory, some darkness from which I flinch. I know where I started, because when they came looking for me, that bar near Bastille is where Pascal picked up my trail. Then or after, I never asked him to help me retrace my steps. Not just because shame flushes through me, still, when I think back to those lost days, although it does. I do not want to know where I was because when I came to my senses immediately after, and in some sense to this day, I was possessed by a terrifying thought: in that lost tranche of time I had been, had become, somehow other. Somehow, both myself *and* not myself. As if some entire identity, inextricably and inexplicably particular to me, for which I bear, have to accept, full responsibility, was born, lived and died into limbo over that three-day span.

I was drinking pastis and whiskey when Nabile came through

the door. From two separate glasses, the weak sunlight from a half-raised metal shutter breaking on both with a terrible clarity. That was the first thing that struck me after the sudden, shocking appearance of my friend and boss in the doorway. The two glasses, lit like stage props. Pastis, I thought, Whiskey, I thought. Bewildered. Then the light from under the shutter. That the shutter was metal. That my state of mind was very strange. That I was in a bar, a dark bar in the afternoon with a number of men, that each man felt sullen and heavy in his individual mass, that these were not good presences. That Nabile was standing in the doorway, that I could make out his face even though it was in shadow, even though my eyes shrank from the rim of bright light around his head and shoulders. I was in the company of two men. Everything was starting to feel more and more *wrong*. These are my drinking companions, these are not good men, I do not know these men, they are rising to their feet and this is not good; all of these things, thoughts, apprehensions, are happening at the same time in my head that is clearing in jumps and small starts. No, not good men, Jesus, paratroopers, yes, on the street, what street, met on the street. Why would I …

Nabile beckoning to me: Joseph, it's OK, it's all going to be OK, come, Joseph. Come. Beckoning, coming no further into the bar. Beckoning.

Not *milice*, no, of course not, but out of the same swamp, the same dark kink, the violence and hatred boiling in them now, one sweeping me backhanded against the wall, the bar so suddenly small as they charged at Nabile, battered him to the ground, fists and boots and strange grunting noises now, everyone else in the bar, not many, crowding out of the way, let them at their work.

Nabile, on the ground, trying to protect himself, curling and flexing, desperate and silent, his eyes …

Beseeching me.

And I stood there, not anyone yet I remembered or knew but it was me, I knew this, and almost retched with horror and shame to know it, it was me, I stood there, I stood there paralysed and watched as they set about beating him to death.

And then I was fully and unforgivingly awake, as the door that had been knocked shut by a flailing Nabile kicking out on the ground came shattering open and Pascal came through with a long baton of some kind already arcing from over his shoulder and the first man went down with a bone-broken skull and the second man took an elbow in the throat that knocked him down and against the bar. Somebody else, a man I did not know, came through and stood in the doorway as the room was gathering itself into a storm against Pascal and when he racked back the slide on the submachine pistol he was holding, that spring-rasp and snap of metal on metal stopped time and stopped everyone in the place.

I was still back to the wall, utterly terrified, and now everyone else was frozen too. Nabile had struggled to his knees, blood pouring from over one eye. Pascal was beckoning to me, very gently, everything is all right now, Joseph. Come now, Joseph. Joseph, come. The man with the gun was glancing back over his shoulder into the street. He muttered something to Pascal. I walked across to them slowly, Pascal passed me by him with a gesture somewhere between a pat, a welcome and a push, and as I went by I saw Nabile lift the arm of the man who'd been struck in the throat, saw him trace down the arm to the hand, past the crude OAS tattoo above the wrist, to the broad band of a tarnished brass knuckleduster. His eyes glanced off mine as he looked up at Pascal, and I flinched though I did not see blame in his eyes, have searched for it since, the rare time I can bring myself to confront this memory, and have not yet seen it;

he shook his head, almost I thought in weary disappointment at the sight of the knuckledusters, then rising to his feet he bent down and stretched the man's arm so that the hand rested on the foot-rail that ran the length of the bar.

Then he stamped on the arm once. Very calm and deliberate.

The man came awake and screamed, the sound of the snap and the scream so close that one sound was almost the other, and then he fainted again. I was being bustled through the door, there was a van at the kerb, one of those corrugated Citroen H types, Pascal was pushing me in, then helping Nabile up and in; I stretched out my hand to him automatically but he ignored me, crawled to the side and curled up on a pile of sacks. I was almost too groggy to notice, too drunk to hold on to the sense of shame.

It was machine gun, minus the weapon now, who opened my apartment door for me, holding me propped against the wall while he did so. I did not look back at the van behind me, nor at the men in the van, when he helped me very carefully through the door up the stairs into our bedroom. Mine and Thérèse's, now mine. He left without speaking and as I fell face down onto the coverlet and began the long slow fall into full and total unconsciousness, I had the fleeting thought that no one had spoken to me or to each other all the long way home, and then I let go of everything forever.

Next night, I had just come awake and was immediately, shockingly paranoid that somehow he knew this, Henri phoned. Go to work tomorrow, you hear me. This is very important. No, I don't want to talk, I don't want to hear you say anything except that you understand. Go to work tomorrow. Do you understand? I understand what you are saying, I said. Do you fucking understand, he asked again. No, I said, I don't understand but I will go to work tomorrow. He hung up.

Next morning, when I walked into the room, Nabile was standing just inside the door. Of course, someone had phoned down to announce my arrival. They were standing all around the room, my workmates. All of them silent as Nabile.

He stepped forward, he put a hand on the back of my head, pulled my head down to his shoulder. I put my arms around him, and after a while he brought his other hand up and held me in a brief, formal embrace.

Late that afternoon, as I was shaking dust off my work coat, I saw him look up at me. He held my look for a moment, then closed his eyes and made an up-jutting gesture with his chin. End of subject, the gesture said, but he knew and I knew that no matter what we intended, did or said, nothing would ever, for either of us, be the same again.

Weeks later, Henri called to the apartment, as if by chance.

He wanted to know how I was getting on. What my plans were. We sat over a bottle of Cahors. He seemed diffident, abstracted, it was clear he had something on his mind, that he was angling to find a way of saying something.

Finally he said: Thérèse will be living in Bordeaux from now on. You can stay on here, of course, no reason not, if it suits. We will halve the rent, of course.

I thought: we? I let it pass.

But really, he said, coming to the point, there is something I wish to ask you to consider, OK?

I thought it prudent to put on some coffee.

Well, he said, like this then: Joseph, after May, you know, the translations, and of course what you do since then, and after … well, you know, that time …, please no, do not be embarrassed, I have been thinking. Certain things you have become aware of, it appears to me. You have noticed, I think, for instance, I am not quite what you might say orthodox, yes? He saw my smile, laughed. Well, let us say you may have noticed. People like me, the Party does not quite know what to do with us. There are primitive cadres who are always trying to expel us, you can imagine. But we stay in. We saw Hungary, we saw Prague, we are not fools; the Gulags – well of course they exist. 'Actually existing socialism'? A black joke, why not say so, eh? Mao is a monster, I cannot believe our great Sartre does not know this. And so on. And so on. But still we stay in. It provides us with ... a host body.

You know what he said, Gandhi, when they asked him what he thought of Christianity? He said it was a very good idea and somebody should try it. So, Joseph, do you follow me? Yes, I think you do.

And now there is this new generation of resistance. Some, I tell you what you already have figured out, some are just crazy, crazy or dilettantes, it does not matter. Much the same. Some will drift off into the banks, the bureaucracy, the ones who all unknown to themselves love what they think they hate; others will retreat from politics but keep some version of their faith. You see what he says, Dutschke? We must embark on the long march through the institutions. All very good, but this means, as they get older, these good souls will become the institutions. Perhaps this is OK, perhaps this is even better than OK, but we old soldiers (I am sorry, I do not mean you of course), we old soldiers do not trust institutions. It's always the institutions that kill the dream. And of course the dreamers too, yes? You, however, Joseph, you I trust.

I was flattered, confused, flattered and impatient.

Henri, I said, what is it you want to ask me?

Ask you? Who said I wanted to ask you anything?

Listen, I said, you have been very good to me, and there have been times I thought that perhaps I disappoint you. Maybe you thought you would look after me for my grandfather for a short while, and then I would go home. Maybe it is a burden to you that I am still here? This I have thought, many times. No, no, please, hear me. Please. On the other hand, I know that there have been times I have made myself useful, yes? So, now it seems to me you have thought of a new way I can be useful. I would be happy to be useful.

The percolator spilled over just then, the raw smell of burnt coffee stinking the air. Henri opened a window while I mopped up, poured, brought cups to the table. There was a bracelet on the table, I remember this, her blue glass bead bracelet. I snapped on the light. I remember wondering what a painter would make of us, looking up from the street, framed by faded shutters, two men in lamplight, heads bent towards each other. An old, grey head, a young dark one. An intense conversation.

Joseph, he said, it is clear to me that you will never go home now, we are agreed?

We are agreed.

Good, I have had this conversation with your grandfather, he is content with this. What he said, he said he never expected you would make your life in Cork, and he is glad you do not live in England or in America. He does not think it would suit you, that you would feel always between two places if you lived in those countries. Better for you, in his opinion, that you have had to choose to remain here, that this is what you chose.

I was uneasy about this, in truth. I did not like the idea of these two old men discussing me. Henri either saw this, or he had anticipated this.

I do not mean I spoke to him, you understand. From time to time we write, from time to time ... never mind. I know his mind on this, is that OK to say? I told him you are very much in this place, that you are not hiding out like some fugitive, that already you have made a life. This is true? Yes, this is evident to me, to us all.

I had a momentary lapse of concentration just then, imagining Marie Louise, Thérèse, Nabile reporting to Henri on me. He could be terrifyingly quick, though: this, he went on immediately, and with emphasis, this I have seen for myself. I do not need to be told.

Let us say, then, that you propose to stay on here in Paris, perhaps for all of your life, OK? Then, we must think, what will you do? I do not mean only what will you do to earn a living, but then work of course is important, it is important to work, is it not?

He caught me off balance there, I thought it was a rhetorical question but he was waiting for an answer. Yes, I said, work is important. It has been good in the library, but I think I have had enough of educating myself – and to be honest I have had enough of menial work also.

I regretted the term immediately, feared I might have given offence. He was ahead of me again: yes, precisely, for you of course it is menial work, because of how you are framed, how you are constituted. Do not be afraid to think this. It would be a waste if you go on doing this work, do you not understand that your comrades understand this? They are proud of you, you know this?

The thought had not occurred to me.

Anyway, see how the time goes! I must hurry, I have to go soon. I am thinking not just of a job for Joseph, you understand? A job for its own sake? But, a job also helps make one to a certain extent invisible, does it not? Here is my suggestion: you should become a teacher.

He sat back and watched to see how I would take this. He anticipated my surprise and confusion. Oh Henri, how artful you were.

I said nothing, knowing that he would continue. Like this, he said: you will set up as a teacher of advanced English, OK? What now they call conversational English. We will help you find an office, always better to have an office people will come to, never have people come to where you live. We will help you find an office in a good location, we will help you find this, help you find pupils. These pupils, they will come ideally from the administration, from journalism, the universities, business, you see my direction? One will recommend you to another: not an American, good; not an English, good – they will like the idea of a cultivated Irishman, it will have a *cachet*, as they say. But a very intelligent young man, they will say, recommending you; well read, well informed, he understands that we are international men of affairs, that we need a very high achievement when we speak in English. You will become their friend, you will become a kind of confidant, you understand me?

I understood him all too well, but I didn't say so. I suppose I didn't need to say so.

He had been looking away out the window as he spoke, and now when he turned to see how I was taking it, he saw me smile. And he smiled, too. Joseph, he said, what a field commander you would have made. I think you are already ahead of me, no?

Yes, I said, very calmly, yes Henri, I think I am already there. My answer of course is yes. But Henri, would you even have asked if you did not already know the answer?

He was already on his feet, bustling into his coat. He looked me right in the eye and said: Joseph, this life of ours it goes by much too fast, never ask a question unless you already know the answer. Is this not the way?

Yes, I said, yes *Maître*, how would we understand the question unless we started from the answer?

He was laughing as I saw him to the door, still laughing

as he wound his way down the uncarpeted stone stairs. From the echoing hall he called up to me through the wrought iron balustrades. Joseph! I forgot to say: I left something out, we are having you evicted from here next month. Now, you see that you don't know everything!

The following weekend Marie Louise came by with Pascal. They cleared out all of Thérèse's things, delicately and swiftly. Pascal squeezed my arm briefly on his last trip, her dresses, her coats, held to his chest as if they'd been dancing and she had just evanesced. Marie Louise, lingering, put a finger on my lips as I was about to say something. Now Joseph, she said. Now, Joseph! If there was a glint of merriment in her eyes, it was not enough to outweigh the sadness she felt for me, let me feel she felt, but Marie Louise was always a warrior and it was to the warrior in me that she appealed when she punched me lightly in the chest, said: and this is our life, eh Joseph?

I too her head in my two hands and bent it forward, kissed her hair. See you soon, I said. Yes she said, gathering herself out the door without looking back, see you soon. And, from the landing: Joseph? Yes, I said. Don't be looking at me like that, she said.

35

I have not mentioned *Madame* who comes and polishes. I am proud of my fine parquet floors, but I am too stiff now to go down on my knees to polish them. Cleaning and dusting, I hold myself to that; from the first day I moved into this apartment, it must be going on forty years now, I have kept it spotless. But polishing, no.

The first day of the month today. I rose early and went to the *boulangerie*, added two almond croissants to my usual order. Time ticks by slowly in these settled quarters, I have been doing this long enough that the bakery woman knows today is my polishing day. She gives me an extra smile as she takes my money, I know it is the smile she reserves for respectable widowers, poor men whose wives have passed on as she would say, for why else would a prudent old soul like me have to engage a cleaner? She takes me for a widower, of course, because on my ring finger there is a worn gold band. I adopted this many years ago, just as I sewed the red thread of the *Legion d'Honneur* into the button hole of my good grey suit. I wear the suit from time to time, not too often, as I go about my local business. The Legion, the ring, the leather folder I often carry, all these things go to make up an identity that keeps curiosity at bay.

Madame was found for me, now that I think of it, by a Maronite priest I would sometimes take a coffee with when we would happen to meet in a bookshop we both frequented. A gentleman, on a break between missionary assignments in the Middle East, he had a quiet passion for poetry, and an eye for those in the parish who had fallen on hard times. I forget his name, but I call his face to mind once a month as I open my door to *Madame* Fatima.

We have our rituals, she and I. She arrives punctually at ten o'clock. I descend the stairs, hold the door open for her. She waits for me to precede her up the stairs, I have caught her wincing as the first tread on each flight creaks, I know she would prefer it not to be so. I open the door of the apartment for her (once, in the early days, I'd left it open behind me for convenience and she scolded me severely for taking such a chance). She advances into the hallway a pace or two, looking this way and that, on high alert. I think she expects, fears, that she may be confronted with a parcel of loose women, disporting themselves shamelessly on the furniture. When she is satisfied that I am still morally blameless, or at least that I have had the tact to dispose of the shameless women before she arrives, *Madame* sniffs once, twice. I close the door behind me, I go to the kitchen while she hangs up her coat, I light the gas under the percolator. On the table, white cups and saucers, an almond croissant on each side plate. She comes in behind me, then goes through the cupboards, opening and closing each one rapidly, ditto the refrigerator, reluctantly allowing that perhaps after all I am not starving myself.

I pour the coffee, offer her milk from the small white jug, sugar from the small white bowl with the silver tongs. These she refuses always, but it is necessary that they be offered. She enquires after my health, is invariably sceptical when I assure her that all is well.

I am required to leave the apartment then, she established this early. She does not want me, as she put it, under her feet. I am not allowed to clear the table, I am shushed out of the place with a series of hand movements that remind me of nothing so much as two sparrows taking a dust bath.

While I am fetching my coat she darts in and out of the rooms, vaguely disappointed that I have indeed remembered to lift the rugs and put them to one side.

I am sometimes tempted to leave a rug down, to see how she would react, but always my courage fails me.

Before I know it, I am heading down the stairs again, amused as I always am by our little pantomime, out into the bright, crisp morning. Now what shall I do?

Normally, I enjoy this morning off. I have a pleasant sense of truancy, I often find that, half unknown to myself, I have squirrelled away some nugget of information – concerning an exhibition, say – that obligingly pops back into my head the night before, so that I have an expedition planned for the morning of *Madame*.

Of course this is absurd, in a sense, since my time has been very much my own these past few years, taking pupils on a whim, and that only seldom. I am free to do anything I like, more or less when and as I like.

Today, though, I am reluctant to leave the area, I am impatient to be back inside. Perhaps I didn't sleep as well as I thought I had, perhaps I am still muzzy-headed, because it takes me a block or two of walking before, somewhere near the Rue d'Ulm, I come to with a start and realise I am impatient to get back to my work, back to my record.

Thinking while walking is a tricky business. Some people can manage it, I used to be able to do it myself when I was young, in Cork. Something would take hold of me, working its way into my thought like a dye spreading through capillaries, and I might be halfway across the city, rapt in my following of whatever it was, before I'd come to myself with a start, almost always be shocked to discover where I was, how far from home.

Now, though, at this age, I am far too easily distracted. Anything might snag my attention these days as I walk, the variousness of things, buildings, noises and sights, not to mention people, liable to whirl me away from myself, from the patient pursuit of a thought.

Old fool, I tell myself, go sit down somewhere, go pay attention.

I take myself into the white stone lofty space of the Maronite church on Rue l'Homond, near the École normale supérieure des Arts Decoratifs. No doubt there is a process of association going on here, with the priest I mean, the one who sent me *Madame* Fatima, but I couldn't care less. I come here from time to time for the quality of the silence it encompasses, a silence made light and mellow because the church itself, solid stone albeit wrapped in a modern block of apartments, is high and bright and spacious. And because it has an anomaly that pleases this crusty old agnostic strangely. Up there behind the altar, seeming to float in the air, there is a statue of the Virgin where normally one expects to find a representation of the crucified Christ.

I have never been religious, I suspect all institutions, yet I have an appreciation of churches. Quiet places, for the most part, where no one is ever turned away. One's presence may be of interest to the old women who come to make their particular bargains with god, but one learns to deflect such attentions. On rare occasions, some priest or other may inquire if one wishes to talk – I strike those churches from my list, having no wish to offend their loneliness, having no wish to have my peace disturbed.

It is, I find, peace of a particular kind – more peaceful, even, than my apartment with its accretions of memory, the dense and busy presence of so much thought contained in my books. And now of course, lately, the swirling phantasmal presences I have called up about me.

I sink into a light trance, then, over there on the right-hand side, by the big, naive painting of Our Lady of Lebanon on her lighthouse ziggurat.

A memory floats to the surface.

Her hands, first. Cool hands, settling my coat, plumping my schoolbag so that it sits more comfortably on my shoulders. Delaying the moment when she must let me go out the door into the world, to school and its terrors, its alienations. Her hands flat on the table either side of me, as she leans over me from behind, to study my exercise book. Her hand reaching to touch my father's face, a gesture full of longing and reassurance (but how did I understand this, so young?). And her face, her face in repose, tilted slightly back, listening to something on the radio; her disappointments, elations, her shrewd sceptical smile at some tale of mine, her avid attention to something my father is telling her, and sometimes a shadow, something nameless flitting across her red round cheeks, darkening her eyes.

To have read too much in a long life is as much curse as blessing, but I know this is not sentiment, still less is it unresolved grief for the lost mother. I think of her from time to time, of course – as I am thinking of her now – but with acceptance, without regret. I had a mother, and she died.

No, dear as she was to me, and she was dear to me, as my father was dear to me though I had less of his time and he had less of my attention, dear as they both were to me this is not about my parents. Something behind them, sheltered by them you might say, ushered forward by them as they regretfully step aside and away. Something … someone …

I am unquiet here, now. I open my eyes, irritated by some intrusion but there is nothing there, nobody else in this white well of quiet. I settle myself again and I see Marie Louise as clear as day, as if I am looking at a cinema screen, slightly over-bright. She is lighting two cigarettes, settling in comfortably, it might be comfortingly, beside me. I see this from above, my own young face passive, staring out the window. She says, probably she will have an abortion.

Probably.

Probably.

I see me nod, accepting this, taking a drag on my cigarette. Tough guy. Alain Delon accepting the blow, too cool to show feeling. Composed.

I took that 'probably' as a strong hint towards what would prove a fact. Let us be cold, I believed it because I wanted to, because I could not imagine Thérèse as a mother, me as a father. Because I could see no future for us together, because as I sat there with Marie Louise, both of us silent, I saw that in a particular sense I had already ceased to have a past with Thérèse. I saw that there had been no Thérèse, there would no longer be a Thérèse, and then I saw that anything could be annulled, that moment by moment each incident in a life could be erased, that we can erase ourselves as we go, that we need never be the prisoners of our deeds, the fated inheritors of our thoughts.

Caught up, swept on by that exquisite and quite matter of fact sadness, I accepted completely that it would be out of the question for Thérèse to bring that child to term.

Yesterday, that self-possessed schoolboy on the street, fascinated for a moment by my cane, looking me thoughtfully in the eye before marching steadily on past ...

She would be, the child would be, what, forty? Her child. Our child. My child.

The Madonna floats in the air, the sun is surprisingly bright through the high windows, the white stone is hurting my eyes.

Steady, man. Take it easy now, breathe deep and slow. Bravo.

No news for years, nobody mentioned her; not out of tact, no, it was because nobody knew what had become of her. I assumed she had left the Party. I thought that perhaps she had found someone, made a life down there in Bordeaux, had become like so many former comrades a melancholy proper bourgeoise, in a dull but not unpleasant marriage to a decent fellow, someone I imagined as tall, reticent and, in an unimaginative way, kind.

Wrong, of course, as I was bound to be. When Mitterand emerged at last from the fog, on his march to ambiguous glory, his Vichy past slipping away from him like the trail a boat leaves on quiet waters, we discovered that our Thérèse had remade herself. Deep in the background of the PS, back there where the grand strategies are conceived and set carefully in play, out of the limelight of office and conference, a steady hand on the helm, our lost Thérèse.

Still single, still – as Henri put it, and not without admiration, even, I thought, with a lingering fondness – always herself.

I could have asked her, I suppose, and from time to time I would consider it: pick up the phone, make my way patiently through the secretaries, invite her to lunch. I could have asked her – but what would have been the point?

Ach!

So now, here, in the comforting aura of the Madonna – and isn't that a surprise, you old agnostic reprobate – here in this quiet place I accept again what I had long ago accepted, even at the very moment Thérèse had announced her pregnancy. Then and after, very simply, I understood that I had no wish whatever to be a father.

Madame will be finished by now, the cups and plates will be put away, the kitchen window propped open to air the place, the white envelope plucked from the hall table, tucked away in her large black handbag. Time to go home.

Of course I wonder, all down the years at regular intervals I have wondered, what it might have been like, to be a father, a husband, a grandfather by now. And not necessarily with Thérèse, there have been other women, and there have been daydreams, fantasies, but after Thérèse left, so finally, so abruptly, I knew deep down that an avenue had closed, that a particular kind of future would not be mine. Did I regret this? Perhaps, fleetingly, at the time, but since then? No.

I have friends in childless marriages who cannot bear to be in the company of children; I have friends, too, who have found in being childless an opportunity to offer shelter and respite to nieces and nephews when things at home become too much for them, especially in the troubled storm passages of adolescence. Myself, I have no such connections and it has never bothered me.

I am aware that I stand outside all worlds defined by family feeling, but it would be misleading to say that I feel this as in any way a diminution. When I wonder what it would be like, to be husband, father, grandfather, I mean simply that: I wonder. It is a kind of questioning without an emotional content or reference. A disinterested curiosity.

The street door, as it falls shut behind me, makes a kind of dull boom. The sound goes up the stairs as the faint smell of lavender polish comes down to meet me, and I climb in a kind of empty content, secure in my building, approaching my own place, my place in the world. I stand in my hallway admiring the sheen on the floor, absorbing the reassurance, the sense of order and neatness that this place always gives me, never more so than in the monthly silence after *Madame* Fatima has done her work.

I put the rugs down in their usual places. I draw a glass of water from the kitchen tap and go through to my front room, the light through the tall windows softened as it reflects back from the spines of my books. I have built this silence, this considered peace around me through the passing years; lovers have stood with me in this room, lain with me in these rooms, and friends have passed long nights of talk here, but mostly I have invested these rooms, this room now, with the silent witness of my own life, with the sense of content I have gathered, accumulated and nurtured in myself.

Sometimes I feel that all this was fore-ordained, that the shape of my life was out there ahead of me from the start, that the child swinging home from the library on an autumn evening in Cork had already some intuition of this exact life, up there ahead of him: these rooms, these high packed bookshelves, this sense of fullness and completion in the self.

And yes, why not say so, this agreeable loneliness.

People, I know, go to great lengths to avoid loneliness – I have never truly understood why. Like all emotions it is transitory, and therefore endurable; it must inevitably give way to some other sensation of the self in place and time. Loneliness is the passing sadness of the solitary, but there are worse, more corrosive forms of sadness.

Putting on my worn and comforting grey cardigan before settling to work, I hear myself say to my journalist friend, in that little café in the Marais: I should have married you. What was that about, I wonder? Out of what unvisited recess ... but I loved her answer, remembering it now puts me suddenly, as if I had clicked through a dimension, in soaring good humour. I'd have slit my wrists on the honeymoon. No she wouldn't; in fact while it lasted we were the most boisterous and cheerful of bedmates, but I know what she means. A born solitary, like myself.

I hope she gets on with Vincent, long-term. Equally to the point, I hope she gets on with Gen. She'll understand that it's a case of both of them together, that they're a team. I shall be interested to see how long it takes them to realise just how powerful she is. I shall be interested to see how they react to being *protégés*. Protected ones.

36

Henri had promised to have me evicted from the small apartment I'd shared with Thérèse – and I'd thought what he had in mind was arranging for me to move once again into a shared house, perhaps even with Marie Louise.

Instead, one afternoon when he'd called to collect some translations on which I'd been working, he told me to collect my coat, to come with him.

It was a short walk. He explained that he had been giving the thing some thought, that it no longer suited that I be so closely identified with Party cadres. He asked if I agreed. I shrugged, I had no particular opinion I told him. I wasn't really bothered.

He was irritated by this, pulled me into a café on Rue Soufflot, the one with the limping waiter, sat me down. Now listen, he said, you're not a stupid person. And you know what I have in mind for you; in fact, let me remind you that you have already accepted. Think about it: you will be meeting all sorts of people; he said it again with emphasis: all kinds of people. Somewhere along the line, somebody will want to know a little more about you, will want to know, for example, where you live. Yes? Show me your identity card. Right, now look at this. This man exists, this Joseph Lyons. You exist for the tax people, the health insurance people, the Sorbonne personnel department. Yes? You agree? You are not just floating on the surface of Paris, you have roots in France, bureaucratically verifiable roots. If someone should think to ask, who is this Joseph Lyons, they will find a birthplace, a birth date, orphanage records, and so on, all this.

What they will not find is a connection to the Party, what they will not find is a young Irishman who came here as a raw boy and has now turned into a Frenchman, one who has, if I may say so, acquired a very French taste for being sometimes flippant and supercilious.

Now finish your coffee, we need to get going.

Well, that rocked me sure enough. I have never rejected outright any negative judgement made on me. I was thinking about this, flippant, supercilious, dark words these, when we turned off the Rue Blainville into a pleasant, quiet street.

Halfway down he opened a door into a tall cool hallway; burnished green tiles, double height ceiling, a curved wooden staircase to one side.

When he eased open the stiff door of this apartment, the very place in which now I am remembering all this, the sound went grating up through what felt like an empty building.

Dust everywhere, high-ceilinged bare rooms, the front room with its twin windows giving on to the street, the spacious cold bathroom, the functional large kitchen with green stains in the porcelain sink.

A single bed in one bedroom, nothing but bare boards in a second, a great high brass double bed, the brass tarnished, in a third, the mattress heavy and thick in what, it was dawning on me at last, would be my bedroom, my apartment, my home.

He was watching me attentively, the smile spreading on his face as comprehension dawned. He flicked a switch: look, light. Come here, into the kitchen. He turned on a tap on the heavy cast-iron cooker: the sour, quick smell of gas.

And ... I queried. No need to finish the thought, the question. He beamed at me: nobody else, Joseph, all this, yours. Welcome to your new home. Then, anxiously, it pleases you? Do you like it?

I felt near to tears.

Embarrassed, proud, obscurely moved himself, he tossed me a bunch of keys.

Now, he said, as I stood there weighing the keys in my cupped hands, some practical business. Tomorrow you will come with me to a bank, we will arrange the loan for you to complete the purchase of this apartment – do not worry, we will get it at a good price. Over some years, you will pay back this loan. My suggestion, you open an account with this bank also, this same branch – between you and our friend the manager tomorrow you can decide how much to pay each month. It is all quite simple.

From tomorrow, Joseph, if you wish, this is your own home for your life.

He was wandering restlessly from room to room as he said all this, smacking a wall with the flat of his hand, rattling doors, stamping on floorboards.

I could not think of anything to say.

You know what, he said, I have a friend who is good at things, you know, renovations? I suggest you have these floors sanded, polished. Good timber, this. Then the walls, a little plaster here and there, paint, a little furniture, pff! Finished.

Yes of course, I said, whatever you think.

Still in a daze.

Now Joseph, certain things I must tell you. I think it is best if you live here very quietly, the invisible mouse, yes? So. You should know, the person who lived here, he has moved away to another city. Not a good man, he was perhaps … compromised – Vichy, all that. He makes a new life, he is persuaded that perhaps he should receive for this place, not what is a good price in Paris but how much would buy him a reasonable apartment in ... where he has moved to.

I heard: he was matter-of-factly threatened.

I heard: live here quietly, draw no attention to yourself, such neighbours as pay attention will not enquire into the business of a self-effacing, serious man.

I heard: you will be ... absorbed.

I said nothing, simply turned, a little at a time, in a circle, seeing into one room after another. On my night walks I had loved to look up into apartments where the yellow light lay on polished furniture, on high packed wooden bookshelves, spilled out over stone windowsills. Now as I stood there I could overlay on the walls, on the floors, things I remembered from that aimless strolling – a bookcase here, lamps there and there, perhaps a low table ... there. As if I had been assembling this very apartment in my mind's eye, and now Henri had given me an empty cave, to fill as I pleased. To make me a shelter for the rest of my days.

Some day, perhaps, you will invite Miguel to visit here, he said.

No, I said, without having to think, no Henri, I don't think so. No.

He was angry, and then he thought better of it – all this in a flash of light and dark across his face. No, he said sadly, no young Joseph, you are right of course. Better the distance, now it is only this distance that keeps you close, eh?

I felt that as a bitter stab, but I bowed my head to the truth.

I put that thought carefully away, I would examine it later, I would be sure to.

Very good, he said, brisk and cheerful again, very good. Now, we have more to do. Come, do not forget to lock up.

The office he had found me was on the Rue Cochin, down near the river, near the Pont Archeveché. Maybe forty square metres, a number of easy chairs, a good, faded rug on the polished parquet. A small bathroom off, shower, no bath, and a tiny kitchenette. Coffee pots, cups, small saucepans, a wheezing fridge. Bookshelves with a decent selection of English books in the main room – histories, geographies, novels, a deal of miscellaneous non-fiction. Rather a smart room – a globe in one corner, I was amused to see. Altogether a professorial room, the few prints tasteful and modern, the framed antique map carefully chosen to evoke France in its grandeur.

I admit I burst out laughing. Henri looked worried: you don't think we've overdone it, do you? Too much?

No, I said, no, it's perfect.

You see, he said, quite serious, these will be conservative people, many of them, they will expect authority, an ambience that reinforces their sense of their own importance.

Henri, Henri, it's OK, it's OK, I get it. Don't worry.

Outside, on either side of and above the wide window, two small parabolic mirrors had been discreetly mounted. To give you a view of the door, he said, but I could see that, scarcely by accident, it gave me also a view of both ends of the street. Seeing my gaze linger, Henri smiled faintly: let me show you the back stairs, he said.

You will have a three-year lease, he said, all business now; three years, indefinitely renewable, payable monthly. You will need to keep careful accounts, all in order. Nothing deflects attention as does regularly paying your taxes. Of course, you need only return your earnings from the students we send you, or the referrals from those students. These will be respectable people, they will no doubt claim you as an expense, you must not be caught in a cross-check, eh? On the other hand, if you take private clients of your own ...

I felt as if I was on a conveyor belt, one moving a little too quickly for my taste. Still, that was Henri, never one to hang about when there was business to be taken care of.

OK, he asked, finally, you are satisfied?

I am at your disposal, dear Henri, I am perfectly content.

He checked to see if perhaps I was mocking him? I wasn't.

Good, he said, looking at his watch, frowning, calculating time against distance I thought. Very well, he said, I have made arrangements for dinner, you do not mind? Then, without giving me time to mind, he said: there is someone who wishes to meet you. Come.

Should I have been surprised, the heavy black car idling in the street below, Pascal at the wheel, Marie Louise in front? They smiled at me briefly, preoccupied. We drove for a long time, out of the city in the swathing dusk that came and went as avenues broadened, streets narrowed to canyons again. I was null and buoyant, content that nobody seemed inclined to make conversation. We came to a stop, angled across the road, at a high wooden gate set in high stucco walls, somewhere, I calculated, out in the western suburbs. Marie Louise stepped out, a little stiff, pushed the gates open, first one, then the other. A courtyard, a great bare tree in a circle of grass, a gravel driveway encircling that. The villa beyond, steps up to the front door. Subdued lights at intervals all around the walls. A car at the foot of the steps, the driver standing by a rear door, then somebody on the steps, a short, round man, his back to us, wearing a hat, a long back overcoat. Down, Henri said, quickly, his hand on top of my head, pushing me. The man at the door had been saying farewell. We coasted to a halt. Henri stepped out, I could hear his footsteps on the gravel, then his voice, resolute and strong, a murmured greeting in response. Steps on the gravel again, a car door slamming, the car pulling away, stopping so that the driver could open the gates again. The dull thump as they closed. I did not hear the car pull away down the street.

A rueful smile from Henri, no explanation. The easiest way out of the car was on my hands and knees. I was dusting myself down when the woman appeared in the doorway, framed by the hall light behind her. My three companions were looking at me strangely, perhaps better to say I simply could not read their expressions. The woman made a beckoning gesture, both arms, and Henri nodded me forward. As I climbed the steps, she stood to one side, gradually letting the light catch her face as I drew near.

When she saw the expression on my face she started laughing, a deep rumbling laugh that shook her body, shook me, too, as she crushed me in an embrace that left me as breathless as I was shocked. Delighted. Confused and almost overwhelmed.

Eleni.

My god, she said, my god but look at what they have made of you in Paris. *Que hombre*! Henri! Is it possible we are young again by some miracle? And here is our dear Miguel, all big bones and muscles, made young again! Ay! Ay! But come, come, the cook has left but the food remains. We must eat, drink!

Gaily she embraced them – Marie Louise, Pascal and then, but first she examined him at arm's length, Henri. Elbow linked in elbow, these two led us inside into a blaze of light, down a short corridor and into a long room. A lavishly laid table at the far end.

Food is a great solvent of confusion, wine even more so. Pascal, unexpectedly suave and debonair, had us bubbling with laughter all through the meal, Marie Louise matching him, sly, dry joke for joke, and I doubt that a single high functionary of the Party escaped unscathed that night with reputation intact. Henri and Eleni, like proud, slightly dissolute parents, beamed on us from where they sat side by side, two to our three across the table.

I simply sat there in a happy daze. Not that I was missing anything – the profound ease these men and women enjoyed in each other's company, the watchfulness in Henri, in Eleni, when they thought nobody was looking, above all perhaps the status

Pascal enjoyed, his lightly-worn air of authority: I saw that I had misjudged him, was shocked when I looked at him closely to see that he was the same age as Eleni and Henri. I was mulling this over when I looked up, found Eleni's eye on me. Ah Joseph, she said, what tales we might tell you if we chose, we three – tales of Spain when we were young and we were believers? Eh, child (this to Marie Louise), can you remember us as we were? Marie Louise smiled enigmatically, but Eleni's eyes had turned back to me. And you, my young *emigré*, my young revenant, I do not imagine you are always so silent? No? I will say this, you have plenty to say in your letters.

She saw me register this, process this; she reached across the table, patted my hand. No, I do not open your letters to Michael John, but he reads them to me, he is very happy for you.

I didn't like the direction in which this was heading; I began to feel uneasy, and this uneasiness communicated itself to the others. There was a rising from the table, a bustling, a clearing away. Eleni signalled that I should join her. We went into the next room, a log fire burning, low lamplight, two overstuffed brocade chairs by the fire.

So, she said, you should know that you can ask me what it pleases you to ask.

Leaning forward, her hunched shoulders, her elbows by her side, encouraging me to be bold.

I could not find words, not just then.

Bah, she said, let us make some clearance. Meetings, you understand, many meetings, all over the place. Some things, you must see the people for yourself, yes? So, yesterday I arrived, tomorrow I go back to Dublin. Here is a happy coincidence, the others (a wave of the hand here, invoking and dismissing my friends) they are elsewhere now, meeting some other comrades. You and I, we have this time, all is very well arranged, no?

How is he, I asked her then. Because she expected me to, because I wanted to know.

He is nearly seventy-five, you know, marvellous, marvellous, what a man. (I knew what age he was, his birthday a month away). She went on in a tumble: so lively, still lively, direct, straight. He spends time in Dublin with me, and you know, I spend time with him in Cork. You know, yes, that the men are gone? Yes, I said, I know all about that. She nodded, so you do, so you do. Well, he takes in people still, practical man, but also to help. A young couple with a baby, waiting to find a house, waifs and strays, waifs and strays – I like this phrase. Oh Cork is changing, you know, oh yes. I go there and there is nothing said, no scandal, no hassle.

I laughed, at her use of 'hassle', at the idea that her coming to stay with Michael – at his age, her age – might cause a scandal.

That earned me a cuff from the lioness, and I had it coming: still a boy, eh Joseph, you think it is absurd, unthinkable maybe, that we enjoy each other still? Still!

I bowed my head in mock penitence; tell him, I said, at his age twice a night is more than enough.

I had delighted her: oh I will tell him that, I will indeed. He will be happy that you consider his welfare but, heh, what about me, eh? You think twice a night is enough for me? Maybe I will not give him your advice after all.

She changed tack with a suddenness that unnerved me. What you do for Henri, what he has asked you to do, you are happy with this?

Yes, I said, after a moment, yes I have thought about it and yes, yes is my answer.

It occurred to me she had asked this question under instruction. That made me uneasy, it made me wonder just who has asked her to check on this.

The old witch! She, clucked. It was Henri who asked me to ask you, you see, I am not the bloody inquisition. Henri. He wishes to be sure, naturally, but also he wishes you to know you can walk away. It is your life, after all. And now, see, you have a question for me?

Yes, I said, why does Henri do so much for me?

Ah! Have you never asked him?

Eleni, I said, I do not know where Henri lives, if he is married, has children, what his precise role in the Party is, why he has never asked me to join, why he trusts me; I do not know if he ever takes a holiday, I do not know if he and Marie Louise are lovers, I do not know if he has blood on his hands ... and I do not know these things because I have chosen not to ask.

Well, she said, well! OK, he and Marie Louise are not lovers, we all have blood on our hands one way or another, he trusts you because you are to be trusted and the rest, it does not matter one way or another. How is that?

Leaning back, now, one hand washing the other slowly, eyes heavy-lidded. A curl of smoke from the fire came into the room, hesitated, doubled back.

That, as far as it goes, is fine. But my question, why does he do so much for me?

She sighed. You could be a very irritating young man, you know this? OK, I will tell you, but first I must tell you that now, who you have become, Henri does what he can for you because he likes and admires who you are. Well, OK, he thinks also you have chosen to become one of us.

One of us? What the hell does that mean?

Ssh, ssh, I will come back to this. First, I must tell you that when you had to go away, when we decided, Miguel and I, to send you to Henri, our friend accepted you because he owed Michael John, as he saw it, what you call a debt of honour.

Michael John would not accept that a debt was owed, he still does not and never will he accept this – in fact, for the love that has been shown to you he considers himself always in debt to Henri.

Of course I looked puzzled, I was puzzled for god's sake.

She sighed again.

OK, I will tell you the story. Come sit here, come, sit.

I sat at her feet, my head heavy, leaning back against the side of her chair. I looked into the fire, I inhaled the woodsmoke.

Jarama, she said, it was just after Jarama. We were in the same detachment, the three of us. Miguel was our section commander. I was proud of myself, I had been given a light machine-gun, a Degtiakov. A good weapon. There was a valley ahead of us, we were dug in on a hill, some ruined walls just below us. We had not eaten for two days, we had very little water. No shade – the olive trees had been felled by shells and bullets, so tortured the olives, so white their flesh, the stumps.

Wave after wave, they came in waves, the Moors, up through the valley, inch by inch. Overhead, the Italian planes, Fiats, Capronis. We had good fighters, though, Russian, we called them Chatos. They beat the Fascists back for us, but in the air only. Still, that was something. They had begun to grace us with commissars, the Russians. We were Communists, of course, me and Henri, but we hated those men, and we knew that they hated us. They were there, this was the official party line, to ensure discipline. Order. Proper military order. There was an English boy, a pale, skinny English boy, a schoolboy we said, no more than a schoolboy, but very brave, very brave. A shell landed just in front of him, he was OK, I do not know how, but then we saw him stand up, screaming, brushing himself and brushing himself as if he was on fire. The comrade who had been fighting by his side, you see, the shell had ripped him apart, all of his flesh and his blood and his guts were all over the English boy. He would not stop screaming, he began to run back towards us, all awkward like a badly made marionette, screaming. And this commissar, he jumped in front of him, his revolver in his hand, he was roaring at this poor boy to go back, to go back, and then this Russian, he stood back, he raised his revolver and he shot that boy right in the face. No retreat, you see, no retreat.

You would have said the entire battlefield fell silent. To us it seemed like that. Henri stood up, he stood up very calmly and he began to walk towards that commissar. He had put his gun down, his rifle, I remember he did it very carefully, so that it would not get dirty. He had a knife in his hand. He was walking towards the commissar, very slow, deliberate. The commissar, this time no shouting, no cursing. He raised his revolver, he held it very steadily, this I remember, and all the time Henri kept walking towards him, also steady, steady.

Her voice in the far away, her hand stroking my hair, stroking my hair. A log spat and settled.

Miguel. Out of the corner of my eye I saw him raise his rifle. He aimed very carefully. He was standing, you see, off to one side, very calm. Then he shot the commissar, once, in the neck. He looked around him, then, still very calm. One after another, the men and women in our section, put our hands over our eyes. We had seen nothing. Nothing. Henri, he too stood there, he looked at Miguel, Miguel looked at him, nothing said, two men standing on a hill in a foreign country, fighting a war we knew was already lost.

Miguel walked over, picked up the commissar's revolver, a Nagant, I remember, I do not know why he had a Nagant, most of the other Russians had the new Tokarev pistols. Heh, what things we notice, eh? He picked up the revolver, Miguel. He tucked it in his belt.

She stroked my hair, stroking, stroking ...

And two of the Andalucian comrades, we called them the two Antonios, they dragged the body of the commissar to the bit of wall down below us, very dangerous but they were lucky, and from below they pushed him up so that his head and shoulders were above the wall. Almost immediately, the machine-gunners from the valley cut him to ribbons.

Next day I got a bullet in the ass and they sent me away.

I looked up, startled.

She grinned at me, sadly I thought, but a flick of the imp in there, in those eyes that had seen so much. Yes, I know, in Dublin I insisted on rump, did I not? Boy, let me tell you, one of the pleasures of age is that we can be as coarse as when we were young.

Soldiers, you see? We were soldiers. Henri is alive because your Michael John, my Miguel, our Miguel, took a soldier's decision. Because we were soldiers, Henri believes that he owes a debt of honour; because we were soldiers, Miguel disagrees.

One thing he has said, he has said it many times, your grandfather: how happy he is for you, that you were not born a soldier.

I was far away then for a while, the boy taking that heavy revolver from its hiding place, the young man in the rain, across the street from the police station ...

I think that I actually fell asleep.

When I opened my eyes, Henri was standing over me, amused.

Eh, Eleni, what have you done to this young man, eh? She sighed: old stories, Henri my dear, I was telling him old stories.

If he suspected, as I think he must have, so heavy and evident the sorrow in the air, the bitter-sweet odour of the unforgotten, he did not show it. Henri had always the gift of grace.

I slept all the way back to Paris. I do not remember climbing the stairs to my old apartment, and I do not remember saying goodbye to Eleni.

She died that following spring. We took ourselves to the Jardin des Plantes, Pascal, Henri, Marie Louise and I. We stood by an olive tree, and Henri took a stone from his pocket, scrabbled a moment in the loose earth and buried it there, fanning the dry earth over the hole with his splayed fingers. We stood in beside him, unspeaking, until he shrugged, looked up at the blank sky, looked at us for a moment, one by one; and then he walked away. We left him to himself.

37

I walk naked into the bathroom. The heating has been on overnight. I stand before the full-length mirror and consider the man I have become.

By an act of will, like an editor cutting together the footage of forty years, I make myself see that man ageing, riffling down through the years to where I stand now. Freeze frame.

Still upright, if bowed in the shoulders. Hair *en brosse*, white where once it was a deep brown. More belly over the not-so-shrivelled genitals, a slight knock in the knees. Good posture, I tell myself, all those years of walking, walking everywhere. Chest perhaps slightly caved in. Jowls slight but perceptible, pouches under the eyes. The eyes. I have never been able to fathom what lies behind my own eyes. Still can't.

What I am looking for, I don't know. That poem by the Russian, Mandelstam:

> What shall I do with this body that has been given me,
> so much at one with me, so much my own?

I remember reading it, the American woman, June? No, Judith, that politician's mistress, a troubled soul. Gave me the book as an apology, had followed her man to his lessons, thinking she would find him with some other woman. A shit, the politician.

Reading that poem, I remember it, when she had dressed and left, walking through into the bathroom, this bathroom, taking a long cold look at this body that has been given me. All those years ago.

And today, I find nothing to hold my attention. What was I looking for, though? Some ... reassurance. Some reassurance in the eyes.

Not there, no, but something I had not expected all the same, not in the eyes, exactly, but in the regard: kindness.

A soft kind of unsettling shock, not unpleasant, to find that I look upon myself kindly. That I can think myself kind, without embarrassment.

Hah. Shower, track suit trousers, tee shirt; coffee, toast yesterday's baguette, slather it with butter. Standing at the kitchen window. Light rain again, freshens the place, light enough I can leave a window part open.

That day, it comes back to me now with a sudden impact, that day when Henri suggested I become a teacher of English, I make it sound as if I simply accepted his proposition, just as I'd accepted his placing me in the Sorbonne, but it wasn't really like that. I see now that I *chose* to accept, just as I chose to accept the offer of this apartment that has been my home for so many years. How to explain this? I don't know. Perhaps it's as simple as this: having no ambition, having never had any ambition, I make instant decisions when presented with a choice. And always I choose what will be *interesting*. Just that. As with, say, Vincent. I could have walked past him, that evening I came across him, fiddling with the car by the Pantheon. I could have walked past, but I felt, just at that moment, that it would be interesting to stop, to talk to him, to see where that would lead.

Anyway ...

Today we have dusting of books. Dyson, the English engineer, what a smart fellow! A shit, I think, but smart all the same. The cyclone vacuum, no bags, no mess, no diminution in sucking power – brilliant. I drag the cheerful yellow machine out of the hall closet and into the front room, ridiculously pleased that I do not creak or groan when I bend to plug it in. Good man!

I built these shelves myself, I studied the Sorbonne shelving carefully, made sure to leave space above the books for dusting.

So much easier with this machine, its brush attachment. Row upon row, bay after bay, humming as I go, pausing every now and then to wonder at where these snatches of song come from.

Madame, of course, has already done floors, furniture, bathroom, etc., but she draws the line at the books.

Finished this room, I nip back into the kitchen for a second coffee from the thermos jug – that old joke, how does it know? – and then the back room.

How elaborately we contrive to deceive ourselves. When I pause, having reached the journals, I accept finally that this is somehow the point of this morning's exertions. It was late last night when I finished typing, late, very late; almost I came through here, I could see myself reaching for the red-bound volumes, the tall notebooks where I recorded, meticulously, things I had heard in that office of mine that seemed to me useful. But I knew I was too tired, I knew it would be better left to the clear light and the clear head of morning.

First things first, I tell myself, finish the work.

I do that, empty the cylinder, restore the laptop to its hibernation.

The journals I have left in a neat pile on the side table.

I pull over a chair, pick a volume at random. But after all, it isn't what the journals contain. No use to me now, all that meticulous note-making, and nothing to be gained from exhuming what time has rendered ephemeral or redundant. I gather the journals together again, patting and tapping, building an unsteady pile. I halve the pile, carry each separate bundle back to the shelves. How the sun over the years has faded the once-rich red of the spines, how the black ink on the carefully placed labels has gone brown with time, the carbon leaching from the ink. I do not know why, but from the start I formed the habit of writing the date on each volume on the last day of the year whose gleanings it contained.

It is enough, I decide, enough for the purposes of my record to note the existence of these journals. Their day-to-day, week to month to year siftings from so many conversations, these are scarcely important except to some specialist in a discipline that has yet to be named and funded.

I set down here that they exist, that down through the years I recorded, for what purpose I could not exactly say, what I gleaned from my clients that might be of interest to Henri and his circle. No client names, of course, it was always my instinct to avoid names, but it would be a simple matter for whoever should have my appointments diary for those years (these, too, exist, I passed them on) to correlate names, dates and times with the journal entries. If anyone could be bothered.

Of course, it would have to be someone capable of reading Irish in the old script we learned in school.

I refuse to explain this.

I walk through this beautiful place that I have made for myself, long since my own, approving of its order, its polished and dusted lustre of home and comfort, its evidence of the life of the mind, its witness that here lived, here lives, a man at home in his body, in his mind, in his place. A man at peace.

The next two lines of that Mandelstam poem:

> For the calm happiness of breathing, for the joy
> of being alive, tell me where should I be grateful?'

Yes, Judith, her name was Judith. A truly dreadful woman, wracked and vengeful; yet not unkind, I suppose, in her desperation, and perceptive enough to choose well with her gift in apology. The small debts we owe to people who float for only a moment into our lives.

I am temporising here, I know it, because I am expecting a call, and when he does call, just before lunchtime, I know that I will be granted a respite from memory for the day. By all means, I tell him; Vincent, I have the afternoon free, give me half an hour to get in some things to make lunch.

An elegant grey silk suit: he hangs the jacket carefully in the hall, the black silk shirt well cut. His manner ... distrait.

How accurate the word, in English and in French. I am inordinately pleased to have it trip on to my tongue. My smile puzzles him, I shake my head: no matter, a stray thought, forgive me.

Very well, I say, clearing the things away, adding the pot of coffee to the tray, let's be comfortable.

He looks pointedly at my house cleaning get-up, smiles genuinely for the first time. Old man, he says, old man ... but his amusement will not let him finish the sentence.

My article appears tomorrow, he said, relieved that we are now down to business.

Good, I say, and I wait.

Your friend, he says, a most interesting woman. I know, I say, and very well connected, I know.

He is suspicious. You know? She has ... you have spoken with her?

No, I say, but I know her, she will have set up some meetings, persons of influence, people who can be helpful? Already you have been meeting certain powerful people.

Yes, he says. He is going to continue but I override him.

Vincent, I tell him, I need you to understand some things. First of all, for your own sake, you need to be very clear, very serious about what you are doing now. I introduced you, yes, but she makes her own judgements. She read the piece, she can see without asking that I take you seriously, but you should understand two things here: she takes a careful look at you, and she likes what she sees. Good. The second thing, you are needed: in the politics of the present moment, the near future, someone like you is needed. And if you are serious, and clever, and clear, that someone can be, exactly, you.

What he says, wounded now, near bitter, you mean a presentable *beur*, passing for white, is that it? What James Baldwin talks about?

You've read Baldwin, I say, and immediately regret the question.

Yes, Joseph, imagine, an Algerian who has read Baldwin. What a shock, eh?

He thinks it is anger, and he gets some comfort from expressing it, but I know, I see it in his posture, he is afraid. Well, that's all right.

Vincent, I say, I am not going to be insulted in my own home. More exactly, I am not going to have my intelligence insulted. I would have thought your generation considered Baldwin old-fashioned; I would have thought it unlikely anyone your age would have bothered to read him. You know fucking well I am not a racist. I will thank you not to insult me.

For a moment I think he is going to strike me. He's on his feet, looming over me, wound up like I don't know what – and then he checks himself, amazed to find he is on his feet, chock full of aggression, about to vent – what? Rage? I see him ask himself: what is this rage? Where does it come from?

Ah would you sit down and make yourself useful, I say, and pour the coffee. Would you like a biscuit, there are some in the kitchen?

And the tension goes out of him, it melts away, it flows away, he watches it flow away, so to speak, entranced with himself. He looks like someone who has just discovered that he can fly.

He's all good humour now, flopping back heavily into the armchair, then pushing himself up again to pour the coffee, add milk and one sugar to my cup.

Laughing, he says: man, Gen is right, you know? You are some kind of fucking witch. Hey, I never heard you swear before, you know that? You sound very Irish when you swear.

Fuck away off with yourself, I say, and he laughs louder, now completely at his ease.

I look at him carefully, content that he is no longer on his guard.

He wants to know, once and for all, who I am.

He wants to know why I want to help him, have helped him.

He wants me to tell him he will succeed in what he desires for himself.

For this, I have set aside the afternoon.

I came here in 1960, I say, and he settles, picking up my tone. He knows he is in for a long story. Some trouble at home (I wave it away, he nods), a friend of my family, old friend, he took me in. I studied, I found that I liked it here, I settled. I set up as a teacher of English, in this way I made many friends. You understand? Over these many years, I made many friends. You see what I am like, yes? That night we met, I decided to make a friend. And here you are. Vincent, all one has to do is endure, you see? One endures, one develops the habits of sympathy, one makes friends. Two of these you have met, perhaps you understand what I mean? A certain sympathy? It pleases me, to make friends, to introduce them to each other. It feels like, oh I don't know, a contribution?

He is nodding encouragingly, I am making him happy. Good.

He motions to be excused, goes out to the kitchen returns with biscuits on a plate. Shortbread. As he is offering me the plate, as I reach to take one, he says, very softly: Joseph, please look at me. Surprised, I turn my eyes up to him.

Holding my gaze he retreats to his chair, settles leaning forward.

Joseph, he says, still soft, is this what you put in the book you are writing?

It is, I say, expanded a little, of course, but yes.

I feel a faint flicker of unease, a tongue darting inside my chest. He tilts his head to one side, he says: then I will not read it. If I want lies I go to the cinema, I watch the news. I have no need of your lies, old man. This kind of shit, I do not need it.

I shot a policeman, I say, surprising us both.

Ah, he says, but his gaze never wavers. And?

It's all in the book, I say.

Ah.

I never went back, I say, because I shot him so that nothing could ever be the same again.

Is that true? He seems concerned.

I don't know, I say, the doubt also is in the book.

You never married?

No.

No children?

No.

I would not have said so, me.

I tense, fearing he is about to make a wrong leap. He sees it, his smile is gentle.

Ah Joseph, I know you have not adopted me, do not worry. Remember, I told you, I also have taken you for a friend. Now tell me, you have been a political man, yes?

I nod.

But not in Ireland, I think, and not for Ireland?

No.

Shall I tell you what I think?

Please ...

I think, Joseph, you are a collector of souls. I think this is what you do, you go about in the world and you collect a certain kind of soul. Me, for instance.

And why, Vincent, would I want to collect you?

What, old man, you think that now I will speak of myself, offer you such an escape? 'My life story, my hopes and ambitions' by Vincent? A little essay? No, but no. I am who I am, and that is what you collected when you collected me. Who I am.

I close my eyes then, I close my eyes and lean back in my chair. I think I am on the point of falling asleep. He waits.

I come back. The room is still sharp, the air clear, light gleams on the edges of my shelves, a softer light on the spines of my books. He gives me time, but he has not finished.

I will tell you what I deduce, Joseph, and you perhaps will tell me if I am right. All over this city, let us speak for the moment only of the city, all over the city there are serious people. Each is serious in a different way, but this they have in common, that they are serious, OK? Many in politics, all different kinds, some in the law, in journalism, some driving buses, some not to be romantic but some sweeping the streets, some clerks in the *Mairies* – hey, nurses, grandmothers, cops, teachers, even a footballer or two, eh? Zidane, eh, I think Zidane is serious? And you are serious. And I am serious. These two friends to whom you introduce me, these are very serious people, I think. One who can make my half-brother appear, disappear, appear again; one who can tell me, two days after we meet for the first time, that I can be a member of parliament, no, that I can, if I wish, be made a member of parliament. That this can be arranged.

You smile, Joseph, but I do not think it is because you think this is funny. I say what I say, you are a collector of souls. And now I want to say something else, OK?

He has been fluid, accurate, clear – and now he hesitates.

You see, dear Joseph, I do not wish to give offence?

I motion him to proceed, proceed. That rolling hand movement.

Joseph, I wish to say very formally thank you. I wish to say,

I will not let you down. I wish to say, I will try very sincerely to be honest, and only to deal with serious people. I shall try to help. I do not know how this happened, but when we met, such an accident, after we met I went home to Genevieve very thoughtful; I would not come to bed, and when she lost patience and asked what was wrong, what had happened, I said to her: all this time we have been awake and we did not know it. You think she got mad at me, asked me had I been smoking hashish again? Eh? No, you know what? She laughed in my face, she covered my face with kisses and she laughed some more and she said: fool! I could have told you that! And when I said, why didn't you, she said, very gentle all of a sudden: because this you have to find out for yourself. This everyone has to find out for themselves.

I think he had not meant to say any of this – perhaps better, had not meant to say so much of this, and very likely not in these words. He sat back, panting, surprised and uneasy to find himself panting, even a moment clawing for breath. Too many words, I think dispassionately, too many words and he will need to be careful with this: the truth in there, but a small truth, and easily lost in the roll of words, the onrush, the heady giddiness. He really will need to watch that. Not by word or look do I betray this judgement. He will have Gen, in any case, to cool him down, to get him to focus on the small, definite things that can be done. But for now, encourage, encourage!

Well, I say, for that thank you, I thank you, but there is no need. As for the seat in parliament, are you ready?

(Yes, I think, I read him right, the rush of emotion already falling away, sobering up, look at him sober up.)

I think so, he said. Your friend the secret policeman, he is astute you know. I think right wing, well of course, but not racist, no, he said an interesting thing: better for the Republic an

Algerian socialist than a sullen Jihadist or a fascist masquerading as a liberal. You see what he is saying here? This, from such as him, this I had not expected.

(Interesting, I think, that he starts with him.)

And your journalist friend, she says – I know she was being funny, but still – when she met me a second time, with Gen, that we would be what the Americans call a dream ticket.

(Yes, she would have taken Gen's measure all right. More than you have, my boyo. Or perhaps I am wrong about this?)

So, yes. I am already a member of the party (are you now?) and after the article appears tomorrow she is having a little gathering, you know, officials, some Ddputies ... so that I can get to know some people.

For a terrible moment I fear I have misjudged him. Not that it matters, if I have made a mistake I will do what I always do and walk away.

Then he says, cool as you like: what do you think, Joseph, do I sound like an ambitious little shit, eh? One of those who starts out with good intentions but loses his soul, bit by bit, until the morning he chokes on the vomit of his own betrayals, his own conceit and vanity?

Electricity in the air, no sound from the street outside, no sound from anywhere. Fires burning inside him, but what kind of fires? Almost I am afraid of him. I consider my answer carefully.

I say: yes, that's exactly what you sound like.

A motor cycle goes roaring past, outside and below, I hear girls squealing, a screech of brakes far off ... Vincent is roaring with laughter, pounding the arm of his chair, even kicking his legs in the air. I have never seen anyone in the real world kick their legs in the air.

Oh Joseph, Joseph, I wish you could have seen your face! I

wish Gen was here! You looked at me as I imagine you would look at a dog that might be about to shit on this very handsome Persian rug! It is Persian, isn't it?

The fucker! Playing with me! If you can convey all that, I say, without ...

... without actually saying it in so many words? Exactly!

I have to say it: I am lost for words, lost in admiration. Now this I had not expected. Ha! (And serves you right, old man, I tell myself, you're getting far too full of yourself lately).

And, I am taken aback. Already he knows what they are like, the kingmakers, their puppets, these public and not so public men. And women. He knows their dead souls and their dreadful ambitions, their vanities and their enmities, their grim satisfactions in petty victories, their undying viciousness, their airless circles of mutual masturbation.

How many years did it take me, to recognise the smooth urbanities of evil? A thought strikes me, it really feels as if I have been struck: Cassady, the first moment I laid eyes on him, I saw him for what he was.

He cannot know what is going through my mind, this Vincent, but he feels me charge up, and he is already electric with earned self-satisfaction – I can accept his admiration of me now, now that he sees so clearly how much I admire and applaud his insight.

Now we're both buzzing with energy, charged up as we are with the nameless knowledge, that stuff you either get or you don't and that makes us sound like such vacuous idiots when we try to put it into words.

We have to calm down, we both know this, we have to calm down now. On the edge of being absurd.

Tell me, he says, your real life, seriously now, is that what you've been writing?

Yes, I say, as much as I can understand of it.

And, forgive me, has it been difficult?

I do not know how to answer him. Has it? I think, I say carefully, I think it has been, but I'm not sure. Not the writing, no; I surprise myself every day, you know? So many words ... but, difficult? I think I will only know when it is finished, you understand?

Will you show it to me? Some day?

I will, I say, when I'm ready.

You mean, when I'm ready?

That, too.

That's fair, he says, that's fair. And, in the book?

Yes?

He hesitates, but from delicacy, not doubt. He gestures towards the shelves, to the row upon row of books on Ireland – history, politics, geography, novels, poetry, the whole shooting works: in the book, will you explain why you turned your back on your country?

Yes, I say, I will try to do that – and all of a sudden, not dramatically, very quietly in fact, I feel a profound sadness, a deep-down dark and heavy sadness, a welling downward of weighted sadness – I know if I tried to rise now out of my chair I could not do it.

Then I say, and I surprise us both, no, I do not think I will do that. I would not know how to do that.

Outside and around this feeling, like something travelling on a band of light, the only way I can find to describe this, myself circling, wondering at myself, looking in on an emptiness.

I am aware that Vincent is stricken, knows he has touched off some terrible quiet implosion, but I am fascinated, not just by this unexpected sorrow, this depth of sorrow, but by this being also outside the sorrow, looking in.

I don't understand, he says finally, thwarted and helpless, upset that I am upset, upset too at his own helplessness.

No, I say, no, how could you? I don't understand myself.

After a while he says, you know what we should do?

I put my hands up.

It's sunny, he says, it's warm, what would you say we walk in the Luxembourg, kick some leaves, maybe go for a beer?

I'll get my coat, I say, leave the washing up.

OK, he says, if you insist. Still grinning as the door closes softly behind us.

Vincent is ahead of me as we emerge onto the street, Mme Frenaud, hurrying by with a heavy bag, almost bumps into him, recoils. I see the look of disdain on her face before she sees me, and realises that Vincent is with me. Confusion, a scurry of feelings like shadows across her face. She bobs me a quick interrogative salute, face freezing over already, before hurrying on, neck rigid.

Vincent is amused, but not entirely. He looks after her thoughtfully. I am not sure that I like what I see in his face.

Come on, I say, prodding him, before the sun goes.

38

So then, my new life as a teacher, if we are to call it teaching ...

Within a month of seeing my new office for the first time, I was installed – with a roster of pupils, not many, enough to get me started.

You see, Henri had said, you must give this some thought. You do not know this, I think, or perhaps you do, but when I look at you, when somebody looks at you, they see a French person. But these pupils, these people who will find themselves recommended to you, they will expect an Irish man, OK? Your accent when you speak English, well it will be, what is the word, inflected, yes? But naturally, you have spent some time here, you are living here. So, how do you become Irish, eh? Tell me what you think.

A Saturday morning, a pleasant little café on the Rue Valette, cramped at a small round table on the pavement. Henri is expansive, unbuttoned, for some reason smoking a small black cheroot. The rank smell of it, his eyes half-closed as he looks up and down the street, a man so thoroughly at home in his life that he might be the *Patron*, relaxing with a nephew after a satisfactory week's business, indulging himself with a lazy morning.

So, young Joseph. He is patient, he has been waiting for an answer.

I know what to do, I said, come visit me on Monday, you'll see.

He likes it when I tease him, something I have only lately begun to do. He smiles, I enjoy his approval.

Good, he says, now what do you propose when they become curious, when they wish to know more about you, eh?

I hadn't thought of that.

You see, ha! What would you do without me, eh? So, listen, I will be your pupil now: I am one who speaks English, I can read it after a fashion, I am ambitious to advance myself and it is now the American century, OK? I do not like this, but one must accept facts. I have given this matter some thought, I decide that what I need is practice, to speak English with a sophisticated person, one who can armour me for the language of politics, the speech of international business. Somebody knows someone who has heard of a serious young man ... yes, yes, and so on. You follow me? Of course you do.

Ah, he is Irish? Good, I am a person who does not trust the English with their superior airs, and as for learning from an American ... After a while, of course, I will wish to know who he is, this Irishman, how he came to be here, so well-informed on world matters, so understanding of our France.

He must tell me something about himself, but I must not be too inquisitive, I must not feel encouraged to take too much interest, eh? So, Joseph, I think what you must be, you must be an ex-priest!

And oh how pleased he is, how he breaks out in smiles when he sees that I get it at once. Ah bravo, Joseph, he says, bravo! So quick!

Ireland, I say. How it begins to close in on one, its narrowness, its elevation of peasant values clothed in piety and fear of the body. One had studied abroad, perhaps in Louvain, one had grown increasingly restive, the idiocy of brute faith, of one's superiors ...

Yes, he says, very good, nobody knows anyone who has ever been in Louvain, continue, continue.

Yes. And the food, and the innocence which grates on one as a kind of stupidity – or, the stupidity that does not recognise itself as innocence, that thinks of itself as worldly, eh? And, life being what it is, one meets a woman ... and then one day, one realises that, let me see now, ah yes, that life is elsewhere. And the woman is married, naturally. The affair takes its course, perhaps she is overcome finally by guilt – you think excessive that she dies tragically in an accident? You are right, too much, she goes back to her husband, penitent, meek – and one is rebuked by one's superiors, perhaps an internal exile, some god-forsaken place, some grey town in a midlands bog? Yes, of course, and one day, one wakes up and realises one does not believe in anything, that one has perhaps never believed, and it is raining, the interminable rain, there is perhaps the smell of boiling meat from the kitchen, there will be supplicants, smelly old frightened people to be visited, and ... one leaves. One simply leaves, without fuss or fanfare. One withdraws one's savings, one leaves for, on a whim, why not, Paris.

And here you are in Paris, a solitary man, dignified, taking the measure of your life, your next steps ... Joseph, you frighten me!

So perfect! Ah but, beware, I see a trap.

We have been sipping pastis, he orders two more.

You see, he says, to a certain kind of Parisienne you will be an irresistible challenge, you understand. Young, grave, handsome – yes, yes, do not interrupt, I say handsome – melancholy, and sexually unspoiled. Yum yum!

Yum yum? I snort pastis onto my knees, half-choking, laughing so hard that I get an airlock in my chest. I recover myself while Henri is beaming. When I am myself again, he makes the same idiot gesture with his scrabbling hands, his upper front teeth frantically nibbling his lower lip. A demented squirrel.

A woman going by giggles, puts her hand over her mouth, totters away downhill on spindly heels. When she goes to cross the road, she looks back over her shoulder; Henri gives her a vigorous wave and she waves back, tentatively, not entirely sure the man isn't mad. I'm not sure myself.

As we part, I am trying to remember if I have ever seen him so light-hearted, and even as I'm wondering I realise that I couldn't, I simply couldn't imagine asking him why he's in such good humour.

On Monday morning he arrives at the office early. I confront him with a sober-looking young man, tweed jacket, shabby but clean corduroys, hair greased back, big horn-rimmed glasses set firmly on his nose – defiantly nervous, nervously defiant, take your pick.

I see I worried you about the women, he says, and when I look at him blankly, he gestures derisively at the mirror in which we are both contemplating my metamorphosis. I can't see anyone much falling for that fellow, he says. But, very good, Joseph, very good. They will trust you and faintly despise you in equal measure.

Now remember, he says, handing me the list of clients, remember to look stony-faced when they pay you. An unfortunate necessity on your part, but one must live. They'll be impressed by how much you're charging, these are the kind of people who measure their status by how much they have to pay for things. And because they must pay you, they will be forgetting you as they go out the door. Until next time, of course. And so on. Now, good luck.

And thus the long procession began: civil servants, functionaries of all kinds, middle-ranked businessmen, female lawyers, bankers, scientists, newspaper columnists, technocrats and politicians, *Enarques* and mid-rank diplomats, wives of all the above but never the husbands of the female lawyers unless they themselves were civil servants, functionaries ...

It was, in a word, astonishing, how many they were, the more so because almost without exception, I found myself dealing with deep-dyed chauvinists, salving their consciences about speaking

English at all by virtue of learning it from an Irishman. To a man and a woman they are French exceptionalists, vengefully disdainful of England, admiring and deeply resentful in equal measure of the (temporary, they assumed) American ascendancy.

But, that said, these were practical people, for them the world was as it is, and English had become unfortunately necessary.

The women lawyers, incidentally, intrigued me: intellectual for the most part, in all the best senses, they felt there would be more oxygen for their ambitions in the Anglophone world, more sorority, more scope. Well, they learned, they learned.

And the information flowed, just as Henri and the comrades had foreseen.

Astonishing what people will tell you in such circumstances. After a lesson or two, I would have established a template with each student. I would ascertain why they wished to improve their English, and then I'd stay one step ahead of them by keeping up with newspapers, magazines, developments in their field. Not as much work as it might seem, since most of them were remarkably incurious about what was happening in the Anglophone world, they wished merely to develop the capacity more forcefully to project their own Franco-centric point of view. They saw the language as conveying or reinforcing their own power to prevail – which meant, inevitably, working with me to learn how to convey what mattered most to them.

With an equal inevitability, I ceased to be a person to them, I ceased to be someone from whom they would think of guarding their thoughts.

With these I soon became skilled at framing our conversations so that my subsequent notes might have substance, might be useful. I rapidly learned to be oblique, to cast my hook into the by-eddies that swirled and doubled around the mainstream of someone's preoccupations, to fish for the judgements and hesitations, the half-thoughts and qualifications that reveal so much when properly understood.

Soon, I was making a good, even a very good living from working a few hours each day. What I heard that I thought might be of use, I meticulously noted in my red journals and at night I would type up what seemed to me relevant or useful.

I would arrive at the office in the early morning, leave the typed notes in an envelope on my desk and go for a coffee. When I'd get back, the notes would be gone.

A simple process, kept going for thirty years. Even after Henri died.

It may seem strange that I never questioned the use to which all this information was being put. So be it. I didn't. I could recognise useful information when I heard it, I presumed that useful information would be put to use. As simple as that, I'm afraid.

At first, I know, my clients were carefully steered towards me; as time went on, I began to get referrals from clients, their friends or colleagues, and these would in time refer others to me. I managed not to get swamped by inventing reasons to dispense with those who had been visiting me longest, almost always by telling them they had achieved a standard of proficiency that made me superfluous to their needs. Bores I gave short shrift to and discouraged, I did not see why I should be bored – and in any case bores rarely had anything of much interest to offer.

Referrals from the comrades became less frequent over time, and thus, as I learned, by the laws of inversion, more important. There was a period when I seemed to be seeing nuclear engineers, a time when Eurocrats were numerous, a time indeed when I seemed to be getting a share of Socialist Party functionaries – a fruitful period, that.

I was off to one side, I put it to myself once like this, off to one side of the graph of French politics, tracking and sometimes even predicting its evolutions. There was satisfaction, I am obliged to say, in this.

Mostly, though, I took my satisfactions on a day-to-day basis; I might enjoy a particular conversation with a particular client, and then it was over. Of no moment to me. Erased.

I was good at what I did, I made sure of that, and I enjoyed it (mostly) as I did it, whether teaching or evaluating and reporting, but I did not think of it as my life. It was simply what I did.

I did not think I was accumulating a life.

I did not think of myself as building a life.

A phrase that I read once, I remember when it was, a winter's day in a bookshop on the Rue Cardinal Lemoine, slush on the pavements, I was wearing a red scarf knotted outside the collar of my overcoat, a phrase that I read once clicked deep inside me, sent me home feeling full to the brim with, well, with life: 'I am a travelling point of view'.

I am a travelling point of view.

For Henri, for his colleagues and comrades, whoever they were, I was a point of view, a source, a purveyor of food for thought.

To myself I was always myself, a travelling point of view who had of necessity to do certain things in order to stay alive, yes, but was neither bound nor defined by those things.

I might have been doing far less agreeable things.

Of course I had private pupils too, so to speak: strays and oddments, men and women who wanted to read and speak English for often *recherché* reasons. Some who were collectors of accomplishments, some who were married to, in love with or perhaps in rivalry with Anglophones, some men and women of independent mind, tuned to the flow of the world and wishing to understand the zeitgeist.

Some of these were, indeed, the women Henri had warned against, but for the most part I found them agreeable, and I did not deny myself the occasional affaire if the attraction was mutual.

Once, why not say so, once only I found I had become besotted – I scheduled this woman for the last meeting on Friday, in the hope that we might extend the session to dinner, to ...

I would sweat, waiting for her to ring on the door; I was never once comfortable in her company; when she'd leave (extricate herself would be more accurate) I would sit like a dead thing staring unseeing out the window. Oh I had it bad, for about two months. One Friday she found me offhand, perhaps even borderline rude, and she never came back again. It would not have been possible to explain that, simply, a fever had broken.

With one man I would sometimes go to jazz clubs, with another, for a while, to wine tastings. There was a woman with a passion for the cinema ...

And so on.

I found that I was not particularly interested in making and keeping friends.

I would go a bit of the road with someone, from idleness sometimes, sometimes because they involved me in some passion of theirs for a while, but my interest would ... fade.

No harm, no blame.

Was I incurious, culpably incurious? It might be said.

Some things one does not need to know.

I adduce this: from time to time, someone would turn up as a student, a client (I never could settle on a term) who was a functionary of the Party. Some hardfaced, greyfaced person who had been designated to represent the Party in some international forum or other.

I knew perfectly well to walk very carefully with these ones, to be bland, a little dull, to affect a certain political naivety, perhaps even (a former cleric, after all) a certain anxiety that made them tremble with a feint enjoyable cruelty.

These had been manoeuvred my way so that Henri and friends could test for themselves, via my reports, certain nuances of personality, certain intentions of policy that were being masked from the rank and file. By this time the Party was well on the way to being sidelined by history, but I had long since figured out that Henri & Co. were a living tendency inside a dying host body that was for the most part entirely unaware of the work they were trying to accomplish. It was useful, I imagined, to know how exactly these apparatchiks were contributing, in their sclerotic way, to the ossification, the murder by boredom, of the ideology whose empty platitudes they continued to mumble by rote.

There might also, of course, have been a question of settling scores – I never made the mistake of imagining that Henri and his comrades were in the business of making omelettes without breaking eggs.

All in all, I consider my work offered an opportunity to exert ... influence.

How it was exerted, whether or not it had any discernible effect, I never cared to know.

This was my life for many years.

39

Dark, and a full moon. I went down to the river a little while ago, down the Rue de Cardinal Lemoine, then across the river, past the house of Abelard and Héloise, then in off the quay to the Rue Cochin. In Paris, they manage to contrive things so that a building, a street, is always changing and yet, somehow, always remains the same. I stood for a long time, wreathed in thought and cigarette smoke, staring up at the window behind which so much of my life had passed. Eventually I grew uncomfortable; it occurred to me that I looked like a character from some bad 1960s movie, staring mournfully at the apartment where love had died, some shit like that, and I took myself brusquely away home.

To this place where so much of my life has passed.

I feel it tonight, the weight of accumulated years. Not as a burden, I must say, not as a burden but simply as a fact. I go from room to room, turning on lights, stopping a while to see if I can attract whatever is stalking me. Nothing.

Right then. I roll up my sleeves, I fill the kettle, plug it in. I put an inch or so of water in a saucepan, a dollop of olive oil, put the saucepan on the gas. (I have always thought in inches and feet, yards, I've just noticed that). Now a heavy pan, a good glug of olive oil, a good pinch of oregano, should be fresh of course but not at this time of year. Fine chop an onion, not too large, six or seven cloves of garlic. Sweat the onion, stoop, not stiff, excellent, to get pasta from cupboard. Now, tin of tuna in oil, drain off oil, run hot tap to wash oil down sink. Kettle is boiled, pour water into saucepan, add pasta. Onions doing nicely, turn down heat, add tuna, breaking into chunks. When pan has cooled down a little, add garlic. Good, now? Ah, so handy these bags of mixed leaves. Shake leaves into bowl, chop and add tomato, that half avocado not too black, chop and add that, so. How's pasta? Coming along, coming along. Cross over, switch on radio, jazz station, fine. Now? Ah, vinaigrette from yesterday, no, the day before. Good shake, add, toss. Pasta ready, drain, back into saucepan, add contents of pan, stir – damn, parmesan. Saucepan off heat, grate cheese, tip pasta onto plate, cover richly with more parmesan, sit. Bravo, Joseph, eighteen minutes start to finish. Good man yourself. Have a glass of wine. Don't mind if I do.

Full immersion in the present moment. Displacement activity. Playing games with my own head. Being sane.

A brandy after in the front room, where I light the lamps and think that perhaps I might take down a book; I walk to the shelves and discover (did I really not know?) what has been haunting me all day.

'... why you turned your back on your country'

Certain things people say have a knack of hanging in the air, of holding, acquiring or drawing to themselves the energy of an afterlife. I almost imagine I see Vincent's question as a small grey cloud, hovering above the chair he sat in.

I cannot be sure this is not how things actually are.

And I know, I know, I am avoiding.

Those first Civil Rights marches in the North. The ambush at Burntollet. Trying to explain, to Henri, to Thérèse, to Marie Louise. Bloody Sunday, the sheer brutal fact of it. The consequences, the inevitable consequences.

The sickness, the rage I felt, the struggle I had to subdue and channel that rage. To understand what was really happening.

The French have a lamentable tendency to romanticise armed struggle in Ireland. I remember quoting Dutschke in some café parliament, the hard sanity of 'the long march through the institutions' – I thought it an original phrase, Marie Louise gently letting me know that Red Rudi had borrowed it from Gramsci. I began to read Gramsci the next day. Nabile, I remember, was impressed – though perhaps sceptical of my ability to understand what I was reading.

I knew it was madness from the start, the bombing campaign, all that followed.

Do you want to go home, Henri asked me, late one night. We had been drinking. There had been a car bomb in Derry, on the news in the bar. I was disappointed, misunderstanding him. Are you fucking mad, I asked him – but what I meant was, I thought you understood me. He did, of course; he had a gentle way of testing my foolishness, of encouraging my tentative sanities.

You know what he said to me once, I said, I knew I was slurring, couldn't quite get a grip on my tongue, you know what Mick said to me once, he said, he said 'I couldn't shoot the men I fought for' – what do you think of that, eh?

Henri propped me against an iron railing, held me there, a palm flat on my chest. I think he was very wise, he said. You were listening, I hope?

I was, it seems, and listening more intently as the long, black years dragged on.

I had left myself behind, the night I pulled the trigger. I stepped away from the life that could have been mine. I saw this clearly from the start of the killings in the North. I had removed myself from much that might otherwise have been possible. Likely, even.

As best as I was able, I asked myself what would have been my responses, reactions, actions, had I decided to make my life in Ireland. I had a certain political formation from my juvenile reading, from growing up with Mick, with the squad; I daresay I would have been swept up into the generational fever –

Guevara, Vietnam, Davis and Cleaver and so on – and if I know myself at all, I more than suspect I could well have been drawn by temperament and analysis to armed struggle against empire.

Drawn, but not committed. To take a life ...

But the truth was, the fact was, I lived at a remove, and that had made all the difference. From time to time, militants who arrived in Paris would address small gatherings. I would hover at the edges, listening, never revealing myself. There was a lot of posturing by ego-driven zealots – harmless or sometimes not; there were a number who were not idiots. I met those also, more accurately I observed those; I was often the one at the closed meetings who sat with some trusted comrade to hear them out, the one who said nothing. I sympathised with their analysis sometimes, I thought their deductions, and hence their prescriptions, naive in the extreme.

I remember a glancing exchange with an INLA militant, as we shouldered together through a narrow doorway: war, I murmured, is the failure of politics, to start from war is to invoke your own defeat. We were speaking in French. I was perhaps a little too pleased with my phrase. No, my friend, he said, level and cool, war is what we turn to when we see no politics. An intelligent man, I thought, but a foolish one.

Shot by his own comrades in one of the feuds that followed.

The ones who came to buy guns I stayed well away from – the French security services are anything but fools; they reserved their full attention for these ones, I had no wish to draw their attention to myself.

Oh how I read, though: histories, tracts, manifestos, pamphlets, newspapers, magazines – I could not explain then to myself, and still I cannot explain, how I managed entirely to repudiate my country, its squalid and bloody travails, and yet to track every twist and turn, to feel on my own pulses the shifts and jolts of the day to day, the slow unfolding of long-buried narratives, grievance, festering injustice.

And not just the war – I watched every glacial shift in the Republic, too, every nuanced and hedged and qualified and tortuous half-step towards the modern, towards the cold facts of the twentieth century, its powers and alignments, its seismic re-arrangements of reality.

Turn my back on my country? Ah Vincent, how much easier it would have been for me had I been able to do so.

But, I never went back. I never set foot there until ...

I must not get ahead of myself.

I must calm down.

I must set this down.

To leave your country is not so simple as to cross the sea.

A letter Mick wrote me, if I go next door now I know the box file that it's in, I can pop the button on the box, riffle down through to where it's laid, a half-moon from a coffee cup on its top edge, a blue sheet of paper, a hurried note from Eleni clipped to it, the clip slightly rusted.

North or south, he wrote, they have no idea of what a Republic is, or could be. This fellow Mitterand, for all his faults, he has some idea. As far as I can make him out – you'd have a better idea yourself. We found that out in Spain, there'll never be a Republic where the people are afraid of god or of themselves.

I had given it no thought, you see; until then I had never actively attended to France as a republic. I remember what I wrote back. I quoted Zhou en Lai, who said it is too early to tell when somebody asked him what he thought of the French Revolution. And Mick replied almost immediately (the next letter down in the file, a short note) to say: I thought he was asked what he thought about the impact of your student revolution.

Good man yourself, Mick, I thought ruefully, when Marie

Louise confirmed that Mick (or Eleni?) was right.

And now, brain sick from trying to make sense of my whirling thoughts, I do go through to the next room, I take down the box and search for that letter, that note.

I was right, he did say that: your student revolution.

Your.

I had occasionally thought of France as my adopted country, and now here was Mick, giving me up for adoption.

I have to go out, I need to walk, I need to get out into the air.

If I hadn't shot that fucker? I need not have stayed in Cork, I could have gone to Dublin, a well-worn trail, or I could have stayed in Cork and worked it out there. Either way I could have spent my life doing some version of what I've been doing here. But could I, though?

Would that have been so bad?

Bah! A saying of Seanie's: if me aunt had balls she'd've been me uncle.

You play the cards you're dealt.

The world is what it is.

Get out, old fool, get out. Walk. Air.

40

Of course I had doubts, constant and recurring. There would be black days when I couldn't get out of bed, would cancel my classes (a call to the concierge, a note pinned to the door), days when a surge of self-pity would come washing through me the instant I opened my eyes. I would feel lost, unhappy and far from home. At times like that, times when my blood felt like slow-moving brackish water in my veins, I would ask myself what I was doing here, I would ask myself what was the good of what I was doing. And then the acid, the mean, insidiously vicious questions: what, really, do I know of Henri? Can I really trust him? This that I am involved in, might it be no more than fantasy, make-believe, mind games played by marginalised obsessives?

Who has not wondered if his life is no more than pitiable self-delusion?

Once and once only I expressed these doubts to Henri. It had become our habit each 17 October, Henri, Nabile and I, to meet at the Pont Saint Michel, to remember the poor souls who had been murdered on that black night in 1961, whose bodies had been consigned to the cold on-rushing mercies of the river.

Nabile would bring roses, red roses, and we would let them fall with the wind into the turbulent brown waters, one by one. We never discussed this, it was just something we did, something we knew to do.

For some reason, this was in 1980 I think, Nabile turned to me and said suddenly, fiercely, you know what a *Harki* was, Joseph?

I thought for a wild moment he was angry with me, was accusing me of something. Henri laid a soothing hand on my arm. No, I said, no, I don't.

Well, he said, calming down, for he was a sensitive man and he saw that he had alarmed me, it's a complicated business. But me, I was a *Harki*. After the Amis liberated North Africa in !942–1943 did you know half of the effective French army was made up of Algerian soldiers? No? Many people have forgotten. We fought in the liberation of France, we fought in Italy, we fought in Germany.

And then came the war of independence. Well, me, I had long since moved to France, but many, many Algerians stayed on in the army to serve France – or, to be honest, to serve themselves, too, some of them. After independence, despite the many many promises, thousands were butchered, horribly, by the FLN. And France, you think France was grateful to men who had served her? You know what he said, De Gaulle? Well, you must suffer.

I could scarcely bear the pain on his face.

I was always glad I had left the army before the independence struggle started, he said, I could not have borne it, to turn my gun on my own people. I was despised by the new breed, and I was betrayed by the men I had fought for.

Not only that, said Henri, sly and quick, you were doubly fucked, you were. A *Harki* and a communist – you couldn't have picked a worse combination, could you?

A wintry smile from Nabile, a puzzled shake of the head.

Why am I speaking of this? Ah, yes. Joseph, you remember Hakim, poor, innocent frightened Hakim?

I said I did.

When they hauled his body out of the river, you know what he had crushed in his hand, do you? A French flag, a small French flag, one of those things they hand out when our glorious army takes to the streets to celebrate itself. The poor bewildered child, he was always asking, did I think he might be able to join the army. Our own people would have butchered him for that flag, and that *salaud* Papon had him murdered for being Algerian. Do you see what I am telling you, do you?

It wasn't a question, this much at least I understood. He embraced Henri, he ... crushed me, held me away from him by the shoulders, glared at me, then cuffed me gently on the side of the head. He turned around, he walked away from us. We stood there, we watched him go.

Ah well, said Henri at last, old Nabile can be a bit temperamental. Myself I think he should have his prostate looked at. But you, Joseph, let's have a brandy and talk about these doubts of yours.

Doubts? I had said nothing about doubts.

Oh for god's sake, said Henri, pick up your jaw and follow me. What the hell do you think prompted that lecture from Nabile, eh? You think that by now we old boys don't know how to read a face?

How old are you anyway, Henri?

Older than you'll ever be, boy, older than you'll ever be. Come on, and don't look at those fuckers in their cage, you'll only arouse their interest. We walked by the stolid CRS in their navy-blue bus, the wire mesh riot screens bolted over the windows. On a whim, not a word said, we fell into lock step, we marched away like a couple of Legionnaires.

Now he said, when we'd settled at the bar, it's like this ... no, better, I'll give you an example. A month ago we sent you a young man (he glanced around) who is of great interest to us. You know the one, rabbit face, cold eyes? I knew the one. Well, you remember in 1968, the one called Rocard wrote a good study on the refugee camps in the Algerian business?

I nodded, yeah, sure, he bottled it, didn't he, he's letting Mitterand go through for the presidency? And he's drifted to the right of the party, yes?

Yes, that one. Well Mr Rabbit is one of his principal advisers, but Mr Rabbit is so far to the left he makes Mao Zedong look like the boss of a knitting circle.

I know I looked puzzled.

Unperturbed, Henri ploughed on: Mr Rabbit considers that Mr Rabbit has a fine mind; Mr Rabbit has a plan; Mr Rabbit considers that M. Rocard will oblige him by introducing, as a right-wing president, measures that, if they were to try them, would get the Left hounded out of office.

So?

So? So, dear Joseph, Mr Rabbit is probably right, but Mr Rabbit hasn't a clue how to get from theory to practice, eh?

Mr Rabbit, incidentally, is a bit of a genius in his own way, and he also happens, I think, to be right.

Right about what? Help me here.

Right about Rocard. He may not make president, but he has a very good shot at making prime minister before 1990. Same thing from our point of view.

I see, I said, but of course I didn't. Our point of view?

Joseph, try to keep up, OK? About what do you speak, you and Mr Rabbit? Yes, exactly. And to whom do you pass on what you speak about? Yes, exactly. And when Mr Rabbit begins to make new friends, and they happen to be friends who admire him, who share his views on what needs to be done, who reinforce his sense of being right? And when his teacher, his sophisticated teacher who is so much in touch with affairs of the world, begins to lend him articles, suggest books he might find interesting? Yes, exactly.

So, dear Joseph, this is your question, at heart: does anything that we do make a difference? This is your question, OK? Well, yes. Yes it does. Everything we do makes a difference, mostly a small difference, every now and then a big difference. OK? Satisfied?

I was. I said so.

Then again, he said, heaving himself down off the bar stool, flicking a note on to the counter, then again, we often fuck things up, too. Ah well, see you.

Gone.

Popped back around the door, said: Didn't I tell you to pick your jaw up? And gone again.

I called for another brandy. There's that guy in politics, I thought, that lecturer Nabile is always chatting to, he'd help me make a list of articles, books. I must call on Nabile tomorow.

41

It's only mid-afternoon but I can't keep my eyes open. I feel that every ounce of energy has drained out of me. I'll close this down, I think I'll have me a little sleep.

42

In the end, it was Pascal who came with the news. A winter's morning, a bright rime on the zinc roofs across the streets, his breath wisping around his upturned face when I answered the bell, opened the window and looked down.

A week before, Henri had said: better you don't go, he's unconscious, he won't recover. Better you don't see him like this, he would not want it. No, no, believe me, believe me, I know this.

Pascal, his first time in my apartment, all these years. Dark pouches under his eyes. His hands cradling a coffee cup, wet marks from his shoes on my kitchen floor.

The young man had phoned Henri, the young man who was living in Mick's house with his girlfriend, their young child. Henri shook his head; I do not know how he had my phone number, where would he have got my number from.

Henri, Henri, I was gentle, I was comforting him, and he did not know it; from Eleni, yes? Eleni had your number? And Eleni gave the number to Michael John?

Yes of course, that would explain, but ...

And you know him, he would have anticipated something like this, would he not? He would have made sure this young man knew who to call.

Yes, naturally. Derek.

What?

Derek his name is, the young man.

And now Pascal at the door again. I throw him the keys, and while he is climbing the stairs I get the packed bag from the back room, take my passport from the desk, check once again that I have my wallet.

Pascal comes in through the open door, and I catch that fleeting expression.

Yes, yes, I know, I say, and I manage a weak grin, bad security, I know.

Ah Joseph he says, and his tenderness almost unmans me, Ah Joseph I am not so bad, eh?

The part of me that stands back always is registering … authority.

I am sorry, he says, Miguel was a good comrade. The best.

I feel dizzy a moment, I have to sit down.

He says: you did not know?

I shake my head, I did not know.

In the Maquis, he says. Seriously, nobody ever told you? Well … You have your passport? Good, there is a car around the block, some roadworks … Lock the door, good. Your ticket is at the airport, Henri …

Black Mercedes. I think: funeral car. A young man, thin and grave, opens the door for Pascal, on the other side for me.

I liked him a great deal, you know, Miguel?

Staring out ahead of him, monitoring the driver without seeming to.

When Henri brought him home to us, I liked him immediately. When we were introduced, you know the first thing he said? He said: Henri told me you would snap my neck if I so much as looked at your sister. His eyes were laughing. I liked him immediately, I said: no, maybe only your arm. The first time.

All the way to the airport we travelled in silence, as if silence was wrapped around the speeding car, a bubble enclosing us.

I was stiff getting out of the car, Pascal helped me, a hand under my elbow. Please, Joseph, he said, look after Henri, yes? I will be here when you come home. The car pulled away, Pascal in the front passenger seat, the driver stealing one sideways look as Henri and I embraced.

I felt as if I was drunk from the knees down.

On the plane we barely spoke. At Cork airport I stood with the bags while Henri made the arrangements to collect the hired car.

I was faintly amused, very faintly, to see he had chosen a Renault. What, he said, seeing my look, does it not make sense to choose something I am familiar with? But he knew what my look meant.

Here is the address, he said, O'Connor's Funeral Home, Shandon Street, you see? You know how to get there?

Oh yes, I know how to get there.

The deep, disorienting visceral pull. The living past in the nearly familiar present.

I keep my eyes closed most of the way, opening them only to check we're on course, reciting directions from the map inside my head, the small world inside my head. Once or twice defeated, deflected by some unexpected one-way street.

Hard, bright sunshine. The green-brown river high, packed between limestone walls. We park by the small green square on the North Mall. I am gripped by a sudden panic: I had not thought of it, surely someone will recognise me?

Henri, mindreader, says: Joseph it's OK, that fucking cop is dead, right? Wear the glasses, the ones you wear for teaching. You packed them, yes? OK, now, an old comrade from the wars and his nephew will call to, what is it you say, to pay their respects. Right? Good. Out of the car. And stay beside me.

Henri, Henri, where are we staying?

What? A hotel, the Imperial, somebody made a booking. Why?

Nothing, it's OK.

How should I explain the sudden fear that had come over me, that somehow I would find myself sleeping overnight in what had been my home?

There was a crowd at the doors of the funeral home, and I thought that perhaps somebody was being removed to a church, but inside the doors the crowd resolved into a murmuring and respectful queue, pressing forward in the hum that comes with a sense of occasion, tense and composed at the same time.

A man in the black suit of his profession spotted us as we hesitated a moment. He managed the trick of being polite and welcoming without ever straying into inappropriate warmth that is, in a way, the highest achievement of his trade. He had spotted Henri from fifty paces, and now, with a dignified nod to me, he ushered us past the wondering queue and into the parlour where Mick was, there is no other term for it, lying in state. All these people, they were here for Mick. All these people …

Mr O'Connor, I recognised him now, led us to the head of the coffin; we were being … announced. I stood unmoving, I did not yet dare look down. Beside me, softly but unmistakably, Henri came to attention. I could feel power radiate from him, a density of being, an accumulation of force, as if he had somehow doubled his weight, his solidity. He looked straight down at Mick, he held that look for a long moment, I could hear the room go quiet, in waves, outward. And then he saluted, a flashing gesture, his rigid hand at his forehead so fast I had barely seen it move. There was a sigh from the people crowding to see, to be part of the moment. Then Henri, I had not seen his hand go down, Henri looked at me and I straightened, I looked down at my dead grandfather, the stone mask of his face, the slight turn of his mouth betraying some incipient amusement, and I put my hand over my heart. I felt nothing at all, but I knew that this was only some unlooked-for discipline of the moment. I knew that breaking grief was only a hand's breadth away, but now, and I knew it, was not the time for breaking.

There was a tricolour standing to one side of the coffin's head, an old man I did not recognise at attention beside it. Henri acknowledged him with a nod, and the old man dipped his head, looked proud and fierce for a moment, and then looked away – at his own past, coming to claim him, that was the feeling I had then.

We marched out, eyes front, and they watched us go, satisfied and puzzled. I should have known, I was telling myself, I should have known.

We sat into the car, the crowd parting for when we would move away. You did not expect this, Henri asked, you really did not expect this?

No, I said, I did not expect this.

Well, he said, do you want to go to the house? I shook my head, no. Not yet.

We went to the hotel, checked in. So strange, checking into a hotel in your own city.

We were in Henri's room, my bags propping the open door. I think, said Henri, we should ring this young man, this Derek, I told him I would. He has taken charge of the arrangements, no, that is wrong, he has been put in charge of seeing the arrangements are carried out. A wintry smile, then: one can believe Miguel would not leave such things to chance. Will you sleep, a little Joseph? And then we phone?

I will, I think, I'll try to anyway.

You were recognised, of course. I can practically hear the tom toms. Does this concern you?

I patted my heart pocket. My dear Henri, I said, I am a French citizen, my passport, my identity card, both confirm this. I do not expect there is anyone willing to risk a diplomatic incident, eh?

Of course, he said, but I was not thinking of that. Bah, that we have dealt with, a long time ago. What I was thinking was more your heart, will there be people opening a wound in your heart?

What a very un-Irish question, I was thinking, even as I reflected on what my answer would be. The men dead, one gone away forever into the Bogs of Offaly, Phil – I do not know if he is alive or dead, as I know nothing of Theresa – and ... nobody else.

No, I said, there is no question of that.

Good, he said, then we should get some rest. Oh and Joseph, I do not think there will be questions but, as a matter of curiosity, how were you planning to explain that Joseph Lyons is not that Joseph Lyons?

Ah sure that's easy, I said, sure amn't I the bastard son he left behind in France? They wouldn't dare harass a bastard at a funeral. And anyway, that other fella never had a passport.

I was glad to close the door on his laughter, though I knew that the same laughter, subsiding, would finally give way to his grief. I do not think I could have borne his grief just then.

Derek seemed to me very young, perhaps in his late twenties, very young and very composed. He sat in the lounge across from Henri, neatly dressed, regarding me steadily.

I don't quite understand, I said. My grandfather had no time for the church, and didn't mind who knew it.

Ah well, you see, he said, the priest was a good friend of Mick's but, eh, a man who wouldn't be gettin' on too well with the bishop, like, know what I mean?

Ah, right.

And, eh, well it won't be a mass, exactly, Not as such, like?

He looked so earnest, it was all I could do not to burst out laughing.

Right so, he said. Removal at seven tonight, we're going to walk to Blackpool, mass, eh, service like, at ten tomorrow. Then straight out to Rathcooney.

Henri staring out into the street.

So, eh, will you be sayin' a few words, or Mister Henri here? He pronounced it properly, a flicker of modest pride there.

I will, said Henri, decisively. I will speak in French, and in English. Joseph will speak at the graveside.

Oh, OK, so.

I wondered what he was smiling at, Derek. He caught my look, held it. I saw that his deference was his good-mannered way of respecting us. I saw the steel behind the shyness.

Well, he said, Mick kinda thought all right ye'd work it out like that. In fact, still holding my look, he said to tell you to make sure the car is facing the right way. For afterwards, like. You know, you'd never know who'd turn up at a funeral sort o' thing.

He looked at me and I looked at him and we both burst out laughing.

Henri looking puzzled.

Never mind, I said, it's a Cork thing.

All the same, I was impressed that Mick had been so impressed with this young man. I could see why, and he knew it, and I was very touched by his quiet pride.

We shook hands, and when we'd watched him go, Henri inclined his head in the direction of the bar.

I'm sorry, he said, I don't know why I said that, about you speaking at the graveside. You don't have to, you know.

Ah that's all right, I said, sure hasn't that young fella the getaway already organised.

You're making a joke, said Henri, but what you say, it might be true. Miguel was always a good judge of a man. And of an occasion.

A hard, dry night. We walked across town, down Oliver Plunkett Street, Prince's Street, across Patrick Street and down through the Coal Quay, The people we passed were incurious, saw only two sombre unspeaking men, heads up, looking straight ahead. I didn't want to see changes; I was registering how much had changed but each doorway, each shopfront was a trap where small insignificant memories still lingered, and I had no time for that. We passed the Bridewell, guards going in and out, relaxed, and Henri glanced sharply at me but I had not the slightest anxiety.

I could see the crowd from across the river, eddying and jostling under the yellow lights in the little square at the bottom of Shandon Street. They moved aside as we walked through, and I knew that they knew, I heard the whispers: the grandson, the grandson. Inside the door, Henri drew me aside. Listen, he said, this is maybe not a good idea? What if they try to arrest you?

Here? I said, gesturing around me, in this crowd? No, Cork is like this, you see, a thing can be known and not known, you understand? There is what is actually known – I patted my breast again, the French passport on me at all times – and then there is what people really know.

He shook his head, still dubious. How to explain this, that the city I had so decisively put behind could still claim and in some sense possess me? How to explain to him what I couldn't explain to myself?

Here's Mr O'Connor now. We're ready to close the coffin, he said – and, as we followed him in, leaning imperceptibly closer to me, he said: your grandfather was a gentleman, Joseph, we wouldn't like to see anything happen.

Henri, who had leaned in frankly to eavesdrop, grunted his satisfaction.

We stood at the head of the coffin, as O'Connor's men quickly and deftly fitted the lid. A couple of old men made a show of striking the flag, of detaching it from its staff, of laying it reverentially on the box before snapping to attention and saluting. It was moving and it was absurd, in equal measure, and then I was ashamed of myself for finding it absurd.

They carried the coffin shoulder high through the thronging crowd, a way being cleared for the coffin bearers and for Henri and myself by sweating men in formal clothes.

There was heat from the people, the many hundreds crowding in around us, but at head height and above the air was cold and crisp, a faint plume of exhaust from the purring hearse swirling through it. We moved off, Henri and I shoulder to shoulder, some men I didn't know on either side of us, young Derek and what seemed a group of his friends in the second rank. We began to climb the hill, and I was pleased to see women step into the ranks behind us, young women mostly, many hand in hand with their boyfriends, and then I could see up ahead and the whole of the Northside, it seemed to me, was crowded thick on the footpaths, their faces turned towards us as we climbed, so many pale discs on a solid dark background, fog now, faint but visible, haloing the streetlights. And as we climbed, in twos and threes, they stepped off the footpaths, joining the cortege, men mostly, but women too, older women now, and still that same low murmur, unbroken, rising and falling, so many eyes meeting mine, a moment; most soft and curious, here and there a hard but not unfriendly stare, a nod.

I glanced right towards Shandon as we passed, and a boy on

a bicycle was stopped up there at the foot of the steps, staring down at us as we passed. A boy on his father's shoulders gave me a tentative wave as we passed Eason's Avenue. At the top of the hill, where the great sandstone bulk of the North Chapel stood gathering its shadows, there was a gang of boys kicking a football across the way outside Dr Shorten's surgery. One stopped, stared, said something sharp and peremptory to the others. They stopped at once, gathered in behind him, stood and stared. I looked back down the long slope of Shandon Street, and as far as I could see, there were men and women walking behind us. Walking the last bit of the road with Mick.

I had not known, I had not suspected ...

Down Gerald Griffin Street, on down Great William O'Brien Street into the heart of Blackpool.

His house? Henri was gesturing towards my home, Mick's home, a dense crowd all around us now as the mourners caught up with us, swelled the numbers already gathered here.

And so this is the famous O'Dwyer's fire escape? You think it worked for him? A grim smile on Henri's face, grim and somehow kind, his eyes soft on me. He leaned in, murmured: you know, one night he whispered to me, Miguel, we were waiting for a German patrol, this was in late 1944, near the end, we were waiting, a night like this, our nerves, you know? And he whispered to me: I was just thinking, I don't know was it such a good idea after all, leaving sweet Blackpool behind me? Sweet Blackpool, he always called it that, you see. Oh we nearly choked to death, trying not to laugh, but then we heard the engines coming up through the valley and ... well ... attention now, here comes that priest.

We followed him into the church, up the plain steps and into the warm half-dark, the tide rising behind us, the dark tide of the crowd pushing on and in. O'Connor's men carried him to the altar, they laid him on trestles, settled the flag.

When the church was full, the priest looked around him, his eyes commanding the quiet that eventually fell.

Tonight, he said, Michael John Lyons will lie here under the eyes of god among his own people. Let ye pray for him tonight, in whatever way means the most to ye. And I will, too.

And that was that. He made the sign of the cross over us, turned on his heel and disappeared behind the altar.

A murmur ran back through the congregation, a muted wave of shock at this break with inviolable tradition – and I knew with a certain grim satisfaction there would be much talk in the pubs tonight about Fr Lynch and his unpredictable ways, a great deal of happy speculation about what kind of mass he would say tomorrow.

It seemed to me that nobody wanted to leave the church until I understood they were waiting for me to leave. When I stood, I could hear them coming to their feet behind me. When I turned to go, and Henri stepped in beside me I could see here and there a familiar or a half-familiar face, people wanting to be recognised and yet tactfully hesitant, not wanting to intrude. I saw that I was at home, and welcome, but that this was only for now, and that I would leave tomorrow and the sea would close in again over the aisle down which we were now walking, steady and slow; I saw that they were already, and not unkindly, prepared to forget that I had ever been here.

We cleared to the house rapidly, Derek leading the way, and when a young woman opened the door to us he said this is Claire, she smiled, and this is our boy, Michael. We pushed into the hall, and Derek pulled the door shut behind us. The boy stared up at us, his eyes moving from one face to the other, thoughtful. Then he stepped aside to let us pass. Five, maybe six?

The table was laid with sandwiches, cakes, tea things, glasses, a bottle of whiskey. The fire was lit, the curtains were drawn.

The room was fresh-painted, the heavy curtains a subdued dark burgundy. A white embroidered cloth on the table, and I knew that under the cloth the worn plain deal would be scrubbed bone white.

Claire came through with a big blue teapot, her hands protected with a draped tea towel. She had long black hair, a sort of wave in it halfway down; she looked like someone Modigliani would have wanted to paint. The child, Michael, stood in between his seated parents and for a moment we were all quiet. I saw, I felt, the grace and the peace they had brought to the house, and though Derek had said earlier in the hotel that they would be forever grateful to Mick for all he had done for them, I saw that they had brought to his last years wonder, and calm, and resolution.

Do you miss your Granda, the child asked suddenly. I do, I said, I do Michael, I miss him very much.

He looked up at his Dad in wonder, said: Da, he knows my name is Michael!

We talked for a while of this and that, avoiding the questions that sooner or later we would have to deal with, but all the time I was waiting for a knock at the door. When it came, I motioned to Derek to stay where he was, looked at Henri, went out to answer.

A man of about my own age, broad in the shoulder, a black wool jacket, a hard look to him but not a thug. Two younger men on the steps behind and below him, a car idling at the kerb. I pointed a finger at him: you, come on in. Then, as the others moved, I said no, you lads stay where you are. They didn't like that, but Henri was beside and behind me and they looked at him and they decided that perhaps they would stay where they were.

In the hall the man went to say something but I cut him off:

I don't want to know your name, I said, I know who you are, the answer is no. He looked at me steadily, he waited. No firing party, I said, I want to be clear. No claiming. Am I clear? You get me? Mick wanted nothing to do with you, and you know that.

I never knew I had such coldness in me. I stared him in the face.

He nodded, he offered me his hand, he softened. I'm sorry for your troubles, he said, you know I was told to ask? I do, I said, you were asked by men my grandfather would not let past that hall door.

He wouldn't give me that. I won't argue with you, he said, I didn't come here to argue with you, but you shouldn't say things like that. I'll say good night.

I opened the door and as he went past I said to him: you can come as yourself, you're welcome to come as yourself. He gave me a curious, twisted sort of grin then, and a shrug, and he patted me on the arm. Ah sure, he said, you start into something and ... you know yourself?

We watched the car pull away, and when I turned to go in Henri looked at me thoughtfully and said: you were very Miguel there for a moment, Joseph. I had nothing to say to that.

Derek was at the window. He turned, said: that was Mick Collins, interesting. Well now ...

You're not serious? Mick Collins?

Oh I am, he said, I swear, an' you know what's the gas thing? All belongin' to him are blueshirts.

Claire laughed, a musical sound. Ah, she said, sure all belong to me were in the British army – except one uncle.

An' the uncle, I asked?

Oh, he was in the Royal Air Force; only he deserted, like.

She saw Henri was shrugging into his overcoat. You know, she said, you're very welcome ...

Ah no, I said, I'd never sleep.

Right so, she said, he said you'd say that an' all.

I glanced at Derek. No, no, she said, not Derek. Mick.

Henri asked for the bathroom. While he was making his way upstairs, I thought of the hidden space, couldn't resist. I stepped under the stairs, found the panel, popped it open. In the dim light I saw there was an envelope. I took it out, read in large block capitals, Nosey Bah! I stuffed the envelope in an inside pocket.

Michael, I said, I'll give you €5 if you can run to the top of the house and back while I count to fifty. But don't fall! You get nothing if you fall.

Derek and Claire looking at me. I used to get a half-crown, I said. Look, I'm going to bail, tomorrow, right after the funeral. I want ye to stay here for as long as ye like when I'm gone. Rest of your lives, if ye like. Ssh, ssh, listen to me. The conditions are that ye keep the place as well as ye have been, and that ye remember what Mick did when he took ye in, if ye ever meet anyone ... ah sure look, I'll get a solicitor to put it all in writing. If ye decide to move on, fair enough, hand the keys back to the solicitor, all right?

I saw they were not quite convinced. Look, I said, what use is the place to me? I'm never comin' back, and I'm fixed up OK. We'll sort it all out in writing when I get home.

There. Then. A blinding, ice cold flash of desolation. I must have staggered under the impact, Claire reached a hand out to cup my elbow, frightened.

Michael burst down the last flight of steps, barrelling past an amused descending Henri. Well, he demanded, panting? I only got to forty-five, I said, fair dues to you. Forty, he said, pocketing the €5 calmly, you were counting too quick. Good night now, Mr Joseph, 'night Mam, 'night Dad. Seven steps up, he turned where the stairs turn. See, he said, looking straight at me, I know your name too.

You do, I agreed, and your French pronunciation is very good.

So's your Cork, he said.

In the street outside a black Mercedes. Mr O'Connor said I was to wait for you, the man said, standing by the car. Where're ye staying?

I looked at him. You're one o' the Mulcahys, aren't you, from Fair Hill? I am he said, you went to school with Donie, me older brother. Then you know feckin' well where I'm staying, so. Ah sure 'course I do, he was amused, sure half Cork do, I just thought 'twould be polite to ask, like.

Tell me, said Henri, settling in beside me, what is this language you speak in Cork?

Your Granda was a lovely man, the driver said, a lovely class of a man altogether. One o' the oul' stock, know what I mean? A pure gentleman.

Thanks, I said, we'll miss him. We all will he said, and then with emphasis: we all will, boy. We all will. There's only a few left.

I give up, said Henri. I need my sleep.

What's your name anyway, I asked the driver as we coasted up to the Imperial. Tomás, he said, what time will I come in the mornin'?

Come an hour before the funeral, I said, say nine o'clock? Ye want to go for a drive around, is it? That's right, I said. Funny now, he said, I thought you might. Welcome home anyway. You know your man died, the guard? I do, I said, I heard. Yeah, four years ago, or was it five? Ah he was a bad fucker anyway, he was no loss boy. His eyes in the rearview mirror flicked to Henri, slumped half asleep.

D'ye mind me askin' now, your friend there, are there many

Frenchmen in America? No, I said, I flew in from Chicago to Paris, we met up there. Chicago, is it, he said, musing, I was never there. Nor Paris neither. C'mere I better let ye get yere sleep. Chicago ... Good night now, good night.

Adjoining rooms. I watched Henri get his key in the lock, walked into my own room, set my travel alarm, stripped, slept.

Tomás is waiting for us in the lobby. Did ye get a good breakfast? I'd say ye did all right. You can't bate the rasher 'n' eggs. Where are we off to?

Audley Place, the top of Patrick's Hill. Another bright, hard, bracing January day. I thought it rained all the time in Cork, Henri said. It does, I said, only today it isn't raining. He laughed. We were standing by the phone box on the high terrace, our elbows on the mossy sandstone wall. Time was, I said, I couldn't see over this wall. Mick would lift me up.

Across the valley, the red and white tower of Shandon with its four clocks, its golden salmon on the domed top turning in the slight south-westerly wind. The brewery beneath, its great brick chimney standing guard over Leitrim Street, the narrow defended gateway to Blackpool. The valley broadening to the right, the church away in there, Mick lying in state all night. Above and to the right, the climbing bulk of Spangle Hill, the white floating tent of the new church with its steep-pitched roof, its narrow soaring spire breaking the skyline. Between that glinting spire and Shandon, the red brick bulk of Farranferris seminary, wrapped in green fields, and below that and to the side of it, red brick again, the Bishop's Palace, then the North Mon, my old school, the Italianate house of the Sisters of Charity, St Vincent's convent. Back to that high church and track along the hilltop to the left, Fair Hill, Churchfield, Gurranabraher with its slope of red roofs falling back into Sunday's Well, the river below that, more fields and many trees, the morning sun burnishing the rising, thinning mists. On the ridge of Sunday's Well, the mass of Blarney Street and Gurrane up above it, the rich green of the distillery fields below, St Vincent's red sandstone church catching the morning light on its green copper roof. Like a castle on the Rhine, Mick used say, when the evening sun would pick out that same roof, the church stepped precariously on the edge of its cliff. Like a castle on the Rhine.

I never tired of this view, its tumble of houses and sheds and churches, its tangle of streets and lanes; I would climb up here all the time, never remembering one day to the next how many they were, the Fever Hospital Steps. I would pick out the houses of schoolmates, fields I had rambled in, lanes I had cycled up and down; I would plot out walks for Mick and myself, retrace walks we had taken, marvel at all you could see and feel and touch and do in our rich, colourful pulsing city of hills. Teenaged, I would come up here in storms, stand in the phone box for the thrill of watching the whole panorama lit and lit and lit again by theatrical sheets of lightning.

It is a beautiful city, Henri said, by way of telling me we had been here long enough. And now let's go.

There were gulls wheeling in the vault of space between Shandon and the North Cathedral, and as I watched the light catch them in their soaring I realised I had never asked Mick why we called the cathedral The North Chapel. One gull dipped for the flat of the city, its wings flashing, and I saw away there in the distance an answering flash from the golden angel on St Finbarre's cathedral in its sea of green.

The priest said for to bring ye in the back, Tomás said. Fr Lynch took my hand, the moment we stepped in the door. Listen, he said, dark eyes humorous under wild and wayward brows, there'll have to be a mass, OK, I can only push my luck with the bishop so far. What I'll do, though, I'll announce there'll be no communion. The old biddies will have murder but sure what harm And I won't come to the grave so there won't have to be prayers. Fair enough? I was off balance, slightly overwhelmed. He pressed on, a man on his own ground who had earned his ground. Look, he said, Mick was a better Christian than ... ah never mind, mustn't be hard on 'em, but he never darkened the door of this church and I wouldn't insult him. The Man Above will make room for him, I know that sure.

You're Henri, yes? I'm pleased to meet you. He was fierce fond o' you, we often spoke about you. Oh don't look so worried, he could be very discreet, Mick could. But he was very fond of you.

And, he pierced me with a compelling eye, he absolutely doted on this fella. Very proud of him, very proud of him he was.

A profound scepticism in that look, but not aimed at me, or not just at me. I could see that this man met his own doubts with a rolling wall of energy, will and good humour, I was glad indeed Mick had been gifted with such a friend.

Now, he said, observing Henri unlatch the slim briefcase he was carrying, only tell me for the love of god that's not the hammer and sickle, I'm in enough trouble as it is.

Henri laid a gentle hand on his arm, no, father he said, do not worry.

And you'll speak after the sermon, the priest went on? You have good English? Ah sure listen to me, aren't we speaking English now. I'm turning into an old fool. Let ye go on out there now, go out this way, and – he motioned to the folded flag Henri had tucked under his arm – let ye do your business.

The church, it did not surprise me, packed. Heat, smell of candles, under-scent of lavender wax, body odour, damp wool. So many avid eyes.

Mr O'Connor saw us come down the steps, glanced at Henri,

moved. Turned the tricolour so that it covered the bottom half of the coffin now, its ends nearly touching the ground. We stood on either side. I read the brass plaque, an oblique light making me squint: Commandant Michael John Lyons, 1895–1985. Henri unfolded the flag, passed me the end. For a moment it floated over the polished wood, a sheet rippling over a bed, then it fell under its own weight, guided by us both, and settled. The red, yellow and purple of the Spanish Republic, the red three-pointed star of the Popular Front, star superimposed on stripes, the flag of the International Brigades.

There was dismay in places when Fr Lynch announced there would be no communion but he drove on through it. For his sermon he chose to recite the beatitudes, not a word of his own added. He motioned to Henri, beckoned him not to the pulpit but to the altar where a microphone had quietly been placed directly above the coffin.

For some reason the word 'catafalque' floated though my mind, the word and some dim memory of looking up from a book, asking Seanie what it meant. I don' know boy, sure look it up in the dictionary, isn't that what he got it for?

Henri on the altar, stone solid, taking his time, looking all of them in the eye. Looking at me, finally. That familiar nod. So.

The man you know as Michael John, he said, the man you knew as neighbour and friend, to me and to my comrades in the International Brigade he was Miguel. Miguel when we spoke to him, when we called him in the morning, when we appealed to him under fire, Miguel, Miguel. But among ourselves, when we spoke of him, we spoke of El Leon. The lion. When we stood together, defending Madrid against the Fascists, I asked him, Miguel, what are we doing here, eh? A person could get killed here. We had that kind of humour we shared, you understand? Bullets like bees, sweat, blood, men falling to left and right of us.

Hungry, always hungry. Thirsty. Forgive me, also stinking – and very, very afraid. Miguel, he looked at me very seriously and he said: If not us, who? If not here, then where?

When that war was over, when we were defeated in Spain, I proposed to return to my country, France. I saw that this war was but a rehearsal – and Miguel, El Leon, he agreed. I will come with you, he said. I had thought, I had assumed, that if we got out of Spain alive, and that seemed unlikely on the night we were speaking I must say to you, I had assumed he would return here, to the city he loved. This city, I have since yesterday seen it with my own eyes, this city where he was loved.

No, he said, I will come with you. Eh, Henri, he said, if not us, who?

In Spain, Miguel Joseph Lyons saved my life. I will not embarrass his spirit, the story does not matter. He saved my life, and he taught me to ask always, always: if not us, who?

He had dropped almost to a whisper, and now his voice soared, three times he repeated it, and each time it was how I imagine a crash of artillery would sound: *No Pasaran*! *No Pasaran*! *No Pasaran*!

It was the priest who led the applause, breaking a silence that had begun to be cavernous, mountainous, insupportable, and the applause rolled in, thunder gaining on thunder, until I thought it would break on the coffin, a monstrous wave, and sweep Mick, Henri, the priest and myself and all of us there away. It was the passion they were responding to, like an audience in a theatre, I knew that, I know that. But still, still ...

We shouldered him down the aisle, Henri and myself at the back, Derek, some other young men taking the leading places. We shouldered him out of the dark into bright hard sun, a crowd there already outside the church. We handed him into the hearse. People, I did not know any of them, were pushing and jostling to shake my hand, I saw Henri in brief conversation with Derek and a tall thin young man with very long hair. Derek all the while looking carefully, searchingly about him. Then Tomás ushering Henri to the black car, beckoning to me. The priest caught my eye, looked away to Henri, looked back. I shrugged, I raised both my hands, palms up. He gave me a wintry smile, a sketched benediction. I liked him for that. The hearse moved off, out on to Blackpool Bridge, then Thomas Davis Street, house of the murdered Lord Mayor falling behind us, a right onto Spring Lane – dead long since, the tortured unhappy Mr Lehane, we passed his house there before the bridge – and out past The Fox and Hounds, out to the high flat top of the hill, to Rathcooney graveyard. Every inch of that road we'd walked, Mick and I, in hail, rain and sleet, in sunshine and in shadow. Long Sundays, long summer evenings, forced marches on blustery winter days, the street lights already coming on when he'd halt, pretend to consider and then say: we'd be as well to turn for home, what do you think? The men'll be getting worried, maybe, I'd offer. You could be right, he'd say, after pretending to consider this wise point, right so: about turn, quick march.

We carried him into the graveyard, the same team as before, crows complaining in raggedy darts in the air above us.

They were at the gate as we went through, a carload of them, the car unmarked, the hard unmistakable faces. It was Henri who spotted them first, a tapping finger on my shoulder alerting me. The same hard faces the world over. The senior man gave me a cold look, a long considering cold look, I watched from the corner of my eye as he bent to speak to a colleague. He watched me watching him.

We came to the graveside, a fine dust on the red-brown earth heaped to one side but I could smell the wet clay all the same, could feel its residual cold. The crowd gathered round, eager now for more drama. The police had followed us in, only three of them, one at the car still, I supposed. I saw Mick Collins, he nodded to me. There would be nothing ... unseemly. I thought suddenly, irrelevantly: that's a man I could have liked.

Faces, faces pressing in, Henri's flag returned to him, folded neatly by Claire. She patted his hand as he took the flag from her, reached up on tiptoe and kissed him on the cheek. I did not see what happened with the tricolour. I wondered sourly which of the old men would be carried under it next, and felt a hot flush of shame at my mean thought.

And now, I allowed myself think (I remember my reluctance, my sense of near-detachment), and now I suppose I had better say something.

I stood out. I had not noticed the sun disappear; all around me I saw men and women gathering their coats around them, conserving heat. They shuffled closer together, a dark mass. All those expectant eyes.

I saw the senior policeman murmur something again to a colleague, they both looked off to the right, towards the city. Henri leaned forward, said softly: reinforcements, they've called in reinforcements. About your passport, I am not so sure as you. All right, I said, we'll go – but there is something I have to say. Of course, he said, of course.

I had a moment's panic then, as if I did not know what would come out of my mouth, words in English or words in French, and then I said: my name is Joseph Lyons. Michael John was my grandfather. Many of you are here today because you knew him. You knew him as a good man, an upright man, a good neighbour, a good friend. He reared me when my parents died, many of you here also know that. You know the man he was, I do not have to tell you how lucky I was, how fortunate I was, that I had the love and care of this good man. And he had mine.

I paused. The boy, Michael, was standing right in front of me, a little away from his parents, his eyes fixed on me, unmoving.

I went on, distracted a moment by a stone clipping a plastic wreath-case, a violent racking cough: many of you also are here today because one way or another you have certain ideas about my grandfather, who he was and what he stood for. The role he played in our War of Independence. When I was a young boy, I asked my grandfather an impertinent question. I asked him why he did not take part in the Civil War.

Now in the crowd, here and there, I saw eyes turn watchful, men gathering in on themselves, tensing.

Here, today, while you consider the words spoken in Blackpool church by his lifelong comrade, his friend and my friend, I want to ask you to consider carefully the answer he gave me. I asked him why, as a soldier for the Republic, he did not take part in the Civil War. And his answer? His answer? 'I could not shoot the men I fought for'. Plain words, plain meaning – but as I grew older I began to understand what lay behind them.

I looked around: silence except for the unsilenceable wind.

I said it again, cold and careful: I could not shoot the men I fought for.

If you have come here today to remember a soldier of the Republic, remember these words. Michael John was an honourable man, he set great store by honour. If anyone here is of a mind to honour his memory, I ask you very respectfully to remember what he believed in. I ask you to remember these words of his. May he rest in peace.

And then I turned away abruptly, startling O'Connor who was marshalling his gravediggers, waving my thanks to him, cutting off any possibility of applause, any response from the crowd that was even now parting to let me through. Henri shouldering ahead of me, I made for the gate, the cops startling ahead of us,

Derek and a moving cordon of young men gathering around us, flowing beside us. At the gate, Derek's friend with the very long hair at the wheel of a red Toyota, engine running, doors open. The cops signalling for their car, watching us anxiously. A man running out through the graveyard gates, heavy-set, balding, waving to me. I hesitated a second and he pushed through to the car. Phil! Jesus, Phil!

I couldn't talk to you last night, he said, not sure you'd want to. Ah Phil, I said, and now at last I was close to breaking down, my hands on his shoulders, Phil!

Here he said, looking anxiously over his shoulder at the oncoming unmarked cop car, here's my card. Call me, call me ... but we pulled away suddenly, Derek hustling us to the car, Henri and I grabbing our doors, yanking them shut. I craned around, saw Tomás swerve the black Mercedes across the road, heard a crunch and grind of gears. Saw him gesticulate angrily at the blaring horn of the blocked cop car: what can I do give me a minute for fucks sake all right all right give me a fucking minute will ya!

I knew I couldn't possibly be hearing all this but ... clear as a bell. I read it from his gesturing hands.

Then we were into the winding lanes down towards Glenville, and somewhere near Watergrasshill we pulled over to where another young man was standing by our hired Renault, smoking a cigarette, casually enjoying the morning.

I suppose our bags are in the boot, I said to Henri, as we made hurried farewells, as we settled into the car. He looked at me reproachfully. Of course they are, I said, forgive me, but naturally they are in the boot.

An hour or so later we were looking sideways at the Rock of Cashel as the car coasted by. Henri, without looking at me, said: I thought you would have more to say. At the graveside, you mean? Yes. I thought so too, I meant to say more, but just there, just then, it came to me, I have not the right. This is not my country.

We sat in silence then, for a long time, the only sounds the low growl of the engine, the hum of the tyres on the road. At one point he laid his hand on mine, briefly, as one who has come to a conclusion after a passage of thought. I saw that he understood, or at least that he thought he understood. It was comfort, of a sort.

We flew out from Dublin. How much do I owe you for the new ticket, I asked. He looked at me over his tilted glasses: what new ticket?

43

I haven't left the house for two days. My mobile's turned off. I snacked and napped my way through yesterday, slept fitfully last night, woke early this morning to continue.

Excavating. Dredging. Pondering.

It feels as if my head is full of wet, dense clay, as if there is dry dust in the air all around when I raise my eyes and look heavy-lidded around me.

I have the heating on, but I feel cold.

There are crows battling over the rooftops across the way, querulous, bad-tempered, rackety and loud.

If I closed my eyes now, I could not say what I am wearing.

How to be sure one has not wasted one's life?

'Sometimes I wonder if I am not wasting my life' – Phil's words, the letter he wrote in response to my note after that brief encounter at the funeral. I have that letter in front of me now, the first in an intermittent series that have mostly to do with business – the personal stuff, very little of that, contained in asides, hinted at in speaking silence. My boyhood friend. That funeral was a long time ago, and only just now, today, have I felt the full impact of Phil's 'Sometimes I wonder ...' – if he felt that way back then, what must the rest of his life have been, how can he have supported it?

I saw a lot of Mick, he wrote once, I saw a lot of Mick and we spoke a great deal of you, your chosen life. I managed his affairs, just as now I am managing yours, and sometimes I'd catch him looking at me with, I don't know, disappointment? I don't know why, why would he be disappointed in me?

Ah Phil, even if I were to write to you now, after this long silence, would you understand?

I could say: you made your father's peace, old friend; he fought for a while and then surrendered, but you surrendered from the start.

But, that would be unfair. I know that Phil was, is, a good man. I would hear from Derek occasionally (I have his letters, too), and he was careful to let me have news of Phil, to let me know how much he liked him; I think that perhaps he hoped that by invoking our buried friendship, trying to advance it, he would tempt me to visit Cork again.

Michael, he'd always say, is always asking after you. I reproach myself for discouraging these advances, these attempts to reach out to me.

I reproach myself not just for being wanting in common friendship; I reproach myself for failing to learn that Derek and Phil, perhaps only subliminally, had discerned in me the damage I would sustain as a result of my refusal to grieve.

I do not think it would necessarily please them to learn that late in life, very late, I did in fact learn to grieve.

What they missed, and I do not blame them for this, was that I could not sustain, I could not bear or sustain the pull and the gravity of tribal sorrow.

I had to grieve as I lived, alone – anything else would have unnerved me, dissolved my resolve, made me unfit for my freely chosen life.

Rain drumming on mansards across the way, a gust of wind rattling the windows. A freshness coming after the thundery, lowering heaviness of the past two days.

Enough! Enough for god's sake. Up, man, up and be doing!

Big, deep scalding bath, heat deep into the bones. Towel and pamper, pat, dress, choosing the clothes carefully. Up and be doing.

Mme Frenaud struggling towards me, a wet, bedraggled crow. I insist, I insist on taking her under the shelter of my big umbrella, I insist on accompanying her to her door. She is worried, a little confused, unsure how to deal with me (that Algerian fellow!) but as she fumbles with her keys, shuffling her bag from one elbow crook to the other, she surprises me with a warm and genuine shy smile. Thank you, she says, her voice steady, composed. Thank you, you were always a gentleman.

By god! I went off whistling, intent on some shopping myself, perhaps a cognac against the weather, dammit perhaps two!

The rain getting heavier, a quick dash across the back of the Panthéon, Rue d'Ulm, down Fosses on to Saint Jacques, the high buildings, the narrow streets giving shelter. An occasional nightwalker like myself, all battling our umbrellas. From above, what a curious dance. Put a helicopter up there on a night like this, dancers under umbrellas down here, in and out the streets. Hmm. The helicopter, would it stay still I wonder, in the gusts? Never been in a helicopter, the noise, wear earphones of course. Something to do, I am not short of money, what am I saving it for, eh? Hire a helicopter, track myself back through Paris down the years. Ha. How do tyres bite down through rain, keep grip? Careful now, crossing, that taxi, behind it, careful, won't slow for anything, mind that boy on scooter. Nearly there, feeling warmer and warmer inside, the closer to home.

Maybe a little bit drunk, Joe? A bit merry? No, not merry. Not merry.

Coffee, Joseph if you please. Whoops, careful. Black coffee Joseph, hot and strong.

I tidy the letters I've dragged out, picking up stray sheets from the floor, re-filing them with care. Everything in its place, a place for everything. The back room still smells of lavender polish – and now I remember, suddenly, the convent corridors of St Vincent's convent, the glossy pews in the little chapel, the corridors down which, on rare occasions, we altar boys would be led to a late breakfast of toast and jam and small iced cakes. Easter Week, that would be, released from school to serve. The severity of the nuns softened as they watched us eat. I stand there and think to myself, not without wonder, that I was once an altar boy.

Not for long, of course. Scepticism winning through, an early appearance.

I pat the letters down in their box file, a small dry sigh as they settle, and just before I flick the holding spring back in place, I fumble for and withdraw that much handled envelope.

Nosey Bah. His name for me when he'd maybe surprise me ferreting at something, nosing out a postcard from behind the mantel mirror, say, craning my neck sideways to examine a part-filled crossword one of the men had for the moment abandoned. Nosey Bah, Cork for inquisitive, always pronounced as if it were one word. Early teens, one day when it occurred to me to write it out (I was going through a phase of writing down things I'd hear, non-standard usages) I realised it was two words – but that left me stumped. Who the hell was Bah, I asked myself crossly, frustrated that I would never know because none of the men knew, Mick didn't know.

How many times have I done this, in the past thirty years? I carry the envelope through to the kitchen, never the front room. I want the hard bare light on the photographs, room to spread them out.

Me on my confirmation, the Mon blazer, first long trousers, rosette on my lapel. That calculating look explained by the custom of giving money to children on the big day. I see clearly I am reckoning up how much I've scored, how much I might reasonably expect to gather in before darkness falls.

Myself aged thirteen or so at Murphy's Rock, one of our

long summer walks, my satchel swung round to the front, one hand inside it. Reaching for chocolate, was I? Fair Isle sleeveless sweater, open neck shirt, baggy shorts. My head back, so that there's too much light on my forehead.

And on, a whole series of me and me alone, the seasons, the years, all recorded.

I spread these out to my left, each photo slightly overlapping the next, two rows.

The next set will be smaller: my parents standing against their bicycles; my parents with strangers, strangers to me that is, evidently friends, all laughing together; my mother holding, it must be, me – the blanket pulled up over the child's head, the photographer's concentration on her rapt, expression, one stray curl half hiding her eye. One shot of Mick and my father, stiff but – I always dwell on this – nevertheless at ease with one another. One shot, taken by Mick I suspect, of my mother at our front door, one hand raised to shield her eyes from the sun, cardigan open over a flowered summer dress. Laughing.

The next set, the men in various groupings: some indoors, shirt sleeves, tea pot, jug, half a loaf on the table, all looking up patiently, humouring Mick and his bloody camera. Affection, for sure, but in one or two faces, and maybe I am supplying this, the shadow of disappointed lives. The men setting out on a cycling expedition, the men at a hurling match, all thumbs up, the men on the fringes of some political meeting, shoulders back, faces turned away. And so on.

And the last set. A snatched blurred shot, out in the hills of West Cork I always think, Mick and the men, grim-faced and somehow haunted, bandoliers, rifles, long coats, soft caps. Mick with his hands jammed in his pockets, scowling at the camera.

Then Mick in bright sunshine, arcades behind in the middle background, a group of men in berets, shirtsleeves, many of them with pipes, one joker levelling his pipe at the camera as if it were a pistol. Mick in a leather jacket, tanned and rangy and very, very grim, looking away down a hillside into a valley, more hills climbing away from us in the background. He has a foot up on a rock, a rifle propped on his knee making a sharp diagonal across the picture. Far and away the best photograph of the lot, properly composed, properly lit and focused, this is the work of an American, Harry Wayland Randall, photographer to the Abraham Lincoln Battalion. I know this because on the back Mick has carefully lettered, I recognise his hand even in block capitals: taken by H W Randall, ALB, Jarama. Two more photographs to go. The first, Henri and Mick, seated in chairs outside a farmhouse. Dark suits, collarless shirts, tanned-looking, worn down but defiant. Their hands on their knees, they stare straight ahead, almost as if defying the camera. You wouldn't cross those two, I remember thinking that, spilling the contents of the envelope onto this table for the first time. A week after Mick's funeral. Not able for it until then.

My family farm, Henri explained, peering over my shoulder when I showed it to him. I had thought this one was also Spain. No, no, he said. I remember that day very well. On the radio, the BBC, the night before, we learned of the landings in Normandy. We knew the worst was yet to come, you see this in our faces, yes? This photograph, we had young Marcel take it because we expected to die soon, we had been talking and realised that we had no photograph of us together.

I don't understand, I said, what do you mean the worst was yet to come?

Oh too difficult to explain, perhaps another time ... And then, seeing my disappointment, he said: ok, like this then, but briefly. Our Maquis group had been careful for years, you understand this. A sabotage here, a small ambush there. So much time spent training the young men, building up weapons, never enough, never enough. There was a calculus, you see? We ambush a German patrol, they burn down a village, maybe they kill everyone. Mick, me, we understand how this thing works, and maybe too we had better minds to understand the overall situation, I mean the whole war? Rifles and pistols against tanks? No thank you. This we had seen before. But the Resistance was beginning to grow, and grow, as more and more people saw which way was blowing the wind. We have a commander who wished to make an uprising, to seize and declare a big piece of territory. This, you should know, was up in the Vosges.

Now we knew, these landings in Normandy, we knew this commander, the eager young men, they would move. They could not be held back. We knew, too, this would mean disaster. Pinned down on the plateau, artillery, tanks, maybe 15,000 Germans in the region. It would be ... annihilation. So, this photo. The same day he developed it, Marcel. Two copies. Sentimental, huh? Also, I should say, we knew, the Party, we knew De Gaulle was in no hurry to see us receiving heavy weaponry, you know? Look, listen, I have to be going. Some day, maybe ...

And the final photograph. I sweep the rest into a neat pile, patting the edges and settling them the way I do when I'm tidying a deck of cards after a hand of patience.

This photograph is of me. I am standing outside the *caves de Panthéon*, my favoured wine shop, bent at the waist, peering in the window. Judging from the fall of light, the fact that I'm in a jacket while the woman just beyond me walking away has a scarf wrapped thickly around her neck, it is autumn or spring. I favour spring. There is something odd about the composition: everything massed to the right, if I might put it like that. I have come to the conclusion that this is because what I have in my hand is part of a photograph, that something is missing.

It took me a long time to work this out. I could not understand how Mick came to have the photograph at all, I confess to some flashes of paranoia about the whole business. One day I was looking away from the photo in disgust and then glanced back suddenly, putting my hand out to catch it, as a sudden gust blew the kitchen window open. Ah. On the left-hand edge of the photo, a long shadow is advancing into the shot. If I guess at a larger, more whole composition, this figure would be front and centre. A long angular shadow – it must be morning, then, on the Rue Saint Jacques – with a hand thrown up, the arm horizontal from the elbow to the face. Who else?

From this I work it out: the photographer stalking the area, waiting for a candid shot of the great man, the shot appearing in some paper or magazine; Mick seeing the photo, somehow contriving to order a print, and then cropping the shot so that I move from the incidental margin to the centre.

No snag marks from a scissors, he must have used a ruler and razor, discarding what was of no interest or meaning to him.

All of the grief that I thought I had been unable to feel, all of the blame and self-loathing I had subsequently heaped on myself, bitterly charging myself with an inability to feel – the first time I saw this photograph, with its freight of mystery, of the inexplicable, I sat at this table under a bright light and wept until I thought, at last, for a terrified moment, that I would never stop weeping.

That one time, but of course never again. I was done. For a long time after I would examine this photograph, this stolen record, and puzzle myself to discover its provenance – until, of course, light dawned.

Now when I take it from its envelope, I marvel at Mick, not for his sentimentality but for the simple resolution it took, having seen the photograph by chance, to acquire a print, to crop it and keep it. No more and no less than reassurance that I was living an ordinary life.

One last thing to note, then, before I put the envelope back in its box of quiet. A brittle paragraph, carefully cut from a newspaper. It records the death in a car accident of Detective Garda Martin Cassady, aged thirty-seven, in a late-night accident near Crossmolina, County Mayo. Garda Cassady was unmarried, had been posted in Mayo for many years. It did not say, as was customary, that he would be missed by his colleagues and the community he had served blah blah blah. It recorded that there had been heavy rain that night, and that no other vehicle was involved in the incident. Almost as an afterthought, it concludes: Garda Cassady when stationed in Cork was shot in the line of duty in 1960; nobody was ever charged with the shooting.

Across the bottom margin, some hand I do not recognise has forcefully scrawled: drunk.

44

The voice on the phone was measured and low. I did not recognise it. I had never received a call at home from anyone I did not know – not even from someone who'd dialled a wrong number – and I was surprised, so much so that at first I did not take in what was being said to me. I had to interrupt the woman, ask her with apologies to repeat herself. There was a pause, then she said, of course, we have not spoken before, you will not have recognised the voice. My name is Delphine, I am the wife of Henri.

Another pause, to allow me to understand.

Ice in my lungs, time slowing. Marie Louise had been calling to the office lately, where once it had been Henri. She had been vague, but I had gathered that he was unwell.

Yes, I said – and I was going to say more but found I could not.

Well, she said, it seems strange to you that we have not spoken before? To me, also. Joseph, he would like to see you. She paused to let that sink in – the detached watcher in me was by now admiring her perfect control of the pace of this conversation. We both knew what was really being said, she was giving me time to absorb all the implications.

I have a pen, I said. Good, she said, here is the address.

Rue des Tournelles, near Bastille, not far.

I'm sorry, I said.

She left what I must call a gracious silence. Today would be good, she said, if you can.

I sat down on the floor. I said, but of course. If there is anything ...

No, she said, nothing. Then: it seems strange, I have always wanted to meet you.

I shall see you very shortly, *Madame*, I said. A sigh: Delphine, she said, please. After all this time ...

Delphine, I said, of course.

Goodbye for now, Joseph.

I will see you shortly, I said. Goodbye. Thank you for calling.

I stood, not without difficulty, my bones somehow seized up, I put a hand on the wall to steady myself. For a moment, I was dizzy, confused, near panic. I had been for days immersed in that death so long ago, and now here is Henri ... I even wondered if I had brought this on him.

Steady, I told myself, steady now.

I went through and splashed water on my head, my hands cupped, handfuls and handfuls, not caring that my collar was getting soaked, that a cold rivulet was running down my back. I stripped off my shirt, checked that my trousers were dry, took a towel from the warming rack by the window, towelled myself vigorously.

The tumblers were clicking over in my head. Sixteen years since Michael John's funeral. Sixteen years. How long since I'd first met Henri, on that dockside building at night, my stomach still fluttering at being on land after that rough crossing? The long journey by night, the house on the Rue Cavé, Marie Louise, Pascal. Thérèse.

And all the years since. The life that I call mine, Henri at every turn of the road. Henri in Blackpool church. Henri in the office in the Rue Cochin. Henri in these rooms when they were bare. Big block of a man, loving and shrewd.

I found I was sitting on the floor again, my back to the folded-back door, the polished boards of the hall running away to the front door. Harsh daylight a line under the door, an accent at the far end of the dark hall.

So many days and nights. Henri so often in this place since

the floors were bare dusty boards, approving each change as I made it my own, eventually stepping in the door as into the comfort of a known place he had somehow made his own, also.

I could have walked, a brisk hard day but not so cold that one would have hesitated to walk. I sat into a taxi at the bottom of Soufflot. The driver was not in a mood to speak. I studied his profile as we drove: he seemed to me a man who had seen too much. I caught myself thinking this and was grateful to have caught myself. One projects one's inner weather onto others so easily, a recurrent fault I have never been able to eradicate. I paid him €10 even though the fare was only €6, was perversely gratified that his response was not pleasure but a slow suspicion.

I rang the bell, and someone bade me enter, said third floor, there is an elevator. Of course there is, I thought, stepping into the hallway – green marble floor, polished mahogany panelling, gilt handles on double height painted doors to left and right. Scissor gates on the elevator, a panelled cabin. I stepped out onto figured carpet, the door directly opposite me open and a young woman standing there, her hand rising to meet mine as I crossed, stretched out my own hand. Charlotte, she said, I am the youngest daughter, you are welcome here. Come, he will be pleased to see you.

I followed her out of the square hallway into a long sitting room, flooded with light; pale blue walls, very high ceilings, paintings, a border of polished parquet to the plain grey carpet. Gleaming furniture, glass fronted book cases, consoles, at the far end a gathering of upholstered chairs. Rising from a silk-covered chaise longue, I could see the weave glisten, a tall slender woman, ash-blonde hair pulled casually back. Like her daughter, her daughters, in a simple dress – hers a deep blue, Charlotte in black, the other daughter, also now rising, in dark green.

Delphine, the woman said, taking my hand in both of hers, and this is Nathalie. I bowed slightly, looked up into ice blue eyes, into warmth and welcome. He will be very pleased you have come, she said, and smiled; since I told him you were coming he is almost his old self, orders, arrangements! Her look conveyed, as she intended, that this rallying would be temporary.

Bah, she said, then, herself rallying to a sudden mischief, we will let him wait a moment or two, eh? The daughters smiled too, at each other, at her, and then at me. Nathalie took my by the arm, we sat. They looked at each other and it was Charlotte who said, looking for confirmation to the others, we have wanted for so long to meet you.

And there was silence, while we considered this. It had sometimes seemed odd to me, that Henri had never introduced me to his family. I could see that it suited us both, of course, not least because I had no wish to be a surrogate son and Henri had no wish to feel for me a father's responsibility, to take on himself a father's duty to judge and advise. Now, sitting here at my ease with these women, sitting here feeling how very much I was at ease, my sorrow at his impending death gave way for a moment to an inexplicable sense of loss, of what was for me an alien feeling, regret for what might have been.

Delphine must have divined in me the loneliness that ambushed me there, then, on the spot. We'll make coffee, Charlotte said, catching her mother's quick look, Nathalie a beat behind her as they ... absented themselves. Like that. Here, gone.

She was beside me, my hands in hers. Enclosed. Henri admires you, you know? Your kindness, this I see for myself, your ... fortitude. As for this – her waving hand encompassed the rich apartment, the whole of the life it had known and encompassed, the life I had known nothing of until now – this he has always protected, so to speak; not from you, understand, not especially from you Joseph, but from the comrades, from his work in the world.

Perhaps we are his sanctuary, do you think? Here he does not have to anticipate disappointment? Perhaps also, I do not know, perhaps also it is like this that he lets us be free to choose ourselves?

I saw that she hoped to find somewhere, somehow, the strength to endure her life when he would be gone, but I saw also, and she saw me understand, that she would fail in this, that her own life energy would weaken and fade, eventually to nothing, when her life's companion would go. Her look said she knew this, had already accepted it and I thought what a marvel it must be, to have such a friend in this life, such company as Henri had enjoyed in this woman, this Delphine.

Ach, she said, rising, disengaging, one must play the cards one is dealt, eh? Those girls, they have grown too timid, too careful of their health, to make proper coffee.

Through there, she said, come to us in the kitchen later.

The afternoon sun lay full on his face where he sat upright by the high window, neat in a burgundy dressing gown the smart collar of ironed pyjamas folded back at his throat. There was a small burnished table between the two chairs, something North African, polished and fretted copper or brass. A large wooden bed on the other side of the room, neither single nor double, a cabinet beside it with a neat array of medicines, away to the right a large ornate wardrobe. A guest room, I thought, looking down into the street as I, too, sat, looking back into the room, looking anywhere but into his eyes.

Tsk, he said, what are you afraid of? Come, Joseph, I am dying, we are all agreed, look at me. Good. Are you well?

He meant it, the question, and I felt I could answer that yes, I was well, but ...

Ah yes, he said, I thought about telling you some months ago, when they told me, but ... you know how it is, eh? You know what I am like.

Not a question.

What was to be seen there, in those eyes? Well, death of course. In that steady regard, in the faint play of amusement that came and went, I saw the dark light of a coming death. Something welling from behind, in the tiniest of unstoppable increments. A figure far off but discernible, marching calmly towards me.

I wonder now at my state of mind, there, then, seeing unmistakably what I saw.

So, he said, when I had grown tired of looking, it comes to us all, eh? The doctor says less than a month, *Madame* the paediatrician – it is not exactly her speciality, cancer, you know – *Madame* the paediatrician, unfortunately, she agrees. You were talking, eh?

Looking away out the window, he said: it would have been impossible, you know?

He meant involving me in his family life.

Impossible, he said again. Oh but often I wanted to, you know. He grew suddenly anxious, Joseph do not think, I beg you, that ...

Trust me, I said, trust me. I understand. And I did, and I saw that he understood that I did.

Good, he said. Now forgive me, I am winding up my affairs, as of course you understand. We must talk, a little. This work we have done together, you and I, well, perhaps that too is coming to its end. Not because I am dying, you understand, no don't make that face, of course I am dying, no, it's just that everything has its time, don't you agree? So, not because I am dying but because maybe something else is dying, too.

I knew where this was going, at least I thought I knew, but I said nothing. Waited.

All these years, Joseph, these years of ... resistance. Shall we agree to call it that, eh? Resistance. Listen, there will be a certain comedy when I go. The Party funeral, the flags, the speeches. The old guard, those salauds will be glad to have outlived me, to see my light quenched. Ha. And the young ones, because I am old they will discount me, have already begun to discount me, without even wanting to know what I have done with my life. Eh, so let it go, eh?

You see, ah but you know this I think, that was never the point, the Party, all that. Listen, when I went to Spain, you know what age I was?

A knock at the door, Charlotte with a tray, a cigarette smouldering in the corner of her mouth. Henri said, you see? Her old man is dying of lung cancer, she comes in here smoking, you see how cruel they are to me? She took the cigarette, from her mouth, grinned, said ah shut up old man, always complaining, handed him the cigarette, left, smiling to herself.

Now, where was I? Yes, Spain. I was twenty, you know in some ways I might have been better suited to the anarchists but ... I was just smart enough to understand the need for discipline. Those fucking Russian communists, though, I came to hate them very quickly. But, somehow I found I had joined the Party – and it was after Spain, you see, that I saw what I would do. I do not presume to bore you with my idea of myself, with my unimportant life.

He broke off, he poured us coffee, he insisted I take a biscuit.

Poor Joseph, he said, sitting back, cup to his lips. You see I have lured you here for a sermon! But, you will forgive me, I continue.

I went to Spain with a boy's heart, eh? I saw, I do not know how, that the world was wrong, that something needed to be fixed. Ah but, this boy's heart I brought out of Spain in an exhausted body, with a man's mind. I saw that I was a soldier, you see, and I saw that I needed to learn, to study my enemy. Already I have said to you, you remember I said it also at the funeral of our Miguel, I have said that it is for some as clear as: if not us, who? And I saw that, inside the Party there were many of us. Of course (and here he leaned over to pat my knee, although my attention was not wandering) of course inside the Party there were also many of them, eh? Of the enemy! But, all things considered, a mechanism, an apparatus.

Now, suddenly, he was tired. One minute animated, present and clear; the next minute, as if a switch had tripped, tired.

He stood up slowly, the sun gilding his whole body, and turning away he unfastened his dressing gown, let it fall. Help me into bed, he said, pass me those pills, there. Good. Let me have a minute.

I propped him up, handed him the pills, a glass of water from the blue carafe. You like that, he asked, seeing me examine it? She bought me that, Delphine, in Venice. Saw my eye linger on it, one afternoon as we passed. The next morning, she was gone when I came down to breakfast, walked in the door of the dining room as I finished, handed me that. Beautiful, eh? Ah so many years ago ...

I was afraid he would be sad, now, afraid that I would not know how to cope.

He dozed for a minute, maybe two. I just stood there, looking at nothing. Eventually I pulled a chair away from the wall, sat.

Then: so where was I? Ah, yes. Miguel, when we had made it to France, when we were holed up with my people in the mountains, the Hitler-Stalin pact, he saw it before most of us did. Nonsense, he said, nonsense: two liars, two monsters buying time. Like, that, Miguel, was he not? Quick. Straight. But I did not leave the Party, and in 1956 I did not leave, and in 1968 I did not leave, after Prague. You see, even after Gorbachev, I did not leave. Now you see why, eh? More of us than you might think, Joseph old man, burrowing in, using the Party as a host body.

Others, the younger people now, they work through other host bodies. An old friend of mine, he said once it was like leaven rising through dough to give us bread.

The long march through the institutions: friend Gramsci said it, friend Dutschke repeated it, no doubt some enterprising young woman will re-invent the phrase soon, eh?

He pushed himself off the pillows, reached for my arm, and gripped: you fear I am rambling, Joseph?

The thought had crossed my mind, I said, but he knew I was teasing him, and if he was grateful for being teased, he was even more grateful that sorrow had not unmanned me.

So, he said, we of the permanent resistance, we have done our bit, I hope. You understand, Joseph? In 1968, in that warehouse, ah what a crazy time that was, eh? You remember, you said you had a question for me?

I remember perfectly well, I said, rocked inside myself by the sudden, near-catastrophic onrush of memories. I remember very well, I said; I asked you: who are we here?

Yes, exactly, who are we here? I am there looking at you, thinking how best to answer you, and I see that I do not need to explain at all. Asking the question, you have already, I see this, understood what is the answer.

So, you will have to go now soon, because this time I really need to sleep. What was it? Yes. Where I started. New times, Joseph, they need new ways, also perhaps new people. Now listen to me, I know that you have chosen to be, what shall I say, yes, part of our work, yes? And I know, because you have told me so, that none of this have you done because of obligation, eh? But, this is not you understand because soon I will be gone, perhaps this part of your life also is over? Perhaps you will wish to let it fade away?

I looked more closely at him, then, our eyes searching each other out, and I saw that indeed he had begun to fail, that he was indeed shrunken, the skin like oiled paper over the cheekbones, the once vigorous hair lack-lustre, the bones retreating inside the body. I had come into the room, I saw now, fearing what I might find but at the same time determined to find the indestructible Henri of old but fearing to see him already in ruins. As I let go of these projections, as I began to allow myself see the dying man as he actually was, he began to smile – and it was indeed the old Henri surfacing from the wreckage, one last time; that old shrewd look, one eyebrow raised slightly higher than the other.

He sent me a good man, El Leon. A good comrade. A good son.

He saw me start, and smiled again, shaking his head. Ah no, Joseph, I never made that sentimental mistake – and nor did you. But, you know what I mean, eh?

He slumped inside himself, then, his eyes falling closed. I got up to go, perhaps I hesitated a moment because he murmured: come again soon, Joseph, I should have invited you long ago.

I bent over the bed, I put my hand on his heart and pressed, very lightly. *No Pasaran*, I said softly in his ear, *No Pasaran*; without opening his eyes, without straining himself in any way, he nodded gently. That's right he said, that's right Joseph. *No Pasaran*.

I took one last good look at him then, without once looking back, I left the room.

Delphine knew, she read it in me, she nodded once, twice, said:

it is good you came here, good. She made a gesture towards visitors who had arrived while I was talking to Henri.

Marie Louise rose, moved towards me without a backward glance, touched my arm briefly as she passed, went on in. Mother and daughters turned away into the kitchen. By some kind of unspoken agreement Pascal and I walked to the window, squinting a little against the high glare. I glanced over my shoulder, at the door into the bedroom. No sound. I imagined her sitting there quietly by his bedside, hands on her lap. Tiny and fierce and utterly calm.

A remarkable woman, Marie Louise, Pascal said. You know how old she is? Seventy-six. Me, I am eighty, the same as Henri. She told you, perhaps, that in the war I was her commander? No, I said, I guessed but I wasn't sure, never asked. Yes, he said. We were both still staring out at the street, the traffic, the people going by below – in 1939 she escaped to England, she was nineteen, imagine; in 1943 she came back, was sent back; we had a cell in Paris ...

Last year we were having dinner together, nothing special, a casual arrangement and she said, Pascal she said, I should have married you all those years ago. Eh, Joseph, imagine! So, who knows why we do these things; I said, sure, marry me then. And she said, OK. I will.

I put my hand on his back, between the shoulder blades, let it rest there. I could think of nothing to say. I patted him once, twice, walked away.

Thank you, Delphine said, opening the door out into the world. Thank you, Joseph. Thank you. She brushed my cheek with the cool back of her hand. Those pale, clear eyes.

I didn't look back, I couldn't look back. I took the stairs.

45

How we see things without knowing at the time that we are seeing them. On the console table in that apartment, a spread of framed photographs. Two of them to one side had caught my eye, for just a moment. I did not remember them until days later, when I opened the stiff yellow envelope that Delphine, seeing me to the door, had given me. Copies, I understood, she had prepared for me. In one, under a harsh sun, arms across each other's shoulders, Mick and Henri, each in a long sleeveless leather jerkin, Henri casually holding a rifle by his side, Mick with a sub-machine gun on a strap around his neck; the other, in a softer light, was of myself and Henri on the steps of the Sorbonne. Nabile took that, I remember it well, my last day on the job. There was to be a party. Henri in a leather jacket, roll neck sweater, caporal jutting from the corner of his mouth, me in a long, light coat, white open neck shirt. We, too, have our arms around each other.

A small wrought iron shelf I bought in, where was it, Porto? Who knows on what whim! I remember retrieving it from a cupboard, fitting it to the wall, standing the two photographs side by side inside the curved protective sidepieces. How neatly they fitted. I push back my chair now, I swivel to one side, to see the late afternoon sun fall in a stripe almost exactly across the head-high shelf.

Porto. Three days, or was it four? And when was that? I have been in so many places, all down the years. Sometimes alone, sometimes with some companion of the moment. What was her name, that young woman I met in Porto, her long black hair swinging back as she reached for this shelf where it sat on a table in a dusty shop reeking of spilt wine? A gift to me.

It lay in the back of the hall cupboard for so many years, an awkward thing; how often did I say to myself: I must throw that out?

Yes, well, I say out loud, and that was then. I have begun to speak to myself; I do not know if this is a good thing or a bad thing, or indeed any kind of thing worth remarking – but I notice it.

I fall into a null moment, not quite sure what it was I had been planning to do.

A long ring on the doorbell. A pause, another, not quite as long.

Saved by the bell, I think, and immediately I scold myself for the cliché. A good sign or a bad sign, this self-scolding? I don't know, but one or the other has broken me free from the null place, the bell or the scolding.

I open the window inward, briskly, lean carefully out, and Genevieve's face is bright as she beams up at me. Pale face, black hair, red leather jacket. A big armful of flowers. Come on, old man, the key, the key!

As adept as Vincent, more graceful though, she waits until the last second before she spins on her heel and snatches the bright keys from the air. Hoopla! Delighted with herself. The first time she has not made me come down to let her in.

I rush to open the door, the better to watch her come climbing vigorously up the stairs, the better to soak in that uprush of buoyant happiness.

A mild, unexpected rush of sexual pleasure from our embrace – such full small breasts, such a trim waist, so pronounced the out-slant of her hips! She lingers a moment, her perfume heady, her cheek nuzzling my neck. She ... permits me. In evident, conscious fondness.

Ah Joseph, she says, melting out of my arms, marching into the apartment, you must have been a devil! And from the kitchen, the laughter still in her voice: evidently you still are!

Devil or not, I am absurdly pleased to observe I can still be aroused – to no end, of course, but what of it? At my age desire is its own delight, its own satisfaction.

Stop it, I say, stop it at once! She is pouting at me lasciviously, her hands open to frame the display of freesias and lilies she has already arranged in my big bowl. Stop it, my heart ...

Oh all right, then, now she is downcast, altogether a different kind of pout. Points at her own face: you see, orphan in the snow, barefoot, turned away from the door ...

Bravo, I say, applauding. Very good, very good.

Right, she says, Genevieve again, smart and efficient. It's a beautiful day out there, you're spending too much time at that cursed laptop, come on. Get your coat. You can buy me a drink if you like, if you're feeling mean and cautious I'll buy you a drink.

Pushing me out into the hall, both palms flat against my chest.

Joseph? Coat? Hello? Come on, I'll turn that thing off for you – going through into the front room.

No, wait, I say, I have to ...

... save and quit, yes of course. I'll do that. I hope you're saving as you go, you have to do that you know, I save every fourth or fifth line, that's what you should do, too. There, done. Hey, big document, Joseph, wow!

I cut her off, I don't want, as they say nowadays, I don't want to go there. Come on, I say, buttoning my coat, let's go then, what's keeping you?

Keys, she asks? I pat my pocket. Right, she says, let's go make all the other old crocks jealous as hell.

She links her right arm into the crook of my left – so's you can flourish that cane, she says. You don't actually need it, do you? No, didn't think so. Suits you though.

Lots of people out today, I say presently.

She looks at me oddly. It's Sunday, Joseph. What, you didn't know?

No, I tell her, I've been ...

... stuck in that book, that memoir, yes?

Out of nowhere, irritation. Not a memoir, I say, surprised myself at the sharpness of my tone. Not a memoir.

Oh god, I've wounded her, she recoils as if slapped, stops, let go my arm. Doesn't know what to say. A couple, harassed, driving two children before them, turn and look.

Come here, I say, and fold an arm around her, feeling her bristle away, then go quiet, lean in against me.

How to explain?

I can't, at least not yet. The question has been drifting against me, no, the questions have been drifting against me, like grains of sand, piling up into a dune, unseen but felt, the weight steadily accumulating.

Gen, I say, I'm sorry – she waves this away, links my arm again, pulls me gently on.

Ghosts, I say, surprising us both, what it feels like, I've been accumulating ghosts.

Ah, she says. And, forgive me, the ghosts are accumulating you?

I don't understand what she means.

I would have thought, she says, picking her words carefully, I would have thought that, a long life like yours, when you summon your ghosts there is the danger, no, that they will begin to summon you?

This time it is I who stop, startled, and I see she has shocked herself, a little, not having meant to say those words.

Wow, she says, where did that come from?

We walk on.

We come on to Rue Mouffetard through an arch way smelling of piss in the sun. Crowds bustling past, uphill and down. We hesitate, then she nudges me as I imagine a tug nudges a ponderous sluggish ship. Down, she says, down first, then against the current back up. More interesting, and the sun behind us for looking at faces. The cafés and restaurants have those light tin tables balanced precariously outside their doors, there are patient queues outside fishmonger and baker, outside the Vietnamese *traiteur*, the butcher, the cheese shop, all with their counters projecting into the street. The young people are all of them eating as they stroll, it seems to me, crepes, kebabs, slices of pizza. Gen is a born shopper, a picker up and scrutiniser of avocadoes and lettuces, a sniffer at fish, a handler of racks of garments.

A faint smell of sewage here and there, bright awnings, sudden dips into light and shade, a rattle as someone re-arranges the bins outside the wine merchant, the babble, no other word for it, of a thousand voices. Then a siren, a burglar alarm or a car alarm, buzzsawing through the air, and under that, getting louder as we descend, somebody singing over an accordion, the sound amplified, getting louder again as we reach the bottom of the road, the hill. Some kind of covered stand, a man in an exaggerated Basque beret, red neckerchief at his throat, the wheezing accordion swaying bony hands. In front of him, white scarf outside black coat, both trailing to her ankles, an old woman in a peaked white cap singing something from ... the 1950s, is it? And dancers, some waltzing, some doing a version of tango, a crowd around all this, many with sheets of paper in their hand, studying the words, singing along. Something absurd about this unexpected scene, something self-conscious, but also, and this I approve of, something defiant, something about it that refuses the car alarm, the news on the television, the present moment.

Gen is entranced, she has her iPhone out and at first I think she is trying to frame some kind of perfect photograph until I see, watching her drift through the waltzing crowd, that she is making a video on the phone.

A very sexy woman in her forties, slender and swaying, comes through the crowd with a bucket, rattling the coins in time to the music. I drop a €5 note in the bucket, her eyes flicker down then up at me. Dazzle! By god, I think, straightening myself up, by god I'm in good form today!

Come on, you! Gen has my arm, that's altogether too much excitement for one day. Over her shoulder, one last time, the chestnut-haired busker favours me with a wicked, forgiving smile.

We breast the tide in single file, Gen's black head weaving this way, that way as the merchants begin packing away their stalls, hosing down the cobbles, turning with only a slight impatience to satisfy a late, importunate shopper.

An interrogative look from Gen, I raise a palm in acquiescence. One of the older, more modest restaurants, agreeably dark and quiet in the back. We order after a brief look at the blackboard, settle on a bottle of white. My choice, a Cotes de Duras blanc sec.

Appreciation from Gen, swilling a mouthful: who's been reading the wine columnists, then?

You have, evidently.

Ouch, she said.

I just happened upon it and liked it, I said.

Like you happened upon us, she shot back.

Upon us, I notice.

Our terrines arrived, we began to pick with our forks.

Did you like the piece in *Libé*, I asked her?

I thought he judged it well, she said, and was going to sweep past but acknowledged my look by saying: well of course, you know this, we talked it over very carefully, he and I, before it went in.

Well of course they did. There would be more, I knew. I sat quietly.

You see, Vincent, here's the thing. On the one hand, the assimilationists, OK? One France, everyone learns it, no matter your cultural background, the colour of your skin, hell no matter even your politics, never mind your gender, never mind your whatever – one France, the Republic one, entire and indivisible. We sink ourselves, all of us sink ourselves, in a common society.

OK. Now, on the other hand, what shall we say, the distinctives? The exceptionalists? One is Ariègeois, one is of La France Profonde, one is – Algerian? Islamic? One is a woman? You see? OK, of course you are familiar with all this, who isn't, eh?

But for us, for Vincent, how to deal with this? You know they have offered him a seat? I mean, a candidacy in a safe seat? Well, not exactly, the prospect is being held out. There are, conversations.

I must have looked impatient.

Of course I know he has spoken of this to you – and it is what you would have expected in any case, yes? But you see, Vincent genuinely wants to reach the young men, yes the young women, too, in the *banlieues*, the tower blocks, those very angry and alienated people. So, to them he must be strong, combative, genuine – you know these kids, this above all they value, their idea of what it is to be genuine. And on the other hand, he must be to others the lawyer, the reasonable young man, the wise head on young shoulders.

Plates cleared away, main courses. I am still waiting.

And she plunges in, straight for the heart.

He is afraid you are going to abandon him. She looked at me

expectantly. I knew this wasn't, quite, true. I did not see that he placed such a reliance on me.

OK, she said, maybe not exactly that. But everything is happening very fast, no?

I want to tell her, none of this is my responsibility. I hold my tongue.

Joseph, what is the point of wondering – how you come to be our friend, all that? But you see, we do need a friend, we need someone to trust, someone who sees things as they are.

She sees I am going to interrupt, raises a hand.

Yes, evidently, it helps of course, why not say so, that you seem to know so very many people. Interesting people. Yes, naturally. But more than this, more than this, why make mistakes that can be avoided, eh? When you can have good advice, in good time, from a good friend?

There is a certain gaucheness in her words, in her manner, that should be annoying me but for some reason doesn't. One shoulder forward, the other held back and down, the legs under the table fidgeting. They are intelligent people, she and Vincent, more than capable of steering the course that history offers his candidacy if he is careful and shrewd – and he is both of these things. And so is she. She stares away into space, and I wonder if maybe she thinks I have more to give. Further useful contacts, introductions. Well, that would be logical, but they will know, surely, that having freely given in the past, I am unlikely to hold back in the future.

Something about this conversation we are having does not ring true.

The coffee arrives and she stirs in a sugar, obsessively driving the spoon round and round the tiny cup.

She lifts her eyes, and the whole atmosphere around us changes. I feel power gathering inside her, her bones getting heavy, her breath going deeper. She straightens, and I imagine I see her uncoiling inside herself.

Joseph, she says, and her voice is very soft. Joseph, she says again, it seems to me you are in great danger of losing yourself these past weeks.

I freeze, my eyes jumping sideways to the busy street. She stops stirring. She waits until I am forced (by what?) to look at her.

We do not know each other very well, she says. But, on the other hand, well enough, eh? I know you see me, you have seen people like me before, yes? And maybe, I hope I do not delude myself, maybe also you see someone good and true when you look at me. As I do, as we do, when we meet you, when we spend time with you. But you know, I also, we also, see you. I see you Joseph, and I tell you that recently I am afraid for you.

I do not know what to say to this. I simply do not know. It is like being in a bubble, everything beyond close range shimmering, not quite in focus. The same with sound, I hear the clear small ring of her spoon as she raps it on the cup, the muted tap it makes when she places it by her scrunched up napkin on the bare table – but of the busy street outside, the chatter of people, the rattle of shutters I hear only a muffled version.

A kind of vertigo – and on the edge of that whirlpool, fleeting, almost not there at all, that grave and sombre regard, those unfathomable eyes, Thérèse.

Then, gone.

Everything crashes back, I wince at the inrush of sound and Gen puts her hand on mine, as if pinning me down very gently so that I do not float away.

You see, she says?

You are making this record, Vincent has told me. Gathering in your life, eh? So many ghosts, I do not doubt it. Do you think we do not speculate what your life has been? Yes of course, so many books on Ireland but you never speak of your country. So perfect, this, this being so French. A mysterious life, for sure. But, you see, we understand this is none of our business. Maybe you are writing this as a book, eh? Maybe someday we will read this manuscript, this book when it is published? Or perhaps it is only for yourself you make this record, who can say? You know what, Joseph? About this, in some strange way I do not care. No! Do not look at me so sceptically! Really, of course I am mad with curiosity but, eh, only curiosity, you know?

She pauses, and I stand outside this conversation. I see how still we both are, I see the turbulence of her energies inside her, a kind of sureness also, and I see inside myself some kind of grey-blue light, a kind of phantom presence of self inside self. Steady enough, but not very forceful. A dryness, a retreat from purpose.

Now she takes both my hands in her hands: Joseph, do not look so stricken. I have gone too far, I am sorry.

Perhaps she has, I am certain she is. I feel a flick of tenderness for her, something tentative but increasingly sure.

I am saying all this very badly, she says, I am sorry. Perhaps like this, OK? You have good charge of your life, even though I say that recently you are in a difficult place. Yes, yes this is true, why not agree with me, eh? It saves time you know! But, physically you are strong, you have good energy, good health. This will not always be so. Come, let us face facts. The world is what it is, eh? So, when it is difficult for you, perhaps when you begin to feel that some ... assistance? Oh of course years from now ... well, that you will permit us to be better friends? To be maybe of some help? On your own terms, of course, certainly, on your own terms, to be sure.

And now she sits back, folds her hands in her lap. Waits. How mysterious people are! She looks so vulnerable, so completely vulnerable to a cutting remark, a coldness, a brusque refusal – and deeper than that, farther away back inside herself, a profound patience, a sureness born of unerring instinct. Does she know, I wonder, how fortunate she is to have that instinct?

Probably.

Well that was very brave, I say, and light blossoms in her face.

Oh Joseph, she says, closing her eyes, leaning even farther back so that I fear she will tip her chair over, you cannot imagine how afraid I was! Terrified! Well – front legs of the chair thumping back to earth – OK, not terrified. We mustn't exaggerate. But, you agree, yes?

And she's back in charge again, of the conversation, herself, me.

What an agreeable sensation this is, I think; and I say yes of course, when I go gaga, when I am crooked and crippled and bedridden you can come wait on me hand and foot. I am miming these infirmities as I speak, to make her laugh of course, perhaps also to comfort myself that the chilling prospect she has opened up might not be so bad. You could come and bathe me, I add helpfully.

In your dreams, she says scornfully. I'm not going to be held responsible for your heart attack!

We pay, we leave, arm in arm.

Mme Frenaud, bound god alone knows where, in a cherry hat and bearing flowers, beams at me as I search for my key. *M'sieu* is looking very well today, she says, offering Genevieve an awkward half-bow. I incline my head gracefully towards her and she blushes, scurries away. Gen looks after her thoughtfully.

Oh and by the way, she says, I almost forgot ...

No you didn't, I tell her severely.

And now she blushes. All right, all right, it was only a manner of speaking, don't look so smug. Vincent and I, we are having a dinner next week, next Saturday. A few people, we would like very much if you would come.

A few people, I say.

She makes a dismissive gesture, back in charge again. You know very well what I mean, of course we want you to give them a look over, tell us what you think, if any of them should be trusted, yes, yes ... that sort of thing. But, Joseph, seriously now, Vincent and I, we would be honoured if you would come visit us in our home.

I took her face in both my hands, I said no, sweet girl, it is I who would be honoured.

And she kissed me. Lightly, delicately, but I ... flowered inside – how else to describe that sweetness?

Here, she said, handing me one of those index cards, blue; directions, the address, Metro and so on. Seven for seven-thirty. Our car's in for repairs but Vincent said to tell you not to worry, he'll find some way to drive you home.

I ruffled her hair, I'd wanted to do that since looking down from my window, hours ago. She winked at me, patted her hair flat, turned to walk away.

Joseph, she called back over her shoulder, Joseph?

Yes, I said?

Don't get cold there.

Freesias and lilies. I open the door wide, a dramatic gesture intended only for myself, and a wave rolls over me, heady and sluggish. Intoxicant. Freesias and lilies. Those pictures of Henri's in the front room, seen through the open double doors, dust on the frames, the glass.

Porto, yes. Pilar. Pilar Galán. Such sorrowful eyes, so slender and golden and fine boned; once when she was coming, she cried out: make me pregnant, I don't care, I shall kill myself.

And afterwards laughing, whatever she'd meant by that gone through her, leaving no trace in memory. From Asturias. Ah yes, I'd said, they say they fought bravely, the men of Asturias, the dynamiters from the quarries. And the women, she chided me, not unkindly, and the women. The women fought also.

Three days and nights. Never seen again, never heard from again. As we'd both wished it, unsaid from the start but between us understood. Porto.

46

I did not go to his funeral, I could not have borne it. That morning I called for the second time to the apartment on the Rue des Tournelles – uninvited, unannounced but not, I think, unexpected.

Once again it had fallen to Pascal to announce a death. We had looked at each other, he told me of the arrangements but even then I knew I would not be present and I was not ashamed, I know that he saw this, even that he approved. I assumed Marie Louise was below in the car, but I did not go down with him, neither when I went to the window did she appear, look up. I saw that Pascal's leg was stiff, as he climbed into the back seat. I imagined her hand stealing into his.

On the morning of the funeral, early, I called to the apartment. The street door was open, some old men in the hall ignored me, heavy with self-importance. I climbed the stairs, I rang the bell, an unseen hand opened the door and they were all three in the hall, facing me, sombre in black but not heavy or dark, perhaps something there of the temporary lightness that comes with release.

I kissed them formally, the daughters, the mother; we none of us spoke. I took from the document case I was carrying the folded flag of the Brigades, I handed it to Delphine, as Henri had known I would when he left it with me, returning from Ireland. A thing I had not known myself, that I would be handing it to his wife, his daughters.

Delphine made a gesture that asked would I like to come in, would I stay a while, but she knew what my answer would be even as her hand rose in the air.

As I was going down the steps onto the street, an empty

hearse came gliding to the pavement – and only then did I realise he was lying there upstairs, perhaps in an open coffin, perhaps with this morning light streaming in across the strong bones of that soldier's face.

I hesitated, almost I turned and went back again, but I knew that my moment had passed and saying to myself that perhaps it was all for the best I turned and walked away in the direction of Bastille. I walked all the way home through streets that were, for the most part, strangely empty.

On the Sunday afternoon, Marie Louise phoned, concerned but not worried. It was a brave day, she said, big crowd, all the dinosaurs going through the motions, fallen comrade, all that old tired stuff. But also, so many others. You know, our own kind of people? In fact, all kinds of people – you should have seen, Joseph, how surprised some of them were to see each other there! It was funny. And, so many of them so young!

A quiet conversation, punctuated by comfortable silences. I asked if she were free sometime in the following week and she said, sure, I'm free tomorrow for instance. I told her what I had in mind and she said: yes, what a good idea, yes we should do that. I will get Pascal to make the arrangements and one of us will phone you later.

I notice cars, I don't know why, ever since I was a child in Cork; I notice their makes and models, I automatically take note of registrations. I notice that Pascal has a fondness for big powerful saloons, always had. Always black, too. Early the next morning, the sun barely catching the zinc cowls on the chimneys across the way, I heard the low a growl of a powerful engine come slowly down the street, stop at my door. Dressed and ready, I was halfway down the stairs when the bell sounded in my apartment above me. An elegant young man stepped back, surprised but recovering quickly when I suddenly appeared.

Elegant, yes, but a bit of a tough, too, I saw. I was smiling as I ducked to enter the front seat, at Pascal's boyish love for these big saloons, his penchant for drivers who carried themselves as bodyguards.

Marie Louise in black wool, a shawl across her knees, Pascal in his usual black leather jacket, a grey silk shirt underneath. I thought they looked very handsome; I thought a policeman, stopping us, would find a reason to wave us on, put us quickly out of his mind. All this Marie Louise picked up on, always so quick. She rolled her shoulders, put on a deep voice: tough guys, huh?

A shy boyish smile from the driver; Michel, he said, reaching a hand to me, and he looked back affectionately at the pair behind us. So, he said, taking your grandparents for a drive, eh? Pascal cuffed him lazily on the back of the head, growled mind your manners, you. Fancy life on the dole, do you?

I settled back contentedly in the luxurious seats.

This isn't stolen, Pascal, is it? I was fairly sure it wasn't, but I knew the question would please him.

The less you know the better he growled. I caught the ghost of a wink from Marie Louise.

We took the road to Chartres, on to Le Mans and Rennes, then Lambale where we stopped for a light early lunch, terrine and salad, a bottle of cider apiece, then Saint Brieuc and, in the early afternoon, Binic.

I'm surprised you remember, Pascal had said, calling to confirm arrangements last night, grumbling about Marie Louise's penchant for springing things on him at short notice: Things should be planned, you know? Carefully.

My god, that must be, what, thirty-five, forty, years ago?

Yes, I said, something like that. I remembered a road sign,

Lambale, we'd come in more or less from the north-west so I went on Google earth and looked at all the ports, to see what might look familiar.

You went on what?

I explained Google earth to him. Eh, he said, you know about all this stuff? Hey, imagine how useful that would have been ... Yes, I said, but it would have been useful to them, too.

Ach, he said, of course it would. Nothing is hidden these days. Nothing. But well done Joseph, eh? Binic it was.

Michel drove us directly to the port. We came off the roundabout onto the Quai Jean Bart, yachts and motor yachts crowding the harbour beside us, and Pascal was confused, leaned forward to tap Michel on the shoulder. I brandished the map at him and Marie Louise soothed him. Then we came out onto Quai Surcouf and he saw the great stone harbour walls encircling the old port and he settled. So many changes, he said, more or less to himself. Everything changes, Michel murmured, surprising us. Everything changes except change

And who might you be, I wondered, taking a good look at him. He smiled without looking at me, said: except for what goes on, eh?

We cruised slowly to where a slipway descended at the root of the great north pier. I saw from the sun that this huge stone structure tended south-east. I had not remembered that. At the far end of the pier, the green-tipped lantern of a small lighthouse jutted above the massive double protective wall. Curving around to meet the lower south wall, this pier stood at a great height over the water. Low tide, I could see now how tricky the channel would be if you did not know your way. Pascal, standing beside me as Marie Louise rooted in the boot for a warm coat, pointed down, then out. You see, Joseph, we liked this place because first, it is a bit away from the town and what happens is to a great extent hidden by this great wall, yes? And second, because it can be difficult to get in here in the dark without local knowledge, well they tend to be – what? Lax? They pay more attention to other ports where it is easier to get in and out, eh? Besides (and this not without a certain complacency) we had good people here, you see. And a good choice of roads, too, you understand me?

Come on then, commander; Marie Louise was amused, gentle. She took his arm, handed me the roses we'd bought in the market in Rennes. Come on then, do not be playing old soldiers with poor Joseph.

It had rained that morning, it would rain again soon, I saw. We climbed up onto the walkway, sheltered by an elbow-high wall from the rising wind on the seaward side. I walked on the outside, conscious of the drop to the pier below, of the even greater drop to the mud and water away down there. Just room for three to walk abreast. To shuffle abreast, as I soon saw. Pascal's hip was evidently giving him trouble, but when he saw I was about to remark on this he shooed me away with an impatient gesture. Marie Louise leaned back, caught my eye, said with her look: you see how impossible he is? But she was smiling, stepping along neatly in her chic black suede boots.

How massive it all seemed, great granite blocks beside us, below us, regular underfoot. I could not imagine a sea that would overwhelm such strength, but then I reminded myself, they would not have built so massively unless they knew that they needed to.

We reached the end of the walk, descended some steps and stood by the white metal railing behind the lighthouse, sheltered from view. A man in a short wool coat, pipe in his mouth, looked at us curiously, saw the roses, nodded in understanding and moved away back down the pier, granting us privacy.

We stood there, accepting the cold, the rising wind, the incoming tide. I could not look at the other two, I slid quietly away into the dark of my own memories.

That turbulent crossing, night and rain, night and fog, the stink of fish, the unending noise of the heavy engine, the stink of fish. And then stepping up onto the granite pier, the night and the fitful streetlights and the dark broad harbour, a rough hand taking mine, the clouds low overhead and then being pulled into a car, and the loft, climbing the stairs under a bare bulb, the interrogation, fear and an undertone of doubt, of unspoken menace. Unsure of, perhaps even frightened of this Henri questioning me, turning my papers over in his hands – this man who is now called René as Henri comes up from the dark at the back of the room and takes me in his arms.

A sudden gust wakes me, and moments later a veil of rain came sweeping in from the north-west. Pascal to one side of me, Marie Louise on the other, not so much crowding, I see, as supporting me. Concern in his dark eyes, her head bent away as she divides the flowers into three. We take a moment, each for that instant unreachable to the others, and we let the roses fall into the dark water. We link arms, we look away up into the wind, to all that is up there, out there, vanishing swiftly into a dark wall of suddenly heavy rain. Then we link arms and careful to keep our balance in the buffeting gusts we round the lighthouse and there is the car, facing away from us, engine throbbing, and Michel struggling with an umbrella, holding it over Marie Louise as Pascal and I scramble for our doors.

Moules marinières, Pascal says, that's what I'd like now, a hot bowl of *moules*. We find a place (Michel seems to know his way around town) and when we have eaten, when we have dunked the last of the rough bread in the lemony herby juices, finished the rough white wine, Marie Louise calls for cognacs. I am slightly breathless, not caught for breath exactly but there is a wooliness in my breathing, a slight pressure in the centre of my chest.

Michel sits up straight, serious now after the banter, the sly jokes, the contented small talk that goes with good food and company. It is not a toast he proposes, it is a salute, and if it is meant for Pascal and Marie Louise, and if it is meant as an honour to our departed beloved Henri, he makes it clear that I, too, am included in his understanding of how things are, and it is this that, finally, brings me to silent tears.

He says: to all those who never surrendered!

We look at each other then, we veterans, and we all four turn to the high windows, to the rain and the wind and the darkening afternoon and perhaps it is more of a prayer than a challenge when Pascal murmurs softly: *No Pasaran*. And again: *No Pasaran.*

In the car, going home, charging between high hedgerows, telephone poles rattling past, a scarp of white wall, some high windows catching the late light, the busy hum of the high-speed roads, we drowsed, we spoke fitfully of this and that. The great bulk of Chartres was chugging along the horizon to the north when Marie Louise said to me, Joseph you will be closing down the office now, I expect? I knew that it wasn't a question. I made her no answer. I fell asleep.

And woke in a kind of panic. Night. The car, idling at a pavement. The back doors open, Michel unspeaking, staring straight ahead. Tired, I realise suddenly, he's tired. Across the street, standing into a doorway, arms wrapped around each other, Marie Louise and Pascal, staring upwards. I craned my head sideways, and then I too was looking up at lit windows in our former home, my first home on the Rue de Cavé.

They got back in. Nobody said a word. They drove me home

and when I moved to get out of the car I saw Pascal look at Marie Louise, nod. She was going to tell me news of Thérèse, I saw it in her face, I felt it in the sudden cold as Michel wound down his window. I looked at her and shook my head, I shook my head no. No. Enough.

I'd left a window open in my apartment. The car was still sitting there below, then as I pulled the drapes across it glided slowly and steadily away. When it was gone the street seemed more than empty. I stood there a long time, and then I undressed, letting my clothes fall where I stood, and I went naked to my cold bed.

Pascal died that winter, of pneumonia, following a fall on ice. I went to that funeral, I stood at the graveside in a sombre crowd, Delphine on one side of me, Marie Louise frail and fierce on the other, and it came to me there, making me feel something of a fool, that all these years I had grievously underestimated Pascal.

If I close my eyes I can still feel their grip on my arms, their nails sharp through the heavy wool.

I was too shy to visit Delphine afterwards, too reticent. I called regularly on Marie Louise. The last afternoon I spent in her company, she was stretched out on a couch in a kind of sun porch Pascal had built on their balcony, I thought she was asleep until she said, without opening her eyes: Ah Joseph, we have seen some times, you and I, such comrades we have been. And then one last time she unhooded those remarkable blue eyes and fixed me in her look, light shining out of her, joyous: weren't we wicked, my god, that day in the Sorbonne! Look at me, Joseph, I'm shivering to remember it!

Michel it was who drove me to their funerals. I still see Michel from time to time, we enjoy each other's company. He is a good man, I think. His books and articles are beginning to be influential.

47

Rain in the night, a steady drumming on zinc roofs. I have always enjoyed the sound of rain on a roof. When I was young in Cork I detested rain, and lying there on my back this morning, completely at my ease, it came to me what the difference is between here and there: in Paris the rain drains away, the gutters are deep and efficient, the soil under the city porous and light; Cork, by contrast, is built on a marsh, and every night's rain seems to add to the sodden mass of the city's foundations. Paris draws air and light, Cork seems to sulk in its bed of rain, gloomy and always damp.

Rain drains, rain accumulates – choose.

I pay little heed to these night thoughts: it seems to me one should be deep wrapped in dreams or fully and consciously awake – the liminal zone is the dangerous place where one is neither alive nor dead to the world. Here, indeed, be monsters.

But ... something in it all the same. I tell myself this as I rise with the light, go through to shower, shave, dress. A bit absent-minded.

Cotton cashmere and silk today, I observe myself choose my clothes in a kind of half-sleep, soft blacks and greys, low-key and dignified.

When I have dressed him (this is how it seems to me just then), when I have dressed him I stand him in front of the full-length mirror, that I may consider him.

Dignified, I think, yes, dignified, sure of himself, relaxed.

Some fucking car alarm goes off nearby and I am suddenly, angrily, fully awake. So much for gliding smoothly into the day.

A hard wind when I open the door to the street, a hard wind, breath of winter on it. At least the rain has stopped, but I should have worn a scarf. Croissants, a baton, *Madame* shivering a little each time the door opens to admit a customer. Winter is coming, eh *M'sieu*? One might say, *Madame*, that it has arrived? She pushes her lips outward, shrugs: one must accept, no? One must, *Madame*, one must.

Across the road from the café there is an unmarked police car, a man and a woman in it. I wonder how he's doing, the Basque boy? I am grimly satisfied my prediction has come true: now that the bird has flown, so to speak, they will waste weeks on pointless surveillance. The woman behind the wheel turns hard eyes in my direction, I see the flick of dismissal as she turns away and am secretly pleased. An old man, a man of no consequence, heading home to his simple breakfast.

Now I am making the coffee, standing there waiting for the percolator to do its stuff. Now I am taking off my jacket, draping it carefully over the back of the chair. I like this sweater, the deep black of it against the grey silk cuffs of my shirt. This cup, too, I like this white cup, cradled between my hands, I have a fondness for fine porcelain.

There is a great stillness in the apartment: the windows are locked down snug, the bathroom door I have closed on the faint hiss of the cistern. I have moved the freesias and roses to the far side of the kitchen, under the window; their scent is fading, more understated now, somehow more comforting for that.

I wash up and tidy away. In the hall, I ease off my shoes, place then neatly at the door to the front room. I like to walk around in socks, in bare feet – polished wood underfoot, rugs, tiles, carpet, such a simple sensuous pleasure.

The desk between the windows, a cool shaded space between panels of light. I sit.

I sit, and with my hands laced in my lap I close my eyes; I consider my situation.

The day Mick came home, the day he appeared on the doorstep that morning so many years ago, I went to my room when the fuss had died down. I kicked off my shoes and lay on the bed, watching the afternoon light play on the ceiling. Hands interlaced behind my head, breathing nice and slow. I felt full of my life, I felt the sureness of being in the exact right place, I felt at home.

In Eleni's house, waking that morning in her daughter's room, lying there, slowly inhaling the faint scent that her daughter's head had left on the pillow, I felt the same sureness. I felt at home.

These past weeks, trawling back through the years, piecing together this record, over and over again I found moments of being at home, so many, so many more than I would have thought to find.

I open my eyes and look around me: I am at home.

It strikes me then, the thought filling inside me, that perhaps I have always been at home.

I would not have said so.

All these long years, if anyone had asked, I would have said my great failing was, I had no power or desire in me to connect with the world, to connect with other people. I would have said: I have been remote, deficient in feeling, unable and unwilling to care. Little more than a travelling point of view.

There is truth in that. I am a solitary man by nature, and I have done my best to honour that nature, to be the self I was given from the start.

And yet, in the address book I will someday bequeath to ... someone, I find so many people with whom I have made, and some with whom I continue to make, a common unspoken cause.

Life is a lonely business, a dance between what we choose and what chooses us. It is what it is. We make the best of it, that is our nature, we play the cards we are dealt. One soldiers on.

But these past weeks, it astonishes me, these past weeks I have found that I was mistaken after all. I was not alone. I was never alone.

Life is our common business, dear Vincent, dear Genevieve, none of us finally matters but everybody matters. You think I am being merely clever? No, you will not think that, I am sure.

I am in good health, as far as I know. I have years in me yet but now, I seem to have decided this in the night, I am done with making this record.

I do not know who, if anyone, will read these words while I am still in the land of the living – not these, at any rate, these final words – but we will have done some work together before you see this, perhaps even I will have shown you what I have written up to now.

I mean to go on from here – this that you have you may think of as a provisional set of accounts, far from a final balance, a final reckoning.

Enough, then, this is as far as I propose to go.

Ach. I stand and stretch. I go to the window. The sky is clearing from the east, the day is softening, the sun is shining impartially on both sides of the street below. Someone, a woman, is turning the corner – flick of her heel, gone

Soon, I think, I will go for a long walk, I will see where my feet take me in this always surprising city.

I go through to the bathroom, I stand there before the mirror, I consider the man who stands before me, and I look into my own eyes. I look back at myself, at ease, a faint smile at the corners of my mouth.

I work my shoes back on without bending to open the laces, a child's habit.

I sit back at my desk, I type these final words:

Once we were in the world. Comrades. We did what we could, for each other and for strangers. We expected nothing. We tried to do good. We did what we thought was best.

My name is Joseph Lyons. I was a man. Once I was in this world. I did what I thought was right. No more, no less.